Copyright © 2020 A. S. Kelly

About Last Night
by
A. S. Kelly

English Edition

Translation by Abigail Prowse

This novel is a work of fiction. Names, characters, places and storyline are the fruit of the author's imagination or are used in a fictional sense. Any similarity to facts, places or people living or deceased is purely coincidental.

Cover Design: Elle Maxwell Design

www.ASKELLYWRITES.com

about last night

A. S. KELLY

1

Tyler

"Everything looks good over here!" I shout to Parker from the other side of the room. I lift myself up from the floor and grab the clipboard, ready to cross off the last few items on our list, before joining him.

"No problems here, either."

"Shall we give the go-ahead, then?"

"Go for it. I just want today to be over." He pushes back his jacket sleeve and glances at his watch. "I have another fifteen minutes before I have to start paying overtime."

"You can go, I'll finish up here. We're pretty much done anyway. I'll do all the paperwork and drop it into the office."

"Thanks, Tyler."

Parker grabs his bag and heads towards the exit of the pub. "Why don't you stop by later on, for dinner? I'm cooking."

"Are you actually cooking? Or are you just heating something up in the microwave?"

"I'm cooking. Spaghetti Bolognese."

"I'm impressed."

"Don't take the piss."

"I wouldn't dream of it."

"I get the sauce from a jar, by the way," he

adds, making me laugh. "But the rest is all me."

"Wow. Don't try too hard."

"You can stay at home if you're going to be an arse about it."

"I'll bring ice cream. And something for us to drink, too."

"Make sure it's something good," he warns, pointing his finger at me, before giving me a quick wave and disappearing from the pub, heading home.

I lean against the bar to start filing through all the paperwork that I'll need to drop off at the office, before heading back to my apartment, taking a quick shower, then paying a quick visit to Supervalu. I promised Parker ice cream and alcohol, and I barely have anything at home, bar a few beers. I was meant to go shopping today, but they called me in for this inspection at the last minute, so I'll have to go tomorrow instead, on my day off. Usually, my days off are dedicated to slightly more adult activities – ones that require two people, or sometimes three or more. Although that isn't really my style – I always prefer to concentrate on one thing at a time. But Parker has just moved into his new apartment, and he's been feeling lonely, even if he won't admit as much. I don't like the thought of him feeling like that, weighed down by his thoughts, a glass of shitty whiskey in hand.

When I get back to the fire station, only the guys working the night shift are there, focused on an intense game of snooker. It looks like it'll be a quiet one tonight – to be honest, it's been pretty quiet for weeks, now. Months, even. Not much goes on around here – not that I'm complaining. We're those classic firemen that get called out to retrieve cats from trees – and no, that's not just an urban legend: it really does happen – or to bust open the front door for some idiot who's locked himself out of his house. That actually happens more often than you'd expect.

I like my job, although I'm not making it sound particularly exciting. But I like the town I live in, too: it's small, safe, and filled with nosy neighbours.

But you know what I like most of all?

My apartment.

I've lived here for almost a year, now. It took me a little while to find the perfect place, and it took just as long trying to save for a deposit. I'm a fireman, not one of those millionaires my mother seems to read about in all her books. We're paid a pretty modest salary, you know.

It's the perfect house for one person. There's a living room with a sofa planted directly in front of my 65-inch TV, where I can watch the game in peace; there's a kitchen, with a two-seater table – in case I ever have guests at breakfast, if you know what I mean. There's a big, spacious bedroom with a comfortable king-size bed; a bathroom with a shower and a bath, because I like both; there's a small garden – extremely small – which I built into the terrace. I use it to grow a few roses and tulips, when the weather is nice enough.

The building I live in has only two apartments, and luckily, the one next door is still empty. Let's just say I'm putting pressure on a certain someone for it to stay that way for as long as possible – or, at least, until I can find someone who can live there without pissing me off at all. Hopefully someone single, like me, with no expectations.

I walk into the Supervalu on the main road which leads into the city, and run toward the whiskey aisle to grab a bottle – a good one, at Parker's request – and a few tubs of ice cream: one double chocolate and one strawberry. I head quickly over to the checkout, before Parker starts to bombard me with phone calls, telling me to get a move on.

"Hey, Tyler!" Carlie, one of the Supervalu checkout girls, greets me. "You expecting company tonight?" she asks, scanning my items.

"Nothing special," I say vaguely. I don't feel like letting her in on all the details of my life.

Carlie has one particular problem: she never seems to understand that you can have too much of a good thing, and that you should stop doing that thing before it stops being good.

"Thanks." I smile at her, but not too much – you never know how a smile could be interpreted around here by the female population. To be honest, I've often found myself in trouble for making the mistake of smiling too much at the wrong people.

"Have a nice evening!"

"You, too."

She sighs.

She actually *sighs*.

And I didn't even smile at her.

Could you imagine what would've happened if I had?

I grab my things and leave the supermarket, sliding into the car and heading towards Parker's house, hoping that everything is still standing when I get there – both his house *and* him.

*****

"Oh, my God, you're here already." Parker opens the door to me, wooden spoon in hand and one of his daughters wrapped around his neck.

"Give her here," I say, handing over the bag of ice cream and whiskey and attaching his daughter to me, instead.

I'm not sure which daughter this is – I can never tell them apart. But they don't need to know that.

"I almost burned the sauce."

He leads me into his apartment, which isn't much bigger than my own. I follow him, a little monkey dangling from my neck. Never use their names: that's my shameless secret, which I apply to a number of aspects of my life. It's always worked for me.

"I'm hungry," moans the girl clinging to my shoulder.

"Me too, but let's not try Dad's patience."

"What?"

"I'll explain another time."

We reach the living room, where the other little monkey is sitting on the sofa watching cartoons.

"Hey!" I say, but she gestures for me to keep quiet.

I sit down, her sister still attached to me, and glance at the TV.

"This puppet again?"

"Shh... I can't hear."

"Sorry." I roll my eyes and try to peel her sister away from me, but to no avail.

"Why don't you sit here and watch TV with your sister while I go and check that your dad is coping in the kitchen?"

"No."

Perfect.

"What if that means that there's no dinner tonight?"

"Our neighbour invited us over," the other girl chimes in.

"Oh, really?"

"But Dad said no."

"How come?" I ask, glancing – with difficulty –

in the direction of the kitchen.

"It's called pride!" he yells from the other side of the apartment.

He didn't seem to care about his pride when he invited me over, not knowing what to do on his own. But I'm not one to throw things in people's faces like that; usually I'm more subtle about it.

"Okay, listen," I say, finally managing to unwrap her arms from my neck. "If you let me go and give your dad a hand, I'll let you have three scoops of ice cream. How does that sound?"

"Two scoops!" cries the dad in question.

"Three," I whisper, holding up three fingers.

She scoffs, before giving in. I get up from the sofa and head towards the kitchen, where an exhausted Parker is attempting to make a dinner almost entirely from scratch.

"Why didn't you go over to your neighbour's?"

I grab the empty *Alfredo* jar of Bolognese sauce – which, I have to admit, I've also bought a few times, myself – and run it under the tap, before dropping it into the recycling bin under the sink.

Parker opens the fridge and hands me a beer. I open the top drawer and pull out a bottle opener, take the cap off, and then glance over at the sauce, which luckily seems to look edible.

Maybe we'll manage to get through tonight.

"We had dinner with her the other day."

"So? It's not like there's a limit to the number

of dinner invitations you can accept."

"She's single."

"Mmm?"

"My neighbour. Divorced. No kids."

"I still don't get it."

"She tried to…"

"To…?" I wait for him to continue, then get there myself. "Oh…"

"It didn't seem appropriate."

"Got it. Well, actually, I don't get it."

"Do I need to remind you why I was living with Mum and Dad again until two months ago?"

"That was a very… specific situation."

"Specifically shit, you mean?"

"Yeah, that too."

"I have to get used to doing things for myself. It's best not to complicate things too much at the moment."

"I agree, but having dinner with your neighbour, spending some time with her every now and then, doesn't sound so bad to me."

"My new babysitter quit."

"Already?"

This is the third babysitter in the past two months – but I don't point this out.

Parker sighs frustratedly.

"What happened?"

"I was five minutes late. Literally, *five minutes.*

And she tried to charge me for an extra hour."

"She wanted overtime?"

"Come on! Fifteen euros for five minutes?"

"You should've just given it to her."

He glares at me.

"What? Now you have no babysitter! How the hell are you going to go to work?"

"I've asked my neighbour to look after the girls tomorrow."

"So you won't have dinner with her, but you'll let her look after your kids?"

"Whose side are you on, here?"

"Hey! I'm just trying to help you out!"

"If you want to help, then put the spaghetti on. The water's already boiling."

"Thank God. I was so hungry..."

I do as he says and add some salt, too. I'm not exactly a chef – I definitely don't take after our mother in that sense, she's an incredible cook – but I can get by. He, on the other hand, is shit.

Oh, yeah. I forgot to mention that Parker is my older brother – older only by eleven months. Our parents always struggled to control themselves when it came to public displays of affection; neither of us want to imagine what they were like in private.

I turn to my brother, whose face has taken on that gaze once again: a gaze which tells me that he doesn't know whether he'll make it to the end of the day without crumbling, or going crazy. I'm growing more and more convinced that the choice I made all those years ago is the only one that makes sense.

2
Tyler

"Are you going to eat that?" Eve asks Zoe, who promptly defends her plate, shielding it with her arm.

How can I suddenly tell them apart? Simple. Parker told Eve to eat with her mouth closed, and I took the hint quickly.

"Stay away from my spaghetti."

"I was just asking."

"If you want to ask questions, why don't you ask Uncle Tyler why Ms. Potter called him a damn bastard?"

My brother almost chokes on his food.

"What... Er... What did she say?"

"Did you go out gnome hunting with my daughters' teacher, by any chance?" my brother asks me, alarmed.

I don't laugh, I swear – but Parker's latest trick of using euphemisms for everything is starting to get out of hand.

"That's not exactly what happened."

"She said that you never called her back," Zoe continues.

"She said that? Really...?"

"Tyler..." Parker warns.

"And what else did…?"

"Do you really think it's appropriate to ask them that?"

I shrug. I'm not the one who brought it up.

"How do you girls know all this?"

"She said it to Ms. Trent at breaktime."

Oh, fuck. Ms. Trent was there, too?

"And she said all this in front of you?" my brother asks, horrified.

"No, we were hiding in the bushes behind the bench they were sitting on."

"What were you doing there?" My brother continues to ask useless questions instead of focusing on the main problem, here: working out whether or not Ms. Potter and Ms. Trent are currently planning my 'accidental' death.

"Then Ms. Trent said something."

I'm sweating, sitting there, immobile. My brother, on the other hand, looks as if he could've just sprouted at least five new grey hairs.

"What?"

I might as well hear it, right? And, besides, it's Parker's problem. He's the one who'll have to explain to his daughters that they can't go around hunting gnomes with anyone until they're thirty.

"Ms. Trent said that it happened two times."

Maybe it was better not to ask.

"And then, Ms. Potter…"

"That's enough," Parker cuts in, trying to prevent an inevitable catastrophe.

"She said that she came three times."

"C-came?" I ask, worried.

She sticks another forkful of spaghetti into her mouth and chews slowly, before speaking again.

"To hunt gnomes. Right?"

My brother's sigh of relief manages even to calm me down, too.

"In one night."

This final statement signals the end of my future in this family.

"She said that you weren't even tired, Uncle Tyler," the other comments, as my brother grips tightly onto my arm.

"Don't say a word."

I wouldn't dream of it.

"Can I have those three scoops of ice cream you promised us?"

Luckily, the conversation moves onto something slightly easier to digest.

"We agreed two," my brother reminds her, getting to his feet.

"That's what Ms. Potter said."

Nope. I'm still not in the clear.

"She said that Uncle Tyler promised her that she'd come two times."

That's true – but now doesn't seem like the

right time to bring up the fact that I'm good at sticking to my word.

"And that she'd enjoy it."

"I'll kill you," Parker hisses, pointing his finger against me.

"And then Ms. Trent said that she could always count on you."

"Well, I guess…"

"Are you done?" Parker threatens.

"Look, I haven't done anything. It was all them."

"I need a drink." He gets up and disappears into the kitchen. I decide to follow him and do some damage control, telling the girls that I'd be back soon with the promised ice cream.

As soon as I catch up with him, Parker waves a spoonful of ice cream in my direction.

"Everything is already difficult enough…"

I let him vent. I realise that it's not just what the girls said that's getting to him; attempting to justify myself now wouldn't help either of us.

"…Without you fucking their teacher, let alone the teacher of another class, too!"

"I'm sorry. Maybe I should've just left it – at least with Ms. Potter – but she's about to move away, and I didn't think she'd stand around in the playground gossiping about her love life."

Parker glares at me.

I lift my hands and take a step back. "You're

right. I shouldn't have done anything."

"What the fuck were you thinking?"

What was I thinking? Not a lot, to be honest, in that moment.

Ms. Potter was going through a difficult time, and I was there to comfort her. But I don't think my brother would consider that a good excuse.

Parker drops the spoon into the ice cream tub, letting his hands fall onto the counter, his head lowered. He looks as if he could fall to pieces in this very moment.

"I don't know what I'm going to do when this whole thing about the gnomes stops being believable."

I step towards him and rest my hand on his shoulder.

"I don't know what I'll do when… God, Tyler! I don't know what the fuck to do!"

"Just take it one step at a time."

"I'm exhausted. I'm angry. I'm—"

"Hey, you'll get through this. It'll just take a little time. And, Ms. Potter aside, you know you can always count on me."

He stands up slowly, flashing me a tired, resigned gaze.

"I'll stay away from their school, I promise."

"It's not your fault. But you are an arsehole."

I take the insult. Right now, it suits me.

"How about I look after the girls one evening?"

"What?"

"I can do it."

"I'm not so sure about that."

"Come on. You know I'm good with them. They love me."

"That's because they know how to manipulate you. They know all your weaknesses, and they use you to get what they want."

"True. But at least they know they can have fun with Uncle Tyler."

Parker shrugs. He doesn't want to admit that I'm right.

"Just for one evening. So you can relax a little. What do you say?"

"I say that sounds like a terrible idea."

"Trust me. I mean, I'm a fireman, right? Who doesn't trust a fireman?"

"Someone who grew up with that fireman," he snaps – but at least he's smiling. It's a start.

"Next time we both have the evening off, I'll look after them. They can stay at mine."

"You're sure you can manage?"

No. But is it worth telling him that?

"Absolutely. I've got this, don't worry."

I feel as if I'm wading through a sea of shit. But I don't tell him that, either.

3

Tyler

As soon as I turn the corner into the road leading up to my building, I realise that something's not right. I don't know how to explain it – it's just a feeling, like a sixth sense. Kind of the same feeling firemen get when they can smell the smoke before the fire has even broken out. Maybe it's the way the leaves sit, completely still, on the trees; maybe there's a slight haze hanging over the street, which dries out your eyes; maybe it's the eerie silence which always precedes a disaster, interrupted only by the rumbling of your car engine. But it's only when I pull into my parking space and see that someone has decided to block it with their damn rubbish bin that I realise that my nice, quiet, uncomplicated life is about to be flipped upside down.

I pull into the next parking space – the one reserved for visitors – and turn off the engine, anxiously lifting my gaze towards the windows of the apartments. To my great disappointment, I notice that there is a light switched on in the apartment next to mine.

I climb out of the car and place my feet on the ground, my shoes dragging heavily along the pavement and towards the stairway which leads to my front door – and, unfortunately, to what is now my neighbour's front door. An enormous box and a plant are blocking the entrance to their apartment, as well as mine.

I'm a nice, polite person – and not just because that's how my mum brought us up, but, of course, because of my job. I can't just go around being a dick to everyone. I can't cause any kind of trouble when I'm in my uniform – or even when I'm not wearing my uniform. Besides, I'm fairly well-known in town; people trust me, respect me. So, in spite of myself, I sink to my knees and pick up the box, grabbing the plant with my free hand. I pull myself together and knock at the door, waiting in the hallway for my *soon-to-be-ex*-neighbour to let me in.

What, you thought I was only helping out because I'm a fireman? To keep up with my reputation? You always have to present the best sides of yourself to your enemies; you especially can't let them see that you're plotting to have them evicted.

After a few minutes of waiting, I rest my ear against the door, concluding that there's no sound coming from inside. Maybe they went down to get a takeaway from the place on the corner, or maybe they've taken their dog out for a walk. Maybe I should stop doing what I find myself doing right now, and picking the lock to their front door – I won't tell you how, it's a trick of the trade. Maybe I should also stop walking into their house and nosing around. But I have the right to know who my next enemy will be – don't I?

Actually, don't answer that. There's no need.

I slip silently into the apartment, and it's only when the door closes behind me that I recognise the unmistakable sound of the shower running in the bathroom.

After quickly calculating that it'll take at least five minutes for them to turn off the shower, wrap themselves in a towel, and step out of the bathroom, I take two minutes to have a quick look around. I put down the box I'm carrying, but keep the plant clasped between my hands – you never know – and I glance around, taking in the characteristic chaos of someone who has literally just moved in.

Not content with what I've already seen – i.e., nothing much – I allow myself another minute to tiptoe over towards the bedroom; but the bathroom door flies suddenly open, catching me in the act. I turn guiltily, ready to spout my usual bullshit about having smelled smoke coming from the apartment; but the figure of my new neighbour turns out to be a pleasant but unexpected surprise. I smile, satisfied. I realise right away that this whole thing could be much quicker and much more fun than I'd anticipated.

"I thought this might be yours."

She looks at me, her eyes wide, wrapping her arms tighter around her chest to hold up her towel.

"Maybe I should just put it down here." I kneel down to place the plant on the floor, before standing back up, ready to unleash all my fireman's charm on her; to show her that I'm a superhero, ready to help any damsel in distress.

She stays standing in the doorway, her hand still resting on the handle, her cheeks red, her eyes unblinking, her shock almost debilitating.

"I'm Tyler, your neighbour. Next door," I say, gesturing towards the wall that divides our apartments. But she still doesn't bat an eyelid.

I allow myself one not-so-quick glance at the enemy standing in front of me, just so I can be prepared. She has bare feet, pink nail varnish shining against the wooden floor. Her legs are long and smooth, her sexy hips, her cleavage on display, large enough to...

"Are you done?"

Her voice shatters my close analysis.

"Excuse me?"

She wraps the towel even tighter around her chest – as if one towel could be enough to contain what I'm imagining is hidden underneath, or as if it could force me to tear my gaze away.

"I don't know how it works around here..." There's no more embarrassment. I think the flush of red across her cheeks has more to do with whatever she's about to yell at me. Now that I think about it, the redness beforehand probably wasn't from embarrassment, either, "...but I'm not used to perfect strangers sneaking into my house, uninvited. It's called breaking and entering."

"It's not breaking and entering. We're neighbours. The door was basically open..."

"And you snuck into my house to spy on me, like the pervert you are."

"I... What?"

"And now you need to leave, before I call law enforcement."

I'm about to tell her that she's standing in front of a member of the law enforcement, but she's already left the doorway and is making her way over to the sofa, where her phone is waiting. She grabs it and starts to dial, her gaze never leaving mine.

"Hey," I lift my hands. "There's no need to..."

"I'd like to report a maniac," she responds to the voice on the other end of the phone. "I can hold. Thanks."

"What the hell...?"

"Yes, he's in my house right now."

"What the fuck?"

"He says he's my neighbour. The address is..."

"Hey, hey! Wait a minute..." I try to step closer, but she moves quickly towards the kitchen, grabbing a knife from the counter and waving it in my direction. It's one of those huge chopping knives you see on the TV shopping channels; the kind of knife which could easily slice a beer can in half.

I raise my hands again and stand still.

"No problem, I'll keep an eye on him," she says, hanging up. "They'll be here as soon as possible."

This can't really be happening.

"I'd suggest you stay where you are. I know how to use this." She waves the knife at me again.

How the hell did I end up in this shitty situation?

I know, I should be scared. I should be a little pissed-off, too, considering the way I'm being treated, and the way this psychopath is putting me in my place – especially after moving into an apartment that isn't meant for her. But something a little further south on my body seems to have other ideas. I've always had an issue with women who grab you by the balls – figuratively, of course – and that's why I make sure to always stay away from them.

"Oh, my God!" she cries, horrified. "You really are a maniac!"

Unfortunately, she also seems to have noticed the argument currently being held between my mind and the stirring sensation manifesting in my trousers.

"Can I just...?"

"Shut up!" She brandishes the knife back in my direction.

"Just let me explain."

"Explain what? That you just go around showing up in poor women's houses and attack them?"

"Attack? Come on…"

"Well, definitely at least to spy on them. You look like a stalker, but you pretend you're all innocent."

"Well, thanks. And *poor women*? You're the one pointing a knife at me!"

"Only because you're being a pervert!"

"Here we go again…" I roll my eyes and sink onto the arm of her sofa.

"Hey!" she cries. "No one said you could sit down."

I scoff and get back to my feet. There's no point trying to explain. I don't even think it makes sense to try and speak to her; she's an absolute nutcase. I reckon she's recently escaped from a mental institution. Maybe she's moving into this empty apartment because she needs somewhere to hide out – although that doesn't explain the plant, or the fact that her stuff is all over the place. But it does explain the knives – I noticed the rest of the set on the kitchen counter. Either way, in a few minutes, the police will be here, and we can finally get this ridiculous misunderstanding ironed out. I'm a member of the law enforcement, too. This will all be brushed under the carpet in three second, and she'll end up looking like an unhinged madwoman. It'll be the talk of the town, and I can finally get my freedom back, without any more crazy neighbours.

I hear the sound of tyres on tarmac and, seconds later, the sound of a car door closing. She moves closer to her front door, never taking her eyes off me; she opens it and glances outside, before turning back to me.

"Clock's ticking."

I don't respond. It'll be more satisfying this way, when I get to see the look on her face as I run my victory lap around her apartment.

"Can we come in?" a familiar voice chimes from outside. "We've received a call."

She opens the door, still wrapped in a towel, and the two most stupid, useless policemen in town step into her apartment.

"Er... Good evening," Ronan blathers, the first of the two idiots.

"Good evening?" she snaps right away. "I called because of an emergency, and you start with *good evening*?"

"How else were we supposed to start?" the other asks. Finn: another old acquaintance of mine.

"There's a maniac in my house!" She gestures towards me with the knife.

"It looks like you've got it under control." Ronan takes off his cap and his gaze lands on me. "Oh, you're going to like this, Finn." He elbows the other, who also turns to look at me.

"Tyler Hayes," he says, slowly. "Still bothering all the women in town, I see?"

"I knew it!" she cries, convinced.

"Bothering? I live next door."

"We know, we know." Finn takes a few steps into her house. "My sister knew that, too."

S. H. I. T.

"I was the one who came to pick her up at sunrise, about a hundred metres from here. Barefoot."

"Listen, I didn't kick your sister out – without her shoes. I'm a gentleman. She was the one who seemed in a hurry to leave."

Ronan laughs, but Finn grows serious.

"Can we please get back to the fact that I called you because this maniac broke into my house while I was in the shower?"

Ronan and Finn study her carefully, and she tightens the towel around her chest again.

"Would you mind concentrating on the problem at hand, please?"

"Could you not have put some clothes on?"

She glares at me.

"I mean…"

"So." Ronan furrows his brow. "Let me get this straight. You called us because of a break-in, and…"

"And that's it," I say, losing my patience, now. This has already gone too far. "I didn't do anything."

"You're still looking at me!"

"It's hard not to," Finn adds.

"Excuse me, but whose side are you on, here?"

"The right one," I say.

"So, Tyler," Ronan says, trying to keep the conversation on track. "Why did you let yourself into Ms...?"

"White."

"Ms. White's house?" he asks.

"Shouldn't you be writing this down?" she points out.

"She's right," I say, glancing over at him.

"Why did you let yourself into her house, Hayes?"

"Because I thought I could smell smoke. I knocked, no one answered, so I thought that someone might be in danger..."

"Smoke? I was in the shower!"

"I smelled it. It must've been coming from somewhere."

"Don't tell me you actually believe this?"

Ronan and Finn exchange a glance.

"You have to understand, Ms. White," Finn begins. "This is a pretty small town. Everyone here knows each other..."

"So you have no intention of following through with my statement?"

"Statement?" I ask, shocked.

This is really going too far, now.

"Listen, I'm a—"

"If you'd like to make a statement," Finn says, interrupting me, "then we are obliged to take him away with us."

"Are you serious, Finn?"

"I don't know. Maybe you should ask my sister."

I let myself fall back onto the arm of the sofa, speechless. I can't believe this.

"Shall we make this statement, then?" Finn asks her.

"Of course we should."

"You'll need to follow us down to the station."

"No problem."

"Maybe... Er... With some clothes on." Ronan lets his eyes fall quickly onto her.

"Give me two minutes."

"Meanwhile, we'll take him downstairs. If you could, you know, put down the knife..."

She looks at the knife in her hand, before moving towards the kitchen counter to replace it.

"Let's go, Hayes," Finn says, stepping closer to me. "You've earned yourself a ride in the Batmobile." He pulls out a pair of handcuffs and waves them in my face.

"You're not being serious?"

"It's just protocol, mate. Turn around."

"This cannot be happening," I comment out loud, as he pulls my wrists together behind my back. "You're enjoying this, aren't you?"

"Honestly, Hayes? I really am. And I think my sister will enjoy it even more when I tell her what's happened."

"Not as much as she enjoyed being next door with me. But I don't think she'll tell you about that."

I should not have said that. I only realise my mistake when Finn begins to read out my rights, adding the accusation of public order offence.

4

Tyler

"Please tell me you haven't actually called me to bail you out?"

"Are you going to keep bringing this up?"

"You're a fireman, for fuck's sake!"

"Are you done?"

"Sorry, I can't help it."

I scoff and shove my hands into my pockets as my now *ex*-best friend, Niall, opens the police station door for me.

"I don't think I've quite wrapped my head around it, yet..." He continues to take the piss, as if all the laughter, comments, and jokes from those four imbeciles in the station tonight weren't enough. Everyone seems to know about this already! I play against them in the law enforcement GAA tournaments; I don't even want to imagine what will happen when the guys in the fire station find out about this unfortunate misunderstanding.

Niall unlocks his car and I climb inside, before anyone else can see me and start taking the piss.

"It was just a big misunderstanding," I repeat, for the thousandth time.

Niall switches on the ignition, still shaking with laughter.

I was such an idiot to get involved with that madwoman, and I was an even bigger idiot to have called Niall to bail me out. But who else could I have called? My brother's looking after the girls, my parents are on holiday, and it's best that my colleagues find out about this as late as possible... I didn't exactly have much choice.

"I thought you were supposed to be my mate," I grumble, leaning my elbow against the window and fixing my gaze outside.

"I am – that's why I left my favourite headmistress at home alone, with no underwear on, and only a white chocolate cheesecake for company."

"Did you really have to go into that much detail?"

"You were the one doubting my role as the best friend."

"I wouldn't say 'best'."

"Do you want me to drop you off here, in the middle of the road?"

"I want you to stop rubbing it in."

"Taking the piss is one of the pillars of our friendship."

I roll my eyes, before letting my gaze land on him. "I still have no idea how the hell this all happened."

"Did you or did you not let yourself into her apartment?"

"Yeah, but—"

"And had she not just stepped out of the shower?"

"You know about that, too?"

"And did you or did you not constantly stare at all the parts of her body that the towel wasn't covering?"

I scoff, irritably. Ever since he's started going out with that absolute goddess of a woman, he's become a little too big for his boots.

"That's all just gossip."

"So they didn't arrest you in her apartment?"

"Apart from that. That part's true."

"And *had* she just stepped out of the shower?"

"Technically, that's true, too."

"And you weren't staring at her with your X-ray vision?"

I don't even attempt to justify myself anymore. He wouldn't believe me even if he'd been there himself, covering my eyes with his hands.

I almost preferred him when he was an absolute train wreck. He had no job, no mates, and no plans for the future. Now he has a job, which actually sounds kind of cool; he has a woman who's even cooler; he has a daughter who makes him look somewhat cool; he has a plan for the future which actually seems to involve some sort of wedding.

What the hell has happened to my friend?

"So, this gossip…?"

"I was just doing my job."

"And what *is* that, exactly? I seem to have forgotten…"

"I should never have called you."

"And done what, instead? Spent the night in a cell? With all those thugs?"

"The only thug around here is you."

Niall laughs, before turning into my street. *Her* damn bin is still taking up *my* parking space. Has no one told her yet that you're supposed to take the bins out on Sunday evening? Or that you're *definitely* not supposed to leave them blocking the parking spaces?

"She's taking over your parking space," Niall points out.

"Oh, really?"

"I'm guessing that didn't go down well with you."

"Not at all."

"You know you can just ask her to move it, right? Just knock on the door like a normal person, introduce yourself, tell her that you're a fireman – you know, someone she can trust…" Niall can't quite hold back another laugh.

"You're really enjoying this, aren't you?"

"So much. It's so nice not to be the talk of the town for once."

"What do you mean?"

"Well, what with the mess you've just made,

and with everything they'll have written up at the station... Tomorrow, everyone will be talking about you, Tyler. And not just the women."

Fuck you, Niall.

I open the car door and stick my foot onto the tarmac.

"Hey!" Niall leans over to the passenger side. "No more bullshit, okay? I have a nice evening planned, and I have no intention of interrupting it again."

"I'm never calling you again."

"See you later, local hero!" He takes the piss one last time before pulling out of the car park and going back to where he came from.

I climb the stairs dejectedly, my head hanging low, resisting the temptation to knock at her door and tell her exactly what I think of her, of her chopping knife, and of her body under that towel. I feel like I'm at risk of being arrested all over again, just at the memory of that body. I unlock my front door, opening it, and settling myself down into my quiet, calm living room. I switch on the floor lamp next to the wall, heading into the kitchen to pour myself a glass – or two – of something strong, something good. And not 'good' like the bottle I took over to my brother's the other day, but the kind of 'good' whiskey I keep just for myself, for special occasions. I'd say this is a special occasion – wouldn't you?

I wouldn't bet on it, you know. I never shy

away from a challenge, and this whole thing feels like a challenge to me.

She's played well so far – she's played dirty, in the most meaningful sense of the word. But she's played well, I have to admit. But I haven't had the chance to show her my cards just yet – and, my dear neighbour, I always have the winning hand.

5

Holly

I open the fridge and pull out the bottle of wine I bought this afternoon at the grocery store down the road, before rummaging around in search of the glasses I bought this afternoon, too, at the same grocery store. There was next to nothing in this house when I first moved in, so I've had to sort it all out myself. The estate agent gave me that stupid plant, and brought me over a few boxes of kitchen utensils – a moving-in gift, he'd said. A gift which is still spread across my floor, apart from the knives, which actually turned out to be useful. I knew I was right to unpack those first. I have a sixth sense for these things.

I open the bottle and fill my glass to the brim, before grabbing my cell and choosing one of my favourite playlists – the one I always listen to when I'm trying to relax – then head out to the balcony. I slide the door aside and step outside, where a little table with two chairs is waiting for me. I reckon this is the only way to salvage what has been a horrible day.

I sit down, resting my legs against the railing, music wafting lightly outside from the apartment. The weather is okay, tonight, too – it's not yet as cold as it is at home, and I don't need a fluffy coat or ski gloves. But maybe I should grab something to cover my legs...

I put my glass down on the table and get up, heading back inside to pull the blanket from my bed. I wrap it around my body and, given I'm already there, I grab the bottle of wine, too. But when I get back to the door I stop right away; there's an unwelcome shadow floating across the floor of my balcony, reminding me of my first impression of the place I now call home. And it was definitely *not* a good first impression. I wait for the shadow to disappear – I have absolutely no intention of running into him, and don't want to have to go back inside and grab hold of another knife, or call law enforcement again. I've been up for more than forty-eight hours, now, and I'm so exhausted that I don't want to do anything but curl into a ball and wake up just in time for my new job.

I wait next to the door for a few minutes, and when the coast seems to be clear, I step outside, finally able to relax a little. I should have gone straight to bed as soon as I arrived, but I tried to put it off at least until the evening, to try and get my body and my mind back onto a normal sleeping pattern. I didn't exactly plan for the fact that, when I was finally ready to go to bed, my maniac of a next-door-neighbour would turn up to welcome me.

I finish the rest of my drink in one gulp at the mere thought of our unfortunate encounter, before hastily pouring myself another glass. The situation definitely calls for another drink.

At the police station, they told me that my new neighbour is actually an esteemed fireman, a pillar of the community; someone you can trust blindly. They said that he only broke into my apartment because he could sense danger. But what danger, exactly? I'd just got here, and I hadn't even turned the stove on, yet – which, by the way, is electric. How the hell did he manage to smell smoke? And can we also mention the fact that he was trying to see through my towel? I know that kind of look, and I know that kind of guy, too. It makes no difference that he's a fireman.

How can he already be home? That means they didn't even keep him in custody for two hours. He deserved an entire night in a cell, just as he deserves the fact that I won't retract my accusation. They asked me to reconsider, and said that if I didn't retract my statement then he could risk being suspended from the force – they said it could have serious repercussions for his career. But that's not my problem. I'm not the one who broke into a stranger's house, right? Besides, he's an adult. He should be capable of taking responsibility for himself. And, yes, maybe I did jump to conclusions without giving him a chance to speak or to explain himself, but come on! I found him *in my house*! Who wouldn't have called the police, in my position?

I have no idea how things work around here. I've only just moved in, and I'm already starting to regret it – but I don't think that it's normal anywhere, no matter how calm and safe a place may seem, to break into other people's houses uninvited.

I gulp down the rest of my drink, hoping that it'll finally calm my nerves and help me get some sleep. I thought that, after two whole days of travelling, I'd have collapsed onto the floor by now, but I can't seem to switch my mind off. And when I can't keep my thoughts quiet, it doesn't matter how exhausted I am. Maybe another hot shower would help, seeing as the last one was rudely interrupted.

Just as I decide to head back inside and jump back under the shower, before crumbling into bed, a voice from the apartment next door forces me to stay another few minutes. Well, 'forces' is a big word – let's just say that I decided to stay and eavesdrop for a while, to listen to whatever he was saying.

It sounds like a one-way conversation, so I guess he's on the phone. I can't hear any other voices, and I didn't hear anyone go in or out of his apartment. I'm wary of the fact that I can hear his voice from my place, which also means that I'd be able to hear when he's home, when he comes and goes, when he has company, when… I jump to my feet and continue with my original plan: shower, then bed.

I grab the empty glass and the bottle, step into the apartment, and slide the balcony door closed behind me. I take a few steps into the living room, but his voice floats through the walls, loud and clear. I even manage to distinguish a few words. *Psycho*, definitely. *Fucking nightmare*, too. And then an *everyone's going to take the piss out of me tomorrow* which instinctively makes me smile. When I can't hear anything else, I head back towards my room in search of something to sleep in, among the chaos of my half-unpacked suitcases. I lock myself in the bathroom, longing for another piping-hot shower – this time, with no interruptions – followed by a night of deep, rejuvenating sleep.

6

Tyler

At half past six in the morning, I'm already up, a cup of coffee wafting beneath my nose, my hands planted on the kitchen counter, and my gaze fixed onto the living room wall ahead of me; a wall which I share with my new, emotionally unbalanced neighbour.

I didn't sleep as well as usual. I couldn't seem to shake off the comments made by all the guys down at the station, or my brother's roaring laughter on the phone – a brother who had obviously been previously informed of last night's events, and who – even more obviously – wanted to be the first to take the piss. He wasn't too happy to find out that he was actually the tenth person to make fun of me, or that Niall had beat him to it. He doesn't like the fact that we're so close, and that I often help him out of difficult situations more than I help my own brother. But what can I do? I just go wherever I'm needed.

When I got home last night, she was already there. I could hear her moving around her apartment. I heard the music she was playing, and I heard the balcony door open. And then, well, I took a peek through the curtains. I didn't see much, just her shadow, but I knew she was sitting outside, and that she'd been there for a while. It's only been a day, and she's already sucking up my personal space. It's bad enough that we share a wall, which means I can kiss my privacy goodbye, but now we also share a balcony: one of my favourite places. Unfortunately, the balcony has no divider – I never thought to put one up, as my lettings agent told me that I'd be informed before any decision was made on the empty flat next door. What use were all those inspections I helped him out with?

I look down at the phone next to my hand. It's six thirty-five; yes, my monologue lasted only five minutes. Is it too early to call him and give him an earful? I mean, I am the innocent victim in this whole situation. He's the one who made this mess, so he should be the one to put it right. I don't intend to share my space with a neighbour – especially not one with a few screws loose, who thinks that I'm a maniac. I don't want her phoning the police every time she hears a woman in my apartment making unusual noises at night – and, yes, I really do mean 'unusual'.

This situation needs to be resolved as soon as possible. My new neighbour has to go, before she's even finished unpacking the chaos she's brought along with her.

I grab my phone in search of my letting agent's number. After four rings, he picks up, panting.

"I already know what you're going to say." I can almost hear the birds chirping in the background. "Can we talk about this in the office later?"

"No, we're talking about it now. I can't wait another three hours. This needs to be sorted immediately."

"I'm in the middle of a run."

"That is absolutely not my problem. What *is* my problem, however, is the fact that you rented out an apartment that was not yours to rent out, to someone who has no right to be living there."

"You didn't enjoy your little holiday in custody, did you?"

I scoff. "How the hell do you know about that?"

"They called me last night. Someone apparently smelled smoke."

Shit.

"Someone who runs the inspections on the entire building."

"So? There could've been a gas leak. Or she could've been in trouble."

"Listen, Tyler. I had to do it, okay?"

"You had to?"

"They offered me a really good commission."

"And you had no other apartments on the market?"

"Not for short-term let."

"Short-term?" My senses sharpen immediately. "How short?"

"Three months. No one else would've taken it. Landlords usually ask for a minimum of one year.

And she's from out of town, too – no one wants an expat in their house with no guarantors."

"How out of town?"

"I can't give you that information."

"I'll remember that next time you ask me for a favour."

"Someone was putting pressure on us, okay? Both on me and on the landlord."

"What kind of pressure?"

"All I can tell you is that they made us give her the apartment."

"So it's all just a series of coincidences...?"

"Exactly."

"Coincidences that you never spoke to me about. How long have you known about this?"

"Well, I don't know..."

"You deliberately didn't tell me, right?"

"I thought that, maybe, once you met her..."

"Oh, believe me. I've met her."

"Listen, I have to go. My muscles are cooling down. If you want to talk about this calmly..."

"I don't want to talk about it. I want you to sort it out for me."

"There's no solution to this, Tyler. It's only three months. What do you want me to do about it?"

Three months, he says.

"I guess I'll just have to sort it out on my own."

"Tyler…"

"Enjoy your run, you traitor. And don't count on me for any more last-minute inspections. You and I are done." I hang up, just to make my threat seem more consistent, and place my phone back on the counter. I grab my coffee cup and take a few sips.

Three months. Like hell.

There must be something I can do to hurry things along.

I'll make sure I get my space back, my independence. Eight days, max, and the apartment will be empty again. I don't care that it's only for a short-term contract – I don't want anyone getting in my way, especially not a woman. Especially not someone who seems to frequently drive herself crazy, someone who is from out of town; someone who doesn't understand how things work around here, who isn't part of the community.

There's always a way to get what you want, and I'm going to make sure I find it. I'm a fireman, and I'm not scared of anything. I don't mind getting my hands a little dirty if it means that I can send *Ms. Kitchen Knife* back to where she came from, as quickly as possible.

7

Tyler

A strange, unsettling silence welcomes me as I set foot in the fire station. The other guys on shift haven't arrived yet, so I head towards the changing rooms quietly, approaching my locker and placing my bag on the bench beneath it. I sit down, ready to get changed for my shift, when the changing room door flies open, making me jump.

"Hayes!" the chief calls.

I leap to my feet.

"In my office. Now."

He closes the door behind him, and I start to breathe again. I thought I was alone, and thought I'd get a few more minutes of peace before the others turned up and began the infernal piss-taking, but I suddenly see a familiar face peering through the glass panel of the door. I realise that the games haven't even started yet, and that today is going to be long and decidedly shitty.

I nod at him to come in – it makes no sense to put this off – and he slips into the changing rooms.

"Just say what you have to say, and get it over with. The chief is waiting for me in his office."

"Maybe it's best if I don't rub it in," my brother says from the doorway.

"What? But you love rubbing it in."

"Not when it comes to a dead man."

"What the hell are you talking about?"

Parker wanders over and pulls a newspaper from behind his back.

"You'd have seen it sooner or later, anyway."

I grab the paper and take a look at the page.

"I don't believe it."

Parker shrugs.

"Who the fuck did this?"

"Someone from the department, I guess. Maybe someone who has it in for you…"

"Finn. That son of a—"

"The one who caught his sister escaping your house in the middle of the night?"

"She didn't escape," I say, clearing things up. "She left with a sense of urgency."

"I don't want to know why."

This time, I'm the one to shrug.

"You'd better get moving, the chief didn't look too happy this morning. You know how much he hates publicity," he says, nodding towards the paper. "Especially when it's bad publicity."

"That arsehole Finn should be arrested."

"You'd know all about being arrested…"

"Whose side are you on, here?"

"Hey, the other guys will be here soon, and I refuse to be on the weaker side."

"I am not weak!"

"Besides, I need something to distract me."

"And you decided to distract yourself with my misery? Couldn't you have found another way to distract yourself? Like, I don't know... Maybe with your divorced neighbour?"

Parker crosses his arms and looks at me. "Don't come crying to me when the angry mob is out looking for you, pitchforks and all."

"Pitchforks?" I can't help but laugh. "That's a good one, really... Especially for someone as old and boring as you."

"Old? There are only eleven months between us."

"I don't mean the age..." I scan him over from head to toe. "The rest, Parker."

"Fuck off, Tyler! I have absolutely no sympathy for you."

I laugh again as I'm heading for the door, leaving the changing rooms and joining the chief in his office. His door is open, and he's standing there, arms crossed, behind his desk.

"Take our time, did we?" He says right away, his eyebrows raised.

"No, sir, I just..."

"Close the door, Hayes, and sit down."

"Yes, sir." I do as he asks and make myself comfortable, as he sits down across from me, on the other side of the desk.

"Tell me that this is all just a

misunderstanding."

I swallow. "It is, sir."

"So you didn't break into your new neighbour's apartment?"

"Well, sir, if you want the full story…"

He lifts one hand to keep me quiet, then pushes the newspaper under my nose – the same paper my brother showed me just minutes ago in the changing rooms.

"Tell me that there's a reasonable explanation to all this."

"There is, sir."

"I'm listening."

"It's just complicated. You need to look at the whole picture to…"

"Let's put it this way. I'm going to ask questions, and you're only going to respond with 'yes' or 'no'."

"Yes, sir."

"Did you break into your neighbour's apartment?"

I thought we'd already moved on from this, but I don't think it's best to point this out.

"Yes, sir."

"Did you, or did you not, smell smoke?"

I have to watch what I say, here.

"I thought that…"

He shakes his head.

"No, sir."

His expression is steady. Mine less so.

"Are you a pervert, Hayes?"

"No, sir."

"A stalker?"

"No, sir. Absolutely not."

"Are you the sort of person who harasses young, single women?"

I need to watch what I say here, too.

"No, sir."

His jaw tightens.

"Did you mistreat a public official?"

"He's a public official, now…?"

He raises an eyebrow.

"In a way…"

He waits for my response, still as a statue.

I sigh. "Yes, sir."

He nods slowly, then lowers his eyes to his desk. He grabs hold of his stamp and slams it down onto a pile of documents, before passing them to me.

I glance quickly at them.

"You're suspended, Hayes."

"Suspended?"

"Until further notice."

"But, chief…"

"There's nothing else I can do."

I slump back into my chair in disbelief.

"I've always turned a blind eye to your bullshit, even when there was that rumour going around about a woman escaping your house in the dead of night."

"It wasn't…" I let it go and decide not to explain myself for the thousandth time – no one believes me, anyway. "It was all just a big misunderstanding."

"As much as I know you're extremely good at what you do, and how serious you are about your job, my hands are tied, here. I'm sorry." He gets up, and I mirror him. "You need to leave the station and fix this whole mess."

"Are you telling me I need to clear things up with her?"

"For God's sake, no. Talk to an expert. A lawyer, maybe."

"A lawyer? Come on, chief! It's just a stupid misunderstanding!"

"Misunderstanding or not, I can't risk the entire squad's reputation for you. Sort things out as quickly as possible, or your suspension may end up being permanent."

* * * * *

Parker walks me out of the building in silence. He doesn't seem to want to take the piss anymore, which is good, as I don't really feel like being a dick anymore, either.

The other guys are starting to turn up, one by one. They wave at us from outside the station, a laugh escaping some of them, with others asking me whether it's true that I was handcuffed. Someone else loudly proclaims that they can smell smoke. Another asks me whether there was a kitten stuck up a tree that needed my immediate attention.

"Don't listen to them."

I shrug. Their piss-taking is the least of my problems by this point.

"In a few days, this whole thing will have blown over, you'll see. It'll all go back to normal. People will forget this whole story and move onto the next exciting piece of gossip."

"Exciting? Around here? I don't think so."

"It happens, every now and again. Besides, it's Christmas, soon. People will be so busy that they'll forget how this whole thing even started."

"How *did* this whole thing even start, Parker? I still don't get it."

"Then maybe it's time to work out why it is that you always end up in these situations."

"Always?"

"The fact that you've managed to stay out of trouble up until now has always been because you happen to know everyone. Everyone knows your… How do I put this…? Your… ways."

"My ways?"

"Do I need to remind you about the whole story with Ms. Trent and Ms. Potter?"

I immediately shut up.

"Speaking of teachers…"

I raise my hands. "I swear, I didn't do anything."

Parker glares at me.

"Just to be clear."

"I need a favour."

"What do teachers have to do with it?"

"Actually, it's about school. I have a dentist appointment on Monday."

"And…?"

"And, seeing as you're now free, I thought you might be able to pick the girls up from school, keep an eye on them for a few hours."

"Why would I do something like that?"

"Because you have fuck-all else to do, and because they're your nieces, and because the last time I took them to the dentist with me it was a nightmare."

"You don't know that I have nothing better to do."

"I know all your shifts and, up until a few minutes ago, you thought you were working."

"So? Maybe I've already made other plans."

"Listen, Tyler." Parker slips into that 'big brother' voice he's been using ever since he became a dad, and I hate it. "I don't want to get involved in your business…"

"Which you already are."

"Okay, then let's just say that I'm forced to get involved so that I can help you out of this particular situation."

I scoff. "Go on."

"Someone made a statement against you."

"Everyone already knows that."

"It would probably be best for you to stay away from anyone who could make the situation worse, just until this whole thing is cleared up."

"You mean: stay away from all women, right?"

"Exactly."

This whole thing is reaching new levels of shittiness that I didn't even know were possible for just one person to achieve.

"This isn't just a way to get me to look after your daughters, is it?"

"My daughters are your nieces."

"Yes, okay, but they're your daughters first. They're my nieces by default."

Parker sighs in frustration.

"Fine, I'll look after them."

"And you need to pick them up from school, too."

"Okay."

"At ten past one, okay?"

"Got it."

"They have lunch at school, but you'll need to make them a snack at maybe three, three-thirty."

"No problem."

"Try to make sure that the snack doesn't have them sitting on the toilet all afternoon or keep them up all night."

"Who do you take me for?"

Parker lifts an eyebrow.

"A little trust wouldn't go amiss, you know."

"I'll only trust you when you prove that I can."

"You're letting me look after your daughters. Why would you do that if you didn't trust me?"

"Because the only other babysitter I found costs eighteen euros an hour."

"That's robbery!"

"Tell me about it."

"Don't worry, I'll take care of it. I'll pick them up from school, make them a healthy snack, keep them entertained, then have them returned to you as good as new."

"Tyler…"

"I'm serious. Come on, they're my nieces. You can trust me."

"I don't really have much choice."

I pat him on the back. "Ever the optimist."

"Oh, and by the way…"

"What now?"

"No more gnome hunting. Not with teachers,

not with teaching assistants, not with secretaries, not with…"

"Hey, hey…"

"I'm serious."

"Me, too. When it comes to my nieces, at least."

"I really hope so."

"Relax. Everything will be fine."

"I'll let the school know, then."

"Let the authorities know, too, while you're at it."

"Tyler…"

I can't help that I always see the positive side to every situation; I can't help that I was born to downplay everything, to joke around. Problems aren't my strong suit: not unless they involve a fire, or a damsel in distress.

"Who do you take me for?" I ask, feigning offence.

"Someone who breaks into other people's apartments."

Touché.

"Don't worry, I'll only sneak in through the school gates. And by gates, I mean the actual gates in front of the school. It wasn't a metaphor for—"

"You've just been suspended."

"So?"

"Does that not worry you? Are you not a little… Angry? Disappointed? Devastated?"

Devastated? Let's not get carried away. It's a little frustrating, okay, but I'll find a way out of this. Just as I'll find a way to get rid of *Ms. Call the Cops,* before the other guys get too used to taking the piss out of me.

"No." Parker interrupts my thoughts.

"What?"

"Don't do anything."

"What are you talking about?"

"I know that look. I know what you're about to do."

"Me?"

"Don't try to fix this your own way, Tyler. You've already done enough damage."

Exactly – I've done quite a lot of damage. I'm hardly going to change now, am I?

I'll get rid of her, I'll get my job back, I'll reclaim my reputation, and, most of all, I'll get my personal space back. *Ms. See-Through Towel* is going to seriously regret ever thinking she could win against me.

8
Tyler

With the rest of the day free, absolutely nothing to do, and not wanting in the slightest to go home and bump into my new neighbour, I have no choice but to visit my good friend Niall. He's the same as me: he has fuck-all else to do for the rest of the day, too.

We meet outside the city centre, at a nondescript café unknown to most people in town, and grab a table inside. The place is almost deserted; it's too late for breakfast, and too early for lunch. Aside from a few pensioners, we're the only people here – the only ones with nothing better to do.

Our future sure is looking bright.

We order two coffees and two sandwiches, given we're already here, before slipping easily into conversation.

"Wow. I really didn't think they'd just kick you out of the squad like that."

"They didn't kick me out. They suspended me."

"How is that different?"

"It's temporary. As soon as this whole ridiculous mess is cleared up, everything will go back to normal."

"Are you doing anything to help it?"

"They've only just suspended me, Niall. Give me a minute to think about it."

"And you're already wasting that minute – which we both know is the most important minute – with an idiot like me?"

I brush past the fact that he's awarded himself the 'idiot' title all on his own.

"Maybe talking things through with someone will help."

"Okay, I can help. I have to say, Tyler, I'm touched."

"Let's not get carried away. We didn't meet up today because I was expecting you to have the answers I'm looking for."

"Now I'm confused."

"You're the only person I know with nothing better to do. Like me."

"I should've known. I'm just your second choice."

"Don't be so hard on yourself. I actually quite enjoy your company."

"Well, thanks. I'm flattered."

"Now that I've stroked your ego, can we get back to my problem?"

"I'm all yours."

"The chief advised me to speak to a lawyer."

"A lawyer? Bloody hell."

"Yeah. He doesn't want me to deal with it on my own."

"Meaning you're not allowed into contact with the defendant?"

"Exactly."

"That's a bit tough, seeing as you're next-door neighbours."

Not for long, I think – although I keep this to myself.

One problem at a time, here.

"I don't know, Tyler. I always think it's best to have a direct approach to these things."

"What exactly do you mean by 'direct'?"

"Well, for starters, I think you need to give her a formal apology."

"Are you kidding?"

"And maybe, I don't know, some flowers, or chocolates, or a cake? Yeah, a cake."

"What the hell are you talking about?"

"And a bottle of wine. That'll go down well, trust me."

"I feel like you're describing your own life, here. Is this how you say sorry when you and Jordan are fighting?"

"And beg. Begging for forgiveness is key, mate."

"I'm not begging anyone."

"No, of course not. Your *skills* tend to speak for themselves."

"You need to stop that."

"It's not my fault that every woman in town – and out of town – knows your ways, my dear fireman Tyler Hayes. Apart from *my* woman. She's too switched-on for your silly games."

"Can we get back to my problem, please?"

"Absolutely."

"Thanks."

"And sex – that's the winning move."

"Sex."

"Especially when you get down on your knees – and not to beg, this time, if you know what I mean..." He winks at me.

"Believe me, I wish I didn't."

Niall laughs, then takes a few sips of his coffee.

"Besides, sex is out of the question. At the very least I'd end up being arrested again."

"Ahh..."

"What?"

"I get it, now."

"What do you get?"

"You've been thinking about it."

"About what?"

"About *her*."

"What *her* are we talking about, here? You've lost me."

"Ahh... Tyler, Tyler, Tyler."

"Why the hell did I ring you?"

"I wish I could say you did it because you knew

I'd have the answers you were looking for. But the truth is that you rang me because I'm the only other person you know who has nothing better to do."

"I'm not looking for answers. I'm looking for ideas."

"In my head?"

"Absolutely not. But I thought that talking it through with someone might help."

"Good point." He takes a bite of his sandwich, then continues. "Is it helping?"

"It's helping me feel even worse, yes."

"Happy to be here for you, mate."

I laugh. There's nothing else I can do by this point.

"But I'd think about it, you know."

"About what?"

"About saying sorry. They can't arrest you just for knocking on the door."

"I guess not."

"And if you take her some flowers, too…"

"I'm not taking her any flowers, or knocking on her door."

The chief told me to talk to an expert, and that's what I'll do. I don't want to make things any worse than they already are.

"Maybe a genuine apology is all it'll take for her to retract her statement. If you admit that you weren't thinking, that you shouldn't have done what you did, that it won't happen again, maybe show her a few of your skills..."

"Can we please cut that out?"

"It was just an idea."

"Why don't you use some of your own skills instead of thinking about everyone else's?"

"I'm not as gifted as you in that department, Tyler. I have many talents, but I think yours surpass all of mine."

I study him carefully.

"You know, right?"

"What are you talking about now?"

"You know my skills?"

"I don't know how to respond to that."

"Leave it. Don't respond, for God's sake. Anything could make this situation worse right now."

"You're right, sorry. I'll stop."

"I'd appreciate that."

"So what are you going to do?"

"I don't know."

"If you have nothing better to do, you could come to training with me later?"

"Do you need someone to give you a hand, by any chance?"

"Yes, please. Those kids are a nightmare."

I laugh. Luckily, Niall is helping me feel better – he always ends up in deeper shit than everyone.

"Is it really that bad?"

"Can I choose not to answer that?"

"Sure."

Niall was the GAA team's coach at the Abbey – the town's secondary school – during their *Intersport* county tournament. Against all odds, he managed to lead the team to victory, which meant that the school – run by Jordan, who is now his girlfriend – received a five-thousand-euro prize. His performance impressed the president of Four Master, the town's official GAA team, and he was offered a permanent position as their coach. Niall played GAA for twenty years for Dublin, one of the best teams in the country, and he was a champion. I had no doubt he'd manage to find his feet here, too. Maybe Four Master isn't his future, but it's a good start, which is exactly what he needed.

"So, are you coming?"

I shrug. I guess I have nothing better to do, and taking the piss out of Niall will keep my mind occupied for a while.

"What time does training start?"

"At five. Please, don't be late."

9

Tyler

After brunch with Niall, I decide to head home, hoping to avoid any unpleasant encounters. But given that her damn rubbish bin is still blocking my parking space, I'd say she probably hasn't left her house yet.

I climb the stairs in silence and reach my front door, inserting the key, but waiting for a few moments in the hallway for any signs of her presence, before letting myself into the apartment and closing the door. I stand there in silence, trying to gauge even the slightest movement from next door, but everything seems calm, peaceful, almost empty.

I head into the living room and over to the balcony door, sliding it slowly aside and stepping my foot onto the terrace to peer into her apartment. The balcony door is closed, the curtains drawn. There's no sign of life at all.

I head back inside, stopping in the middle of the living room, my hands on my hips and a strange sensation seeping into my body. Is she still alive? If she'd died in her sleep, for example, and no one had noticed she was gone, and her body started to decompose... Okay, maybe my imagination is running a little wild, now. Maybe I should just ignore her, pretend she doesn't exist, and contact a lawyer like the chief suggested. Maybe I should find a peaceful way to resolve this whole issue, so that I can get back to my job and my life as soon as possible.

* * * * *

I spend the rest of the day in total boredom. I'm not used to staying at home, and I'm not used to feeling nervous, either. I tried to go for a run, got as far as the park, and walked home. I was tired, exhausted. A little shaken up. I hate feeling like this, and I hate the fact that someone I don't even know has made me feel like this – someone who judged me before getting to know me. Okay, so maybe I *did* break into her house. And, fine, I did see her practically naked. And maybe I did try to take a little peek – you'd have done the same, in my position – but she was the one who pulled out a knife, for God's sake. She called the police! Here. In town. She could've at least given me the benefit of the doubt.

I take the stairs two at a time and step into my apartment. More deathly silence. Should I be worried? Should I knock at the door, and see if she's still alive? Or maybe I could go in through the balcony, and... And end up in trouble again.

I scoff in frustration – at what, I'm not sure – and peel off my sweaty clothes. I step into the shower and wash myself quickly, before wrapping a towel around my waist and drying my hair with another. I head into my room, rummaging through my wardrobe in search of something to wear whilst I give Niall moral support, and leave the house again. I'm a little early; I needed to get some air, and I need to be with someone, to help keep my spirits up. I decide to send him a message to tell him I'll pick him up, and after ten minutes, I'm pulled up outside his house, waiting.

The automatic gates to his parents' house open, and he slips between them to join me. He opens the passenger door and drops his bag onto the back seat, before sliding in next to me.

"You were bored, right?"

"Yes," I admit.

"Okay. Let's get this adventure over with."

I pull out of his parents' driveway and glance at him in amusement.

"Adventure?"

"You have no idea what you're in for, mate."

* * * * *

"Isn't it a bit weird that your daughter's boyfriend plays in your team?"

"Hey, hey... Watch your words."

"What words?"

"'Boyfriend', for a start."

"So he's not Skylar's boyfriend?"

"Absolutely not."

"What should I call him then?"

"Friend. Friend is fine."

"Friend with benefits?"

"Are you looking to get arrested again?"

"For what?"

"Aggression."

"And who am I being aggressive to?"

"Me, after I've tried to punch you in the face, but inevitably missed."

I laugh. I knew Niall would be the perfect distraction.

"Besides. *Playing* in the team? Let's not get carried away…"

"He doesn't play?"

"He's part of the team, but I have a feeling he might end up on the bench for the first match."

"Why have you put him on the team if you have no intention of letting him play? He was great during the tournament."

Carter is Skylar's boyfriend – Niall's fifteen-year-old daughter. He's a nerd, a bit of a loser, but he seems to have a few tricks up his sleeve. He was part of the school team during the tournament and was called up to sub for the unlucky goalkeeper during the last few matches, somehow miraculously pulling it off. I thought his GAA career would've ended with that tournament, which he clearly only took part in to impress Niall and Skylar.

"I think he might be trying to impress someone."

"By someone you mean you, right?"

"Don't tell me."

"I thought you liked Carter?"

"I liked him when he was tutoring Skylar, and I thought she would beat him up if he stared at her for too long."

"And now things have changed?"

"He's getting more and more confident every day."

"And what are you planning to do about it? I'm sure you already have something in mind."

"For now, I'm just going to keep a close eye on him."

"Okay."

"And you can help me."

"How am I supposed to do that?"

"You can help me out here."

"Here?"

"I need an assistant."

"What?"

"The old coach took his assistant and his physiotherapist with him when he moved over to his new team."

"So...?"

"I need a hand."

"You need someone to reattach your balls?"

He glares at me.

"You can always ask Carter to help."

"I can't. My daughter says I can't treat him like a slave."

"Does that mean you've already tried?"

"I only asked him to collect the damn balls and put them back in the damn bag."

"So now you're asking me to touch your balls?"

"Is it just me, or has this conversation taken a very weird turn?"

"Pretty much the same as every conversation I have with you."

"Let's start again. Okay?"

"Okay."

"I want you to be my assistant, Tyler. Please?"

"Would the chairman be okay with that? I've only ever played in the law enforcement team. I'm not a professional, and I never have been."

"The chairman gave me the task of finding someone who would be good for the role. As for your experience, no one is asking you to run around kicking a ball – you just need to help me with tactics, organising the team, and keeping the kids in line."

"I don't know…"

"Come on. It's not like you have anything better to do."

"I'm hoping that won't last long. I want to get back to work as soon as possible."

"You will get back to work, and when you do, we'll find a way to make sure the two don't clash."

"Are you really that desperate?"

"Yes. But not as desperate as you."

"What have I got to do with it?"

"You're thinking about it. And you're about to say yes."

"I never said that."

"And for you to be my assistant in a team full of teenagers who only think about one thing – not sport, but something that could land them in a whole heap of shit that…"

"Niall."

"Sorry, got carried away, there. Are you in? Or not?"

I scoff, glancing out at the kids, who have just finished their warm-up lap, and are heading in our direction. How desperate would I have to be to agree to something like this?

"I'm in."

And I already know that there won't be a single day that passes where I don't regret this.

10
Holly

After three intense days spent lounging around in bed, interrupted only by quick snacks – mainly consumed in bed – and calls of nature, I feel refreshed, ready, and excited to start my new job. I get up early, take a lukewarm shower, eat some cereal straight out of the box, and get dressed, buzzing and anxious to get started. I walk slowly down the stairs, grasping the railing to stop myself from slipping on the dewy morning ground. The last thing I need is to end up with my butt on the floor, attracting the attention of my nosy neighbour, who has obviously been spying on me through the windows. He seems to be ignoring the fact that he already has an arrest hanging over his head; it would only take one word from me for that to become a permanent problem. I haven't even managed to do that, yet. The guys at the station are waiting for me to make a statement, but I was too tired to leave the house, and I had no intention of putting an end to my well-needed rest. Now, I just want to concentrate on work.

I slip quickly into the taxi, trying to avoid being seen. I don't have my own car, so for now, I'll have to get around like this – at least until I can get my bearings on everything. I thought about maybe renting a car, but I'm not sure it's the right choice. I have a driving license, which I miraculously managed to get hold of a few years ago, in case of emergency, but I'm not a huge fan of driving. And this damn country! How the hell do they manage to drive on the wrong side of the road?

Besides, it's a small town, and it's not particularly well-connected with public transport. I don't like having to depend on taxis – I like to have my independence. I guess it'll just take a little patience and some getting used to, and I just have to try not to run anyone over in the process.

The taxi driver already knows where to go; I guess everyone here knows exactly where everything is. He parked outside the gates of the Abbey – the school I'm about to start working in. I step out of the car and check the time: I'm a little early, but I head through the entrance anyway, towards the principal's office.

I was lucky enough to only have to wait a year for this opportunity, in this exact town. Even though the contract only lasts a few months, I'm excited to have the experience, to try my best. I want this to be something unique – something I can refer back to in the future.

I love kids, and I love teaching. I never wanted to do anything else, and I don't think I ever could – despite my mother trying to drag me into one of her usual crazy schemes.

"You must be Ms. White." A woman welcomes me as I step into the corridor.

"That's me. But, please, call me Holly."

"Nice to meet you, Holly. I'm Anya, Ms. Hill's

assistant."

She shakes my hand enthusiastically.

"We spoke over the phone."

I nod, waiting for her to tell me what to do.

"I see you followed my instructions to a T. This is Ms. Hill's office – she's the headteacher of the secondary school campus, which we're standing in right now," she says, gesturing around us. "At the moment she's standing in for Ms. Cole, who's gone on maternity leave. She actually shouldn't have left so early, but they put her on bed rest, and they needed a last-minute substitute, so Jordan…"

"Anya." A voice from behind us makes us both jump.

"Am I talking too much again?"

"A little."

"Sorry," Anya says to me. "I always get so carried away."

"No problem, I talk way too much, too."

"I like her already," Anya says, turning to the principal.

"Shall we make ourselves comfortable in my office?" she says, gesturing towards the open door behind her.

I join her and shake her hand. "Holly White."

"Jordan Hill."

She nods at me to enter, and sits behind her desk.

"Well, you've had quite a journey."

"About two days of travelling."

"Wow. That's a long trip just for a temporary contract in a school."

"I wanted a new challenge, so here I am."

"And, trust me, it definitely will be a challenge. We have a big senior infant class this year. Fifteen kids in total – ten girls and five boys."

"I can't wait to get started."

"I'm glad you were able to take the job, and so quickly, too, despite the upcoming holiday season. This exchange programme is a great opportunity for everyone. We've had some amazing teachers from all over the world – it's been so inspiring, very motivating."

"I totally agree. That's exactly why I jumped at the chance to add my name to the list. And thank you so much for helping me find an apartment at such short notice. I know the school contacted agencies for me, and acted as my guarantor."

"It was the least we could do."

"I'm so happy to be here, and to get started. I can't wait."

The principal smiles at me, before speaking again.

"Can I ask you something?"

"Sure."

"Why Ireland? Why Donegal? This town? I know that you only applied to places on this side of the country."

I take a deep breath, before speaking, calmly and peacefully. "Because I have the feeling that there's something waiting here for me."

* * * * *

The teacher working alongside me, Wes, is also new. He started at the beginning of the school year, at the end of August, but, like me, he's not from around here. He comes from Dublin, and was also looking for a change. He seems alright – actually, more than alright. He seems like someone I'll be able to easily spend time with. Hopefully I'll be able to build a constructive relationship with him, where we can collaborate and work well together – maybe even become friends. Not that I should have any problems with that; from what I've understood, Wes bats for the other team. My biggest problem has always been in forming relationships with men, when they're interested in a very different kind of relationship.

I have nothing against men – more against rejection. And not just in that sense. I mean rejection in all senses. I've tried over the years, but with poor results. Maybe there's something in my family's DNA – my mother was always rejected by men. Maybe it stems from the fact that I was raised only by her, which meant I witnessed a lot of her failed relationships over the years. I'm just convinced that I wasn't cut out for these things, that it's not worth trying when you're only ever faced with disappointment after disappointment.

But, I'm here. Trying. Taking a chance on myself. Maybe I didn't have to travel all the way to the other side of the world, but I feel that there's something here that can help me understand the things about me that don't quite fit. I have to find out what those things are.

11

Tyler

Spending an afternoon with Niall and his team of nerds actually wasn't that bad. Watching someone who has it decidedly worse than me helped to put things into perspective. After being with him on the pitch, and then having dinner at his house, with his parents and his daughter, I got back to my own apartment feeling calmer and more positive about my future.

I had a nice, relaxed weekend, spent enjoying the company of the person I love most in the world: myself. I had time to reflect on everything with a clear mind, and I've decided to call a lawyer and try to reach an agreement with my nutcase of a neighbour. I have no idea what kind of agreement – I'm not the lawyer, here – but I'm sure he'll be able to help me find a reasonable solution to this whole mess. And after he's found it, everything will go back to the way it should be. I'll make sure I personally take care of getting that psycho out of the building, so that she never sets foot in here again.

I slept well – eight hours straight – and this morning I woke up early, as always, to go for a run. I had just taken a shower and sat at the table to have breakfast when I started to hear noises coming from the apartment next door. Music, similar to the other evening, followed by gentle steps, like someone was walking barefoot through the house. At about quarter to eight I heard the front door close, and the sound of heels climbing down the stairs. I wish I could say that my longing to get up and run over to the window was overruled by a good dose of logic, but I'd be lying; and I'm not the world's best liar. I got up and scurried over to the living room window, which looks out onto the street, and pulled back the curtains just in time to see her reach a taxi, open the door, and climb into the back. Her legs were the last thing I saw before she closed the door behind her: it's an image that has, unfortunately, accompanied me through my lonely morning, as I wait to go and pick up my nieces from school.

I spend my free time cleaning the house, then I go to the supermarket in search of healthy snacks for the girls, as requested by my brother. I grab a few tubs of yoghurt adorned with coloured faces which I assume are cartoons; I also pick myself up something to drink. I know I'll need it later. I head quickly home to unpack the shopping, eat a sandwich, then rush out to school to pick them up.

I climb into the car, follow the road into town for about fifteen minutes, then head in the direction of the school. I park in the parents' car park, then step out of the car, wearing a pair of semi-useless sunglasses and a leather jacket. I plaster a smile across my face that says *your fireman has arrived*, sauntering through the playground like someone who knows how to make an entrance.

I head towards the gates, where a few of the mums are standing in groups, and stick my hands into my pockets, ready to pick up my – *not so* – angelic nieces.

"Hayes." One of the mums pulls away from the group to say hello.

Callie, I think. Yeah, Callie. Divorced. Two kids under seven. Too many issues, and too willing to stay until breakfast the next day. Luckily, I have a good memory, which prevents me from making the same mistake twice.

"I haven't seen you around for a while."

I smile kindly at her, but don't respond.

"What are you doing here? Are you here to meet someone?" Her slightly strained voice gives away her assumption.

"My nieces," I clarify.

"Oh... Nieces..." she echoes. "What class are they in? They might be with my Bray. You remember Bray, right?"

"They're in Ms. Potter's class," I say right away, brushing past the assumption that I wouldn't remember the name of her son.

"Oh, Ms. Potter left. Didn't you know?" Her voice takes on a particularly unpleasant, almost bitter tone now.

"Of course..." I knew she was about to go away for some big project, but I didn't know what or when. I didn't go into details; I was too busy

82

getting onto my knees to… Well, I'm not going to go into detail now, either.

I wish I could say I slept with Ms. Potter because I knew she'd be leaving soon, and it wouldn't cause any problems with my nieces – but I'd be lying about that, too. It's not my style.

"Who's the new teacher? Someone from around town?"

"Why do you care so much?"

Ah. Someone must've heard the same rumour as my nieces.

"It doesn't matter," I snap, trying to take a few steps back, but Callie has no intention of letting me off lightly. I thought divorced women would've been a good choice – that maybe, after a failed marriage, they wouldn't have wanted to get involved in anything serious. Apparently, I didn't think things through properly.

"I think she's from out of town," she adds. "A foreigner. Who'd have thought?" she says, almost outraged. "The school year hasn't exactly got off to the best start."

"What do you mean?" I ask, curious.

"Too much change. It's not good for the kids. First the headteacher, now this whole teacher exchange thing…"

I shrug. "It happens, right?"

"Like what happened to you a few nights ago?"

I wondered when this would come up today.

"There have been rumours going around that you had a little trip to the police station, and that…" she steps closer, so that she can whisper, "…that you were even handcuffed."

Just so you know, I got the suggestive remark.

"Oh, there they are," she says, luckily, pointing towards the playground where the kids are lining up with their teachers, waiting for their parents to show up.

"That must be her."

I turn towards the class in search of my nieces, and when I see them waving at me from a distance, their new teacher by their side, I can't do anything but wave goodbye to my newfound positivity and surrender to the enormous heap of shit which has just been upturned over my head.

12

Holly

After the first three hours with the kids I feel a little disorientated, so Wes and I sit down together in the cafeteria as he tries to bring me up-to-speed with the class. I have no idea how they manage to learn Gaelic when they can barely even write or read correctly in English yet, but Wes explained that it's an important part of the education system in this country.

He talks me through the different classes, and points out some of the troublemakers who tend to stir up their classmates. He tells me they're a little rowdy, but curious and quite bright – that they're really good at subjects like art and maths. I'm pleased, because those are my strong points.

"They're still young, and completely undeveloped. It's normal for them to be a bit excitable," I add, biting into my sandwich, which I bought from the vending machine.

There isn't really a proper cafeteria here, even though that's what they call it. You have to bring your lunch from home – even the kids – and I had no idea. Wes covered me for a few minutes, which was just enough time for me to jog over to the other side of the building and find a vending machine.

"Have you always worked with young kids?"

"Up to the second grade."

"I don't really understand how it works for you guys."

"It's pretty much the same, we just have different names for each class. For us, they're called grades, but the ages are the same – apart from the last few classes of high school."

"You'll really like it here. It's very relaxed, and the headteacher, Ms. Hill, is lovely. It's a great place to work, and definitely a good place to start over."

"What makes you think I need to start over?"

"You've come quite a long way to be here."

"I'm here to experience something new, that's true. But not necessarily to start over."

"I'm here to start over." He pushes his salad around for a few moments. "I wanted a change of scenery, to breathe new air – I'm not sure if that makes sense."

"It makes perfect sense."

I know exactly what he's talking about. My mother needed 'new air' every three and a half months.

"Maybe this is the place for me. Besides, it's a nice place to live: the town is nice, the people are always friendly – if you like small towns where everyone knows everyone."

I don't really know what that means. I've never been in one place long enough to find out, but that's exactly what this period of my life is for: to work things out about myself, my family, my roots. Everything that was taken away from me.

The bell rings too soon – I didn't even manage to finish my lunch.

"You'll get used to that, too," he says kindly, as he gets up to call the kids back into class. I get to my feet and follow him as the kids line up. They seem to follow instruction from him, but not me – although this is normal, too. They don't know me, yet, they don't trust me. It'll take a little time and patience.

The last hour before the end of the school day is easy, enjoyable. The kids are working on an art project, painting pictures that Wes tells me will be used in a winter exhibition that the school puts on to raise money.

"Apparently, it's really fun, something that the whole community takes part in. There's a Father Christmas who gives out gifts. Everyone has to join in somehow."

"It sounds great."

"I hope you love Christmas, because from what I can gather, it's a real event in town."

I don't particularly love Christmas, but there's no need for him to know that. I'll do my best: for the kids and for the school.

"Five minutes left," he says, pointing to the clock on the wall. "I'll start to collect their paintings."

"I'll get them all ready to go."

We help the kids put on their jackets and shrug on their backpacks, before Wes leads the procession outside as I follow up with the last of the kids.

We reach the playground and line ourselves up, waiting for the parents to show up to collect their kids. Two girls, who are basically identical, approach me, dragging me into the centre of the crowd.

"There he is! You see him?" one of the girls asks.

I lift my gaze and my jaw almost hits the tarmac.

"Come on, let's go. We don't have all day," the other says, dragging me towards the school gate, where my *neighbour-local pervert-probably single dad* greets us.

"You."

I cross my arms once the girls have finally let me go, throwing their arms around him.

"Me."

"I didn't know you had kids."

"We're not that close."

I open my mouth to speak, but Wes appears at my side.

"Their dad called. It's okay, they can go with him." He steps back towards the line of kids, leaving me only with *him* and the two girls.

"Who on Earth would trust you with their

kids?"

He smiles. "My brother."

Oh my God. He smiled.

Someone should ban him from doing that.

"This is Uncle Tyler," one of the girls says. "Uncle Tyler, this is our new teacher, Holly White."

"Holly," he repeats. The letters of my name slide sensually from his lips.

"Well, as long their dad spoke to Wes…" I turn to leave, but he brushes his fingers against my arm.

"Do you really think that's appropriate?" I point out.

"Uncle Tyler, don't hustle Ms. White."

"Hustle?"

"Hassle," I suggest. "And she's right. I shouldn't even be talking to you."

"Why not?" the other asks. "Did you go gnome hunting with her, too, Uncle Tyler?"

"Gnome hunting?"

"Please, don't ask. It doesn't paint me in the best light."

"I get the impression that nothing paints you in the best light."

He smiles again. Apparently everything I say amuses him.

"You should make sure that we stop having these little… Encounters."

"I swear, it was a coincidence."

"For some reason I don't believe you."

"Can we go, Uncle Tyler?" one of the girls asks, catching his attention.

"Yes, honey. Just let me say goodbye to Ms. White."

"Don't make me call the police again."

He rolls his eyes, then floors me with another one of those smiles – this time, it lights up his eyes.

"Danger is my job, Ms. White. I thought you already knew that."

Yes, they may have mentioned that he's a fireman. Now I understand the risks he takes every day. But no one thought to mention the risk I'd be taking; because I know that smile can capture lonely young women, flooding the entire town – no, the entire *county* – with light.

13

Tyler

"Do you girls reckon it's possible for your dad not to find out that I already know your new teacher?"

All three of us are splayed across the sofa, each holding an overflowing bowl of chocolate ice cream, topped with chocolate syrup. And, yes, I've already ditched the 'healthy snack' idea – that went out the window the moment I found myself standing in front of Ms. White. Well, their dad's the one looking after them later – it's his problem, not mine. I needed some comfort food, and I needed to bribe the girls.

"That depends," one of them replies.

I don't know which one is speaking. They still haven't used each other's names yet. I think they're doing it to get one up on me.

"How did you meet her?"

"Trust me, it's a story that doesn't make me look good."

"I'll take your word for it," the other says.

I don't even have the energy to respond.

"You didn't go gnome hunting with her, too, did you, Uncle Tyler?"

"Absolutely not!" I protest, raising my voice a

little too much.

The two girls exchange a long glance, as if they were silently agreeing on something, before one of them speaks again.

"What happened with the smoke?"

I swallow nervously.

"What... smoke?"

"Dad was talking to Grandma about it on the phone."

"What? When?"

"She called last night."

She called him and not me. Fantastic.

"And he said that you got caught breaking into your new neighbour's house."

"And he said that the police were there," the other adds. "And that they took you in."

"He told Grandma all this?"

"Took you in where?" one of the girls asks, looking over at her sister, who shrugs.

"I don't think this conversation is appropriate," I say quickly, before serving them each another scoop of ice cream to keep them quiet.

"And how did you know that this whole story involves your teacher?"

"We saw her through the window."

"What?"

"While you were in the bathroom."

"She didn't see you, did she?"

"Yeah."

"Perfect."

I serve myself another scoop of ice cream, too, while I'm there.

"Did she say anything to you?"

"She just said hi."

I sigh, relieved.

"She seems nice."

"Mmm?"

"Ms. White."

"If you say so…"

"Today in the cafeteria she spent the whole lunch break talking to Wes."

"Who's Wes?"

"Our teacher."

"Why don't I know anything about this Wes?"

They both shrug.

I see my crazy neighbour is starting to make friends, so I must be the problem. And all because I was worried about the safety of our building?

"Uncle Tyler?"

"Mmm?"

"You're not going to go gnome hunting with her, are you?"

"I don't think so, honey."

"No one is hunting any gnomes around here. Not now, not ever." Parker's voice floats in from the doorway. "Why is it that we always end up talking about gnomes when you're around?" He wanders over to kiss the girls.

"You should be grateful that we were talking about gnomes, and not about—"

"For God's sake, stop."

"Whatever."

Parker sits on the arm of the sofa, next to his daughters. "So, girls. How was school?"

"We met our new teacher."

Fuck! That didn't take long. Weren't we just talking about keeping this a secret?

"What's she like?"

"She's okay, I think," says one of them. "But maybe Uncle—"

"Who wants more ice cream?" I leap to my feet, interrupting her. "I have strawberry in the freezer."

"Ice cream, Tyler? Seriously?"

At least his attention has shifted onto something I can deal with.

"They're my only nieces. Let me spoil them a little."

"They'll be bouncing off the walls after all this sugar."

"That's not my problem." I head into the kitchen, followed by my brother.

"Arsehole," he hisses through his teeth.

"Nice, Parker. And in front of your daughters, too!"

"You're a dickhead."

"It just gets better and better," I say, winding him up. I close the freezer door and place the tub of ice cream on the counter.

"So?" he asks, leaning against that same counter. "How was everything at school?"

"Great."

"The school remembered that you were the one picking them up, right?"

"Uh-huh."

"I didn't know their new teacher was starting today."

"Mm-hmm."

"What's she like?"

"What?"

"The girls' new teacher. What's she like?"

"How should I know?" I shrug, tearing my gaze from him. "She's a teacher, Parker. What's she supposed to be like?"

"What's with all this fake disinterest?"

"Fake?"

"Well, a few days ago, you seemed to really care what the girls' teachers were like."

"That's not true."

"So you *didn't* go gnome hunting with Ms. Potter and Ms. Trent?"

"That was a coincidence."

"Two coincidences," he says, holding up two

fingers to echo his point.

"Okay, two. That doesn't mean anything."

"What have you done with the girls' new teacher, Tyler?"

"Me?" I'm sweating, visibly nervous. This is what happens when I try to lie.

"Come on. Who is it?"

"I don't know what you're talking about."

"Don't make me ask the girls."

"You wouldn't dare."

"Girls!" Parker heads quickly towards the living room, and I'm hot on his heels. "Did Uncle Tyler behave himself today?"

"With us? Or with our new teacher?" one of them quickly responds.

You can tell that these girls have been brought up by my brother.

Parker glances at me, but I don't give in. He turns back to his daughters.

"Why? What happened with your teacher?"

"Is this the secret you wanted us to keep, Uncle Tyler?"

I scoff, scrabbling to at least salvage my role as uncle to these two girls, without dragging them into the messes I make.

"It's her."

"Her... who?"

"My neighbour. She's their teacher."

"No."

"Yep."

"I don't believe it."

"I couldn't have known."

"I'm not so sure about that."

"Oh, come on, Parker!"

"You're unbelievable."

"I don't think that was a compliment, Uncle Tyler," one of the little traitors chimes in.

"Come on, girls. It's time to go home." They seem to understand that now is not the time to make a fuss, as they shrug their jackets on quickly. "Grab your backpacks." They follow their dad's instructions like two robots, before heading for the door, ready to leave.

"I'll fix this, I promise," I say to my brother, before he opens the door.

"You won't fix anything, Tyler. Why are you always like this?" he asks, pointing to me. "You're incapable of taking anything seriously, of working hard to get what you want."

"That's not true. I work hard at my job."

"Then make sure you do something to keep that job, Tyler. Because if you carry on like this, you could end up losing it."

14

Holly

By the end of my first week at work, the principal calls me into her office after class.

"Come in, come in." She gestures for me to enter, and I sit myself down across from her.

"Has something happened?"

"I just wanted to have a chat about how everything is going. Are you settling in well? Is there anything I can do for you?"

"Everything's going well – actually, really well. Wes is helping me out a lot, and the kids are starting to get used to me."

"Good, I'm really happy to hear that. Wes hasn't been with us for long, but I think he's amazing. He's so great with the kids."

"Yeah, he is."

"What about everything else?"

"Everything else?"

"Have you been into the centre of town yet? Are you getting your bearings? Do you like it?"

"That's a lot of questions..." I say, feeling a little uncomfortable.

"Sorry, let's take things one at a time. What do you think of our town?"

"To be honest, I haven't really had the chance to go out yet. I've been concentrating so much on work."

"Of course."

"I was waiting for the weekend to get out and see the sights."

"If by 'sights' you mean a pub to get drunk in, where you can meet someone and take them home, then I have a few suggestions." Anya appears in the doorway of the principal's office.

"Straight to the point, Anya."

"You're wasting precious time." Anya joins us, hopping up to sit on the principal's desk.

"What's going on?" I ask, confused.

"It's Friday," Anya explains. "We're officially out of school hours."

"Okay…"

"And we want to take you out for a girls' night."

"W-what?"

"Friday is our night out," the principal adds. "Just girls. Ready for anything."

"Should I be worried?"

Anya raises an eyebrow. "That depends…"

"On what?"

"On how well you can handle your alcohol."

"Oh… Pretty well, I think."

Anya slides down from the desk and steps towards me. "You're in Ireland now, Holly. Here, drinking is a serious sport."

"Now I'm really worried," I say, turning to Ms. Hill.

"What Anya is trying to say is that we want you to come out with us tonight. You need to get to know the city."

"Thanks, but—"

"No 'buts'," Anya says, interrupting me. "Tonight you're coming out with us. It'll be fun – we'll get drunk, and spend the whole evening gossiping about the men who populate this half of the county. And, believe me: they're not even the worst you could come across."

I laugh, in spite of myself.

"I'll come by and pick you up," Ms. Hill adds.

"Thanks. I still haven't quite worked out how to get around town yet."

"No problem. I know where you live, anyway," she says, with a feigned indifference that almost feels like a warning.

I have to admit that they're really starting to scare me.

"And we know about the whole story between you and Hayes," Anya adds.

"Everyone in town knows. But that shouldn't shock you. It's normal – word spreads quickly around here, and rumours don't tend to die down," Jordan continues.

"I'd noticed."

"I'm hoping you'll fill us in a little more on

what happened tonight."

"There isn't much more to add."

"We'll be the judges of that."

＊ ＊ ＊ ＊ ＊

I leave my apartment and wobble down the stairs in my heels, heading towards the car waiting for me. I climb inside and her warm smile welcomes me.

"Thanks for coming to pick me up, Ms. Hill."

"Please, only the students call me that." She starts the engine and pulls out onto the road. "I'm just Jordan."

I relax into the passenger seat after clicking my seatbelt into place.

"You're aware that Hayes was spying on you from behind the curtain, right?"

"Absolutely. He does it every day."

Jordan laughs, and takes a right turn.

"Typical Hayes."

"Do you know him well?"

"Everyone knows him well."

"That doesn't seem like a good thing."

"It depends on your point of view."

"I don't think I particularly want to have a point of view when it comes to him."

"Unfortunately, I don't have a choice. I've

known him since we were at school, and he also happens to be my boyfriend's best friend."

"Ah."

She laughs, glancing over at me. "He's harmless, trust me."

"If you say so. I'm not so convinced."

"He's just a little, you know... He's one of those men who will never grow up. But he's a good guy. You can trust me on that."

"He didn't exactly give off a good first impression."

"So you're planning to follow through with your statement?"

"I don't know. It all seems a bit ridiculous."

"When Hayes is involved, things tend to be a bit ridiculous."

We stay silent for the rest of the journey. Once we get to the parking lot, Jordan pulls in next to another car, which I then discover belongs to Anya. We both climb out and head towards the entrance of the pub.

"There isn't really a lot of choice around here," Anya says right away. "There aren't many places to go. But this place is decent enough, if you want to have a few drinks, have fun, maybe even dance a little."

"Okay," I say, taking a mental note of her advice.

"I don't think it's the best place to meet guys,

though."

"Anya!" Jordan says, stopping her.

"What? Didn't we want to find out whether that's what she was looking for?"

"Trust me, it's absolutely not what I'm looking for," I say, as we push past a small crowd and sit down at an empty table.

"Bad break up?" Anya asks, immediately curious.

"I never really got far enough into a relationship with anyone for there to be a break up."

Anya turns in search of a waiter and calls him over.

"I think we already need a drink. I get the feeling it's going to be a long night."

Jordan and I laugh as the waiter wanders over. They order for me, too – I have no idea what they've chosen. I just told them I was happy to drink anything, and I don't know whether or not that was a good idea. But I'm here, surrounded by people who seem genuinely interested to get to know me. I'm free. I'm single. I'm ready: ready to accept anything this adventure can offer me.

* * * * *

By the third round, I still have no idea what I've been drinking, but I feel ready to vomit the entire contents of my life story over this table, in a pub whose name I've already forgotten.

"You were telling us about your relationships," Anya says, encouraging me to speak.

"What relationships?"

"I don't know. Tell us."

"So you tricked me into coming here and forced me to drink so that I'd spill all my secrets?"

"We brought you here so we could spend the evening together – no tricks, no ulterior motives," Jordan says calmly. "As for the drinking, you told us you could handle your alcohol, and we believed you."

"You two aren't normal," I say, making them both burst out laughing. "But I like you both a lot."

"So, these relationships you were talking about... Were you maybe batting for the other team?" Anya asks.

I laugh. "I don't like you in *that* way."

"Not that we'd have a problem with that," she adds hurriedly. "But you should know that I'm a sucker for a di—"

"Maybe you should lower your voice." Jordan's hand covers Anya's mouth. "Or we'll end up with every single man in town queuing up by our table."

"I don't think I've ever spent an evening like this," I say, suddenly a little sad.

"You didn't go out with your friends much?"

"I didn't really have many friends. I moved so often as a kid, and then as a teenager, too, that it was difficult to maintain friendships. Growing up, I always thought it wasn't worth going to the effort of meeting new people."

"Why did you move around so much? For your parents' jobs?"

"My mother. She was the one who raised me, and she had this obsession with always needing to go looking for something new."

"Did she ever find that something?" Jordan asks, kindly.

I shake my head.

"I think we need another drink," Anya states. "This is making you depressed."

I smile at Anya, who immediately gestures to the waiter to bring us another round.

"You don't need to tell us anything if you don't want to, Holly. We just wanted to spend some time getting to know you, just us girls."

"Unless you want to tell us about what happened with *Mr. I Think I Can Smell Smoke*," Anya says, nodding behind me, towards the entrance of the pub, where my *neighbour-local fireman* has just walked in with another guy, a smile plastered across his face.

"I don't believe it." Jordan gets up. "Excuse me for a minute." She heads quickly over to the guys, and I turn my gaze to Anya, who is laughing.

"You see that guy there, with Hayes? That's Niall Kerry, Jordan's boyfriend. And Jordan's gone over there now to tell him off for coming here, to the same pub as us."

"Why?"

"He knew we were coming here, and he knew that you'd be here, too."

"Sorry, but I don't get it."

"He did it deliberately. To make Hayes uncomfortable."

"But aren't they friends?"

"Exactly."

I don't know by this point whether to blame the alcohol or this strange little town.

Jordan comes back over to us, almost purple in the face. "I swear, I'll kill him."

"It doesn't matter." I gulp down the rest of my drink. "He's the one with the problem, not me. He's the one who should be avoiding *me*."

"Well said!" Anya clinks her glass against mine, before emptying hers, too, in one sip. "We need another round."

"I don't know if I can handle another round."

"Let's get some nuts, too, to line our stomachs." Anya calls the waiter over again.

"Are you sure it's not a problem?" Jordan asks.

"Absolutely. It's as if that fireman, with his *I can do whatever I want to you* smile doesn't even exist."

"Er..."

"Did she really just say that?" Anya asks.

"What? What did I say?"

"Maybe it's best if we leave," Jordan suggests, but I grab the glass which has just been placed in front of me, and lift it into the air.

Jordan and Anya follow suit. "To new friends and new beginnings," I say.

We clink glasses then drink, although they drink much faster than me. I take my time; otherwise I'll barely be able to make it to bed once I get home.

"Good evening, ladies." A voice interrupts us.

I lift my gaze to see Hayes, standing there with his friend.

"I wanted to introduce myself to the new girl." Even though I'm drunk, I can still see that he's trying not to laugh. "I'm Niall Kerry: almost a celebrity around here."

Anya bursts into laughter, as does the fireman; at the sight of him laughing, I can't seem to contain my own laughter.

He notices, and immediately makes the most of the opportunity.

"Hello, Ms. White."

"Hayes."

"I hope you're having a good evening."

"It was." I take a sip of my drink, and the corner of his mouth begins to twitch. I feel as if he's set me alight, laid me out on the floor, then set me alight again. I thought firemen were supposed to put out fires, not start them – but I also thought I'd be able to handle my drink, and here I am, fantasizing about flames and smiles and firemen.

This country is already ruining me, and I've only been here a week.

"Can I get you the next round, then? To make your evening better."

"Could you turn around and walk out the door, instead?" I suggest.

"It's a pub, I can come in whenever I like. Besides, I'm not aware of any restraining order."

"I should've asked for one."

"They'd have laughed in your face," Niall says, making the entire table laugh. "And, seriously – Hayes? He wouldn't hurt a fly even by accident. Well, actually, maybe if it was an accident..."

"You're not helping, Niall," Jordan says.

"When *does* he help?" Hayes responds.

Damn. He's always so quick-witted: another sure-fire way to set you alight.

"We'll take you up on those drinks, by the way," Anya says, "right, girls?"

"Absolutely," Jordan agrees, emptying her glass.

Hayes looks at me. He knows I'm the one who'll give the last word.

"I won't change my opinion of you just because you buy me drinks, you know."

"I never thought you would."

"In that case," I say, emptying my glass, too, and placing it down on the table, "let's get another round."

15

Tyler

Niall parks along the street, not far from the pub.

"Tell me the truth. We only came out tonight because you didn't want to sit around at home on your own, right?"

Niall came over to mine with the clear intention of dragging me out this evening; just like old times, he said, like two mates, just the two of us. But on the way here, he admitted that Jordan was out with Anya, his daughter was out with Carter – who is *not* her boyfriend – and his parents were having dinner with friends.

"Why, did you have anything better to do?"

"That's not the point."

"Then what *is* the point?"

"You know what? It doesn't matter."

I open the door and climb out of the car, and Niall does the same. We walk side-by-side towards the entrance of the pub. After all, I can't really be annoyed at him; I turn up at his house when I'm bored, too.

I hadn't yet thought about what I was going to do this evening when he knocked at my door. Following my brother's advice – and the chief's advice – I've been trying to keep a low profile to avoid making the situation worse. I haven't been out pestering any women, or been pestered by any myself – and believe me when I say that happens – but I think that a quiet evening out with my best friend will do me good. I don't think it'll do any damage. At least, that's what I'd convinced myself of during the three minutes it took to walk from the car to the pub, because it doesn't take me long to land myself in even more trouble; trouble that my *maybe-now-ex*-best friend has offered to me on a silver platter.

"You came here deliberately, didn't you?" I ask right away.

"What are you talking about?"

I point to Jordan, who is approaching us quickly, her expression furious.

"Oh. This? I had no idea they'd be here."

"Please, don't get me involved in your stupid games. Have we come out tonight so you can check on your girlfriend?"

Niall laughs as Jordan appears before us, hands on her hips, and a clear desire to wrap her hands around his neck in frustration.

"Kerry."

"Hello, my beautiful headmistress."

"Flattery won't help you, here."

"What if I get down on my knees later?"

Jordan can't quite hide her smile, and I roll my eyes.

"Stop trying to distract me."

"That was never my intention."

"You knew we were coming out with her tonight."

At Jordan's 'her', I let my eyes roam the pub. I make my way around the room twice before finding their table.

"You're a dickhead, Kerry."

"I never doubted that."

"You're aware I have an arrest hanging over my head, right?"

"I know. But I also know that you'll manage to find a way out of it."

"And how am I supposed to do that?"

"How am I supposed to know? Aren't you the one with the *skills*?"

"I can't use my skills on her, Kerry."

"Why not?"

"Do I really need to explain it to you?"

"It would help."

"I'm going back to our table. You two," Jordan says, pointing to each of us in turn, "try not to cause any more damage. This is our evening. And she's my new teacher."

We both lift our hands innocently as Jordan turns her back and strides back over to their table.

"So," I say, looking at him. "You're having fun, aren't you?"

"Not yet. But I'm sure it won't take long."

"Why are you doing this?"

"Because I get bored easily."

"Remind me why we're friends, again?"

"I don't know. You decided to be my friend. I just played along."

I shake my head, but can't help but laugh.

"Shall we go over?" He nods towards the pub. "Or do you need a little push?"

I ignore him, and head confidently towards their table. Niall appears immediately by my side; he wouldn't miss this.

I say hello to my neighbour, who looks sexier tonight than every other day this week, when I've watched her leave her apartment and take the stairs. I offer them a round of drinks, and she seems hesitant to accept. Her cheeks are red and her eyes are bright, probably due to the alcohol, and her mouth… Bloody hell, I shouldn't be thinking about that mouth in the way I'm thinking about it right now, or I'll end up being arrested again. But my little friend below my waistband is already starting to stand to attention.

I feign disinterest – or, at least, I try – as Niall continues to be a cretin – he doesn't need to try. Finally, my dear Ms. White – did I really just say *my* and *dear*? – gives in, and lets us sit down. Anya calls the waiter over to order our drinks.

"He's paying," she says immediately.

Niall and I each order a beer, and the girls

order the same drinks they've been nursing all evening. I make the most of the opportunity to sit closer to Ms. White, and attempt to have some form of civil conversation with her.

"I'm seriously considering that restraining order, you know," she says, crossing her arms and closing off any kind of contact between us.

"You watch too many American TV shows."

"I'm Canadian."

"Canada... Isn't that pretty much the same thing?"

She glares at me.

"Is this what you guys do, over there? Arrest the first guy you come across, issue restraining orders, abandon your families...?"

She watches me warily.

"Scratch that last part."

"You're a really weird guy, Hayes."

"Is that a bad thing?"

"It is when it means you break into your neighbours' houses..."

"Listen. I really did smell smoke, and I didn't know anyone was in."

"You were carrying my plant."

"True. But I didn't know whether someone was at home in that moment. The lights were off – or, at least, I thought they were, from the outside. The apartment is attached to mine. We're basically only separated by a wall anyway."

"Does that mean you can hear everything I'm doing?"

Lie, Tyler. Lie.

"Absolutely not. The walls are thick – really thick. I wouldn't even hear you screaming for help at the top of your lungs."

She studies me, unconvinced.

"I really was just worried about the smell of smoke. I'm a fireman, right? Do you really think a fireman would risk his career, his reputation, for something like that? Just to spy on his new neighbour?"

Our drinks arrive then, interrupting our conversation – the only civil conversation we've managed to have since she turned up here to ruin my basically-perfect life.

She reaches for her glass and takes a few sips.

"I don't believe you, Hayes," she says, seriously. "I don't believe you, and I don't believe men, period."

"Well, I don't believe women. Period."

Her mouth curves into a slight smile.

"I guess we have something in common."

She drinks again, forcing me to stare at her mouth as it rests against the rim of her glass.

Apparently, we do have something in common. And, apparently, that means that I'm pretty fucked. But it's best that no one knows that.

* * * * *

I head over to the bar to order another pint and sink onto the stool, waiting to be served. I glance around, towards the dance floor, where Niall and Jordan are dancing. Then I let my eyes wander back over to our table, where Ms. White is sitting with Anya. I ask the barman to fix two more drinks for the girls, then look back over towards them. From here, I have a perfect view of Ms. White. She's sitting with her legs crossed, her calf muscles tensed from her high heels. Her skirt has ridden up her thighs, showing glimpses of something very interesting. Her elbows are resting on the table, her chin in her hand, and her sensual mouth moving as she speaks to Anya.

Please, don't say anything. I already know what you're thinking.

The barman places the glasses down in front of me, and I ask him for a tray, before taking the drinks over to our table.

"Oh, look," Anya says, winding me up. "You've already found a new job." She takes her drink and immediately takes a few sips.

"Another job?" Ms. White asks, her eyes landing on me. They're narrow now, almost closed. I get the impression she can't quite focus on my face. I have no idea how much they've drunk, but I'd take a guess that she's a little over the limit.

"Did they not suspend you from the squad?" Anya adds, plunging us further into embarrassment.

"How would you know?"

"It's not a big town. People have nothing better to do." She gets to her feet, drink in hand. "I'm going to go for a wander around the room. Can you deal with him for just a few minutes? Until Jordan comes back?"

"I can deal with him perfectly well," Ms. White says, slurring each syllable.

Anya walks into the crowd, and Ms. White turns her attention back to me.

"I didn't know they'd suspended you."

I take a sip of my beer. "It's one of the risks of my job."

She smiles a little, then traces her small, seductive fingers around the rim of her glass.

"I didn't mean to cause you all these problems."

I sit there in silence, unsure of whether or not to agree. Until yesterday she was out to get me, and I think the alcohol might be speaking for her, now.

"It's just that... A woman should be able to defend herself."

"I totally agree."

This time, she's the one to fall silent. She glances over at the dance floor, where, until a few minutes ago, only Jordan and Niall were dancing, wrapped around each other; now, there's a crowd obscuring them from our sight. Anya has disappeared to God knows where, and the two of us are alone at the table.

"Do you want to dance?" I ask, nodding towards the dance floor.

She scrutinises my expression carefully.

"We're in a pub full of people. What do you think will happen?"

"I don't know, but you definitely don't seem like the kind of guy I'd normally dance with."

"What kind of guy *would* you usually dance with?"

"I don't think we're intimate enough for me to answer that."

"Intimate?"

I can't deny that the word has had a seriously worrying effect on me, and on my little friend down below.

"Close. I meant we're not close enough."

This is definitely not helping the situation. By this point, I don't think anything can help.

"Besides, I don't dance. It doesn't matter who I'm with. I'm really bad at it."

I can't seem to wrap my head around the idea of Ms. White being bad at something, even if I'd seen it with my own eyes.

"You can't be that bad."

"And you can't be naïve enough to think that

I'd fall for it."

"Fall for what?"

"Fall into your trap."

I laugh. "Trap?"

"Is this how you hit on women? Your jokes, your smile? You lure them into bed…"

"Bed?"

"Come on. I've met guys like you. I know what you're like."

I, on the other hand, don't know enough women like her, and I'm starting to like it a little too much. But I'm still a fireman and, as I said, danger is my middle name. So I get to my feet and reach out my hand.

"Show me what you can do."

Colour leaps into her cheeks.

"I… I don't…"

"On the dance floor, I mean," I add, smiling – although I get the feeling that this could be one of those times when smiling lands me in a whole heap of trouble. "I don't bite."

"You'll keep your hands to yourself?"

"I promise."

She studies me for a few moments, then gets up. Ms. White is small, despite the heels, but I like it. I like the fact that she has to tilt her head back to look at me.

"I'm not drunk enough not to know what you're up to, Hayes," she says, following me towards the dance floor. We find a space big enough for the two of us, not far from Niall and Jordan.

"What am I doing?"

I place my hand on her waist before sliding it slowly up her back, my fingers pressing lightly against her skin.

"I know your intentions, you know."

I can assure you, Ms. White, that you'd never be able to imagine all the intentions rushing through my mind right now.

She slides her hands down my chest, and I pull her closer, pressing harder against her back.

"We're just dancing."

"That's not true. We're basically standing still in the middle of the dance floor."

"That's how you dance in a couple."

She lets her gaze wander the room as I rest my other hand gently on her waist.

"See? It's not so bad."

She turns her gaze back to me, tilting her head back completely to do so. Her eyes are small and tired – I'd imagine the alcohol is starting to take hold of her senses. I need to take about fifty steps back to avoid even more trouble.

"Do you think?" she asks, hesitantly. I can't help but smile.

"You're perfect, Ms. White." My voice is low, intimate. I don't think she hears me amongst the chaos around us. I hear it, though. I can feel it running through my body, through my hands, making me tighten my grip on her, bringing her closer to me. Ms. White doesn't pull away; she rests her head against my chest, next to her hands, so small and so delicate. She starts to lose herself in the slow, rocking movement of our bodies.

"You're the one doing everything." I feel her voice vibrating across my chest, and smile, instinctively.

"Just let yourself go. Let the music take you away. Let me take you away."

Ms. White sighs, her hot breath seeping through my shirt.

"Is this okay?" she asks, lifting her eyes to mine.

I look down at her. "You're doing great."

She bites her lip shyly, before pressing her head against my body, as we both lose ourselves in this moment of perfect madness.

16

Tyler

Once we get back to the table, we sit in silence for a while, intent on finishing our drinks. Dancing was a really bad idea – but it felt so nice to hold her close to me, as if she were someone to take care of, and I were the one to take care of her.

We sit there, watching the others dancing. Niall and Jordan can't tear themselves away from each other, and Anya seems to know how to move, and who to move towards.

Ms. White seems tired now, maybe a little uncomfortable, too. She looks like she can't wait to get home. I hate when people feel uncomfortable, especially when they're with me, so I try to break the tension.

"Tired?" I ask, my eyes seeking out her own.

She doesn't look at me. She sits there, staring at the people on the dance floor.

"A little. It's been a long week."

"Do you want to go home?"

"Maybe that'd be best, yeah."

"Do you know how you're getting back?"

"I came with Jordan, but she looks a little busy."

"I can give you a lift, if you like."

She looks at me, lifting an eyebrow.

"You can trust me. I'm a fireman, a member of the community. And, until you showed up, I had an untarnished reputation."

"Until you broke into my house, you mean."

"Touché."

"Well," she says, getting to her feet and placing her hands on the table. "We danced together and I didn't even have to knee you between your legs."

"Would you really have done that?"

"I don't think you want to know the answer to that."

I laugh, amused, and get up, too.

"Well, seeing as you already know how to keep me in line…"

"I think you're my only hope of getting home tonight."

"Does this mean you trust me?"

"I've drunk a lot tonight, Hayes. And I'm on my own, in a country I don't know. I'm tired, and I want to go home. The principal of the school I work in knows that I'm with you, so…"

"So you're willing to take a chance."

"Don't forget that I know how to handle a knife."

"I doubt you have any knives in your bag."

"Don't challenge me, Hayes," she says, lowering her tone. "You have no idea who you're up against."

And I don't have to find out, I tell myself, as I'm rummaging around in Niall's jacket pockets.

"What are you doing?"

I pull out his car keys. "I came with him."

"So you offered me a lift home when you don't even have a car?"

"I'm a resourceful guy."

"I don't doubt it."

"After you," I say, gesturing for her to lead the way.

"Hands where I can see them," she warns me, before sauntering ahead of me, her hips moving seductively.

I follow her, fully aware that I'm heading towards another disaster, but also aware of the fact that certain disasters can't be avoided.

* * * * *

She falls silent again in the car. I can't tell whether it's because of our unexpected closeness, or because the effects of the alcohol are already starting to send her into a trance. Her legs are tilted slightly towards me, her coat partly covering her. Unfortunately for me, she still has a fair amount of skin on show; unfortunately for her, I'm not the kind of guy to look the other way.

I sent Niall a message to tell him I was taking Ms. White home in his car, and that I'd drop it off with him tomorrow morning. He responded saying that Jordan warned me not to do anything stupid.

"So, your first night out?" I ask her, glancing quickly in her direction. Her gaze is fixed out the window.

"Yeah."

"How did you like it? The place, the people…? Apart from me, obviously."

I glance over at her again. She's smiling.

"I definitely think you drink too much over here."

Now I smile. "I definitely think you're right."

"How the hell do you not all have liver damage?"

"We all have a spare."

She laughs. And not to impress me, but because she's genuinely having fun.

"You know what we say around here?"

She turns to look at me. Although I don't meet her gaze because I'm driving, I can feel the electricity of her eyes all over my body.

"Drink 'til you're Irish."

"Seriously?"

"There are even T-shirts, mugs, glasses…"

"I'm sure there are."

"And, you know, I need to buy you a pint glass."

"Why?"

"As a welcome present."

Yep. I'm stupidly ignoring all the signs, I know.

Ms. White doesn't respond. She falls back into silence for the last few minutes of our journey home, until I park outside our building. I switch off the engine and climb out of the car, wander around to the other side, open the passenger door, and offer her my hand.

She eyes me suspiciously.

"Trust me, I'm a gentleman. And if we'd met under normal circumstances, you'd have noticed sooner."

Or maybe her opinion of me would've been even worse – but I don't think I want to know. I also don't think she'd particularly like to know the opinions other women tend to have of me.

She takes my hand and gets to her feet, wobbling a little.

"Are you okay?"

"What the hell do you put in your drinks over here?"

I close the door behind her and lock the car.

"Only the good stuff," I say, jokingly, at which she shakes her head.

"Can you manage?" I ask, nodding towards the stairs.

"Oh, my God, those stairs."

"Do you need a hand?"

"I think I'm still capable of managing by myself, thanks." She lets go of my hand and bends down to take off her shoes, planting her bare feet onto the tarmac. "That's better." She heads towards the stairs, grabbing hold of the railing as she slowly leads herself up to her front door. "And don't look up my skirt," she says.

Does she know nothing about men? That's like telling me not to eat a freshly-baked cake.

I follow behind her, one step at a time, and when she reaches the penultimate step, she loses her balance a little, teetering backwards. I stretch my arms out to grab her, quickly breaking her fall. I lift her up a little, easily, and pull her into me.

"This isn't going to change my opinion of you, either."

"I never expected it to, I swear. I didn't plan for this."

I could never have planned such a perfect moment; usually, I try to run from moments like this. But tonight – and I mean *only* tonight – I want to grant myself the luxury of enjoying every second of this madness.

I climb up the last step with her between my arms, and stop in front of her door. She jangles the keys at me, then slips them into the lock. The door opens before us.

"Can I come in?"

"You're asking my permission, now?"

"I don't want to get arrested again."

"You can go in."

I take two steps inside and close the door behind us, leaning my back against it. We're plunged into darkness, and I'm still holding her in my arms. One of her hands is resting on the back of my neck.

"You can put me down, now. I'm safe."

"Yeah, you are," I say instinctively.

I let her slide slowly down, her feet landing on the wooden floor of her living room.

"Thanks for the lift." Her hand is still pressing lightly against the skin of my neck.

"Thank you for not calling the police again."

She smiles. I can't see it, but I can tell by the way her breathing changes.

She steps back, and her hand leaves my skin, slowly. Her fingers brush delicately against my neck, and I shiver; it runs the length of my spine.

"Can you get to your room by yourself?"

"Is that a subtle way of telling me you want to see my bedroom?"

I smile. "No. It was a genuine question."

"I can manage. But thanks anyway."

"I guess I'll be going, then."

I open the door behind me and stop in the hallway.

"Lock the door behind you and use the chain, too. You never know what kind of people are out and about – especially in this part of town."

She steps forward, the lights outside the building illuminating her smile.

"But I live next door to a fireman. I don't think there's anywhere safer than that."

She's right – for her it's definitely safe. But I'm not so sure the same applies to me.

17

Holly

At eight o'clock on Saturday morning I'm already up, thanks to a hammering headache, brought on by my inability to handle my alcohol the way I thought I could. At least, that was until I set foot in this country. I'd got out of bed in the hope of finding some kind of painkiller somewhere, but after a few minutes of searching, I abandon the idea, and slump onto the couch, hoping to fall back asleep. I lie there on my back, cursing myself for going out last night; but a knock at the door forces me to drag myself back to my feet. When I open the front door, there's no one outside – but on my doormat, there's a takeaway coffee and a pack of pills. I bend down to grab hold of everything and close the door. *Ms. White* is written on the cup, and attached to the medicine package, which I gleefully discover to be paracetamol, is a note.

I hope these presents make you feel a little better.

Your local fireman.

I burst out laughing, which makes my head throb, before reading on.

About last night...

I brought you home, safe and sound, but I couldn't help looking up your skirt. Nice choice.

Next to the writing is a smiley face.

I'm assuming by 'choice' he's referring to my underpants. I guess I should be angry, go knocking on his door and maybe throw this coffee all over him – but right now, I don't have the energy. I just want to take my tablets and drink my coffee in bed, and spend the rest of the morning doing absolutely nothing. I especially don't want to think about yesterday, or about the fact that he liked my pink polka-dot underwear.

* * * * *

After another few hours of dozing, I decide to go for a walk around town. My apartment isn't too far from the centre – it's quite a long walk, but it's definitely doable. It's short enough to make me forget about that stupid idea of renting an expensive car that would be impossible for me to drive without crashing.

I follow Main Street, which leads into town, the whole way, before stopping outside the window of a café. It's lunchtime – or, at least, I think it is. I still haven't worked out the timings around here just yet. But judging by the lack of empty tables in the café, I'd say it's pretty close. I'm hungry, too – all I've consumed all day is the coffee Tyler dropped off this morning. I was still feeling a little nauseous from the headache, but after the paracetamol and a little rest, I feel good enough to try keeping my food down.

I stand there, looking through the window of the café, undecided on what to do. I don't know if I'm ready yet to dive into the past – into someone else's past – but someone opens the door and steps outside with a blackboard proclaiming today's specials. I stand there, frozen, staring at him. He places the board on the sidewalk, says hello to a few people, stops to chat to a few others, then heads back towards the entrance. He opens the door again, but stops to look at me.

"Everything okay?"

"M-me?" I ask, pointing to myself.

"You've been standing outside for a while."

"Oh... S-sorry."

"What for?"

"I don't know?"

He bursts out laughing, throwing his head back, which makes me laugh, too.

"Come in," he says, nodding towards the café. "You look hungry."

"That's true."

"New in town?"

I nod.

"In that case," he says, gesturing for me to step inside, "let me bring you your first lunch here, on the house."

* * * * *

"All the tables are full, but there's space up at the bar." He pulls out a stool, and I sit down. "I'll be right with you. Meanwhile..." He passes me a menu. "Take a look at this."

He paces towards the back of the room, towards what I imagine to be the kitchen, and I try to relax into my extremely uncomfortable stool. I look quickly around me. The café seems nice: simple but intimate, familiar. Something I've never experienced. I get so distracted by my thoughts that, before I know it, he's already back by my side.

"Seen anything you like the sound of?"

"Oh, I haven't had the chance to..."

"Can I help?"

"Yes, please."

"Today's special is fish and chips. Haddock, to be precise."

"Haddock?"

He looks at me, raising an eyebrow.

"I'm not from around here," I say, embarrassed.

"Believe me, I'd already gathered."

I laugh, and he starts guessing.

"Are you American?"

"N-no," I say, my heart hammering. "Canadian."

"Seriously?" Something like pain flashes behind his eyes. "Which city?"

I swallow, nervous. "Montreal."

"I've been to Canada once, but I never made it to Montreal..." His eyes grow cloudy, his voice losing confidence. "A long time ago."

"How come?"

"I was looking for someone," he says, smiling sadly. "But I won't bore you with stories from my youth."

"I don't mind," I say, too quickly. He studies me suspiciously. "I don't know anyone here," I add. "I only moved here ten days ago, so it's nice to chat. Honestly."

He holds my gaze for a moment, then holds out his hand. "Angus," he says. "I'm Angus."

I squeeze his hand. "Holly."

"Holly," he repeats, smiling. "Let me go and pass your order on to the kitchen. Then, if you like, I can take a five-minute break and tell you all about the sights of this beautiful place."

I push aside my anxiety. "I can't wait."

* * * * *

"Wait a minute," Angus says, stopping me at the climax of my story. "You mean that *you* were the one who called the police on Hayes?"

I can't help but contain my excitement at his enthusiasm.

I dip another French fry into my garlic sauce.

"Wow. Everyone really does know everything around here."

"I would've loved to see his face." He laughs again, taking a sip of coffee. "I can tell you think that he's a hopeless idiot, but I can assure you, Hayes is harmless."

"Everyone's told me that."

"Everyone?"

"My colleagues, my new friends – if I can call them that."

"Where do you work?"

"I teach at the Abbey – the senior infant class. It's actually for a school exchange programme, for teachers. I'll only be here for a few months."

"And you came all the way over here for...?"

"I needed a change of scenery."

"Broken heart?"

"Yeah." I guess, deep down, that's true. My heart *is* broken – but it doesn't matter who the culprit was. "I just needed a change."

"Well, I'm sure it'll do you good. I hope you find the answers you're looking for."

"How do you know I'm looking for answers?"

"You moved to a different continent, my dear. And you're here, in this place, which is – let's face it – in the middle of nowhere."

"I don't mind."

"Neither do I. But I was born here. For visitors, it's a different story."

"I can imagine."

"But there's one thing I'm sure of," he says, getting up and grabbing my now-empty plate. "I know you'll feel at home here."

I can't help but hope that he's right.

18

Tyler

I take the chicken nuggets and potato smiles out of the oven, and place them on the counter. My brother is trying to get the girls to wash their hands, and I'm here, staring at those stupid smiley faces, wondering what the hell has been happening to me these past few weeks.

Here I am, on a Saturday night, at my brother's house, with two five-year-olds, heating up frozen food. Not only am I heating it up, but I am also *eating* it – my brother's culinary skills are non-existent. I can get by, but my nieces are fussy eaters. They only eat pizza, chips, burgers, and spaghetti and meatballs. I think that's everything. Oh, wait: chicken nuggets. It's a boring and restrictive menu, which pretty accurately reflects the current state of my life – a life which has suddenly undergone an abrupt change of pace since my sexy new neighbour decided to complicate things. Wow, we've gone from 'crazy' to 'sexy' in just one night – you're landing yourself in even more shit, here, Tyler.

I'm following the advice given to me by the chief, my brother, and my lawyer – I'm even following Niall's advice. Isn't that pathetic? What's happened to the fearless, handsome fireman who saves everyone in town, and keeps lonely women company?

"Uncle Tyler," one of the girls says, tugging at my shirt to get my attention. "Your phone is ringing."

"Oh, yeah?" I look around in search of it.

"You left it on the sofa."

"Thanks. I'll be right back." I leave her dangerously close to the food and go to pick up. The chief's name lighting up my screen doesn't scream good news.

"Hayes!" he barks from the other end of the line.

"Sir…"

"I have an unofficial message for you."

"O-okay," I say, growing more worried.

"I've received some information from the police."

Oh, fuck. I knew it. She's turned me in. It's because I admitted to looking up her skirt. Or maybe it's because I carried her up the stairs. Or maybe…

"It seems everything was all a big misunderstanding."

"What?"

"The official announcement is being released on Monday."

"Oh… Okay." I don't know what to say.

"That means I'll put you back on the rota for next week."

My brother appears in the living room and

plants himself in front of me, anxious to know what's happening.

"What... What's happened?"

"From what I can gather, the defendant went down to the station this afternoon, confirmed that everything was just a huge misunderstanding, and apologised for wasting everyone's time."

"Really?"

"We'll find out more on Monday. I'll be waiting for you in my office."

"Of course. Thank you."

The chief hangs up, and I look at my brother. "Apparently it was all just a big misunderstanding."

"Seriously?"

"The chief said he'll be waiting for me on Monday down at the station. He's going to put me back on the rota."

"That's amazing news, Tyler! What's with that face?"

"I don't know."

Parker studies me curiously. "You haven't done anything, have you?"

"Like what?"

"You haven't used any of your skills on her?"

"What are you trying to say?"

"I don't know. But I know you, and from your expression, I think there's something you're not telling me."

"I haven't done anything. I just dropped her home."

"What? When?"

"Last night. I went out with Niall, and she was at the pub with Jordan and Anya…"

"Why is Kerry always involved in these things?"

"Nothing happened. We had a few drinks, chatted, then I took her home. That's it."

"You're sure?"

And we danced. I danced with a woman. And when I held her, my hands were almost trembling. Then this morning I brought her coffee and painkillers, and I left her that stupid note. And I admitted to looking up her skirt.

"Absolutely."

"Well, in that case… We have to celebrate."

"Weren't we supposed to be drinking Coca Cola tonight?"

"I have some rum in the cupboard."

"Now we're talking."

"You start laying the table, I'll grab the alcohol."

I go back into the kitchen to fill our plates, and find my nieces there, digging into the still-warm potatoes in the baking tray.

"Hey!" I complain. "Those are for everyone."

"You two wouldn't stop talking and we were hungry."

"Well, you're both getting a smaller portion, now."

They scoff and step aside to let me pile the food onto our plates, before helping me bring them over to the table, where Parker has already poured our drinks.

"You should thank her," Parker says, sitting across from me.

"Mmm?"

"The teacher. You should thank her."

"Why would I do that? I'm not the one in the wrong here."

Parker raises an eyebrow.

"Fine," I scoff. "Maybe I *am* the one in the wrong. But her reaction was still way over-the-top, right?"

"I'm not so sure about that."

"What do you suggest I do?"

"Flowers and chocolates."

"Yeah, chocolate!" my nieces cry in unison.

"Not for you," their father says, keeping them quiet.

"Forget it. I don't think so."

"Or maybe wine would be better. Yeah," Parker says, shoving a forkful of food into his mouth. "Flowers and wine."

"Not happening."

"You should do it, Uncle Tyler!" one of the

girls says to me.

"What would you know about these things?"

"Well, you have to say thank you..."

"These girls are too switched-on for my liking," I say to my brother.

"That's your fault."

"Aren't you the one raising them?"

"It's not my fault that everyone in town is talking about their uncle."

"Every *woman*," I correct him, pointing my fork in his direction.

Parker rolls his eyes.

"And, no. No way am I getting her a present. What am I supposed to be thanking her for? I dropped her home last night, she got back safe and sound. I made sure of that."

Parker studies me carefully.

"Not in that way."

"I hope not, for your sake. Don't forget that she'll be the girls' teacher for the next few months."

"But then she's leaving."

"Tyler!"

I lift my hands. "I was just asking..."

"Don't even think about it."

I stick a chicken nugget into my mouth.

"I'm serious, Tyler. Keep your hands off my daughters' teacher. And no gnome hunting."

"I promise, that was never my intention."

"Good. That's best for you, and for us. And it's definitely best for her."

His last point doesn't offend me. My brother knows me – he knows that I'm no Prince Charming. At least, not outside the bedroom; I think the rumours about my skills speak for themselves.

"Actually, let's forget about the presents for a minute. Even a handshake would be good."

"That's exactly what I was thinking of."

"And that's it. Okay? Good morning, goodnight, and goodbye."

"Can I wave?"

"I'm being serious, Tyler."

"Me too, don't worry. I won't go near her. I won't knock on her door. I won't use any of my skills. I promise."

"What skills, Uncle Tyler?"

I laugh, and my brother grows purple with rage.

"I won't have any contact with my neighbour, with your daughters' teacher. You can trust me."

* * * * *

Two hours later – just as I promised my brother – I'm knocking at her door. I didn't know whether to go for flowers, chocolates, or wine, so I went for the full package. Luckily, my nieces have dinner really early, so the Spar – which, equally luckily, sells everything – was still open. I managed to make it home at a reasonable enough time to knock at my sexy neighbour's door without risking another arrest.

When I find her standing in front of me, wearing a pair of sweat pants and a hoodie from a university whose name I can't make out, her hair gathered messily on top of her head, I realise that I should've taken my brother's advice and just waved at her from afar. Suddenly struck by the effect she has on me, I shove the bunch of flowers under her nose, hoping that she'll take them and whack me over the head with them, followed closely by the bottle of wine.

"Thank you," I say, pulling them away from her face for fear of seeming rude. I wave the wine and chocolates in her direction.

She studies me warily.

"I heard you retracted your statement. I wanted to, er…" I hand over the gifts. "Please, take them. I feel stupid."

She smiles, triumphantly, before reaching out to take the flowers.

"And these." I hand her the box of chocolates and the bottle of wine.

"You didn't have to do this."

"I thought it might be a good opportunity to re-introduce myself. Like a good neighbour."

"Oh, yeah?"

"We got off on the wrong foot."

"You think?"

"And I really… Well, let's just say I didn't give off the best first impression."

"So what impression am I supposed to have of you? This one, right now? Or the impression from last night, maybe?"

"Trust me, this impression is much closer to the real me."

"Thanks for the coffee, and the paracetamol. I couldn't find any at home," she says, gesturing behind her. "I haven't had a chance to unpack properly yet, and, to be honest, I can't be bothered."

I smile at her honesty.

"As for the note…"

"Please, don't."

"So, should I invite you in? Now that you've proven you can be a good neighbour?"

No, absolutely not. That's the last thing you should do.

"Exactly."

Sorry, Parker, but you know what I'm like.

"I don't think I will."

I laugh and shake my head. "Good choice."

"Thanks for… Everything."

"It was my pleasure, Ms. White."

"Holly. Just Holly."

"Holly," I repeat. "Well... See you soon, Holly."

"Goodnight, Tyler."

She closes the door, leaving me standing in the hallway like the dickhead I am. I head back into my apartment.

Dark. Silent. Lonely. Mine.

I take off my jacket and hang it in the entrance, leaving my shoes next to the door and heading towards my bedroom. I get undressed slowly, casting my clothes onto the armchair next to the bed, before slipping on an old pair of jogging bottoms and a T-shirt. I wander back into the living room and over to the bar, to pour myself something to drink – considering I have nothing else to do – when music begins to waft in from the apartment next door. I stand up, my ear pricked as I listen to the balcony door sliding open. I feel it: her presence, just a few feet away from me. I pad quickly over to my own balcony door, barefoot, and slide it slowly aside.

I place one foot on the freezing cold tiles of the balcony and peer outside – just as indiscreetly as before – and find her smiling down at her glass.

"You can't take 'no' for an answer, can you?"

"I actually didn't ask you a question."

"You're right." She places her glass down on the table and turns towards me. She's wrapped in a blanket, but her feet are bare, like mine.

"Are you drinking the wine I gave you?"

She shrugs.

"Do you like it? The wine, I mean. Is it good?"

"Are you seriously asking me whether I like drinking?"

I laugh, and bring my other foot onto the tiles. I've come out onto the balcony in just a short-sleeved T-shirt, barefoot, with my mind blazing.

"I'm asking you what you like."

"Why should I tell you? And, more importantly, why would you want to know?"

"I'm just planning for the next time I have to apologise for something."

"Do you intend to do that a lot?"

"That depends."

She waits for me to go on, but I have no intention of doing so.

"Do you want to stay and keep me company?"

"I was just about to pour myself a drink, too."

She gets up and goes to disappear inside, but I stop her.

"I'll do it."

I run back into my room and grab a hoodie from the wardrobe, pulling it on quickly, before taking a glass from the kitchen and rushing back towards the balcony. I stop for a second – I don't want her to realise that I'm scared she might leave – before placing my foot outside again. I should've grabbed a pair of socks while I was there, but she's barefoot, so I guess I should be, too.

I sit down on one of the chairs I keep out here, and she reaches out to pour me a glass of wine.

"Thank you."

"Thank *you*," she says, brandishing the bottle. She places it down on the table and hands me the box of chocolates.

"We could've done this inside, you know."

"This is more original, and less effort."

I take a whiskey-flavoured chocolate and put the whole thing in my mouth.

"Effort?" I ask, my mouth full.

"I still haven't figured you out, Tyler Hayes," she says, popping a chocolate into her mouth, too.

"So you'd rather keep me at a distance while you figure me out?"

"Exactly."

"You know, right, that I could just jump across this balcony and slip into your house without you even noticing?"

"Are you suggesting I sleep with a chopping knife beside my bed?"

I'm giving her ideas – ideas that could land me in even more trouble.

"Forget it. Pretend I never said anything."

She takes another sip of wine, then grows sincere. "I should've given you the benefit of the doubt, before calling the police."

"Yeah, you should have," I agree, before adding, "but you did the right thing. You never know who could be lurking around, and you'd just got here. I..." I look at her, her eyes shining in the dark. "I'd really like for us to start over."

"Because we're neighbours?"

"Yeah. And because you're new in town, you don't know anyone. You might need... I don't know, to borrow some sugar."

She bursts out laughing, throwing her head back.

"Or maybe a bottle of wine, for when you run out."

She dries her tears, and straightens up in her chair.

"Basically, it's always nice to have a friend nearby."

"A friend?"

"You can ask around: I'm one of the best."

Her lips begin to curve into a smile.

"I'll believe it when I see it."

She pours herself another glass of wine, then reaches the bottle out towards me, filling my own glass nearly to the brim.

I can't see this friendship ending well.

"Maybe we could give it a test run."

I gulp down my wine, trying to drown the thousand responses which are bubbling up in my mind.

"Just to see whether it's worth the effort."

It would definitely be worth the effort, my sexy,

alcoholic neighbour. But I'm scared that it might turn into something too big for either of us to deal with. And I don't know whether I can run that risk.

19
Tyler

Niall puts down the knife and looks at me. "I don't get it."

"What is there to get?"

"I thought you just said you offered to be her friend?"

"I did."

"You?"

"Me."

"Friends with a woman?"

"I'm Jordan's friend," I say, gesturing over at her, in the kitchen.

"Are you?" Niall asks, before turning to Jordan for confirmation.

"I don't want to get involved in this conversation," she says.

"You came here for a glass of wine," I remind her, "and apparently you've stuck around just to eavesdrop."

"Eavesdrop? I'm standing right in front of you. It's not like I'm spying on you."

"Here's your wine, honey," Niall says, handing her a glass.

"Are you telling me to leave the kitchen?"

"I would never," Niall says.

She seems unconvinced, but leaves anyway.

"Where were we...?" Niall turns back to me.

Where *was* I? What the hell am I doing?

I'm at my friend Niall's house – his parents' house, to be precise, where he still lives, at the tender age of thirty-nine, along with his teenage daughter. I'm here because it's Sunday, I was on my own, and I came to have lunch with him. My parents are still on a cruise, I was at my brother's last night for dinner, and I had nothing better to do.

"We got off on the wrong foot."

"You and Ms. White?"

"She's my neighbour. My nieces' teacher."

"A neighbour who, until yesterday, you wanted gone."

"Gone... Let's not get carried away..." I stick a carrot into my mouth.

"Did you not want to get rid of her so that you could have the next-door apartment empty, just as you like it?"

"I never said my plan was concrete."

Niall crosses his arms.

"I just said that we got off on the wrong foot. There's no reason for us not to be civil."

"So you suggested being friends?"

"What's wrong with that?"

"You like her."

"Who?"

"Who have we just been talking about, Tyler? Concentrate!"

"I don't like Ms. White."

"I heard that." Niall's *adorable* daughter appears in the room. "You men are worse than little kids. You'd do anything to hide the evidence."

"What evidence?" I plant my hands on my hips and turn to face her.

"Come on, Hayes. You? Friends with a woman?"

"She's right," Niall says quietly, earning himself a sharp glare.

"What's wrong with being friends with women?"

"Nothing," Niall says, trying to salvage the situation. "Unless…"

No. He's not salvaging anything. He's making it worse.

"Unless what?"

"Unless you're so scared to show her you like her that you're playing the 'friend' card."

"Where did he come from?" I ask Niall, gesturing towards Carter, his daughter's *non*-boyfriend.

"I didn't mean to…" Carter begins to panic.

"Don't listen to him," Skylar says. "He's just trying to shift the attention away from himself."

"I don't have to shift anything," I say, defensively. "I was just chatting to my friend." I nod towards Niall.

"Are you talking about Holly White?" Niall's mother appears in the kitchen.

"That's the one," Skylar responds.

"Such a lovely girl." Niall's mum pours herself a glass of wine. "I saw her yesterday at Linda's."

My ears prick up.

"Oh, really...? What was she doing?" I ask, feigning nonchalance.

"Loser," Skylar hisses at me. I ignore her.

"Having lunch."

I clear my throat. "On her own?"

"I'm completely okay with whatever nicknames my daughter is about to give you from here on out," Niall says, high-fiving Skylar.

They really shouldn't let just *anyone* become a parent. Especially not him.

"She was sitting at the bar, Tyler. I don't know if she was with anyone. The place was packed."

"I was just wondering."

"Too late, Hayes. You're already screwed," Skylar says, making her father and her *non*-boyfriend burst into laughter.

"If you're so interested in what Ms. White does

in her spare time, why don't you ask her to spend some of it with you?"

"What do you mean?"

"Ask her out!" Skylar cries. "You're even worse than *him*."

"Why is your daughter speaking to me like that?"

"Because you deserve it," Niall says plainly.

"Besides, I'm not interested in going out with her.

"Of course you are!" Carter exclaims.

"Do you even want to play in the next match?" I ask, threatening.

Niall laughs. He's really enjoying himself, here.

"Why did I bother coming here today?"

"Because you didn't want to be at home alone in case you ended up knocking at your neighbour's door?"

That may be partly true, but it could also be partly influenced by the conversation floating around this kitchen.

"She doesn't have a boyfriend," Jordan says, her voice attracting everyone's attention. "If that helps."

"Why should it help? I'm not asking anyone out."

"Fine. Do whatever you like, Hayes."

"Of course I'll do what I like. I always do."

"Then why are we all sitting here talking about your neighbour?" Skylar asks.

"I'm here because I was invited over for lunch. God knows why you guys are here, too."

"Come on, now…" Niall says, taking control of the situation. "Too many cooks," he says, patting me on the back. "I'll take care of it."

"Now you're really in the shit," Skylar adds. I'm fighting a losing battle, here. But what can I do? I'm here now. Everyone sees through my bullshit – and I know I've been spouting more than usual in trying not to give into the temptation of inviting Ms. White to go gnome hunting with me.

Everyone already knows, right? At least that's one thing I'm good at.

"I really need to talk to this Ms. White."

Everything is calm again in the kitchen, now that it's just the two of us. Niall has gone back to chopping vegetables.

"I have to tell her that she can definitely find a better friend than you."

Not just as a friend, I want to add; instead, I just stick another carrot into my mouth.

20
Holly

My second week at school goes much better than the first. The kids are getting used to everything, and, thanks to wonderful Wes, I'm starting to feel comfortable myself. I haven't been teaching for long, but I like being assigned to a younger class. I love helping kids take their first steps into education, helping them grow, and watching them mature. I love watching their curious faces light up at the discovery of something new. Admittedly, things here are very different: teaching methods, curriculums. But Wes and I make a good team, and I know that we'll be able to make the most out of this experience. I'm lucky to have such a welcoming, adaptable partner – someone the kids love. It's easy to see that they all love him, that they trust him. They see the two of us as a team, which has helped them accept me as their teacher.

"This is for you, Ms. White." Caleb, one of the shyest kids in class, hands me a flower. "It's from my garden."

"Oh, thank you," I say, smelling it. "It's beautiful. I love this colour."

He smiles, satisfied, his cheeks a little flushed, then runs back to join his friends at their table.

"See?" Wes says right away. "You're already

winning them over."

"You think so?"

"Absolutely. Give them another two weeks and they'll all be inviting you over for Christmas."

"Seriously?"

"It's a small town. Almost like a big family."

His words remind me of something I heard a few days ago. It's strange how the word *family*, here, seems to have an entirely different meaning – a meaning I never seem to have learned.

"Ms. White?"

I turn my gaze towards the classroom, where I see a hand raised in the air. I head over to its owner, one of Tyler's nieces, whose name I still haven't learned. They're basically identical.

"What's the matter, honey?"

"I don't get it."

"What?" I ask, glancing at the maths worksheet: they have to colour the exact number of animals dictated by the simple sum.

"Don't we have to write the number?"

"No, love. Just colour in the right number of chickens."

"What about the next one?"

"Then you have to colour in the cats."

"Mmm... And the next one?"

"Butterflies."

"Got it."

"Good," I say, leaning back, her eyes still following me. "Is there something else you wanted to ask me?"

"I have a question."

"Yes?"

"Do you go gnome hunting, Ms. White?"

This seems to be a recurring theme in this family.

"Oh... I... I don't think..."

"Uncle Tyler always goes gnome hunting."

"Your uncle goes gnome hunting?"

She nods, before her sister joins in.

"He went twice with our old teacher, Ms. Potter."

I sit in silence. I think I've just worked out what they're talking about.

"Not two!" the other cries. "Three!"

"I thought it was three times with Ms. Trent?"

"I can't remember."

"So?" the first asks. "Do you go gnome hunting, too?"

"I don't think that..."

"Maybe you should ask Uncle Tyler to take you. He's really good. Our old teachers were happy they came so many times with him."

I swallow nervously, feeling my face flush for absolutely no reason.

"I don't think I'm going to go gnome hunting."

They look disappointed.

"Do you have any more questions?"

They both shake their head, and I head back to my desk, where Wes is waiting, confused.

"Gnome hunting?"

"Please, don't ask."

"I don't want to ask, believe me. But your face..."

"What's wrong with my face?"

"I don't know. You look angry, or disappointed."

Disappointed is the right word. Just like the girls. Although I have absolutely no valid reason to feel this way.

* * * * *

For some unknown reason, at the end of class, I head to Anya's office.

"Your face already tells me I don't want to know," she says, as soon as she sees me. She gets up and walks around to the other side of her desk, leaping up to sit on it, as I sink into the chair. "Actually, that's not true. Tell me everything."

"To be honest, I don't even really know what to say."

"Mmm..." She glances at the time. "It's too early for a drink. We need another solution."

I smile, despite my terrible mood.

"Let's try this… What brings you to my humble office?"

I consider my answer for a few moments, then tell her.

"Have you ever heard of gnome hunting?"

"Oh, no."

"Oh, no, what?"

"Don't tell me he used his skills on you?"

"Skills? What skills?"

She studies me for a few moments, then shakes her head. "Forget about the skills. Tell me… Where did you hear about the gnome hunting?"

"In class."

"Ah. The Hayes girls."

"So you know?"

"That depends. I don't know exactly what I'm supposed to know, and I think it's probably best if you don't know, either."

"You're confusing me."

"Sorry, you're right. Let's go through this step by step."

"Okay."

"Did something happen between you and that hopeless fireman?"

"Something?"

"Did he not take you home?"

"Yes."

"And…?"

"And nothing. He dropped me home. End of story."

Apart from the fact he carried me into my apartment. And then the next morning and that evening…

"I can tell from your expression that there's more you're not telling me."

"I retracted my statement."

"That only makes me less convinced."

Anya lifts the phone on her desk to her ear. "I need you. Right now." She hangs up, leaving me in total confusion; two seconds later, the door flies open and Jordan appears from her office, just a few feet away from Anya's.

"What's happened?"

"She retracted her statement."

Jordan heaves a sigh of relief. "I thought something had happened in class." She sits next to Anya, on the desk in front of me. "I already knew that, by the way."

"And you didn't think to tell me?"

"Sorry, it must've slipped my mind. Tyler was at lunch at Niall's on Sunday."

"Interesting…"

"More than you think."

"What… Who *are* you two?" I ask, alarmed.

Anya laughs, as Jordan studies me, smiling.

"We're your new best friends."

I smile, too. I can't help it.

"And we're ready for anything," Anya adds.

"I don't know whether to be worried, or…"

"Worried? About us? Absolutely not. As for Hayes…" Anya says. "You need a fast-track course on him. Right?" she asks Jordan.

"Let's start with today."

"T-today?"

"Tonight. Dinner. At mine," Jordan explains.

"Oh, I… I don't know…"

"I'll come and pick you up at six," Anya says. "I'll bring the wine."

"Don't bring too much. We have to work tomorrow."

Anya laughs, jumping down from the desk. "We're not the ones who have to study."

Jordan laughs, too, before placing her heeled shoes down on the carpet.

"What should I bring?" I ask, a little uncomfortable. I'm not used to their way of doing things – although I think I like it.

"You only need to bring yourself. And dessert, if you like."

21

Holly

I haven't seen Tyler for a few days, but I can feel his eyes all over me every time I leave the house. I'm actually not sure whether he really is spying on me through the window, but I always get the feeling I'm being watched, whether I'm going up or down the stairs.

I climb into Anya's car, a chocolate cake in hand, which I bought just after school finished.

"Good choice," Anya says, glancing at the cake. "Jordan's a chocolate addict."

"Good to know."

She switches on the ignition and we sit in silence for a while, before Anya starts speaking.

"You know, right, that he was watching you from the window?"

An unexpected shiver passes through me – I don't know whether it's a good or bad thing.

"Oh, really?"

"Are you going to play this game with me, White?"

I laugh, and she echoes me.

"There's no pretending between friends. Not even about how much weight we put on over Christmas. It means we can cry about it together."

"Friends..." I whisper, a strange emotion

seeping through me. "I don't think I've ever really had any. Not as an adult."

"That's so sad."

I shrug.

"Well, luckily, you're here now," she says confidently, as we follow the main road into town. "And here, my dear Holly, you definitely won't feel lonely."

"I never said I felt lonely."

"Certain things don't need to be said out loud. Sometimes, a friend just knows."

I smile, a little sad and nostalgic, although I'm not sure what for. I've never felt that I was missing anything, and I've never really felt lonely, simply because it's always just been me. Even when my mother was around.

You can't miss something you've never had, and you can't regret things that you've never done.

* * * * *

Jordan opens the door to us with a glass of wine already in hand; she looks as if she got tired of waiting for us to start drinking.

Anya hands over a shopping bag containing bottles of wine, and I pass her the cake, a little shy.

"I knew I liked you," she says, making me laugh. "Come in, come in. Make yourselves at home."

I take off my jacket and drape it over the arm of the couch, echoing Anya's movements, before joining them in the kitchen, where I find her intent on pouring another two glasses of wine. She hands it over at the exact moment something soft brushes against my calves.

"Who's this?"

"That's Caramel. She's a girl."

I bend down to stroke Jordan's cat, and she immediately shows her appreciation. I've never had pets – we moved around too much, and too quickly. I could barely have even looked after a goldfish.

"Dinner's nearly here," Jordan says. "I ordered Chinese. I hope that's okay, Holly."

"Of course. That's perfect."

"I thought we could eat in the living room, sitting on the floor around the coffee table."

"Whatever you guys prefer, honestly."

Anya heads into the living room, followed by Caramel. She kicks off her shoes and kneels down on the carpet, next to the coffee table, on which she places her glass of wine.

"Come on, we haven't got all night," she calls us, just as someone knocks at the door.

"That'll be dinner. You go and sit down," Jordan says to me, before heading into the hall.

I head shyly over to the table, before kneeling

down next to Anya, uncomfortable and unsure of how to act. I've been to dinner with colleagues before, but only at restaurants. I've never eaten like this before.

"Here we go," Jordan says, settling herself down on the floor with us, her arms laden with takeaway boxes. "Fork or chopsticks?"

"A full glass," Anya says, wiggling her empty one.

"If you have another one, you won't show up at work tomorrow, and I'll have to pretend not to know why."

"What are best friends for?"

"I left the wine in the kitchen."

"I'll go and get it."

Anya leaves us alone for a few moments, as Jordan opens the containers. An inviting aroma of spices and something deep-fried wafts into my nostrils.

"We have spring rolls, fried chicken, prawns, rice, and I think there's some pork here, somewhere, too."

"It all looks perfect, Jordan. Thank you."

"You're welcome. It's only food."

"No. I mean thanks for this."

She studies me curiously.

"For the way you guys are making me feel."

"How are we making you feel?"

Anya sits back down with us.

I look between them, a little embarrassed. "At h-home. You make me feel... At home."

And I never knew it could feel so good.

* * * * *

"We never had a real home," I say, chewing another mouthful. After my confession earlier, they obviously asked more about my life, about my family. "It was just me and my mother."

"What about the rest of your family?"

"I don't know much about them, and I don't think I've ever met them. My mother was a bit of a free spirit."

"Like how?"

"A hippy. I'm not sure what you call them over here."

"Interesting..." Anya takes a sip of wine. I still haven't seen her eat anything yet. "And we use 'hippy', too, by the way."

"Did you move around a lot?"

"We lived in so many cities I actually don't remember them all."

"But..." Anya takes another sip, which doesn't go unnoticed; Jordan stuffs a spring roll into her mouth and Anya scoffs, swallowing, before taking another sip. "I guess your father..."

"I've never met him. To be honest, I don't actually know anything about him. My mother was always really vague whenever I asked about him. She said she had no idea who he was."

Jordan strokes my hand, and I smile.

"I could never make friends. At the beginning, I tried, when I was a kid. But over time, after moving around so much, I started to lose interest. As if it wasn't worth the effort."

"Of course," Jordan says, understanding.

"So I stopped, and concentrated on studying instead, until I was able to choose for myself. So I decided to stay put."

"Then what happened?"

"Then I was scared that I was starting to become more and more like my mother," I say, bitterly. "And then I found out that I was exactly like her. And I only seemed to want to run away from everything."

"Do you think she was running from something?"

"From responsibility, from the idea of any kind of relationship. She didn't want to be tied down to anything."

"That can't have been easy."

"I have no roots, no ties. I have no family."

Anya fills my glass again. I start to worry that I'll be the one who doesn't turn up for work tomorrow.

"I've never... Never been in a relationship," I say uncomfortably.

"What?" Anya cries. "You don't mean that...?"

"No, no – not like that." I lower my gaze in embarrassment. I never thought I'd be able to talk about this, and I certainly didn't think it would come out tonight – but these two women together are seriously dangerous.

"I've gone out with guys, but nothing serious, nothing that ever remotely resembled a relationship. I'm an absolute disaster when it comes to this kind of thing."

"What do you mean?" Jordan asks kindly.

"I can't... Can't..." I exhale deeply. "I'm terrible at having conversations with men, with approaching guys, with flirting. And I'm terrible... Well, also at *that*."

"I can't believe that," Jordan says resolutely.

"Me neither. You could never be terrible in bed," Anya confirms.

"I'm totally hopeless."

"Says who?"

"Well, guys aren't exactly lining up outside my door. No one's ever called me back... That could be an indication, don't you think?"

"That doesn't prove anything," Jordan says, refilling everyone's glasses. "Maybe they just weren't right for you, or..."

"Maybe I wasn't right for anyone."

"Or maybe we should test your theory." Anya gets to her feet, wobbling dangerously. "And I know exactly who to test it out on."

"Why do I feel like this is getting out of hand?" Jordan asks, worried.

"You should've known this would happen when you invited us for dinner."

Jordan stabs at a piece of cake. "True."

"I'm sorry. I didn't want things to go this way – I didn't mean to go on so much about my pathetic life."

"That's what evenings like this are for. Besides, your life isn't pathetic at all. You just need to get to the root of the problem, and solve it!" Jordan says, determinedly.

"And I know exactly how to do that." Anya empties the bottle into her glass. "And the solution is right at our fingertips – actually, it's right outside your front door."

"Are you joking?" Jordan asks.

"Why not? He's the ideal candidate."

"Who?" I ask, anxious.

"Your peeping-Tom neighbour."

"What? Absolutely not. No way..."

"Him and his skills," Anya says, convinced, at which Jordan gives her a sharp kick under the table.

"What?"

"You know nothing about his skills."

"What, like you know better?"

"You know he's never had any effect on me at all."

"What's this about his skills?" I ask, alarmed. I'm lost.

"There are a few rumours going around."

"Anya..."

"She'll find out anyway. It's best for her to be prepared."

"Prepared for what?"

"Your neighbour, and his habits."

"What habits?"

"Let's just say that our fireman is pretty well-known around town. And not just for his job helping out in the community."

"It depends what you mean by 'helping out'," Jordan adds, before ducking behind her glass.

"Does this have anything to do with gnome hunting?"

"Bingo!" Anya says, lifting her glass in my direction before taking another sip.

"So are you saying that...?"

"He's fucked half the city? Yes." Anya gets straight to the point. "Not us," she adds. "He has a different type."

"Type? Like what?"

"Lonely, desperate women. Women who've just gone through a break up, or been cheated on..."

"I'm not following. And I don't think it's because of the alcohol."

"Tyler Hayes has quite a specific talent," Jordan says, taking over. "He seems to be able to cheer any woman up."

Anya stifles a laugh.

"And the best way to do that is…"

"Sex," Anya finishes. "And I've heard he's pretty good."

"Oh…"

"And I think he'd be perfect for you."

"What?"

"He's an expert. He's good looking – no one can deny that."

"No, that's true," Jordan agrees.

"He knows how to use the tools at his disposal. You can always count on him."

"And he'll never ask you for anything more," Jordan concludes.

"What do you mean?"

"Tyler Hayes isn't cut out for commitment. Of any kind."

"A little like you," Anya adds. "That way, neither of you are risking anything."

"You can't seriously be suggesting I sleep with him?"

"We're just suggesting you use him to work out whether or not *you're* the problem."

"Is that not the same thing?"

"My definition is definitely more subtle."

Jordan nods, then turns to me. "It's not a perfect plan, but we can always give it a try."

"Try to do what?"

"You should try to seduce him."

"Me?" I stare at Anya in disbelief.

"We can see whether you have an effect on him. The fact that he spies on you through the window already gives us a pretty good idea."

"I could never seduce a guy. And it's not going to happen."

"Don't you like him?"

"That's not the point!"

"So you *do* like him."

"I never said…" I get up, losing my patience. "I have no intention of using my neighbour as a test dummy."

"It was just an idea. No one said you had to use him," Jordan says, trying to calm me down.

I scoff and sit back down. Anya passes me my glass and I gulp down the rest of my wine.

"We're friends now – or, at least, he said he wanted to be my friend."

"Friend…" Jordan says, reflecting aloud. "I guess you could try starting off like that."

"Friends with benefits?" Anya asks. "The best kind."

"She doesn't *have* to sleep with him."

"Oh, no?"

"But you could use your friendship, and his *knowledge*, if we can call it that."

"Like a teacher?" Anya asks. "Is that what you're suggesting?"

Jordan shrugs. "Maybe getting a guy's opinion wouldn't be the worst thing…"

"Are you seriously telling me I should ask for his help with… With what, exactly?"

"To help you understand how men work. How to approach them, how to strike up a conversation, how to seduce them. And then…"

"No way."

"I think it's a great idea," Anya agrees.

"I think it's a terrible idea."

"It would only be terrible if you liked him," Anya says, suggestively. "But you don't. Right?"

"Absolutely not."

"Then what's the problem?"

"He's my neighbour. I barely know him, and…"

"And?"

"I'm embarrassed," I say, covering my face with both hands. "I'd never be able to ask him something like that. I could never…"

"What?"

I slide my hands away from my face and lower my eyes.

"If he ever found out that…"

"That you're no good in bed?" Anya finishes.

"I don't know if I'd ever live it down."

"Aren't you curious to know what's stopping you, or what's stopping the men you like? Don't you want to find out what isn't working for you in terms of relationships?"

"I'm not sure. Maybe I just take after my mother."

"Or maybe not," Jordan says, her tone softening. "Maybe you've just convinced yourself of that, and you need a little push in the right direction. It takes courage, and you've already proved you have loads of that."

"Really?"

"Look at you. You're here; you've travelled halfway across the world and moved on your own to a place you don't know. You already have friends."

I smile.

"And you also have a next-door neighbour who spies on you through the window," Anya adds. "You've taken some big steps, don't you think?"

"I guess so."

"And maybe that means you can take a few more steps."

"I don't know."

"Just think about it. Hayes isn't going anywhere."

He isn't going anywhere, but I might – even

though I don't want to. Not until I've managed to piece together the broken shards of my past, and work out exactly where this all started.

22

Tyler

When I offered to look after the girls for an evening, I didn't think my brother would've been inconsiderate enough to accept. But here he is, standing at my front door, holding two overnight bags and two school backpacks. He must be really desperate to have asked me.

"Please," he says again. The girls are already settled on the carpet in front of the TV. "No horror films."

"Just comedies. Got it."

"No rom-coms. Nothing with sex."

I scoff. "Fine. Cartoons."

"I'd also like to remind you that my daughters don't know how to keep a secret – not even when you bribe them."

"Trust me, I know."

He glances behind me towards the girls, then sighs heavily.

"If you don't trust me, why are you letting them stay here?"

"I couldn't find a babysitter, and I couldn't find anyone to switch with me for this night shift."

"I'd have swapped with you, but I don't start until tomorrow."

"This time, it's fine. But the next time this

happens, I'll work something out," he says, unconvinced.

"You only need to sort yourself out until Christmas, then Mum and Dad will be back."

"I need to find a more permanent solution. Someone I can trust. I can't keep running to Mum for help."

I don't see anything wrong with that, but my brother has a different opinion. He wants to prove to everyone at all costs that he can do things on his own. I think it's his way of ridding himself of guilt – not that he has anything to feel guilty about.

"Call me if there are any problems."

I don't think I'll be doing that – but I don't say that. "Go to work, or you'll be late."

He blows the girls a kiss from the door, then finally decides to leave. I watch him climb down the stairs and head towards his car. I wave goodbye, glancing quickly over at the next-door apartment. I haven't heard any sounds coming from inside, but the living room light is on. I can see it seeping out from under the door. I'm not spying on my neighbour – I'm just checking, as a fireman, that everything is okay, and no one's in danger. I think I've made that pretty clear, right?

I turn back into my apartment, strangely lost in thought, and even more strangely agitated. My nieces pick up on this right away.

"What's wrong, Uncle Tyler?" one of them asks

me – I'm not sure which. I should ask them to wear name tags, like the ones they have at meetings or conferences, but I'm scared they'd mix them up deliberately, and I'd spend the whole evening looking like an idiot.

"Nothing, niece number one. I'm just thinking."

"Niece number one?"

"Only because you spoke first."

Luckily, she laughs, attracting her sister's attention.

"What are we having for dinner? I'm hungry."

"Already?" I glance at the clock. I guess it *is* six o'clock, and they usually eat dinner pretty early. "Well, I guess I can start cooking now."

"Nah," says the other. "Let's order a pizza."

"Your dad said no junk food."

"Pizza is junk food?" the other asks, horrified.

"No, pizza isn't junk food. It's just not healthy."

"Not even if we ask them to put vegetables on it?"

I try – with difficulty – not to laugh.

"You know what?"

They both shake their heads as I move closer to the coffee table, where I'd left my phone.

"Let's order a pizza tonight."

"Yay!"

Their enthusiasm makes me feel like the coolest uncle in town – which I guess is true.

"Just don't tell your dad."

They both mime zipping their lips shut, and I laugh, scrolling through my phone's address book for the pizza place's number.

"I think he gave in too quickly – don't you think?" one whispers – or, thinks she is whispering – to the other.

"I think he's up to something."

I pretend not to be listening and turn my back to them, so that they don't catch me smiling proudly.

They're right – I *am* up to something. But, like I said, I'm a resourceful guy. And I've just found an ingenious way to check up on my sexy neighbour, without looking like an idiot.

* * * * *

After forcing myself through about forty minutes of Disney Channel, there's a knock at the door.

"I'm starving!" one of my nieces complains.

"Me too!" the other echoes.

I head over to the door, more nervous than I'd like to admit, and plaster one of my signature smiles onto my face.

"Oh…" I say, feigning surprise. "I wasn't

expecting a special delivery."

The corner of her mouth twitches.

She's fucked.

"I believe these are yours?"

"I guess that depends. Did you order three pizzas all to yourself? Or maybe you have guests...?"

The other corner of her mouth twitches, too.

Maybe I'm the one who's fucked.

"Your name is on the box."

She hands it to me, and I take it.

"They got the wrong apartment. I tried to stop the delivery guy, but he was in a rush."

"You could've kept them. I'd already paid."

"I wouldn't steal your dinner."

"Is the pizza here?" my nieces yell from behind me.

"And I definitely wouldn't steal *their* dinner."

"If you want some, by the way... I mean, if you haven't eaten..." I open the door a little wider to invite her in.

She thinks about this for a moment. "I don't think that's the best idea."

"Please, look at me. My nieces are here. You've caught me off-guard."

"I don't want to intrude on your family dinner."

"I'm babysitting. I'm also getting pretty

desperate."

She laughs, shaking her head.

"Come on. One of the pizzas has hot dog pieces on top."

She lifts one eyebrow.

"And pepperoni."

"A nice light dinner, then."

"And my pizza is extra-large."

"And you'd share it?"

With you, I'd share anything.

"I'm a generous guy."

Especially when it comes to the bedroom. But I don't think that's appropriate right now.

"Hey, Ms. White!" one of my nieces cries, noticing that I have company. "Did you order pizza, too?"

Ms. White laughs. "No, honey. They delivered yours to me by mistake."

"And you didn't eat it? I'd have eaten it."

Ms. White laughs again, and I feel something begin to churn inside me – although it's a feeling I could get used to.

"I'd never want to steal your food."

"Why don't you eat with us? Uncle Tyler ordered an extra-large pizza. No one could eat it all on their own."

"Oh, really?" she asks, turning back to me.

"I need a hand."

My Ms. White smiles.

And yes, I said *my*. Please, pretend you never heard that.

"In that case..." She smiles at me, and I feel something painful and all-consuming explode inside me. "Just let me go and get dressed."

"Stay like that," I say, swallowing. "You look great like that."

Ms. White looks at me for a moment, her eyes sliding down to her bare legs, before moving to meet my gaze.

"I'll grab my keys, then. And maybe a bottle of wine."

Go and get anything you want, Ms. White. Take me, if you like. Like I said, I'm off-guard, desperate, and harmless. You're the one who isn't harmless, here.

* * * * *

Ms. White steps into my humble abode, looking around. "It's exactly the same as mine."

"They're mirror-images of each other."

"Is your bedroom the same, too?"

I swallow nervously.

I should try to avoid associating Ms. White with my bedroom.

"Uh-huh."

"Ms. White, come and sit next to me," one of my nieces cries, attracting the attention of our guest.

"Of course, Eve."

My jaw hits the floor.

"How the hell can you tell who's who?"

Ms. White laughs. "It's a secret."

"And you don't want to share it with me?"

"It could come in handy one day."

Smart. And sexy. And witty. And totally out of my reach.

I watch her as she wanders over to my nieces and sits down at my table. I shouldn't be looking at her arse in those shorts, should I? It's not a wise move – especially because I've just said she was out of my reach. She's the enemy, someone to be conquered – and not in bed. Besides, she's my nieces' teacher, and I promised my brother that I wouldn't do any damage. Friends. Just like I suggested yesterday. We can manage that. I can do this.

It can't be that hard. Can it?

"White or red?" I ask her, standing in the middle of my living room.

"White would be perfect."

No, what's perfect is the shape your lips make when you say the word 'perfect'.

"Are you coming, Uncle Tyler?"

"What? I'll be right there. Let me just go and

get the wine." I head into the kitchen, where I stand for a few moments until I feel steady again.

"Do you need a hand?"

"Ah!" I jump, one hand flying to my chest. "And you..." I move to place my other hand on the counter, but miss, almost ending up on the floor. "What... Are you... Doing...?"

"Are you okay, Hayes?"

"Me? Perfect."

"You're being weird. Did you inhale some smoke or something?"

Why does she have to do this to me?

"Nice."

She smiles, satisfied, and moves closer. "Can I help?"

"How?"

"With the bottles and the glasses." She studies me, concerned.

"Of course."

"Are you sure you're okay?"

I'm fantastic, my sexy, *out-of-my-league* neighbour.

"Glasses." I grab them from the cupboard and hand them to her. "I'll bring the bottles."

"Okay..." She studies me, unconvinced. "I'll go back in and see the girls."

"I'm just coming!" I say, the word making me cringe. That word should be banned from all conversation – and from my head – for the rest of my life. "Just a minute."

She walks off, joining my nieces, and I follow her, bottles of wine in hand, my head spinning. I sit down at the table with them.

"Are you okay, Uncle Tyler?" one of the girls asks me. "You look weird."

"I'm great, honey. I'm just hungry."

"I've already had a slice," the other says guiltily. "I couldn't wait any more."

"That's okay," I say, reaching out to grab a slice from the box. But it just so happens that Ms. White has reached for the same slice, my fingers landing gently on hers.

"Ladies first."

"Thanks," she says, taking the pizza and bringing it to her mouth.

"I'm a gentleman," I say, pouring her a glass of wine. "But I'd already told you that."

"You know, Hayes," she says, chewing slowly, before wiping her mouth with her hand. "I'm starting to think you may just be right."

"O-oh, really?"

"Sometimes, first impressions can be wrong. And things can grow from the strangest situations."

"Th-things?"

She shrugs, taking another bite. "Like a friendship."

I don't even attempt to repeat that word.

"I mean, I don't have many friends. Guy friends, especially."

I seem to have stopped breathing.

"It's something new. It's nice."

I'm sure it is, Ms. White. It's just a shame that my mind has already gone somewhere else – somewhere much further than you could ever imagine.

"So," she says, wiping her hands on a napkin and grabbing her glass. "To friendship."

I pick up my glass, too, clinking it against hers. I smile at her, taking a sip – just one, though. I seem to have forgotten how to swallow.

"Can friends go gnome hunting together?" one my adorable nieces asks, innocently.

"I don't think so, Eve," she responds kindly.

"Why not?"

Wait: what does she know about gnome hunting?

"Friends can't go gnome hunting together. They go separately, with other people."

"Why?"

"It's bad luck," I say, attempting to salvage the situation.

"Ahh," she says, luckily accepting my explanation.

I turn my gaze back to Ms. White, who has been dangerously silent, and try to look for a sign

– something to help me work out exactly what she knows about gnome hunting. And, especially, *why* she knows about it. But she meets my gaze and smiles, and I forget about all the stupid questions floating through my mind. You know what else I forget about?

"I like it," I say. She furrows her brow in confusion. "Friends. I like it."

I forget about doing anything that could hurt us both.

Ms. White sighs – a sigh I can't read into, for fear of tumbling back into that whirlwind of thoughts about her, about my bedroom, about *coming*, and about gnome hunting.

"I like it, too."

* * * * *

When the girls collapse onto my bed, I join Ms. White out on the balcony. It's strange to see a woman sitting there, so calmly, at my table, a glass of wine in hand, her expression so relaxed, and with no intention of asking me to go to the cinema next Saturday, or to go ice-skating, hand-in-hand.

I sit down next to her and pick up my glass.

"Are they asleep?"

"Out cold. It's a miracle. You did well not to let me give them any ice cream – I think sugar is the problem, just like my brother says. I never listen to him, though."

"I never thought you would."

I smile, sipping at my wine. "Aren't you cold out here?"

She shakes her head. "I'm perfect."

"It's fucking freezing."

She laughs and looks at me. "Back home, there's already about four feet of snow."

"Back home?"

"In Montreal."

"That's where you're from?"

"Yeah."

Ah. Now I understand that strange way she pronounces her *r*'s, which makes my hairs stand on end. But it's best not to concentrate on that little detail when she's sitting right next to me, or something else might start to stand on end, too.

"And…" I clear my throat. "Is your family still there?"

"My family is all here."

I furrow my brow, and she flashes me a sad smile. "In front of you. It's just me."

"Oh… I didn't…"

"It's fine, Tyler."

Is it just me, or does my name sound different when she says it? It must be that damn accent. Maybe she should take pronunciation lessons – for me, not for her. She's already perfect as she is. I'm the one with the problem.

"It's been like that for a while. I'm used to it, now."

I pretend to believe her, because we're not close enough for me to ask any more questions. And because we'll never be close enough for her to answer them.

"What made you choose Donegal?"

"They were offering a job exchange at the school, so…"

"So you'll be here for…?"

"Three months."

"What then?"

"Then we'll see." She takes another sip, staring out at the darkness ahead of us. I don't ask any more questions – not even stupid ones – because I get the impression that the evening could end up heading in a different direction. Neither of us can let that happen.

"Have you ever watched a GAA match?" I ask her, out of the blue.

"What's that?"

"The national sport. Along with rugby. But everyone can play rugby – not everyone knows how to play GAA. It's called Gaelic football. They don't play it anywhere else."

"Is it serious?"

"Extremely." I sit up straight and turn my body towards her. "And it just so happens that I've just been asked to be the assistant coach for the local team."

"Wow, you're full of surprises…"

You have no idea how many surprises I want to give you, my dear Ms. White. But I've already promised you that we could be friends, and I intend to stick to my word – until death do us part.

"We have a match on Sunday morning."

"Are you inviting me to watch?"

"Entry is free. I know Jordan will be there. Niall is the head coach, so…"

"You two are really close."

"Too close, trust me."

She laughs, then gets up. "It's getting late."

I get to my feet, too.

"Do you think you can manage on your own?"

I used to be able to do everything on my own, Ms. White. Now, I'm not so sure.

"Of course."

She goes back into my apartment, grabs the keys she'd left on the table, then heads for the front door. I follow her, a strange sense of nostalgia coursing through me. It's as if I'm missing something I already know I can never have.

"Thanks for dinner, Tyler. Your extra-large pizza was great."

"Thanks for keeping me company."

She steps closer and I stand there, frozen, as her

soft lips plant themselves onto my cheek. It's a sweet, spontaneous gesture, which she does with absolutely no hidden agenda.

"Goodnight, Ty."

Ty. She called me Ty.

"Goodnight, Holly."

She opens the door and leaves my apartment, as I stand there, listening to the sound of her heading back home.

My door closes softly as hers opens, before closing behind her. I listen to her footsteps on the floor, my stomach in knots. I hear the fridge door opening, then more footsteps. I stay standing there, my breath catching in my throat.

I close my eyes and rest my forehead against the door, no longer sure that I'll ever be able to do anything alone again, the way I've been doing for all these years.

23

Tyler

Niall turns to face me, his hands on his hips, and his expression unreadable. Maybe I should've waited until the end of the match to tell him what happened the other night.

"Coach, should we start warming up?" one of the kids asks.

"Shh," Niall says, lifting his hand, his gaze glued to me. "Don't interrupt us."

"But, coach..."

"We're talking about game tactics. It's very important."

"Game tactics?" I ask, as soon as the kid has wandered off.

"Yep. Yours."

"I'm not playing any games."

"Oh, no? Then why did you invite her over for dinner?"

"She's my neighbour."

"She was in your house, Tyler. For. Dinner."

"My nieces were there, too."

"Okay, let's rephrase this. She was at your house. For dinner. With your family."

"I still don't understand why you're making a big deal out of this."

"How many women have you invited round for dinner?"

"Do you really want me to answer that? I've never kept count. I'm a gentleman."

"Let's rephrase that, too. How many women have *actually* eaten dinner in your apartment?"

"I don't see what..."

"And how many have met your family? And by 'met' I mean been introduced to, spent time with...?"

"She's my neighbour. She's the girls' teacher. She's not from here, she hasn't made friends, yet."

"I don't know how else to explain this to you, Tyler. So I'm just going to say it, okay? You're fucked, mate."

So direct, Niall.

"All you need to do now is to invite her to watch a match, and..."

My expression speaks for me.

"Don't tell me."

"I don't even know whether she's coming."

"Tyler..."

"What was I supposed to do?"

"The problem isn't what you were supposed to do, but what you're *planning* to do."

"I'm trying to be a good neighbour, a good friend. She's alone, in a foreign country. Let's not forget that I'm a fireman."

"A fireman who narrowly avoided being jailed for being a 'good neighbour'."

"Er... Coach?" The same kid as before interrupts us again.

"What?" Niall asks, impatiently.

"We should really start warming up soon."

Niall turns to me, his finger wagging in my face. "You and I need to have a long, hard talk."

I bow my head in defeat, as Niall gathers up the kids before heading out onto the field. I follow them, bringing up the rear, as we pass the changing rooms and step out onto the grass. I look around; there are already a few anxious parents watching from the stands, yelling at their kids to run faster, or yelling at Niall to fuck off. There are a few people there who obviously don't want to be there; and then there's...

"You're really in the shit, now, Tyler," Niall points out, waving at Jordan, who is sitting next to Ms. White. "I can't even come to your defence here, you know."

"No one's asking you to defend me. Who says I need help defending myself?"

"She's sitting right next to Jordan, Tyler."

"So?"

"They're pretty close. They're already basically best friends."

"I still don't see the problem."

In that moment, Ms. White waves shyly at me.

And I, being the dickhead I am, plaster a smile onto my face – one of those smiles which only proves that I really *am* in the shit, this time.

"Do you see it now?" Niall asks.

"I'm just waving at her."

"I hope so. For her sake."

"Not for mine?"

"I just hope that you can keep your *skills* under control."

"My skills aren't an option, here."

"Are you sure?"

"Without a shadow of a doubt."

The referee blows the first whistle before I can spout any more bullshit.

"In that case... You wouldn't mind, then, that Anya has organised a night out for them both?"

We head towards the bench to talk to the kids before the match.

"Why would I mind?"

The kids gather around us. Niall quickly goes over the tactics, and reminds them that if they lose, he'll set fire to their underwear and send them all home commando, before turning back to me.

"Because it's *that* kind of night."

I shrug, indifferently.

"It's game on, Tyler."

"What the hell...?" I say, before the lightbulbs

begin to switch on in my mind.

"Exactly." Niall knows I've worked out what's going on.

"It's none of my business," I say, unconvincingly.

"If you say so..." Niall turns back towards the field and starts to yell at the kids even before the first kick.

I cast my eyes back towards the stands, where my sweet, sexy, young and single Ms. White is sitting, coffee in hand, her cheeks pink from the cold, her breath steaming up as she chats to Jordan.

"You have five days to do something. Actually, make that four and a half."

"I don't have to do anything," I respond, annoyed, turning back to gaze out at the match.

"Whatever. I just wanted to let you know."

"It wasn't your job to let me know."

"I just wanted to help my best friend. Or are you only *her* friend, now?" he asks, nodding towards the stands behind us.

"What's your problem? Am I not allowed to have other friends?"

Niall bursts out laughing. "I'd actually be happy to see you making other friends."

"Am I starting to annoy you, by any chance?"

"Not at all. I'm just trying to help you."

"I can be friends with whoever I like. Actually, I

have a date tonight."

He studies me, one eyebrow raised.

"With who?"

"Since when have you cared about what girls I go out with?"

"Never. I just wanted to make conversation."

"Shouldn't we be concentrating on the match?"

"We are."

"It doesn't seem like it."

"Okay, then yell something at them."

"Why?"

"Because that way, you'll grab your teacher's attention."

"I don't need to grab anyone's attention. I can assure you that if I did want to get her attention, I wouldn't need to play stupid games like this. You, on the other hand…"

"Sure, sure. The local fireman whips out his infamous *skills*."

"Are you done?"

"No. Oh, that's right. You guys are friends. You can't give friends special treatment like that."

"I'm this close to leaving you alone on this bench."

"You wouldn't dare."

"Don't tempt me."

"Coach?" Carter, Skylar's *non*-boyfriend, interrupts us.

"What do you want, benchwarmer?"

Carter doesn't bat an eyelid. "One of the guys is on the floor."

"Oh, for fuck's sake!" Niall leaps to his feet. "Why didn't you tell me right away?"

"I did."

"He's even useless on the bench," he hisses to me.

"Shall we go and see what's going on?" I ask, nodding towards the field.

"If we have to…" Niall heads towards the centre of the pitch.

Who the hell entrusted him with a whole team?

I pull on my cap and sneak another glance over towards the stands, where Ms. White is intent on following the match – so much so that she hasn't even realised I'm staring at her again. Which means I'll definitely be staring at her for much longer than I should.

24

Holly

"He's looking over here again," Jordan points out.

I take a sip of my coffee and quickly cast my eyes in his direction.

"Are you sure nothing happened between you two?"

"I told you. They delivered the pizzas to the wrong address, and he'd ordered an extra-large…"

"Uh-huh."

"And he was babysitting his nieces."

"And you helped him out."

"I just had dinner with them. He's my neighbour, and they're my students. We made it perfectly clear that we just wanted to be friends."

"Is that what we're calling it now?"

"He's nice."

"I don't doubt that."

"We're friends."

"You've made friends pretty quickly, then."

"Well, things happened pretty quickly with you and Anya, too, don't you think?"

Jordan shrugs. "That's what it's like around here. We don't waste any time. If we like someone, we make them feel at home."

"It's nice."

"I was just lucky to have been born somewhere like this. Or unlucky, depending on your point of view."

"Do you feel lucky?"

"I love this place. I love feeling like I'm part of something."

I smile, a little sad; maybe I'd have liked to feel that way, too. But I never had the chance to find out.

"So the fireman didn't show you his skills…?"

"No. Absolutely not."

"And you didn't even consider the idea of using this friendship to your advantage?"

"No."

"Okay," she sighs, taking a sip of her coffee. "But you decided to go out with Anya?"

"I don't think it's possible to say no to Anya."

Jordan laughs, shaking her head. "I've known her for over twenty years, and I've never been able to say no to her."

"I thought there'd be no point even trying. Besides, it can't do any harm. Right?"

"That depends on your intentions."

"I don't really have any intentions. For now, I've just decided to trust her. Do you think I shouldn't have?"

She laughs again. "I'd say you've done well. As long as you're sure you have no hidden agenda."

"What do you mean?"

"That you're not looking for a relationship."

Definitely not. Aside from the fact I don't know how these things work, it would make no sense. I won't be here forever, and I don't want to make my life more complicated – not when I still have to work out what I'm doing with it.

"I'll only be here for a few months. I want to make the most of this experience, maybe spend some time working on myself, understanding what does and doesn't work for me…" I stop, suddenly hit by a wave of sadness.

Thinking about her only makes me sadder – and I'm never sad. Or, at least, I never used to be, until I began to find out what I'd been missing.

"I get the feeling you're here for something more than just the school exchange."

I smile at her. "I'm here for loads of reasons. I just hope they're the right ones."

Jordan squeezes my arm.

"You'll work it out, in time. And, whenever you need it, remember that you always have a friend here, ready to listen."

* * * * *

Once the match is over, I tell Jordan I'd rather walk home than accept her offer of a lift, so I head towards the centre of town. It's a grey day, without even a hint of sunlight, and the air is pretty chilly – although it's nothing compared to the temperatures I'm used to, back home. To be honest, I've lived in so many different climates that I get used to the weather pretty quickly. I never really complain about the heat, or the cold, about snow or rain; I always know that, sooner or later, it'll change.

Being brought up by my mother, with her constant need to run away from things, didn't exactly help me plant my roots; it definitely didn't help me form relationships, either. I've never really had trouble meeting people, but when you don't stay in one place long enough, you don't tend to put in the effort to build up a friendship – it isn't worth it. Especially not with men. And the only example I ever had to follow wasn't exactly helpful.

My mother wasn't a bad person, and in her own way, she never left me wanting for anything. But she did hold me back in many ways, raising me in a way that suited her, and her need to travel, to hide from responsibility. She raised me with a fear of never being enough. I never admitted this to her, and I only realised it years later, when I was already an adult myself. I began to realise that I felt uncomfortable in my own skin. My mother probably kept running from everything because she felt that she was never good enough. I wish I'd understood that sooner – I wish I could've helped her, when I still had the chance.

Now I'm alone, in control of a life I barely recognise. I can't shake the feeling that I'll never find my place.

"Good morning, Holly!" An already-familiar voice brings me back down to Earth, to the street I'm walking along, to the place my legs have brought me without me even realising.

"Looking for somewhere good for lunch?"

"Is it already lunchtime?" I glance at my watch. I'd completely lost track of time.

"We don't really have a set lunchtime around here, you know… I open at ten and close at seven. People just come and eat whenever they want."

"I like that."

"Me, too. It means the café is always busy."

I look through the window, then my eyes fall back onto him. "Any spare tables?"

He smiles at me, and for a moment – just for a moment – I dream. I hope. I wait.

"Would you be alright up at the bar with me?"

I believe.

Truly.

"That would be perfect."

25

Tyler

"What do you mean she left?"

"She said goodbye, and said I'd see her tomorrow."

"Yes, but why?"

"Should I be worried?" Jordan asks Niall, pointing at me.

"It's just his way of processing and accepting things."

"Got it."

"Processing and accepting what?" I'm starting to lose patience with him.

"This is part of the process, too. If I told you now, you wouldn't get it."

I forget about Niall, who isn't helping at all, and turn back to his more useful girlfriend.

"Why did you just let her leave like that?"

"What was I supposed to do?"

"I thought we were friends."

"I hope you realise that this is only making me think that…"

"Yeah, yeah. All that 'acceptance' bullshit."

I bring my hands to my hips and glance around, as if I could somehow see which way she went. I disappeared for about thirty minutes after the match, thanks to Niall, who dragged me into the changing rooms. If I'd just gone straight over to the stands, I wouldn't have missed my chance.

What chance am I talking about?

It's best if I don't say. It's all part of this damn acceptance process.

"She said she wanted to go for a walk," Jordan says, as I turn back towards her. "In town. And then she wanted to walk home." She smiles cheekily at me. "I believe you know the way?"

* * * * *

I know every street in this town, and in the suburbs. I know everyone who lives here, their family, their address, and almost every other detail about them – it's probably best if I don't disclose that now. But, more importantly, I know myself. You might say that's hardly big news, that everyone knows themselves. But it's actually not that simple. It's often easier to ignore, not to listen, to pretend you don't understand. Just like I'm trying to pretend that my sexy neighbour has no effect on me; just as I'm pretending that I'm not remotely interested in spending time with her; just like I'm pretending that I don't need a disaster like this in my life. But when I see her through the window at Linda's, sitting up at the bar, smiling and chatting with Angus, my mind is already made up. I push open that damn door and step into the abyss, only to smile just a little of her.

Ms. White turns towards the door, as if she could feel my eyes on her.

"Ty?"

"Ms. White! What a nice surprise!"

I head towards the bar, where Angus wastes no time.

"Haven't seen you around for a while."

"What are you talking about?" I say, glaring pointedly at him. "I always come here."

"I haven't seen you for months."

"Maybe you just didn't notice me."

He crosses his arms and studies me. I hold his gaze, willing him silently to mind his own business.

"Are you here for lunch?" Luckily, my sweet, pure Ms. White breaks our uncomfortable silence.

"Yeah." I sit on the stool next to hers. "I'm here for lunch."

Ms. White laughs, her soft, perfect hair – which smells like shampoo – wafting in front of her face.

How do I know so much about her hair?

I'm not going to tell you.

Okay, maybe I will tell you. I smelled it, that night, when I took her home, and carried her into the apartment, and... And that's it.

"Are you...?" I clear my throat, Angus' eyes still glued to me. "On your own?"

"Yeah, I'm on my own."

"Do you want some company?"

"Sure! I was just about to ask Angus for today's specials."

"I'd love to hear them, too."

"You already know the specials. You know all the specials everywhere around here."

I don't like his tone, but I have company. So I pretend not to have heard his inappropriate comment.

"Would you mind reminding me?"

Angus scoffs, then recounts a list of dishes I already know by heart. He waits for us to decide.

"I'll have the soup of the day, and a sandwich."

"Good choice." He turns to me. "For you?"

"I don't know. Could you tell me the specials, again?"

Angus glares at me, as Ms. White gets up to go and wash her hands.

"What are you up to, Hayes?" Angus asks right away.

"You're the one who's up to something. You're old enough to be her dad!"

"What the hell are you…?"

"You should be ashamed of yourself."

"I'm just trying to be nice to a customer, to make her feel at home. She's here on her own, she has no family…"

"How do you know that?"

"You know, Hayes, when you're interested in more than one thing, you end up actually getting to know people."

"Are you telling me you're not interested at all in that way?"

"God, no! She's almost still a teenager! What the fuck is wrong with you?"

"I was just wondering."

"What about you? Are you sure of what you're doing?"

"It's none of your business."

"She's a great girl."

"How would you know?"

He glares at me.

"So what?"

"You're an arsehole."

"Here I am." Ms. White sits down next to me. "Everything okay?"

"Fantastic," I say hurriedly. "I'll have the soup, too. And a chicken Caesar wrap."

Angus heads off towards the kitchen, but before disappearing inside, gestures that he's got his eye on me. I ignore him, and turn my attention back to Ms. White, who is sipping her coffee.

"You're not exactly popular around town," she says, placing her mug back on the counter.

"Angus can be a little grouchy."

"You think? He seems so nice, to me."

"You've been here before?"

"Once before."

"You know there are much better places in town? Just ask. I'd be happy to take you somewhere better."

She shrugs, wrapping her fingers around her mug – but she doesn't drink. She just stares down at the liquid inside.

"I like it here."

"Seriously?"

Linda's is pretty much a diner: it's always busy, and it's not the best place to have a quiet meal.

"I like the atmosphere."

Her tone is strangely sad.

"Does it remind you of home?" I ask cautiously. I don't know much about her, and I don't want to touch a nerve.

"In some ways," she says vaguely. I decide to drop the subject. I don't want to pressure her.

"So," I say, trying to lighten the mood. "Did you enjoy the game?"

"I didn't really understand what was going on."

I laugh at her honesty.

"It's not all that different from football. We just use our hands, too."

"I don't see why."

"We like to use everything we have available to

us."

Ms. White blushes, and I can't hide my satisfaction.

"You're always like this, aren't you?"

"Attractive?"

"...Explicit."

Explicit? She thinks *this* is explicit?

My dear, sexy, innocent neighbour. I really hope you never discover *my* definition of 'explicit'.

"I'd say it's more... honest."

"Honest..." She thinks about this for a moment, then timidly asks: "Are you always honest?"

It feels like a trick question, but I respond anyway.

"Of course. Honesty is one of the most important traits you can have, in my opinion. It's the base of every relationship. Especially between friends."

She nods slowly, then sits in silence until Angus brings over our food. We thank him, and he walks away, but stays close enough to eavesdrop onto our conversation. It doesn't matter too much – I have nothing to hide.

I just want to have lunch with Ms. White. And then, maybe, drop her home. I have no other plans, no hidden agenda. And it would be best for it to stay that way; but, my dear readers, no one can predict these things. Not even yours truly.

26
Holly

I head home with Tyler in the late afternoon. We stayed at Linda's for a few hours; I had nothing better to do. After the match, I thought I'd grab something quick for lunch, then spend the rest of the day relaxing at home. But my unexpected meeting with my neighbour shook up my plans.

I didn't mind his company – and that's the problem. The more time I spend with him, the more I start to enjoy it. I just hope I don't start to like him in a way I can't control.

Anya and Jordan's words were churning around in my mind throughout our lunch, and his way of speaking – so spontaneously, so suggestively – only made it worse. It made their suggestion seem almost plausible.

I'd have to be out of my mind to ask Tyler to help me with this. I'd have to be even more out of my mind to think that he could be the answer.

We get out of the car and walk towards the stairs in silence. Tyler nods at me to go ahead, and I start to climb, only to stop halfway up and turn suddenly to face him.

"You're not doing this to ogle me, right? I'm not even wearing a skirt today."

Tyler laughs, a sexy dimple which must have

previously slipped my mind appearing on his chin.

"I'm a gentleman. I've already told you that, more than once."

I turn back to the stairs and wander up to my front door, pulling my keys out from my purse and sliding them into the lock.

"Thanks for lunch, and for the lift. And for your company, too."

"Well. I am the local fireman."

I laugh, pushing open the door. Tyler stays standing in the hallway, his hands in his pockets, his eyes sparkling, a smile still plastered across his face.

"What?" I ask, curious. I get the impression he has something to say.

"Your arse," he responds, drily. "I made you go upstairs first so I could look at your arse."

My mouth falls open in shock. I have no idea what to do with that confession.

"I told you earlier I was honest. But I'd have let you go first, anyway. For chivalry."

"I'm starting to think your chivalry always has an ulterior motive."

"You're starting to get to know me, then."

"I don't think it takes long to get to know guys like you."

"Guys like me..." he repeats, amused. "What would you know about guys like me?"

Nothing. To be honest, I know nothing about

any kind of guy. That's the problem.

"You're going red."

My hands fly to my cheeks. "That's not true."

"Your face is on fire."

I let go of my cheeks and shake my head.

"What? What's the problem?"

I'll never tell you, Tyler Hayes. It's already embarrassing enough. I don't want you to start making fun of me.

"There's no problem."

"If you say so..." He takes a few steps back and heads towards his own front door. He pulls out his keys and I move back into the hallway, stopping at my doormat.

I want to say something, but I don't want to look like an idiot. So I opt for something simple.

"I like spending time with you."

Tyler looks at me. His expression isn't amused, anymore. I'm scared I've said something wrong, so I quickly try to make up for it.

"As a friend," I say, nervously. "Spending time with you as friends. I like having friends. Guy friends. I like having girlfriends, too. Obviously. But I also like having guy friends." He tries to stifle a laugh, but I notice anyway. "Forget it."

I try to rush back inside, but Tyler stops me. His fingers wrap around my forearm.

"Hey." His voice is sweet, now, caring. "You haven't said anything wrong."

I don't look at him. I'm too embarrassed. "I'm not so sure about that."

"You talk too much when you're nervous, don't you?"

I shrug. My eyes are still glued to my shoes. Tyler's fingers slip away from my arm and move to rest delicately under my chin. Gently, they guide my gaze up and onto his face. I'd never noticed the colour of his eyes before. I thought they were blue, but now that I'm looking at them up close, I realise that they're green: a clear, sparkling green. They're the kind of eyes that undress you without ever touching you; the kind of eyes that could really get you in trouble.

"I like being your friend, too. And I like it when you can't stop talking, when you make no sense. When you're embarrassed. Like right now."

My cheeks burst into flames.

"And when you blush like that."

I wish I weren't smiling, but his words have touched me in places he shouldn't even know about.

"You're honest, you're genuine. It's pretty rare."

"It's stupid."

"No. Nothing about you is remotely stupid, Ms. White."

The way he says *Ms. White* sets off all my alarm bells. Even the ones I didn't think I had.

"Holly. I said you could call me Holly."

"You did say that, but Ms. White…" He sighs, his breath tickling my face. "It's a whole different story."

His words trail down my spine, making me shiver – and it's nothing to do with the cold.

"It's sexy."

I bite my lip at the way he pronounces the word *sexy*.

"It suits you."

Is he telling me that he thinks I'm sexy?

Just when I think this conversation could take an unexpected turn, Tyler steps back, depriving me of his touch.

"Maybe a friend shouldn't say things like that."

I don't respond. I don't know what to say. Disappointment seeps through me, and I'm certain that it's the worst thing I could feel right now. Disappointment means that there was something inside me, a sense of hope: something entirely unexpected. I can't start to hope like this – I'd never be able to handle it. Especially not when it concerns my sexy, charming, fireman neighbour, who I've already told I want to be just friends.

"I'm going to go now. I have to be at work in a few hours. Night shift."

"Sure."

"See you soon, Ms. White."

He steps into his apartment, and I step into mine. The sounds and movements are almost identical.

We both close the door, take a few confused steps into the living room; we probably both look around in search of something – who knows what. Then we both head into our respective bedrooms, each thinking of the other.

I stay in my room almost for the rest of the afternoon. I take a shower, I wash my hair, I paint my nails, I look in the mirror, and I let my thoughts carry me away. Only later that evening, when I hear him moving around in his apartment, I leave my room and sit on the couch, entranced by his movements, by his presence. I can hear him wandering around the house, without knowing exactly what he's doing, until I hear him walk towards the front door.

Curiosity gets the better of me, and I get up and run towards the window. Instinct tells me to open the curtains. Longing assails me when he turns back to look at the window. An unexpected sense of happiness seeps through me the moment he waves. Madness makes me hold my breath as I wave back.

But as soon as his car leaves the parking lot, pulling out into the street, I'm hit by a different emotion: fear.

I'm scared that I'll never be able to come out of my shell; that I'll never be able to build a life for myself that's healthy, calm, and – why not? – happy. I'm scared that I'm exactly like my mother, that I'll never be able to stop sabotaging anything good that happens to me. I'm scared that I'll keep running away from any kind of commitment, stability.

I'm scared I'll never be able to tell the difference between the person she left behind and the person I really am.

I'm scared that the first thing I've ever really wanted in my life is desperately out of my reach.

27

Holly

At the beginning of the week, all of the teachers at school have a committee meeting to go over suggestions for the Christmas show. Wes had already told me that the school organises a Christmas fair every year, with games, arts and crafts, a Santa's grotto, and a cake sale, alongside the Christmas show. I have no idea what to suggest – I'm not a huge fan of the holidays, and I'm not sure how they celebrate around here. Besides, the kids are so young, so it's not easy to find something suitable. Luckily, Wes seems to have come prepared.

"Frosty the Snowman," he says, confidently, as Anya takes notes. "I think it would be well-suited to their age, and the lyrics to the song just repeat over and over, so it'll be easy to memorise. We can make our costumes out of coloured paper, and we can choreograph dances – don't forget the dancing."

I smile at his enthusiasm.

"Sold!" Anya says, turning to the rest of the teachers.

"You came prepared." I nudge him playfully on the shoulder.

"It's a classic, especially for the first few years of school. Trust me, it'll be great."

"You're the boss."

"Did your old school never organise anything like this at Christmas?"

"Definitely not like this," I say, referring to the fair, the sale, the Santa Claus. "We put on a few little shows, but it was usually something every class took part in, and the little ones were just part of the choir."

"Okay… Well, like I said, Christmas is a huge event here. You'll see."

I don't know whether I should be worried about the fact that he's always so clued-up about the things I know nothing about, or whether I should just be reassured by his presence.

"I'd be lost without you. You're always so confident. And you're so good with the kids."

"Thanks, but you're pretty amazing, too. You just need a push in the right direction to let go a little."

"You think?"

"I think you're heading down the right path, but with a little help…"

"What do you mean?"

He considers this for a moment. "Do you want to have dinner at mine?"

"Oh," I exclaim, surprised.

"I'm assuming you've worked out by now that I actually bat for the other team."

I smile. "I thought you might, yes."

"So you shouldn't be worried about my motives, here."

I nod, listening.

"What you *don't* know is that I'm great in the kitchen, and that I love cooking for other people."

"Interesting…"

"Come to mine tonight."

I reflect on this for a moment.

"We can have dinner, maybe a few glasses of wine, talk about school, or about you."

"Me?"

"I get the impression you've had a really interesting life."

I laugh, shaking my head.

"What do you say?"

"Why not?"

"Perfect!" He smiles at me, satisfied. "I'll send you my address later."

* * * * *

When I close my front door behind me, on the way to Wes' apartment, Tyler is just stepping into his own.

"Good evening, Ms. White."

Since our strange, unexpected moment out in the hall, we haven't bumped into each other again. He hasn't even appeared at the window as usual, to watch me leave the house. I actually haven't even heard him moving around at home over the past few days.

"I haven't seen you around for a while," he says, as if he could read my thoughts.

"Have you… Been busy?" I ask, shyly.

"Work. I've been working double shifts, covering for a colleague. I've only just made it home."

"Got it."

"I feel like I haven't been home in weeks."

"You must be exhausted."

"A little. What about you? Where are you off to?"

"Dinner."

He raises an eyebrow.

"Out. I'm going out for dinner."

"Out," he repeats, his voice steady.

"Out of the house, I mean. They've invited me over for dinner," I say, starting to babble again. "One of my friends is cooking for me. At his house. So I'm going to dinner at his."

Tyler's expression tells me that I've explained this really badly.

"A colleague," I add, which doesn't seem to help. "He's from Dublin." I don't know why I'm telling him this. He didn't ask. "He's new, like me. Well, he's actually been here since the beginning of the year, but he already seems to know everything.

He's so good with the kids, and he's really kind, too. He's offered to help me. So I'm going to his."

Tyler doesn't move a muscle.

"I really should…" I nod towards the cab which has just pulled up onto the street. "You should go to bed." The word 'bed' sends both his eyebrows shooting up into his forehead. "Alone." Now he's staring at me as if I'm crazy. "To sleep. Right?" The corner of his mouth starts to form a smile.

I can't seem to control my tongue, and I'm starting to look like a total idiot.

"Have a good evening. Well, have a good sleep."

I head quickly down the stairs to avoid saying anything else, and climb hastily into the taxi. I tell the driver the address, then sink back into my seat. Before we pull away, I glance out the window, only to see Tyler standing in the same position I left him in, his gaze glued to the cab. I lift a hand stupidly to wave at him as we drive away, but he doesn't wave back. When we stop at the crossroads, I will myself not to turn around and check whether he's still there, watching me leave. Instead, I force myself to forget about this whole meeting, these crazy thoughts, and concentrate on the evening ahead of me.

28
Tyler

"I thought we were friends."

"Hello to you, too, Tyler."

"Fuck you, and your 'hello'."

"What's with you?"

"Why didn't you warn me?"

I sink onto the arm of the sofa and take a few sips of my beer. I haven't even changed my clothes, yet; I just chucked my bag into a corner, grabbed a beer from the fridge, then called my *ex*-best friend, in search of an explanation.

"What are you talking about?"

"She's having dinner. With a colleague. At his house."

"What dinner? What colleague? Who are we talking about?"

"I've just got home from a really shitty shift, Niall. Don't test my patience."

"I'm going to guess we're talking about your new *friend*, because I'm assuming this reaction is all part of the infamous 'process'."

"Can you please just be useful for once?"

"I wish I could, believe me, but I was in the middle of a really good film, and..."

Niall's voice fades away, immediately replaced

by someone else's.

"What's your problem, Tyler?" Jordan asks me, directly. "Is it that she's going out? That she's having dinner with a colleague? That she's at his house? Or is it that...?"

"What? What else?" I ask, running out of patience.

"That you're not the one she's having dinner with?"

I keep quiet. Sometimes that's the best response.

"So you knew?" Niall's voice floats in from the distance.

"I don't know anything. I just connected the dots."

"You're so intelligent."

"Is that not why you're marrying me?"

"Of course. And because you're sexy, and..."

"Hey! I'm still here, you know. Can we concentrate on my problem, please?"

"I didn't know you had a problem."

Niall is winding me up. He's waiting for me to start spouting more bullshit, but that's not going to happen. If you can't keep quiet – like I said – then there's nothing you can do but deny everything until you're blue in the face. It's your only hope.

"Then let's try to get a move on." Niall's voice appears back in the foreground. "First I'll get rid of you, then I can go back to my main job."

I scoff, frustrated at Niall, at the thought of her, in someone else's house, and at the fact that I'm so bothered by this thought.

"How long has it been since you last slept?" Niall asks me suddenly.

"I can't even remember. What's that got to do with anything?"

"Why don't you go and get some sleep? And then we can talk about this calmly tomorrow?"

No, Niall, we can't talk about this calmly. We can't waste any more time. I can't.

"Because by tomorrow, it could already be too late."

I just say it. Denying everything isn't going to help me, at this point.

"This process is really starting to speed up," I hear him tell Jordan. I don't even try to contradict him. I'm already contradicting myself enough as it is.

"I'm sorry, Tyler. I have no idea who she's having dinner with." Jordan is back on the phone. "All I can tell you is that, if it's a colleague, you can relax. They're all wonderful people, very professional and trustworthy."

Does she really think that'll make me feel better?

"I'd like to remind you, however, that if you have any intention of showing her that you're interested – and I mean *really* showing her – you need to start making a move. She won't stay single for long."

"How do you know?"

"Come on, Hayes," Niall says, taking the phone from Jordan. "There aren't many young, charming, single women around here. And she's from out of town, too! She's new and attractive. They'll be flocking around her like moths to a flame."

"You're not helping," I hear Jordan whisper.

"She won't be on her own for much long. Tonight she's at dinner, tomorrow she's at the cinema, next week she could even be—"

"Please, don't!" I stop him before the thought of her – of her curves, her hands, her mouth – pressed against someone who isn't me, starts to drive me insane.

"That's what's going to happen, mate. Why the hell don't you do something about it?"

Something. Yeah. I can do something. It's just that I'm not sure that my 'something' is the same 'something' that they're implying.

"I'll talk to you tomorrow, okay?"

"What? Wait, Tyler, what are you…?"

I hang up and throw my phone onto the sofa, before getting to my feet and pacing up and down my living room. I can think of about a hundred good reasons why I shouldn't be with Ms. White – I'm not even going to attempt to list them, now. I think you've probably worked them out. But there is something I can do. I can make sure that no one else even *thinks* about wanting her.

Does that sound like a good idea?

Come on, I'm a fireman. I have a few tricks up my sleeve, and I have my sources. I intend to put all my efforts into this.

You'll be out of *everyone* else's reach, my dear, sexy neighbour – I'm going to make sure of that. And I'm also going to make sure that it stays that way, until the day you leave, and then... And then I don't even want to think about a time when my only goal in life isn't to protect you.

29

Holly

Wes lives right on Main Street, in a small apartment above the flower store. It's the perfect size for one person, or maybe for a young couple, but it's nice, and welcoming. He says it was like this when he moved in, fully furnished and, luckily, decorated just the way he'd have done it himself. He offered me a glass of wine as soon as I stepped through the door, then told me to follow him into the small kitchen, where he was just finishing up with dinner.

"Salmon, potatoes and asparagus. I hope that's okay?"

"It sounds perfect, thanks."

I sip at my wine and quickly look around. He hasn't got many personal items; there are no photos, no signs of any personality. I'd imagine his life is similar to mine, in that respect, even though he's been here for longer, and probably isn't quite as disastrous as me.

I decide not to ask. Not yet, anyway. I'll save the questions about his life for later.

"I could have come and picked you up," he says again. I told him I'd make my own way here – I didn't want to bother him. "But I'll drop you off at home tonight, okay?" he says, waggling a spoon at me. "You're not leaving this house on your own."

I smile at him, taking another sip of wine.

"It'll be another ten minutes. If you want, we can go and sit in the living room."

I follow him and we both sit on the couch. Wes has already laid the coffee table for dinner.

"I hope you don't mind eating here?"

"No, not at all." I smile and grab one of the shrimp appetizers he offers me. "Everyone here seems to have the same habits."

"What habits?" He chews an appetizer and waits for me to respond.

"I was at Jordan's – Ms. Hill's," I say, correcting myself. I have no idea what kind of relationship they have, "and we ate sitting on the floor, next to the couch."

"So you were at the boss' house…?" he says, curious. "Tell me. What's she like?"

"I don't know… Kind, friendly. She knows how to make people feel comfortable."

"So you're… Friends?"

"Something like that, yeah. Her boyfriend is best friends with my neighbour, so…"

"Neighbour? The one who got arrested?"

I nod, drinking some more.

"How are things going with him?"

"Good, I think. We're friends. Or something like that."

"Interesting." Wes crosses his legs and studies

me, amused. "Tell me about this friendship."

"It's just friendship. He's a good neighbour."

"Are you telling me that? Or are you also trying to convince yourself?"

"W-what?" The room starts to spin, and I don't think it's from the wine.

"I've seen that fireman, Holly."

I shrug, feigning indifference.

"Believe me, there are a lot of things I want from that man. But friendship is definitely not one of them."

I can't help but laugh.

"And I'm not buying this whole 'friendship' thing. Not even when you pull that innocent face."

"What are you talking about...?" Another sip.

Thank God he's dropping me home.

"I'm just saying that tonight we're going to lay all our cards on the table, my dear Holly White. I want to know everything about that fireman, your weird friendship, and, especially, I want to know about you."

* * * * *

Two glasses of wine later, and I don't think there's much more left to learn about me – or about my stupid thoughts when it comes to that fireman.

"Well, the girls' suggestion isn't the worst

idea."

I glare at him.

"Even though I refuse to believe that you have no luck with men. I think a professional opinion – maybe from a fireman – could be helpful."

"Please, don't start. I should never have told you."

"I wish I could tell you that that was the worst thing you've told me tonight, but I'd be lying."

I cover my face with my hands.

"There's nothing to be embarrassed about, Holly."

"I'm not so sure about that. To be honest, I'm not so sure about anything anymore. Not even where 'home' is for me."

"That's where I come in."

"This is why you insisted I come over tonight, right? You knew it would end up like this," I say, struggling to my feet, Wes propping me up. "You did it on purpose. You wanted to know about me and *him*." I take a few steps into the living room, still supported by Wes. "About me and him..." I repeat quietly. "About me. And. About him. Separated by huge, fat full stops."

"Honey, you're babbling again."

"That's what happens when I'm nervous, or agitated, or... Or with a guy. A guy I like. I told you I'm a mess."

"A beautiful mess," he says, brushing a strand

of hair from my face and tucking it behind my ear. "Who just needs a few hours of sleep."

"Absolutely." I wander around in search of my coat. Wes helps me put it on, then grabs his car keys.

"I didn't even help you clear up."

"I'll do it tomorrow."

"Thanks for tonight, Wes. It was really fun."

"Thanks for coming. I just hope that next time you organise a night out, you'll invite me, too. I don't want to miss out on all the fun."

"You'll be there next time, I promise."

* * * * *

I say goodbye to Wes again before attempting to climb up the stairs. But when I place my foot on the first step, my head starts to spin dangerously, making me teeter on my heels. I grab onto the railing to stop myself from ending up on the floor, but before I've realised what's happening, two strong, steady hands land on my hips, making me jump.

"A woman should always be walked to her front door." His warm, reassuring voice makes me tremble. "What kind of men are you going out with, Ms. White?"

"The only kind that want me," I find myself saying, bitterly.

He scoops me up in his arms as if I were lighter than air, and my hands grab onto his neck.

"The ones that want you, Ms. White," he repeats, his tone laden with bitterness, too – a bitterness that really doesn't suit him.

He climbs the stairs, carrying me in his arms like that first night – the night he brought me home.

"They'll prove it to you, those men. They'll make you see, in a thousand different ways, so that you never question yourself again."

He places my feet on the ground, my back to the door, and stands just a breath away from me.

"Well, up until now, no one has ever wanted me," I say, caught somewhere between sadness and anger.

He closes the distance between us with just one step, his hand resting on the wooden door behind me, beside my face.

"Maybe that's because no one has ever really deserved you."

In the darkness, I see his eyes shimmering with something I don't know how to describe; but it lights something up inside me, as if he were in control of my master switch.

"What... What are you doing here? Weren't you supposed to be sleeping?"

"I wanted to make sure you got home okay."

"I-I am home."

"Good."

He doesn't move from the door, and my eyes never leave his. Neither of us has any intention of leaving this hallway.

"I have to…"

"Yeah, you have to."

Neither of us has any intention of letting the other go.

"Tyler…"

He lowers his gaze for an instant, before finally pulling away, making me feel stupid for ever having considered that something could happen.

"I'll wait until you're inside."

I peel myself away from the door, my knees trembling, and rummage around in my purse for the keys – but my fingers are shaking harder than my legs.

"How much did you drink, Holly?"

My name slides seductively over my skin.

"Just a few glasses of wine."

He reaches out a hand, and I pass him my purse.

"May I?"

I nod, embarrassed.

Tyler sticks his hand into my purse and pulls out my keys, dangling them in front of me, before opening the door.

It's not the wine, you stupid, sexy fireman. You're the one confusing me, making me nervous.

You're the cause of this.

The door opens and Tyler hands me back my bag.

"If you'd gone out with me, instead, Ms. White, you wouldn't be coming home like this."

I swallow. My throat is dry, scratchy.

"If you'd gone out with me, Ms. White," he says, stepping closer again, his hands sliding through my hair, "then you'd never have gone back to your apartment."

He lets me go, taking my last breath, my senses, my thoughts; then his own front door bangs shut.

I lay awake the whole night, my eyes glued to the ceiling, my hand resting on my hammering heart, trying to work out when we stopped being friends, and when Tyler Hayes started to play games with me; trying to work out exactly when I realised that I want to let him into my hiding place, my safe house.

30
Holly

For the next few days after our little encounter in the hallway, our meetings are brief and strangely formal. We saw each other yesterday, at the door. I was coming back from school, and he was just leaving. He was wearing a tracksuit, so I guessed he was going for a run, or maybe to the gym, but I didn't ask. This morning, we both left at the same time. We walked down the stairs, side-by-side; my arm brushed against his for a few seconds. He asked me if I needed a lift, and I said I'd rather walk. He told me to have a good day, and I did the same. And now I'm sitting in Anya's office eating hazelnut chocolates, because she doesn't like hazelnut.

"Do you realise what he's given me?"

"He couldn't have known."

"There's absolutely no chance now of me answering his calls."

Anya is talking about the last guy she went out with, who apparently has just missed his chance to go out again. Why? Because she doesn't like the chocolates he bought her – the ones I'm currently eating for her.

"Luckily it's Friday."

I watch her, waiting for an explanation.

"The best day of the week."

I'm not sure I like where this conversation is going.

"You and me," she says, pointing to us both. "We're going out."

"Oh... I don't know if..."

"Didn't I say I'd take care of you?"

I nod, a little frightened.

"And seeing as you have no intention of taking advantage of your neighbour..."

I shake my head violently.

I'm more sure of that now than ever.

"I have to be the one to help you spread your wings."

"Why do I feel like you're trying to spread your *own* wings?"

Anya laughs and gets up from her desk, before moving to stand in front of me.

"I've been spreading them for a while."

"And you're not tired of flying, yet?"

"What else is there to do around here?"

"You could always accept the chocolates that men keep sending you?"

"Who gives a girl chocolates, in this day and age? Come on!"

My sexy neighbour, for example. But it's probably best if I keep that to myself.

"A bottle of wine would've been better. Or prosecco, maybe."

He also gave me a bottle of wine. But I don't mention that, either.

"So. Tonight. I'll come and pick you up at seven. It'll just be me and you, Jordan's busy with Kerry's family."

"Anya, really…"

"I'm looking after you, now."

That doesn't make me feel any better, but I don't want to offend her, so I keep that to myself, too.

"And we're not going home until we've each found someone to go home with."

"What?" I ask, worried.

Anya smiles cheekily at me. "Have you ever heard of gnome hunting?"

"What?" I ask, leaping up from my seat. "No, no, I can't—"

Anya grabs my arms and shakes me, bringing my attention back to her.

"I'm not saying you have to sleep with someone tonight. Please, just relax."

I take a deep breath. "Okay."

"But we need to start working on you, on your confidence. On trusting yourself."

"It sounds so complicated."

"You are my mission, young, innocent Holly White."

I can't help but smile.

"And when Anya's on a mission… Nothing can

stop her."

* * * * *

Anya shows up at my door.

"Weren't you supposed to message me when you left?"

"I thought I'd come and pick you up at the door, like a true gentleman."

I laugh and gesture for her to come in.

"Where's your hopeless neighbour?"

"I don't think he's home. I haven't heard anything."

"Does that mean you can hear everything he does? Even when he…?"

"When he?"

"Come on, Holly."

"Oh, God, no!"

"Maybe guys like him don't bring girls home."

"You think?" I ask, suddenly interested.

"I have no idea how it works for him. For me, it makes no difference whether we back to mine or back to his… I don't have a problem either way. But for someone like Hayes, I'd guess it's a little different."

"What do you mean?"

"Well, I've heard rumours that he's allergic to any kind of relationship."

"Like everyone."

"But I get the impression he's particularly opposed to these kinds of things. He's the kind of guy who will only spend one or two nights with someone – never more. And when you're that kind of guy, you never want any indication that something could lead to more. Do you know what I mean?"

I nod, perplexed.

"So. We ready?"

"Yes," I say, a little sad.

"What's with that face?"

"What face?" I grab my jacket and slip it on.

"This whole Hayes thing is bothering you, isn't it?"

"Absolutely not!" I cry, a little too defensively.

"If you say so…"

I grab my purse and head towards the door, opening it. "It's none of my business. I have nothing to do with him, or who he decides to sleep with!"

"Good evening, Ms. White."

His voice from behind me makes me jump.

I turn suddenly, my cheeks on fire, embarrassment clamping my tongue.

"I wasn't talking about you!" I immediately regret saying that. "I was talking about someone else."

"Someone else."

"A guy."

"Okay."

"I thought he was interested, but then he did a runner."

"What a coward," he says, making fun of me.

"Never trust anyone who gives you chocolates, or who pretends to be a gentleman, or who has eyes which..." I hold my breath the moment his own eyes begin to deepen.

"Eyes which...?"

I swallow my anger, and voice my disappointment. "Lie."

His expression changes in an instant.

"I'd say it's probably best if we get going," Anya interjects, before I can say anything crazy. Maybe it's already too late – but it's pointless dwelling on that, now.

"Where are you ladies off to this evening?"

"None of your business, Hayes," Anya says, her voice hard. She wraps her arm around me and starts to guide me away. I close the door and follow her down the stairs and over to her car. When I'm sitting inside, I fix my eyes on the windscreen, ignoring the temptation to look back at our building. I stay strong, keep my face neutral, and try to salvage at least a little of my dignity.

Anya starts the ignition and pulls out into the street. It's only when I start to breathe again that I realise I haven't done so since the moment he looked at me.

"All those things you said – they were about him, right?"

I nod, still looking ahead.

"You know he was waiting for you to turn around, right?"

I don't move a muscle. Anya sighs.

"We're going to have to call a cab tonight. I don't think I'll be able to drive."

I smile, grateful that she's here with me, and grateful that I don't have to spend this evening alone and sober, after yet another encounter in the hallway.

* * * * *

"Maybe it would've been best to have dinner first," Anya says, gesturing towards my already-empty glass.

"I don't need food."

"Then what do you need?"

"A guy."

"Any guy? Or the guy who made a scene outside your apartment earlier?"

"It wasn't a scene."

Anya raises an eyebrow.

"Can we please just concentrate on the men that are here?"

"Are you sure about this?"

"Did you not bring me here for a reason?"

"Yes, but then I thought that, maybe..."

"Maybe what?"

She sighs, then grows suddenly serious. "That you were already thinking about someone else."

I shake my head, and cast my gaze around the room. The drink I just finished isn't helping, and the thought of him, of what I said to him, of what he probably thinks of me now...

"Holly." Anya's hand rests on mine. "If you like him, we can—"

"No."

"There's nothing wrong with it."

"It's just a silly little crush. Come on! You've seen him, right? He's charming, and he knows what he's doing. He lives right next door. I see him every day! It would be hard for me to think of anything else, right?"

"I guess so..."

"That's why we're here."

Anya looks at me, confused.

"I need to get him out of my head."

"What are you talking about, exactly?"

"I want... I need to..."

"Don't tell me you're looking for a one-night-stand?"

"Why not?"

"Because that's not what you want."

"Actually, it's exactly what I want."

"Your words don't seem to reflect your actions, you know…"

"I need to stop."

"Stop what?"

I bite my lip, anxious. "I need to stop… Thinking about him. Can you help me? Please?"

"Are you sure this is what you want, Holly?"

I don't even have to think about it.

"Absolutely."

* * * * *

"So, Tyler, you were saying…?"

"Trevor," he corrects me. Again.

"Of course, Trevor." I smile nervously and take another sip of my drink, under Anya's watchful gaze.

"I was wondering why a girl like you is here alone on a Friday night."

"Well, I'm not exactly alone. You're here, now."

He brings the bottle of beer to his lips and smiles, satisfied. Maybe I'm encouraging him a little too much, but is that not why I came out tonight? To throw myself in at the deep end, to spread my wings, just like Anya said?

"Can I borrow her for two minutes?" Anya asks, helping me up. "I'll bring her right back." She drags me towards a corner of the pub, then checks whether Tyler – damn, I mean *Trevor* – is watching.

"This wasn't exactly what I had in mind when I suggested we go out tonight."

"Didn't you want me to throw myself into this?"

"Not at the first guy you come across."

"Tyler isn't the first guy I came across."

"Trevor!"

"Sure, sure, Trevor... Their names are too similar," I laugh, nervously.

"Now let's grab our things and go."

"It's still early. And tomorrow's Saturday."

"You've drunk too much."

"No more than you."

"But I'm Irish. You're not."

"Good observation."

"Please, Holly, let's go. We can go back to mine, make ourselves a hot chocolate. Whatever you want."

"Why don't you want me to have fun anymore? Why don't you want me to meet someone?"

"Because it's not the right thing for you."

"You don't know me that well."

"True. But I saw you tonight, and I saw what

was happening... It's not okay. Please, just trust me."

I scoff. "Okay."

"I'll go and grab our things. Don't move, okay?"

I nod, and Anya heads off in search of her stuff. I stay put for a moment, before striding over to the table we were sitting at before, where I'd luckily left my things.

"Let's go," I say, grabbing his hand and pulling him to his feet.

"Where?"

"To mine."

"What about your friend?"

"She can get home on her own."

Trevor grabs my coat and helps me put it on.

"After you."

* * * * *

By the time we get to my front door, doubt started to creep up on me. When we were in the car and his hand was resting on my thigh, I was already certain then that this was the wrong thing to do.

I stop in front of my door and turn to face him. I'm not ready for this.

"Listen," I say, feeling all the alcohol attempting to slide back up my throat. "We've had fun, we had a few drinks…"

"And we can keep having fun."

He plants his hand against the door and moves closer. His breath reeks of beer, and he smells like a mistake: a colossal, irreparable mistake.

"I'm tired."

"Maybe we can lie down for a while…"

"And maybe it's time for you to piss off."

His voice paralyses me.

"Before I break that fucking hand you've got resting against the fucking door."

"Hayes?" he asks, turning towards Tyler.

"Fuck off. Now."

"What the hell is wrong with you? Why do you care what I do?"

Tyler scoffs, and before Trevor can add anything else, his fist has made contact with his face.

"What the hell…?" Trevor brings his hands to his nose, as I stand at the door, frozen. "You're out of your fucking mind, Hayes!"

"I warned you. Now piss off."

"You're a bastard."

"And now I'm a bastard who has a problem with you, arsehole!"

Trevor walks off, swearing under his breath. Tyler watches him leave, then turns to me.

"Inside. Now."

I shake my head, dizzy.

"W-what?"

"Get inside, now."

"You can't tell me what to do."

"Okay, you're right. Let's try again. Could you please kindly get your arse inside?"

I cross my arms.

"Inside *my* apartment," he clarifies.

"I don't think so."

"Holly…" His tone softens as he says my name. "Please. Come inside with me."

"Why?"

"Because I want you to sober up, and do so somewhere safe."

"And your apartment is safe? Remember I called the police on you, Tyler."

The corner of his mouth starts to twist into a smile.

"I can assure you there's no place safer than this." He stretches his arms out as he speaks, as if he's not talking about a specific place – definitely not his apartment – but about something else. Something intimate, scarily beautiful. And I'm stupid enough to fall for it, hard.

31

Tyler

"What the hell were you thinking?" I ask her, as soon as I've closed the door behind me.

She looks at me, confused.

"Bringing that guy home."

"I don't think that's any of your business."

"Oh, no?" My voice raises involuntarily.

The truth is that I can't stand the thought of what might have happened if I hadn't intervened.

"You don't even know him."

"Yes I do! His name is Tyler."

I furrow my brow; now I'm confused.

"Trevor, Jesus! His name is Trevor! These damn names..." She sinks onto the arm of the sofa. "They all sound the same."

I rest my hands on my hips and study her, sitting in the middle of my living room.

"He's a nice guy. Trevor, I mean. Not Tyler. Tyler's not a nice guy at all."

I wish I could stifle my laughter, but I can't.

"See? He's a bastard, too."

"You know Tyler is standing right in front of you?"

"Says who? There are loads of Tylers in the world. They aren't all firemen, and they don't all live next door to me, and they're definitely not all arrogant, or sexy, or arrogant. Especially not sexy."

"Did you just call me sexy?" I ask, amused.

"Not you! Another Tyler."

"Which one?"

"A hypothetical one."

"How much have you drunk tonight, Ms. White?"

"I don't know." She shrugs. "It's not my fault. Your alcohol is different over here."

I laugh and step closer to her, before bending down to take off her shoes.

"What the hell are you doing?"

"I'm helping you get comfortable."

"Is this so that you can look at my underwear again?"

"It's so that we can go to bed."

"Oh no." She leaps up, stumbling. I get up, too, and grab her before she loses her balance. Her small, soft hands are splayed against my chest, a little uncertain, but curious to explore. Her body is warm against mine; my fingers are pressing lightly against her hips. Her bright, innocent eyes ignite a hope in me, a madness.

You're playing dirty, Ms. White. And you don't even know you're doing it.

"I-I'm not sleeping in your bed tonight."

"Yes, you are."

"Why should I?"

"Because, like I said, I want to make sure that you're okay."

And because I want to make sure that no one comes anywhere near your apartment without my consent.

"I live right next door."

"That's not good enough for me."

Her eyes reflect the hope in my own; I should push it down, keep it quiet. But it's sparking something unusual and unexpected within me. It's something I want to keep feeling, just to understand what it means.

"What about you?" she asks. Her breathing grows heavy. "Will you be sleeping with me?"

The mere thought of it hurts.

"On the sofa. I'll sleep on the sofa."

Disappointment flashes across her expression, making me smile unexpectedly.

"Come on," I say, pulling myself away, against my will. "I'll take you to bed."

I feel her shiver, even though I'm no longer touching her.

"You'll take me to bed?"

I feel as if I'm dying, but seem to still somehow be breathing.

"Me, Ms. White. Only me. No one else."

* * * * *

She lays down on my bed, fully clothed. She only let me take off her shoes. I offered to lend her a T-shirt, but she refused. She turns onto her side, her hand resting under my pillow, her hair spread across my bedsheets.

"I could've managed by myself, you know."

"I'm sure about that." I laugh, pulling the covers over her.

"I'm serious."

"Me, too." I think about this for a moment, then decide to take the next step in Niall's beloved 'process'. "You definitely could've handled it on your own – but he couldn't have."

"Are you worried about me, Hayes?"

"I'm a fireman."

"But there's no fire."

"That's not all we do."

"Do you also rescue damsels in distress?"

"Only one at a time."

"Should I be flattered?"

"Get some rest. Tomorrow you'll have a migraine and a lot of regret to deal with." I get up and head for the door.

"It was nice," she says then, her voice tired, laden with sleep.

"What?" I stop, waiting for her response.

"Seeing you turn up like that. Like a knight in shining armour, defending my honour. I didn't need you to…"

"I know."

"But it was nice. Men usually run away."

"Run away?"

"From me."

I turn back to face the bed, because this sounds interesting. I sit down and her eyes land on me.

"I'm a disaster. With men. In every way." She blushes, then continues, without looking at me. "In *that* way, too. Especially in that way. Actually, I know literally nothing about that."

I don't want to know whether *that* means sex. I don't know if I can handle a conversation like that.

"I'm sure that's just the alcohol talking."

"I've never had a boyfriend."

Oh, fuck.

"N-not like that…"

I know I'm not going to want to hear this, but I try to stay strong.

"I've dated a few guys here and there, but I've never really had… a *man*."

I was right. I didn't want to hear that.

"I've never had a real relationship."

"I don't think now is the best time to have this conversation…"

"Anya offered to help me."

"Help you do what?" I say, my voice growing louder before I can attempt to control it.

"To spread my wings, she said."

I'll. Kill. Her.

I clear my throat and try to speak calmly and confidently, but that's a lot of information to receive in a matter of seconds; I wasn't ready, I need time to think. I need to step away from her for a moment.

"You need some sleep," I say, getting up. "Everything will feel better in the morning, and..."

"Why don't you help me?"

"W-what?"

She lifts herself up and sits on the bed. "You're a man. And you're an expert," she says, biting her lip nervously. "I've heard the rumours about you."

"They're just rumours."

"Really?"

"No, but I don't want to talk about it."

I turn back towards the door and hear her settle herself back into bed.

"I thought we were friends," I hear her say.

"That's true, we are friends. And if I help you get what you want, then we can't be friends anymore."

Holly doesn't respond, so I turn around to see whether I've offended her in some way. It's only then that I realise she's fallen asleep. I don't whether or not she heard my response, and I don't know whether she'll even remember having asked me for help by the morning – but I'll remember, and I already know I won't be able to think of anything else.

* * * * *

The balcony slides open behind me: a sign that my overnight guest is awake.

"Good morning." Her shy voice greets me.

I turn around to say something stupid, to try and alleviate the awkwardness of the situation, but when I see her standing there, deep grooves across her face from the covers, her hair in disarray, and her expression telling me she has no idea how to act, everything I wanted to tell her disappears. I've never seen anything more beautiful in my life.

"Good morning." I opt for simplicity. "How are we feeling?"

She wraps her arms around herself. "Well, I'm in one piece. I think."

"It's cold out here, let's go inside. There's still some coffee in the pot."

She takes two steps back, and I join her in the house.

"Not only did I steal your bed, and waste your time, but now I'm stealing your coffee, too?"

She follows me into the kitchen as I pour her a mug of coffee and place it on the counter. I open the fridge and hand her the milk carton. I don't say anything, I don't even try to reassure her about 'stealing' my things; I'm still in shock from the effect she's had on me, finding her there, first thing in the morning, in my house. I don't think I'd ever be capable of saying anything that didn't make me sound like a dick.

"Thanks." She picks up the mug and brings it to her lips.

"How are you?" I manage.

"I think I'm okay. Apart from being totally mortified."

I gesture towards the living room and we both sit on the sofa. She sinks into the cushions, and I perch on the arm, a safe distance away.

"Everyone does stupid things sometimes."

"I can't believe I tried to bring that guy home. What the hell was I thinking?!"

"Nothing happened."

"Thank God you heard me come home."

That's not entirely true. I'd been waiting by the window for you to come back, Ms. White, because I had a strange feeling – and not because I'm a fireman. Then, when I saw you come back with a guy, it felt as if the Titanic had crashed into my stomach. It was a horrible feeling, which seems to be surfacing again now that I'm thinking about it. It's something I never want to feel again. That's why I made a decision, last night, when I was standing in my bedroom doorway, watching you sleep.

"I'll help you."

Her eyes widen.

"I want to help you."

"I don't get it."

I take a deep breath. "I don't like the idea of you coming home every night with a different guy, just to..." The Titanic plunges into me again. "I'll help you."

"Are you saying you'll help me go out with other guys?"

God, *no*.

"I'll help you realise that there's absolutely nothing wrong with you."

I categorically refuse to believe it.

"And how do you intend to do that?"

I hadn't thought about that. But it's taken me all night, and all my efforts, just to come to this decision.

"We'll work it out together."

Ms. White studies my expression for a while. "Are you serious?"

"What else are friends for?"

Other than murdering every guy who tries to take you home.

She gets up from the sofa and leans towards me. I have no time to move and, to be honest, I'm not sure I'd have moved even if I *did* have the time. So I absorb every inch of her hug, breathing in the scent of her, mixed with the scent of me. I bask in the heat radiating from her body.

"Thanks, Ty."

God. Help me.

"No problem, Ms. White."

She pulls away from me – *too quickly* – and studies me curiously.

"Why do you keep calling me Ms. White?"

Because it's sexy, and because I'm the only one who does.

I shrug. "It's just a name."

Maybe that's true of every other name in every other language – but not yours, Ms. White.

"You're a strange guy, Hayes." She sits back down on the sofa.

"Strange in a good way? Or strange like someone who should be arrested again?"

She laughs. I'd never realised before that when she laughs, she laughs with her whole body, in a way that means she can't stop.

"I'll tell you soon enough, but I'm leaning towards it being a good thing – otherwise I'd never have asked you to help me last night, and you would never have offered to help me today."

"Speaking of which," I say, clearing my throat and growing serious. "If you want me to help you..."

"Yes...?"

"Try not to go out too much."

And meet any other arseholes.

"You want me to lock myself in my apartment?"

If you don't lock yourself in, I'll lock you in.

"You can spend time with me, instead."

She tilts her head, scrutinising me.

"Just until you're ready to go out with someone," I add. "I'll keep you company until then."

"Until I'm ready...?" she asks, worried.

I force myself to say it, as if someone were holding a gun to my head.

"Until you're ready to spread your wings."

Her face relaxes immediately.

"Thanks, Ty. You're the best."

Friend, I add in my head. Best friend.

"At your service."

She smiles, then gets to her feet. "I think it's probably best if I go home."

I get up, too.

"Thanks for everything."

"Stop thanking me, honestly. I didn't do anything."

She heads towards the front door and opens it.

"I can't wait to get started."

Get started sleeping with other guys, my mind finishes. Am I really about to help her spread her wings? We all know what that means for Ms.

White – although it also means she'll end up landing in the arms of the wrong person. But who am I to stop her? And besides, it's better to be able to supervise the situation than to leave everything to Anya, right?

Right?

Please, just agree with me.

"I'll leave you to your day. I guess you have a lot to do."

I only have one thing to do, Ms. White: think about how to avoid this catastrophe. For me and for you.

"Have a good day, Ty."

Another hug: one that could've melted the iceberg which struck the Titanic, were it not lodged firmly into my stomach.

"You, too."

The door closes behind her, and I'm alone in my apartment, thinking about the inevitable disaster I've just begun. And when disaster is on the horizon, there's only one person to call.

32

Tyler

"Have you lost your mind?"

"Shh, please. I don't want everyone to come running into the kitchen."

"You've just offered to help her do *what*?"

"Shut up, for fuck's sake!"

"You're an idiot, Hayes. And I always listen to you because, hey, who doesn't trust a fucking *fireman*?"

"Can you please lower your voice?"

"This is how you deal with the situation? If you like your neighbour, just ask her out, like a normal person!"

"Cut the crap!"

"What part of that is crap, sorry? Oh, right. The fact that you're a normal person."

I glare at him, but he ignores me, sending down half his beer in one slug.

"Slow down, it's only midday."

"Oh, *I* need to slow down?"

"I don't understand why this bothers you so much."

And I don't understand what the fuck I'm doing at Niall's house. Oh, right. Ms. White slept in my house, I spent the entire night staring at her as she snored softly, and when she woke up this morning, looking dangerously beautiful, I started telling her all that bullshit.

"You're not telling me you're really doing this to help her? Come on, Hayes. I thought that with your *skills* and..." he gestures at me, "everything else, you'd be able to get a girl into bed without all this crap."

"I'm not trying to get anyone into bed, Niall. And, please, stop talking about my 'skills'."

"Why? Does it make you uncomfortable?"

"When you're the one talking about them, yes. A little."

Niall rubs his forehead with his hand, before taking a deep breath and speaking seriously, in a way I've only seen him speak a few times in the past.

"Let me tell you what I think."

I scoff. "If you have to..."

"I see a broken heart in your near future."

I roll my eyes.

That's it, Niall? I thought you could do better.

"So?" I ask, challenging him. "What else?"

"And I also see another broken heart, mate." His tone is concerned. He points his finger against my chest before continuing. "And I'm not sure that it'll be easy to fix. I'm not sure if you see what I'm getting at."

"I have no idea what you're talking about,

Kerry. I should've stopped listening after the whole 'process' thing."

"What are you so afraid of?"

"Afraid?" I laugh bitterly. "Do you have any idea what I do for a living?"

"Not really, to be honest. I only ever seen you cleaning the fire engines."

"Very funny…"

"But we're not talking about work, here, or about your calling – I'm guessing that's what inspired you to become a firefighter."

I shrug.

"I'm talking about something much more difficult to manage – and I'm saying this from personal experience."

"We're not all as lucky as you, Niall."

"There's no doubt that I've been lucky, but that doesn't mean that it can't be the same for everyone."

"I don't think there are many women like Jordan around."

"That's true," he says, smiling. "But maybe what you need isn't another Jordan, but a Ms. White." He winks, making me laugh.

"I'm not interested in Ms. White, Niall, or in anyone else."

"Why not?"

"Because we're not all cut out for these things. For commitment, stability, a family."

"I thought I wasn't cut out for it, either – remember? And now look at me. I cook lunch, my daughter invites her *non*-boyfriend round, and Jordan goes out shopping with my sister. I'd say that, for someone who could barely even commit to getting a cat, I've taken some pretty big steps. Don't you think?"

I smile at my friend. "We're not all like you. We're not all capable of taking those steps. Not even if…"

"Not even if?"

"Not even if it could be worth it."

Niall nods slowly.

"Why, then?"

"Why what?"

"Why knock at her door, invite her to your house, offer to help her *spread her wings*? And we both know which wings you're talking about."

Because I desperately need to spend time with her, firstly. And also because I need to stop Ms. White from ending up in the wrong hands. And also because I need to convince myself that she's not worth it, before it's too late.

"Because she needed a hand, and I was there to help out."

"Ready to push her into the arms of the next arsehole that comes along?"

Ready to push her into the arms of someone who isn't me.

"I'll make sure they're the best of a bad bunch."

"This is a really shit idea. You know that, right?"

"As are most of our ideas."

Niall leaves me alone with my thoughts for a few minutes as he starts to make lunch. He said he wanted to challenge himself with something new, and I'm starting to bitterly regret accepting his offer of staying for lunch.

"Can I ask you something?"

"Sure."

"And will you respond as my friend?"

"What does that mean?"

"Will you be honest?"

"I reckon I can manage that."

"Why, Tyler? Why have you chosen this?"

"Chosen what?"

"A life with no ties, no emotional involvement or commitment."

"I'm just not cut out for it, that's all."

"Have you ever tried?"

"There's no need."

"How can you say that?"

"Hey, these are a lot of questions. I only agreed to one."

"You're right. But let me ask you another, then I swear I'll stop. Mainly because I really need to start concentrating on lunch."

I nod at him to continue.

"Has something happened to you over the past few years? Did a relationship end badly, or did someone break your heart? I don't know what it is, but something seems to have scarred you..."

"No, Niall. Nothing like that. But I've seen up close what happens when you lose everything. And I have no intention of feeling anything like that myself."

33
Holly

The following Monday at school, I'm pretty quiet. After that disastrous night out, my horrendous attempt at bringing a guy home, Tyler's intervention, spending the night at his, and how strange it felt to wake up there – and let's not forget about the fact that he agreed to help me... I definitely have a lot to think about, and not a lot to talk about. I'd have no idea where to even begin in untangling this absolute mess. And I've only been here for a few weeks. I can't even bear to imagine what could still happen.

We spend almost all day practicing the songs that the kids will have to sing for the Christmas show, and chopping up carrots for the snowmen's noses. It's a creative, enjoyable day – for the kids and for us.

"Someone's thoughtful this morning..." Wes hisses into my ear, in between carrot-chopping. "Has something happened? Do you want to talk about it?"

"No, nothing."

"Will you tell me at lunch?"

I laugh, and look at him.

"You know I won't stop until you spill the beans."

I glance at the clock on the wall, realising that there are only a few minutes left until the bell.

"It's basically already lunchtime."

He smiles cheekily at me. "I couldn't have waited another minute."

* * * * *

"This weird chemistry between you and your neighbour..." he comments, slowly chewing his chicken salad. "I'm not convinced at all."

"No one said anything about chemistry."

"Please, honey. I can feel it from here, and I've never even seen the two of you together. I don't even want to imagine what it's like in real life."

"It's not what you think. Like I said, we're just..."

"Friends. Sure."

"I'm being serious."

"We," he says, gesturing between us, "are friends. But you and your sexy fireman are definitely *not*."

"He's not even that sexy."

"Hey, I've taken a good look at Hayes."

"Oh, have you?"

"A few days before you got here, we had the Fall Dance at the secondary school. He was part of the security team. In his uniform. And, trust me, I couldn't think about anything else for days."

I'd have been the same – but I don't tell him this, or the situation could take a serious turn.

"I'd never want to be friends with a guy like him. I'd end up trying to jump into his bed at every chance I got."

I've been in that bed – but I keep that little detail to myself, and I think it's the right decision.

"So the night you went out with Anya was a disaster."

"A total disaster."

"You really need to start doing something to bump up your self-esteem, Holly."

"That's exactly what I want to do. Speaking of which…"

Wes sits up straight.

"I may have asked someone for help."

"May have asked?"

"Okay, have asked."

"Who?"

"T-Tyler."

"Oh…"

"Please, don't say anything."

"How can I not say anything? We've just been talking about him!"

"*You've* been talking about him."

"Yeah, yeah… But let's get back to the point. You asked Hayes to help you with what, exactly?"

To be honest, I'm not entirely sure myself.

"I wasn't exactly specific. I just told him I have some problems with men, and that..."

"Wait, wait. You told him *what*?"

"The truth."

"Aside from the fact that I think this is just something you've convinced yourself of, which hopefully he will soon prove wrong..."

I glare at him.

"What are you expecting him to do about it?"

"Give me advice, maybe a few pointers."

"On what?"

"On how to attract men. And, maybe, how to make them stick around."

"I can't believe you asked *him* for help with that."

"Me neither."

"You must've been really desperate."

My glare grows sharper.

"And I can't believe he said yes."

"I didn't think it would happen, either. To be honest, when I asked him, I thought he just thought I was totally insane."

"Then what happened?"

"Then he changed his mind, like this," I say, snapping my fingers, "and offered to help me. As long as..."

"As long as what?" Wes' curiosity is almost

embarrassing.

"As long as I agree to stop going out with lost causes, like the guy from the other night."

"And you fell for it?"

"What do you mean?"

"You actually believe that he wants to help you spread your wings?"

"Shh..." I say, glancing around. "Lower your voice."

"I can't believe you're actually that naïve."

"Why? What do you think he wants from me?"

Wes wiggles his eyebrows.

"Oh, no. Definitely not. Not with his infamous *skills*."

"Why wouldn't he want to use his skills on you?"

"Because he could have any woman in town – probably in the entire county. Actually, think he's already had them all."

"Exactly. So..."

"So, what?"

"He's missing someone from the list."

"No, I can assure you, it's not like that."

"Something doesn't seem right, here, Holly, and I intend to get to the bottom of it."

"What do you mean?" I ask, worried.

"Tonight, we're going out. You and me."

"Tonight? But it's only Monday?"

"So that means we can't go out for dinner?"

"No, but—"

"We need to talk about this whole thing, and about your fireman and his *skills*, without people eavesdropping, if you get what I mean."

"I get what you mean, but there's really no need."

"Let me be the judge of that. We need to work out what your sexy neighbour is up to, and we need to work it out now."

34
Tyler

Parker opens the door with a look on his face that tells me that he did not invite me over with good news.

"What's going on?"

"Come in, Tyler."

"Okay," I say carefully, doing as he says. "Where are the girls?"

"With my neighbour."

I raise my eyebrow.

"I needed to speak to you alone."

"Should I be worried?"

"You tell me, Tyler, whether someone in this room should be worried."

"Shall I sit down?" I ask, nodding towards the sofa.

Parker just stands there, frozen, so I make myself comfortable anyway, just to be safe. He watches me, a serious expression on his face, before sitting on the coffee table across from me.

"What did I ask you, Tyler?"

I swallow. I have no idea what he's talking about, but I'm sure it promises nothing good for me.

"When, exactly?"

His face tells me he doesn't want questions. Only answers.

"You ask me loads of things... Can you give me a clue?"

"What did we talk about, the last time you came for dinner?"

"I just want to point out, here, that we actually spoke about loads of things, and that it could be..."

"I asked you one fucking thing!" His voice fills the living room.

Now I understand why the girls aren't here.

"Parker..."

"No more teachers, Tyler. I was clear about that. You gave me your word."

Oh. Fuck.

"T-teachers?"

Is it just me, or is it way too warm in this apartment? Has he whacked up the thermostat?

"I know about your latest little trick."

"What... Er... What trick?"

"The girls were hiding under the teacher's table today in the cafeteria."

Do you hear it too, reader? That sad, foreboding music in the background? I think it's called *Requiem for a Fireman*.

"So..." He gets up and starts to pace slowly around the room. "You offered to..." He turns to face me, scratching his chin. "How did they put it?

Hang on... I think... Something to do with wings? Oh, yeah, that's it: you offered to help their new teacher *spread her wings*."

I'm taking a quick mental note of all the escape routes from this apartment, but the only one which seems possible right now is the window. I could throw myself through it – it's just one floor down, I could manage that. Or maybe I could misjudge it, and then gain my brother's sympathy...

"Tyler."

"Yes, Parker?"

"Did you, or did you not, offer to help the girls' teacher spread her wings?"

What do I do, here? You know I'm no good at lying. And I can't exactly make my nieces look like liars, can I?

"Absolutely not."

Okay, fine, so I loaded all the blame onto them. They're easily forgivable – unlike me.

"Tyler."

"Parker."

"Don't make me ask again."

"It's not what it sounds like."

"If I've learned one thing from you, Tyler, it's that things are *always* exactly as they sound."

I should be offended by his words, but the truth is that I have no right to be. My brother is right.

"I swear, nothing happened between me and

Ms. White."

"Are you two seeing each other?"

"No. Well, technically yes, but not in the way you're thinking."

"Are you telling me you're not trying to sleep with her?"

I sigh. "No."

And I've never been more sincere.

"Are you telling the truth?" His expression is suspect, but his voice has softened a little.

I reach out my arms and flash him a smile. "We're friends."

"Seriously?"

I nod, and Parker sits back down.

"Then what's this whole thing about spreading her wings?"

"It's a long story, but it's not the kind of story you have in mind."

"Then what's going on?"

"I'm just trying to help out a friend. That's all."

"Help her out with what, exactly?"

"With learning to trust herself."

Parker sits in silence for a moment.

"Why the hell are you doing that? I mean, you're getting nothing in return... Why do you want to help her with... well, with what? Finding a boyfriend?"

The Titanic is inching back towards my

stomach. I can feel it.

"I don't... I just want to..." I scoff, frustrated.

"Oh, my God!" Parker cries, leaping to his feet. "I don't believe this."

"What?"

"You like her!"

I leap to my feet, too.

"Who?"

"Don't try to throw me off with your little games, Tyler! You like Ms. White!"

"W-what the fuck are you t-talking about?" I say, turning my back to him and starting to pace around the living room, too. "I don't like anyone. Ever. You know that. Actually, no: I like everyone. That's my problem. Right?"

"I'd actually say it's the opposite."

I turn quickly to face him.

"The problem is that you never like anyone. No one ever holds your attention, no one..."

"What?"

"No one makes you think of stupid things like pushing them into the arms of someone else, just because you're scared you won't be able to hold them up yourself."

If I stand here, frozen, maybe I'll be able to pretend his words haven't hit me.

"Do you really think that spending almost forty years with you has taught me nothing, Tyler? Do you think I don't know you?"

"Maybe you think that..."

"I don't think. I know. Just like I know you have trouble believing it."

"This again..." I shake my head and sit back down. I take a few deep breaths, before deciding to try and understand how I'm feeling, maybe even say it out loud, to someone. "I don't even know her."

"You think it might be a matter of time?"

"I don't know what I think, Parker. I only know that..."

"What?"

"That this can't happen to me." I lift my gaze to meet his. "This can't happen to me, *too*."

Parker smiles sadly. "So that's your problem, then."

"I didn't think I had a problem until you started telling me I did."

"This doesn't mean it'll definitely happen to you."

"But... What if it does...?"

"That's life, Tyler. You just need to go with the flow."

"Then what? What if I end up like...?"

"Like me?"

"I didn't mean... Sorry, I didn't..."

"It's okay."

"It's not okay, at all. You, them. What she did

to you. None of that should be okay. And I don't want to find myself saying that it's 'okay' one day for me, too. Because it isn't."

"You know what isn't okay for me? That someone else's choices can influence your life. That someone else's suffering can stop you from being happy."

"Have you ever considered that maybe I'm happy just the way I am?"

"Not for a second."

"Well, you're wrong." I get up again, and head into the kitchen, opening the fridge and pulling out a beer. I open it and take a few sips.

"What's going to happen when Ms. White spreads her wings, Tyler?"

"What do you mean?"

"Are you just going to let her fly?"

I take another sip, hoping that the beer can wash down my bitterness.

"You can't hold anyone back, Parker. I've learned that from you. And, no offence, mate," I say, studying his expression, which is as serious as my words, "I don't want to make the same mistake. Not now, not ever."

35

Tyler

There it is. That feeling has come back again. The feeling which promises impending disaster, like the calm before the storm, the unnatural colour of the sky before a downpour. Like when a dickhead – and, of course, I mean myself – realises that he's just a dickhead, and that he deserves every disaster that comes his way; disasters he's created with his own two hands. I pull up next to a car I don't recognise, which has been left in my parking space. There's a guy waiting inside. He doesn't even lift his head to look at me – he just sits there, his eyes glued to his phone, typing away. I climb out of the car and slam the door, hard, hoping to grab his attention, but still he doesn't turn to look at me. Unless I break into his car, risking yet another arrest for God-knows-what, I can't work out what the fuck he wants with my Ms. White. Because there's only one reason this guy would be here – and I'm not saying this because of my sixth sense for these things, but because we are the only two people that live here, and this guy is definitely not here for me.

I head towards the stairs leading up to our front doors, but when I place my foot onto the first step, the door opens, revealing Ms. White, looking more beautiful than ever.

Yep. I said it. I'm not ashamed of it, and I

definitely don't take it back.

She walks slowly down the stairs, grappling onto the railing, her red coat hugging her body in a way it's best for me not to describe – especially when I can't seem to look anywhere else.

"Hey, Ty."

Her tone is a little embarrassed.

After my offer, we haven't seen each other.

"Ms. White," I say, nodding. "Where are we off to, looking so...?" So beautiful, Ms. White. So stunning, and so far from my reach. "...So rushed?"

She smiles kindly, then glances behind me, towards the car which contains the town's next 'accidental' casualty.

"Dinner."

I clear my throat. "On... Er... On your own?"

She bites her lip nervously. "With a friend."

Surely she didn't actually say that word. Not to me.

Friends don't exist, Ms. White – men and women can't be friends. Not when you're the woman. There's only one thought on everyone's mind when you're involved: a thought centred around something I probably shouldn't mention right now.

"He'll be waiting for me," she says, nodding towards the car behind me.

"Sure," I say, stepping aside to let her pass. She

continues down the stairs, before I start to lose her completely; to lose her before ever having had a chance to have her.

Her perfume leaves me breathless; watching her get into a car that isn't mine makes me never want to take another breath again.

She waves goodbye before climbing into the car. A few seconds later, they disappear down the road. A few seconds after that, I'm sitting in my own car, following them like a madman.

*****

"I'm doing something I absolutely should not be doing."

"Oh, Tyler. My *ex*-best friend. What can I do for you?"

"I'm sitting in my car."

"Okay..."

"Parked outside the Manhattan."

"The restaurant on Main Street?"

"That's the one."

"I'm scared to ask anything else."

"I'm scared to tell you what I'm doing – mainly because I have no idea what the fuck I'm doing."

"Let's take it step-by-step. Are you there because you're hungry?"

"Niall..."

"Okay, let's get straight to the point... I'm guessing you're following the 'process' in your own way."

"I think I've just sped up the fucking process quite significantly."

"What are you doing there, Tyler?"

"I'm spying on them."

"On who?"

"Ms. White and her friend."

"Oh, for the love of God!"

"What? Are you about to tell me I've fucked up?"

"There's no doubt about that. But I was actually about to tell you that you've completely lost your mind."

"So? Are you coming?"

"I'm already on my way."

* * * *

Niall sits himself down next to me and passes me a Tupperware tub.

"Apple pie. Mum made it."

I look at him, confused.

"If we have to wait..."

I shake my head and open the container, taking a slice, before handing it back to Niall.

"So. What's going on?"

"Do you really want to know?"

"I can try guessing if you want."

I bite into my pie and turn my gaze back to the door of the restaurant.

"There's nothing we can do but wait. We can't go in. Every table would see us."

"Mmm, that's true. There are no blind spots."

I scoff nervously, as Niall bites into his pie.

"Who is this friend?" he asks, his mouth full.

"I have no idea."

"Where the hell has he come from? And, more importantly, when? Did you not just offer to help her with this stuff?"

"Exactly," I hiss.

"He must be a new entry."

I glare at him.

"What? I'm just guessing."

"Don't."

"Did you, or did you not, call me to help?"

"I don't know why the fuck I called you, to be honest. Maybe I was just bored."

"Or maybe you needed a friend – and I'm talking about a real friend, not *that* kind of friend…" He gestures towards the restaurant, making bile rise up my throat.

"Sorry," he says, realising his mistake. "That came out wrong."

"What am I doing, Niall? Why am I following

my neighbour, spying on the door to the restaurant?"

"Do you want me to tell you?"

"If you start talking about this bloody 'process' again…"

"You like her, mate. That's the only explanation."

I sit there in silence, staring through the windscreen.

"And this might just be the first time you've really liked someone."

"I've liked loads of women in the past, Niall."

"Not like this, though. You always liked them enough to sleep with them, but this…"

I turn to face him.

"We're talking about a different kind of 'like', here."

"What would you know about it?"

"I've been with a fair few women, as you know. And, apparently, as everyone in town knows," Niall says, referring back to his past reputation as someone who had made his way around the locals. He'd had a few successful years in that department, until he realised that Jordan was the one for him. "And, as you know, I started from scratch – back to the only woman who'd ever made me feel something in here," he says, touching his chest. "Some things you just know right away, mate. And they're the things that make you do stupid shit like this."

"Are you sure?"

"Look where we are."

I let my head fall against the steering wheel, under the compassionate gaze of my friend.

"You need to take the process into your own hands."

I turn my head to face him.

"Then what, Niall? Then what happens?"

"I can't tell you. But I can tell you that it's not always bad."

"That's not hugely encouraging."

"Do you really need my encouragement?"

"I need support."

"More than this? I'm in your car, helping you spy on your neighbour."

I sit myself up straight and shrug. "Well, yeah, I guess…"

"You need to make a decision, Tyler. Either you confront this, or…"

"Or?" I ask, although I already know I won't like this *or*. *Or* is never good.

"Or you let her spread her wings on her own."

I don't even have to think about it for a second.

36
Holly

Talking about my private life has never been easy for me. I was so reserved for so long – maybe because I never really had any friends, and maybe because I was ashamed to tell anyone about my hopelessness with the opposite sex. But since I moved here, I haven't been able to hold my tongue, and the more I bring up every minute detail of my awful love life, the easier it is to talk about it. I didn't have too much trouble talking to Jordan and Anya about everything, and it seems to be the same with Wes. I never thought that talking so openly about everything would do me so much good; would help me see things from another point of view. From a guy's point of view.

"Straight or gay, we men are pretty simple," Wes says, digging his fork into his dessert.

We've had a nice evening. We ate delicious steak, and each had a glass of wine – after all, it is still Monday, and we have a long day ahead of us tomorrow at school, from the Christmas songs to the papier-mâché costumes.

"It's probably less complicated than you think. As a woman, I'm sure you tend to over-analyse everything, and conjure up rom-coms in your head, which then turn out to be exactly what you think they are: daydreams."

"I don't think I idealise things too much. Or maybe I do, a little. But that was when I was younger. Now it's a bit different."

"Maybe you're just anxious. Maybe the idea of a relationship makes you nervous, or you put too much pressure on yourself and start to babble, think about things too much instead of living in the moment."

"That sounds about right."

"Your mum really did some damage," Wes says, finishing his dessert and resting his fork on his plate. "What does she think about your moving here?"

"I think she'd be proud," I say, smiling sadly. "She died about a year ago."

"Oh, honey. I'm so sorry. I shouldn't have said those things..."

"It's okay, you didn't know. And it's true: she did do some damage."

"Nothing that can't be fixed," he says, reassuringly. "We still have time to get back in the saddle and start galloping."

"I think galloping might be a bit much for me."

"Let's take it step-by-step. Get back in the saddle first, and the rest will come."

"Are you sure?"

"Absolutely. New place, new friends, new experiences."

When Wes says the word 'friends', my mind

runs to Tyler: to his offer, to the fact that I'm excited to spend time with him. I'm too excited – excited in the wrong way.

"Speaking of friends," Wes continues, as if he could read my mind, "I don't think *Mr. Sexy Fireman* was happy to know you were out having dinner with another guy."

"What do you mean?"

"Did you not see the way he eyed me up when he got home? I pretended not to see him, obviously, but I can promise you he was not happy at all to find me there."

"Now who's the one daydreaming?"

"Don't tell him."

"Tell him what?"

"That I'm not interested in women."

"I don't understand how that helps."

"It'll help you find out what his real motives are."

"We're friends, Wes. Like you and me."

"Like you and me? No, honey. I really doubt that."

"He's not interested in me at all. Not in that way."

"Okay. If you're so convinced, why don't we put your theory to the test?"

"Because I don't do things like that. I'd have no idea where to even start. That's why we're here."

Wes smiles cunningly. "You just leave it all to

me."

* * * * *

Wes pulls up by the sidewalk outside my building. I open the door and he does the same, before moving around to the other side of the car and helping me out.

"Thanks for tonight."

"Thanks for being such great company."

He bends down to kiss me on the cheek. "See you tomorrow."

He gets back into the car and waves, before pulling back out into the street. I wave back, before heading towards the stairs; it's only when I place my foot on the first step that I realise he's sitting at the top of the stairwell.

"Hello, Ms. White."

"Ty? What are you doing here?"

He gets up, shoving his hands in his pockets.

"I wanted to make sure you got home safe and sound."

His honesty leaves me speechless; the warmth and intimacy of his voice leaves me breathless.

"I am your neighbour, after all. And I'm a fireman, remember." He smiles, and something melts inside me. "And I'm your friend."

"Y-yes. Yes, you are."

"And, as your friend, I feel I have a right to tell

you that you shouldn't go out with other friends."

"What?"

"I'll help you. I'll help you do... What you asked. But let's start with the basics – the fundamentals. Like in when you're playing a sport. And that means no going out with anyone who could make you lose sight of the end goal. Not until you're ready for the next step."

"O-okay," I stammer.

"I told you I'd help."

"Yes, you did."

"But you have to respect my rules. As if I were your coach."

I join him in the hallway. Tyler brushes my hair from my face; I can feel his fingers slipping through it, letting it tumble gently down my back.

"You're only allowed to go out with me, Ms. White."

"It doesn't feel like you're actually asking me out."

"I'm not. It's one of the rules. It's essential for our plan."

"And what is our plan?"

"You know exactly what it is. You were the one to come to me, remember?"

I remember perfectly – but I'm not so sure anymore of *his* plan.

"So you get to decide when I'm ready to go out with someone?"

"You'll realise on your own. I'm just here to help out where I can, and to check that no arseholes come near your apartment without my consent."

"Does that mean you'll be interrogating all my potential dates?"

"Exactly."

I can't help but laugh, making him laugh, too. The tension between us finally lifts a little.

"Do you want to come in for a drink?" he asks, his hands in his pockets, his head sinking back into his neck. "Maybe you can tell me about your disastrous date."

"How do you know whether it was a disaster?" I ask, following Wes' advice.

"Come on. A kiss on the cheek? At the bottom of the stairs?"

I shrug. "What's wrong with that?"

He takes a step towards me and I lift my gaze; his eyes are bright and alert in the darkness, like a predator ready to pounce.

"First of all, you *always* walk a woman to her apartment." His voice grows deeper, inviting me to keep quiet. "And then... And then, a woman like you, Ms. White, should be kissed up against the door, until your knees give way and you can't catch your breath."

My knees start to tremble at the mere thought of it, the breath snatched from my lungs the moment his lips say my name.

"I don't think anyone's ever kissed me like that before."

His eyes are dark, dangerous.

"Well, I guess it's time to do something about that. And I promise you that I'll make sure you get everything you've never had."

37

Tyler

"Please, just explain it to me one more time." Niall tosses a bag of apples into his trolley as I grab two bottles of wine for mine.

"What didn't you understand the first time?"

"It's not that I don't get it. I just don't *get it*."

I glare at him.

"I understand what you told me, I'm not an idiot. But I have no idea what the fuck you're doing!" He raises his voice, attracting the attention of the other customers in the supermarket.

"I've just invited her over for dinner, Niall. Relax."

"In your apartment."

"She's already been over."

"Exactly!" he cries, agitated. "Why don't you go out somewhere?"

"Because it's more intimate at mine."

"Right there!" He points at me, satisfied. "I knew it."

I rest my hands on my hips and stare at him.

"You're trying to seduce her."

"What the hell are you talking about, Niall?"

"Don't play dumb with me. Save it for someone

who might actually believe you."

"Maybe you're forgetting that I've offered to help her be more confident, so that she can..." I can't even say it.

"She can...?" Niall encourages.

"She can do whatever she wants." My tone plummets with my mood.

"You're really in the shit now, mate. With no way out."

"And you're getting carried away, as usual."

"What are you going to cook?"

"Why do you care?"

"Hey! You're the one who asked if we could go food shopping together."

"I know you're the one who usually does it, so I thought to myself, why not spend a little time with my best friend? Although I'm starting to doubt the whole *best* friend thing..."

"Why don't you want to tell me what you're cooking?"

I scoff. "Steak with whiskey sauce and gratin potatoes."

Niall raises one eyebrow.

"What?"

"Sounds like an intimate dinner."

I laugh, trying to mask my nerves. Thankfully, I've avoided telling him that I've also bought eclairs, which I'm going to fill with cream and cover in melted chocolate. I'd never hear the end of it, otherwise.

"Be careful, Tyler."

"Or?"

"Or someone could get hurt. And I already know you're not going to like it."

"I can take care of myself."

"I know you can. But I also know that you'd rather hurt yourself than hurt others. I just don't want that to happen."

* * * * *

At seven o'clock on the dot, Ms. White appears at my door, holding a bunch of flowers.

"You told me not to bring anything."

I smile at her choice and take the bouquet from her.

"Thank you. I don't think anyone's ever bought me flowers before."

I close the door and she steps into my living room.

"Well. I guess you could say I'm your first time."

I turn to face her, standing in front of me. I really want to say something stupid, to lighten the mood, to make this moment fleeting and unimportant, like every other moment I've experienced in my life so far. But I couldn't do it, even if I tried with every cell in my body.

You're my first time, Ms. White. That's for sure. Just as I'm sure you'll also be the last.

Ms. White is standing in the middle of my living room in her dark jeans, torn at the knees, wearing pink trainers – I think this is the first time I've seen her without heels – and a hoodie in the same colour. Her hair is tied up, messy, her face pink and her expression genuine: she seems a little embarrassed, but happy to be here. And her mouth... God, that mouth. It's full, pink, curved into a delicate smile. I don't think I've ever stopped to really notice the particular features of a woman like this, but believe me when I say that there isn't a mouth in the world more beautiful than hers. Not even in a work of art. It would be impossible to recreate.

"Wow, it smells amazing." She tears me from my daydream. "You weren't lying when you said you could cook."

No, I didn't lie about that, Ms. White. But I'm worried that this might be the only truth I'll ever tell again.

"I hope you like steak."

I lead her into the kitchen, and she follows close behind. I lift the lid of one of the saucepans, letting the smell of meat and whiskey waft into our nostrils.

"Now I'm starving."

I smile, replacing the lid, lowering the heat, and checking on the potatoes in the oven.

"Still needs a few minutes." I open the fridge and pull out a bottle of wine. "Do you want a glass?" I ask, showing it to her.

"Why not? I don't have far to go to get home."

I pour us both a glass of wine as she approaches me. I hand her the glass, and her wide eyes, the same colour as a fallen autumn leaf, leave me breathless.

"Besides," she says, her voice warm, intimate. "Aren't I in the safest place in town?"

The safest place in the world, Ms. White. Just for you.

"You are." I clink my glass against hers and take a sip. "You can go and sit down, if you want," I say, gesturing towards the table at the other end of the living room.

"First I want to put these in a vase." She grabs the flowers she gave me, which I'd left on the counter. "I'd like to put them on the table, if you don't mind?"

"Not at all. I just don't think I have a vase. Sorry – people aren't usually nice enough to bring me flowers."

"Mmm…" She considers this for a moment. "Let's see what you've got." She peers through the glass cabinets of my kitchen, scanning my glasses and plates. When she finds something that could be useful, she opens the cupboard and pulls out a pitcher. "How about this?"

"I usually use that for margaritas, but I think,

this time, I could dedicate it to a more noble cause."

She laughs, holding the pitcher under the tap and filling it up, before grabbing the flowers and arranging them inside. They're beautiful: colourful and bright, just like her.

"I'll take them over to the table."

She walks into the living room, and I stand there, watching her, like an idiot, as she places the pitcher in the middle of the table.

"Do you need a hand?" she asks, realising that I'm just standing there, doing nothing.

"I've got it all under control." I grab the glasses and carry them over to the table. "Make yourself comfortable. Dinner will be ready in a minute."

"Okay."

I head back into the kitchen to check that everything's ready, when her voice floats in from the living room.

"Is this one of your famous skills?"

"What do you mean?" I call.

"Cooking for a woman. Is that one of your skills?"

My skills, my dear Ms. White, all went to shit the moment I met you.

"No. This is just for friends."

She appears in the doorway and studies me.

"Special friends."

She smiles.

"Very special."

She rolls her eyes and heads back over to the table.

Unique. Maybe that was the right word. Because you are unique – I don't need to get to know you any better to know that. Just like my friend Niall said: some things you just know right away. Just like I know I'd only hurt you, and that you'd only hurt me, and that, together, we'd be something dangerous. But I want to find out how many times you can be my first, and how many times you could be my last; just because I'm enough of an idiot to know that I'm already in way too deep – so much so that I need a minute to work out how to get myself out of this without causing any more pain.

For you, Ms. White. Not for me.

All hope died for me the moment you came bursting into my life, without permission.

38

Tyler

I never invite women over for dinner. It's too risky, too familiar. A situation that could result in an intimacy that leads to something more. Space for their things in my wardrobe, their toothbrush on my sink, their bra hanging from my bathroom towel rail, Christmas spent either with my family or with theirs. Long-term commitment. Women do come over, but only – and exclusively – to sleep. Or, something like that. The next morning, I make them coffee, or breakfast, but that's where it ends. I'm always clear right from the beginning, and I've never messed anyone around. Sometimes they've tried to call me again after a while, or they've turned up at the fire station, or, even worse, turned up here, at my front door. I always try to be nice when that happens; I try to explain the situation, to point them in a different direction. I'm good at dealing with people – and not just because of my job. I think it's one of my hidden talents. I know how to make people feel comfortable, make them open up and relax. I make them feel good – with me, of course, but also with themselves. And that's what I'm doing with my dear Ms. White.

I refuse to believe that she's as awful with men as she claims to be – I wouldn't believe it even if I'd witnessed it first-hand. I'm sure that there's just something holding her back. Maybe she's just insecure. I hope she's not insecure about the way she looks, because, fuck: when she looks in the mirror every morning, she should be happy with what she sees.

I writhe around nervously on my chair, trying to quieten my thoughts and concentrate on her, instead: the way she slips her fork into her mouth, then pulls it between her lips. Her tongue darts between those lips, too. The same lips that are perched at the rim of her wine glass.

"This sauce is... Mmm..." Her tongue roams seductively around her mouth. "You're really good!"

You have no idea how many things I'm good at, Ms. White, and I swear, I'd love for you to discover them all. But I don't know whether I could bear that.

"Whiskey," I say, taking a sip of wine. "Whiskey sauce."

"Oh, wow! With the wine, and now this sauce... It's like you're trying to get me drunk." She laughs, taking another sip. "If we weren't friends, and you hadn't just offered to help me, I'd say you were trying to get me into bed."

I cough loudly, attempting not to spray my mouthful of wine across the table.

"Ridiculous, right?"

"R-ridiculous? What's ridiculous?"

"The idea that you would even think... Come

on, Ty. I've heard the rumours. I know the kind of girls you usually go out with."

"Oh, do you?"

"And I'm definitely not your type."

"W-why not?"

"If I were, you'd already have tried it on with me. We live next door to each other, we're both single…"

"That doesn't mean anything."

"If a guy like you were attracted to a girl like me, then I guess that… Well, we…"

"What? We'd have already slept together?" I say it, because I have to know what this woman is thinking.

She blushes suddenly, hiding behind her glass.

"If I have to help you spread your wings, Ms. White, then first you have to be able to say what you're thinking. You can't be scared to talk about sex."

"You're right."

"You need to be confident. You need to trust yourself, and what you can do."

"What I can do? Oh God… I don't think I can do much."

"We're definitely getting off on the wrong foot, here."

"You're right about that, too." She places her glass down on the table. "Let's get started, then. What do you think?"

"Get started? Just like that?"

"Is that not why you invited me here?"

Fuck, no.

"Yes."

"I'm ready."

"Are you really?"

"Maybe after another glass of wine..." she says, smiling.

"Let's get settled on the sofa with dessert, and then we can get started – if you really want to."

"Dessert? You made dessert, too?"

"It's nothing special. Just some chocolate eclairs."

"You're full of surprises, Tyler Hayes."

This isn't the first time I've been told that, but it's the first time someone has said it with no ulterior motive – and I like it. I like it a little too much. Just as I like her mouth a little too much, when it presses against my cheek, before she disappears into the kitchen to clear the plates.

I like her. Fuck, Niall was right. I like Ms. White, and now I have no idea how to make sure that she never likes me.

* * * * *

Ms. White seems to relax when we're on the sofa. She kicks off her shoes and crosses her legs, turning her entire body around to face me. She ate four eclairs – seriously, four. I had two. No one could've eaten four. And, of course, the whole thing really turned me on: seeing her sitting there, next to me, so comfortable, her cheeks flushed from the alcohol. I'm even turned on by the fact that all those things have turned me on. It must be the novelty of it all, the discovery of something unexpected. The magic of that 'first time'.

And I was definitely not expecting you, Ms. White. But you turned up all the same, and now all I can do is try to find a way to make sure that you leave, without causing too much damage.

"Please, take these eclairs away from me, or I won't be able to help myself."

I laugh, sipping at my wine. "You can eat them all, if you want. I made them for you."

Her eyes grow soft.

"I can't eat any more. I'll explode."

She takes another sip, too. I've lost count of how many glasses of wine we've drunk – and of how many erections I've had this evening.

"So," she says, impatiently. "Where do we start?"

With you, taking off that damn hoodie, and showing me what's underneath.

"I guess we should start by getting to the root of the problem."

"Okay."

"Why don't you start by telling me what the

real problem is?"

"I've told you, I'm not cut for relationships."

"That doesn't help."

She reflects on this for a few moments. "You know when I start to babble, saying embarrassing things...?"

"I vaguely remember, yes."

"It happens every time I'm with a guy. I guy I like. I just get all nervous."

"That doesn't sound so bad to me."

"It is when you say out loud that you thought that..." She lowers her voice, as if someone could overhear her. "That his... Well, that his..." She stifles a laugh. "That you thought he'd be bigger *down there* because of the bulge in his pants."

My mouth falls open in shock.

"I know, I know, it just came out..." She shakes her head, covering her face with her hands. "Not only did I manage to tell him that I thought he had a small package, but I also admitted that I'd been staring at it."

This time, I can't help but laugh.

"Stop making fun of me!"

"I'm not, I swear. But I'd imagine that he—"

"It's not funny."

"Sorry, you're right."

"He left me there."

"What do you mean?"

"We were just about to... Well... Have sex. And he just left me there. He got pissed off and left. He called me a bitch, too."

"What a gentleman."

"I guess I did offend him."

"You were nervous. It just came out wrong."

"Would you have carried on anyway?"

"M-me?"

"Would you have left me there, too?"

"I don't think..."

"Come on! Tell me. What would you have done, if I was lying, naked, in front of you, and I'd told you that the size of your package wasn't quite up to scratch?"

"What... What would *I* have done?"

She nods, waiting.

"I'd have proven to you that size doesn't matter."

Her eyes light up.

"And I'd have kept proving it, over and over again, through the night, until you'd taken back everything you'd said."

"Oh."

"And then I'd have proven it again the next morning, just to be sure."

"Ah."

"But, you know, Ms. White..." I lower my voice – I can't help it. "I'd have left you so breathless that you couldn't even have spoken in the first place."

Her lips part softly, her eyes waiting for my next move.

"I'd have taken every breath in your body, without ever giving them back."

39

Holly

Now I finally understand what this man's skills really are. Don't get me wrong, I'm sure his skills are equally impressive lying down – or standing up, or upside-down, or even hanging from a lampshade – but I get the impression that he is capable of anything. And thinking about it now, after a good few drinks, sitting on his couch, with only my thoughts for company, isn't helping matters.

"Your cheeks are bright red."

I bring my hands to my face.

"We'll never get to the practical side of things if you can't handle the theory, Ms. White."

He's talking about putting theory into practice. *With me?*

"It's the wine," I say, defensively.

He raises an eyebrow.

"Fine, but the wine doesn't help. Sorry, but I'm terrible at this stuff. I told you."

"You just need to get used to it."

He slides along the sofa towards me, taking my glass and placing it down on the coffee table.

"What are you...?"

"It's best if we try not to say too much."

"Oh... Okay," I say, a little disappointed.

"Not with me, and not to me. I like words. Especially yours."

I feel my face catch fire again.

"And I like this, too," he says, stroking my cheek with the back of his hand. "But we need to learn to control it."

I nod; otherwise, I'd start one of my embarrassing monologues again, and he's just told me to stop – even though he likes them.

My monologues.

He likes my monologues.

"Let's see…" He thinks about this, narrowing his eyes a little to scrutinise my expression. "What can we do to calm your nerves? I don't think imagining the other person naked would help in this case. This isn't like stage fright."

Oh, God. Imagining him naked actually would help me, but only with one particular thing – and now is not the time to be thinking about that.

"How about something funny?"

"F-funny?"

"No, you're right, that's a shitty idea." He grabs the bottle of wine and pours us each another glass. He hands it to me, and I accept, silently. I'm worried that if I even utter a single word, the dam would burst, and I'd end ruining this absolutely perfect moment. The first perfect moment I've ever experienced. With a man I definitely shouldn't be experiencing it with.

"Something relaxing. Is there something in

particular that makes you feel relaxed when you think about it?"

I shrug. My only thought at the moment is whether he gave me that speech about size for any particular reason, or whether it was all just made-up.

I gulp down half my wine. I'm so full I could explode – from the food and the wine – but I keep drinking anyway. I need to be able to survive this evening,

"We can work on it."

I'm not so sure what 'it' is anymore. Maybe it's the wine, or the whiskey sauce, or maybe it's the smell of him, or the dimple in his chin, or his words. Maybe it's the fact that Tyler Hayes is morphing into something I never expected – something I'm not sure I want to live without.

"Maybe it's best if I..." I get up too quickly, the wine and my thoughts swirling around in my mind, making me lose my balance. But I don't fall, either back onto the sofa or onto the floor; I just find myself in his arms, again, like a scene from a rom-com. Maybe even a Christmas rom-com, just to make it that little bit more perfect.

"Maybe we've had a little too much tonight." He helps me stand up straight, but his hands linger on my waist.

"Maybe I should stop pretending I'm Irish and just admit that I'll never be one of you guys."

He smiles.

Jesus Christ.

"It's the company. And the food," he says, one of his hands leaving my waist to brush a lock of hair away from my face.

It's you, Ty. *Oh, my God.* It's you.

"We'll take things slower next time."

I'll never be ready for a 'next time', and I'll never be ready for any man. That's just the truth. Because I'm only realising now that I just want one man: the one I convinced myself I would never want. The only one who makes me feel comfortable. The only one who really makes me want a man at all.

"I'll walk you to your door."

"You don't have to."

"Of course I do. Remember, a man should always walk you to your door. If he says goodbye in the street, Ms. White, he's not the right man for you."

I smile.

"Let's go," he says, nodding towards the door. I follow him, plunged into sadness.

I don't want to leave. I don't want to go back to my apartment. I want to stay here, with him. I want to sleep in his bed. I want...

Oh, no. Oh, no, no, no.

My eyes widen suddenly, and Tyler studies me, concerned.

"Are you feeling okay?"

I nod my head.

"Your face tells me otherwise."

"I'm... Fine."

He opens the door and I step outside, the icy night air immediately bringing me back to my senses.

I pull my keys out of my pocket and stick them into the lock.

"Thanks for tonight," I gabble, opening the door. "And for the advice. And for..."

"Hey." Tyler steps in front of me, stopping me from closing the door and finding refuge inside. "What's going on?"

I shake my head sharply.

"Have I said something? Did I do something wrong?"

I shake my head again. My breath thickens and tangles in my throat.

"Holly." He rests his fingers gently under my chin. "What's wrong?"

I look at him for a moment, before madness pushes me to do something I never thought I'd be able to do. I lift myself onto my tiptoes and bring my mouth to his, pressing my lips delicately against him. Terrified, I wait – I wait for a sign, a breath, anything to tell me that I haven't imagined all this, that it's not something I invented in my head. His breath tickles my lips for a moment, but Tyler doesn't take that step towards me.

Feeling disappointed, and more stupid than ever, I take a step back, wanting to bury myself under my duvet and cry over my naivety until the morning. But Tyler takes my hand and pulls me back to him.

"Not like this, Ms. White. Not... Like this..." he whispers onto my mouth, before pressing his lips against mine. I stand there, immobile, breathless, until Tyler speaks again, onto the part of my mouth which is still buzzing from his touch. "Not like this," his voice warm and laden with promise – a promise I desperately want to believe in. A promise I want him to keep.

"Goodnight, Ms. White."

He goes back into his apartment, and I hide myself away in mine, confused, electrified, and excited, because I almost kissed Tyler Hayes. Because he almost kissed me. Because I get the feeling that he can't wait to do it again – at least as much as I can't wait.

* * * * *

The next morning, while I'm sitting in the middle of my bed, a cup of coffee clasped in my hands, wondering whether I imagined everything last night, I start to hear strange noises outside my front door. I get up and pad over to it in silence, opening it just enough to stick my nose outside. When I realise that there's no one there, I drop my eyes to the floor, where a takeaway coffee, a box of paracetamol, a Tupperware tub of eclairs, and a note is waiting for me.

I head back inside, put everything down on the kitchen counter, and begin to read, my heart hammering.

I thought you might need some of these essentials this morning. And, by essentials, I mean my eclairs.

Please, don't tell anyone I can cook - especially not desserts. Otherwise, I'll end up with a queue of women - and men - outside my door.

I laugh like an idiot.

Have a good day, Ms. White.

And, about last night...

We're taking some really big steps.

I hug the note to my chest, overwhelmed, and stand like this for a few minutes feeling, maybe for the first time in my life, truly happy.

* * * * *

At lunchtime – or, somewhere around lunchtime – I step through the doorway of my favourite café. Angus notices me right away, and waves at me from the bar. I head over and sit at one of the stools.

"I was starting to think you weren't coming."

I study him, confused.

"You always come on Sundays, roughly around this time."

"Seriously?"

He nods, wiping down the counter with a cloth.

"If you want, there are a few tables free. I can set one up for you?"

"I'm fine up here."

"You'd rather eat at the bar?"

"Uh-huh," I say, vaguely, taking off my jacket and laying it across my legs.

"In that case..." he glances over at the clock, "I reckon I can keep you company."

* * * * *

Angus tells me that the café has been handed down through his family. His great-granddad was the one to set it up.

"My mother left it to me about ten years ago."

"Oh, I'm sorry."

"For what?"

"I thought that maybe she..."

Angus bursts out laughing, throwing his head back.

"She left it to me because she said it was time for me to settle down."

I touch my chest, where my heart is hammering manically. "So she's...?"

"Alive and kicking."

"And she never comes into the café?"

"She's not stupid. She avoids this place like the plague."

I smile at the way he speaks about his mother.

"I'd love to meet her," I say, without thinking, to which Angus raises an eyebrow. "Well, I don't know many people around here, and... Everyone seems like one big family, and..."

His expression softens.

"Sorry. That was rude of me."

"No, it wasn't."

I gather my courage and decide to tackle this, head-on.

"My mother died last year."

"I'm sorry, Holly."

"She was the only family I had. I have no brothers or sisters, no uncles, aunts, cousins, grandparents..." I sigh, sadly. "It's just me."

His hand rests gently on mine.

"Sorry, I don't want to bore you with my story."

He passes me a napkin, and I dab at my eyes.

"You're not boring me. If you ever need to talk to a friend, I'm always here. Seven days a week."

I smile gratefully at him.

"What about you?" I ask, changing the subject. "Don't you have a family?"

"To be honest, I never really thought about it. And now, well…" he gestures around him, "I'm a little too old. But once… Once, there was someone."

"Oh, really?" I ask.

"She was beautiful. Full of life, and crazy – damn, she was crazy."

"What happened?"

"She didn't want all this," he says, stretching his arms out.

"What do you mean?"

"She wanted to travel, to see the world, to live… She didn't want to be trapped in a little town like this, with someone like me, who fries fish and waits tables for a living."

His story makes tears prick in the back of my throat.

"Now I'm the one making you sad with my stories."

I shake my head. "No, you're not."

"It was a long time ago."

"Have you never tried to find her?"

He smiles sadly. "I went all the way to Canada for her."

"Really? What happened?"

"She sent me home again."

I slump back into my chair, defeated.

"Why?" I ask, close to tears.

"She didn't love me."

I bite down hard on my lip, trying to curb my sadness.

"She never loved me. I was just a summer fling to her. I spent every penny I had on that trip."

"I-I'm sorry."

"It was a long time ago."

"And you never found anyone else?"

He shrugs. "No one was like her. No one could ever be like her."

* * * * *

I walk home in the rain, slowly, sadly, disappointed. Thoughts are ricocheting around my mind: about her, about him, about everything that was taken from me, about everything that other people have been deprived of. It's something I'll never be able to understand. Something I know I'll never have.

When I get home, I'm totally soaked, robotically placing one foot in front of the other to climb the stairs, with no desire to do anything at all. But when I get to the final step, the door next to mine flies open.

"Holly, what the hell...?" Tyler steps outside his apartment. "What happened?"

I look at him, and all the tears I'd been holding back pool into my eyes.

"She never loved him."

"What are you talking about?"

"She used him. She…"

I close my eyes and let the tears trail down my cheeks. Tyler's arms close around my body. I rest my head against his chest and grasp at fistfuls of his T-shirt.

"Shh, it's okay," he says, stroking my wet hair and resting his warm lips against my forehead. "I'm here, okay? You're home, now. You're home with me."

40

Tyler

I walk her into her apartment and help her peel off her wet jacket.

"You need to warm up." I leave her in the living room for a moment to whack the thermostat up as high as it can go, before going back to her. "Maybe you need to take a warm shower. What do you say?"

She nods, and I stroke her face with both hands, bringing her gaze to meet mine.

"Hey," I say, gently. "It's going to be okay. Whatever it is, I promise you it'll be okay."

She nods again, then leaves me to head into the bathroom. She closes the door behind her and, after a few minutes, I hear the shower running. I look around, not knowing what to do, then decide to head back into my own apartment to grab something that could make her feel better. I go back to hers the moment I hear the water stop, and wait impatiently in the living room. I see her step out of the bathroom, wrapped in a towel, and stop in front of the door. Water is dripping onto the floor, her face tired and emotional. Her eyes are swollen from crying, and her lips are trembling as if she were on the brink of crying again.

She seems smaller than yesterday, defenceless, vulnerable. She seems more alone. I'm gripped by a devastating need to hold her close to me, to show her that I'm here for her; but I'm scared that I can't do anything to help her feel better, to make her laugh again.

"Holly." She looks at me, sadly. "Tell me what I can do to help."

"Could you hug me?" she asks, her voice choked with tears.

I walk over to her and wrap my arms around her, pulling her into me. She rests her head against my chest, her breath tickling the sensitive skin of my neck. I guide her into her bedroom and lay her down on the bed, sitting myself up behind her and holding her close to me. Her back is against my chest, now, my lips gently brushing against her neck. I can hear her breathing heavily, trying to hold back tears.

"You don't have to do it with me."

"W-what?"

"Be strong. You don't have to be anything you don't want to be."

I feel her begin to tremble in my arms, and I hug her instinctively tighter.

"You're in your safe place, remember?" I tell her, a new, terrifying emotion coursing through me. "You can be anything you want to be."

I hear her start to cry again, sobbing, trembling, before starting the cycle all over again. I simply hold her to me, waiting for the storm to pass, ready to take her hand and help her back to her feet.

* * * * *

When she starts to calm down, I convince her to dry her hair and put on some warm clothes, as I lay a blanket out on the sofa, a tub of triple chocolate ice cream on the coffee table, alongside a bottle of whiskey and two glasses. I wait for her to come back, and when I see her appear in the living room, I'm crushed by a pressing need to hold her tight, to kiss her eyes until the swelling goes down. It's impossible to ignore, this feeling, but I try – I know that, right now, among this confusion, everything I do could be taken the wrong way, teetering towards an enormous mistake that could ruin everything forever.

"Here," I say, nodding towards the sofa. "Come here." She joins me, and I sit down, before taking her hand and gently pulling her next to me. Holly sits, letting herself fall onto my shoulder, lifting her legs and stretching them out on the sofa. I make myself comfortable, one arm wrapped around her, her hand resting lightly on my chest.

"I've brought you some comfort food."

"Comfort?"

"Uh-huh. Chocolate ice cream. And whiskey."

"That sounds more like suicide than comfort. For my liver and for my butt."

"Your butt is perfect just as it is," I say

suddenly, relieved that she feels good enough to make jokes. "I can't do anything to help your liver, though. You kissed that goodbye the day you bought a plane ticket to Ireland."

She laughs. It's not a hearty laugh, but it's something.

"Thank you." Her hand slides down my torso and around my waist. "I'm happy you're here, Ty."

There's nowhere else I'd rather be, Holly. And this is another of those famous 'first times' you keep giving me.

"I'm your local fireman. Always at your service."

"You're much more than that, and you know it."

I close my eyes and take a deep breath.

And you, Ms. White, are the most unexpected, terrifying thing that could ever have happened to me.

"Do you want to tell me what happened?"

"Maybe after a few glasses of that." She gestures towards the bottle on the table.

"If you say so." She lifts herself up a little so that I can reach over and grab the whiskey, pouring us each a small glass, and handing it to her. "Drink it slowly. This stuff is strong."

She finishes it in one gulp, then pulls a face.

"Thank God I told you to take it slow!"

"Wow, that really *is* strong!"

"One of the best." I drink mine, too, but without grimacing. "It's from Connemara. Do you know where that is?"

She shakes her head.

"Don't you know anything about this country?"

"I know the airport, and I know this town."

"Then why?"

"Why what?"

"Why are you here, Ms. White?"

She sighs deeply, and hands me her glass. I realise that she needs a little more encouragement, so I do as she says, and pour her another drink.

"I get the feeling your choosing to come here was based on more than just work. Right?"

"It's a long, sad story."

"I'm here. And..." I try to take a breath, as the most terrifying thought begins to take shape in my mind, seeping into the other parts of my body. "I'm not going anywhere."

Holly looks at me, her eyes brimming with warmth, a little frightened, like a deer who is lost in a wood: alone, cold, and hungry. As if she desperately needs to believe in the man who has come to save her; but as if she's also scared to let herself go.

"Trust me."

I'm so sincere that I can almost feel the words

as they come out of my mouth.

"Why are we friends?" she asks. She's sincere, too; I can't help but be honest in my response.

Don't forget: I'm a useless liar.

"Because you can do it."

She lowers her gaze. It wasn't what she wanted to hear, and it wasn't what I wanted to say.

"And because we're not really friends," I add, my chest hammering, fear pulsing through my fingers as they stroke her face. She lifts her eyes to meet mine; they're wide, so sweet. They look like hot chocolate, to heat you up during even the darkest and loneliest of nights.

"Then what are we?"

I smile at her. "I have absolutely no idea."

She smiles, too.

"But I know that I like it."

"You like it?"

I nod, determinedly.

"I like it, too."

41

Holly

He just said that we're not friends. He just admitted that there's something between us. He hugged me while he said all these things, and now he's here, with me. And I like it, and he likes it, and now I feel overwhelmed with all the wonderful and terrible emotions from today, from the past weeks. I feel like I need to talk about it with someone. And I know that I want that someone to be him.

"You're right." I grab the spoon and delve into the chocolate ice cream.

"I'm always right. But explain to me what you're referring to, now?"

"I'm talking about the fact that I didn't chose this place by chance. Like I said, I'm on my own. I have no family."

He nods, but stays silent.

"Or, at least, I thought that was the case. When my mother died, I had to sort through her things, decide what to give to charity, and what to keep..." I sigh sadly at the memory of those days, alone with her memories, the ghosts of her past. "She told me she didn't know who he was."

"Who are you talking about?"

"My father. She told me that she had no idea who he was, that she'd had a few different flings that summer. She lied to me."

"How do you know that?"

"I found her old travel diary – the one she used to take on all her trips. And one of those trips was here, in this town."

"And you found out who she was writing about, right?"

I nod, biting my lip.

Tyler smiles at me. "The owner of the café in town."

I nod, still hurting.

"That's why you always go there, why you always sit up at the bar."

"I just wanted to get to know him."

"What about him?"

"He doesn't know I exist. He has no idea he has a daughter. He…" I can feel the tears rushing back. "He loved her."

"How do you know?"

"He was telling me about a woman he'd followed…" I dry my eyes. Angus' words start to press down on my chest. "She told him that she never loved him, that he was just a summer fling. And she never thought to tell him about me."

"Are you sure?"

"He seemed sincere. He had no reason to lie."

"I guess not."

"And he told me that he'd never loved anyone after her."

"I'm so sorry, Holly."

"She deprived us of each other, you know? She kept me from part of my family, my roots. She stopped me from having a past."

"I don't know what to say."

"She couldn't stop running away. From places, from men, from responsibility. From me."

"She was probably just trying to run away from herself."

"I can never forgive her."

"Holly..."

"I can't. She's the reason I'm such a disaster."

"You're not a disaster."

"My relationship with others, with men; my insecurities, my inability to form any ties."

"You're not like that."

"She always told me that men were fleeting, that no one sticks around. That no one really wants you. She told me that they just use you, replace you, and that... And that no one would ever really love me." An uncontrollable sob escapes me at the memory of those words, which my mother repeated for years.

Tyler moves closer on the sofa and pulls me into him. I let myself crumble into his sweet embrace, melting into an ocean of tears.

"I'm a disaster, Ty. In every way. I'm just like her."

"You're a beautiful disaster, and anyone who

hasn't realised that in the past can go fuck themselves. And if they don't go on their own, I'll make sure I'm the one to send them packing."

"You'd really do that for me?"

He sits there in silence. The incessant beating of my heart intertwines with my breath.

"There's nothing I wouldn't do for you."

I close my eyes and stay like that, slumped against his body.

I don't need to hear anything else. There's nowhere else I need to be.

* * * * *

Later, towards the evening, once we've finished the ice cream and drunk another few glasses of whiskey, Tyler orders a pizza. An extra-large, for us both, with sausage and pepperoni on top. We eat on the sofa, accompanied by a few bottles of beer.

"So, what are you going to do?"

"I came here thinking I'd find a man who wanted nothing to do with me. But I've found out that Angus was kept away from such a huge part of his life – just like me."

"Are you going to tell him who you are?"

"I don't know. I mean, what would I do? Just turn up, tell him who I am, and wait for him to throw his arms around me?"

"Why not?"

"Because I'm scared."

"Of what?"

"Rejection."

"I don't know Angus that well, but he seems like a good guy. I don't think he's the kind of man who would shy away from responsibility."

"I'm not ten years old, Ty. He wouldn't have to provide for me, or take me out every other weekend."

"Then what's stopping you?"

"If he tells me that he doesn't want anything to do with me, that he'd rather just send me back to Canada – back to someone who doesn't even exist anymore..." I look at him. "I have no one, Ty. I came here hoping that... I don't know. I'm so stupid."

"No, you're not. And please don't ever say that again."

"There's nothing more for me, here. And there's nothing more for me in Canada, either. I don't have a place. I don't—"

"Here." He reaches his arms towards me. "There's always a place for you here."

"I only have a three-month visa, Ty," I tell him, fear seeping into every cell in my body. "And it's already been a month and a half."

"We can think about that in another month and a half."

"Ty."

"And we can also think about how to tell your dad that he'd be insane not to want a daughter like you in his life."

"You really think so?"

"I'm deadly serious."

"I don't know whether I'm ready to tell him. Not yet."

"Okay."

"I need to think about how to do it."

"Of course. Take all the time you need."

I sigh with relief and reach for another slice of pizza.

"I'm sorry I've taken over your day. Did you not have things to do, or somewhere to be...?"

"Actually, I was supposed to go to work."

"W-what?"

He bites into his slice of pizza and chews slowly. "I asked someone to swap shifts."

"I had no idea."

He shrugs, taking another bite. "I owe my brother, now, but that's fine."

"Your brother?"

"He covered for me. And to be able to do it, he had to leave the girls with his neighbour – his divorced, single neighbour who's been trying to get her hands on him for months."

I cover my mouth with my hand, trying to stifle

a laugh.

"He'll be after my balls, now."

"I'm so sorry, Ty. For you and for your balls. You really didn't have to go to all this trouble."

"My balls will survive. I couldn't let you go through this alone."

I bite my lip.

"I'll never let you feel lonely, Ms. White."

"You can't say that."

"I say what I feel, and what I want. And what I want, right now, is to help you spread your wings in the right direction."

I swallow nervously.

"And what direction would that be?"

He's not smiling now. His gaze is deadly serious.

"You'll find out when you're ready."

42

Holly

While we're in the hall for the Christmas show rehearsals, one of my students waddles over to me, holding a biscuit tin.

"For you, Ms. White," he says, shyly, handing me the tin.

"Oh... What...?" I take it and open the lid: inside are cookies in the shape of reindeer, their little noses iced in red.

"My mum made them."

"And she made them for me?" I ask, my hand flying to my chest.

He nods, scratching his nose, and I bend down to my knees to give him a hug.

"Thank you so much. I'm sure they're delicious."

"She told me you have to eat them with hot chocolate."

"Of course, I will."

He wanders back over to the others, as Wes looks at me.

"I've never been given any homemade cookies."

He wraps his arm around my shoulders.

"I don't know what to say. I'm... Speechless."

"Trust me, this is nothing."

I look at Wes, my eyes soft, emotional.

"These people, this town… It's special."

I'm starting to realise the truth in this – especially when I think of Tyler, of everything he's done for me, of the way he stayed with me the whole evening and into the night. We fell asleep on the couch together, me leaning into his body. This morning I woke up and he'd gone, but I found one of his notes on the coffee table in my living room.

About last night…

I meant every word I said. Even when I said my brother would be after my balls. I don't know what I'll do without them, but I'll find a solution. I'll find one for you, too.

I smile now, at the thought of it. Like an idiot, I stuck the note in my purse, to keep it with me. It's one of those things you re-read over and over, because you know that every time you read it, you'll feel something different.

"What's that dreamy look for?"

"Mmm?"

"You look like you're daydreaming."

"No, not at all. I was thinking about those cookies, and hot chocolate."

"Biscuits and hot chocolate you'll be eating on your own?"

I feel my cheeks start to flush.

"I'm guessing that's a no."

I shake my head and look over to the stage, where the junior infants have just appeared.

"It's our class soon," I say to Wes. "Try to concentrate on the rehearsals."

"Has someone taken a few steps, by any chance?"

"What steps?"

"I saw him, you know. Sitting on the stairs."

I should've guessed.

"He was waiting for you."

"He wanted to make sure I got home okay."

"How thoughtful of him... But I guess that's what friends do, right?"

I sigh heavily. "He said we're not friends."

"Oh, wow. I wasn't expecting that."

"Trust me, neither was I."

"And what do you think? How did you take it?"

"I still don't know. A lot has happened in the past few days," I say, vaguely. I don't really want to talk to Wes about the whole story with my family. "Things are a little bit confusing at the moment."

"Okay."

"I need a little time to work things out."

"Work out what's happening between you two?"

"Work out what to do," I say, sadly. "I only

have a three-month visa."

"What are you trying to say?"

"I have no reason to stay here, Wes."

"Not yet."

I smile at his optimism. "We all know the fireman's reputation."

"That's true, we've heard the rumours about him. But we don't know his version of events. We don't really know him."

"Exactly. I don't know him."

"That doesn't mean that you can't get to know him. You still have another month and a half, right? Make the most of it."

"And then?"

"And then you can decide what to do."

"What if I realise that I like him, but he realises that he doesn't like me?"

"I think that it's pretty clear by now that you both like each other."

I shrug. "It's not enough just to like someone."

"No, but it's a good start. Try to work on it."

"You're forgetting my problem with men."

"Did he not offer to help you with that?"

"That was before."

"Before?"

"Before we realised that we're not really friends."

"I don't follow."

"We need to concentrate on the show."

Wes lifts himself away from the table he was leaning against and plants his hands on his hips.

"You're right – but this conversation isn't over."

He takes a few steps forward and claps his hands, calling the children's attention. I join him and lead the kids onto the stage for their rehearsal. Wes stays in front of us, acting as a prompter, as I stand next to the two youngest in the class – the ones who need a little help. I lift my gaze and see Jordan, standing in the middle of the hall, ready to help out with the performance. She smiles at me, flashing two thumbs up for encouragement, before the music begins, and the kids timidly start to sing, prompted by Wes, who mirrors their movements. I find myself singing and dancing along with them, happy to be here, in this school, in this place; happy to have had the chance to get to know these kids, these people, and maybe, finally, to understand who I am, and where to go from here.

* * * * *

When I used the rest of my savings to buy a one-way ticket to Ireland, I had no idea what I'd find on the other side. It was a dark time in my life. My mother, the only family I had, had died, and I was on my own. Discovering that, actually, she *wasn't* my only family member shook my world. The first thing I felt was anger, then disappointment, then, lastly… Lastly, pain. All of a sudden, though, the pain I felt wasn't for the fact she wasn't there – it was for everything she had taken away from me. I know, it's horrible for me to even think that, but that's how I felt.

My mother kept part of my life away from me. She told me that my father was just a good-for-nothing, like all the other men she'd been with. She said she wasn't even sure who he was, that she knew he'd never wanted me. She said that men were all the same; they all say they want you, until they've had you. Men abandon you, reject you, cast you aside.

I believed her. She was my mother, and she was all I had. Even though she took me from my friends, from the places I'd begun to love, from the life I'd always dreamed of having, I loved her. I followed her everywhere she went.

And I believed her for so long. I believed her until I found out that she knew exactly who my father was, and that she'd decided not to tell him about me.

Now I feel cheated. I feel like I'm not *me* anymore. I can't help but wonder how my life could've been if my dad had known about me, if I'd grown up here, maybe, in Ireland, with him, instead of wandering around aimlessly with her. I wonder how it would've felt to have a parent who puts their daughter's needs before their own. How it would've felt to have a family.

No. I never had one. My mother wasn't exactly a family. She never made cookies at Christmas, for example. She never bought a Christmas tree. She never bought any presents, or told me about Santa Claus. I am called Holly, though. Maybe it's a cruel trick of fate, or maybe it was deliberate. *Holly White*. It's almost like a joke – but my mother chose it for me.

She chose not to let me know part of my family, my roots; she chose not to give me a stable upbringing. She chose to make me unhappy.

I don't know whether I'll ever be able to forgive her for it. And I don't know whether I'll ever be able to make up for everything that was taken from me – but I'm here to try. I'm here to find all the answers I've been looking for.

43

Tyler

"I haven't seen you for a while," Parker says, as he helps me check the equipment on one of our fire engines.

"You're seeing me right now."

"You know what I mean."

"Actually, no." I check the pressure of one of the extinguishers. "And I don't want to know. Next topic."

"At ours, I mean."

"You mean I haven't been round for a while to cover your arse and look after the girls?"

"Actually, I think I was the one to cover *your* arse."

"All this because of a shift swap, Parker? Really? How many times have I covered your shifts over the years? And how many times have I taken a double shift for you?"

"I have two daughters, Tyler."

"Is that my problem, now?"

"What's keeping you so busy?"

"I don't think that's any of your business. Otherwise I'd have told you on the phone when I rang you, asking for a favour. One fucking favour. In how many years?"

"Exactly. You never ask me for favours."

"I guess there's a first time for everything."

"So…"

"So, what?"

"What did you have to do?"

I scoff and turn to face him. "I had to help someone out with something."

"Who?"

"You don't want to know the whole story."

"Now that you mention it, I *do* want to know the whole story."

"Fine," I say, lifting my hands, before putting down my clipboard. "Someone needed me."

"A man or a woman?"

I stare condescendingly at him.

"Are you telling me that I covered your shift, left my daughters with my clingy neighbour, and promised her a dinner at my house, just so that you could fuck one of your latest questionable conquests?"

"First of all, 'questionable' my arse. They're all certified."

"Tyler!"

"And, secondly, no. It's not what you think. I really had to help someone out with something." I take a few moments to study my brother's expression. "I wanted to help a friend."

Parker lifts an eyebrow. "Don't tell me this is about *that* friend?"

I sigh heavily.

"God, Tyler!"

"What have I done now?"

"Did I not ask you to stay away from her?"

"You asked me not to sleep with her, and I didn't – I swear!"

"Am I supposed to believe you?"

"Do you want to ask her?"

"Don't tempt me!"

I scoff, exasperated. "Why can't you just believe me?"

"Because I can't imagine you just *helping* someone." He waggles his fingers in air-quotes.

"I swear, this was totally selfless."

"Why should I believe you?"

"Because if I'd wanted to sleep with her, I already would have, and everyone in town would know about it."

Parker thinks about this. "I guess that's true…"

"Listen, I can't tell you anymore, because it's nothing to do with me. It's her life, and it's private."

"And she trusted you?"

Now I'm the one to glare at him.

"Sorry if I find it hard to believe, but I've known you for thirty-nine years."

"Well, she hasn't. And that works in my favour."

"What do you mean?"

"She met me as a blank slate."

"Okay…"

"She doesn't know much about me, or what I've done, even though rumours seem to be flying around everywhere. She trusts me, from what she's seen so far. Do you know what I mean?"

Parker stays quiet, his expression unreadable.

"It's like being able to start over again. Like I can be someone else entirely. Or maybe…"

"Maybe?"

"It's like maybe I can finally be myself."

"Are you telling me that you like my daughters' teacher, Tyler?"

"Your daughters are my nieces."

"Stop changing the subject."

"And she's not just the girls' teacher. To me, she's Ms. White."

"What is this, some kind of weird porn thing? Like a teacher telling off a naughty student?"

"God, no!"

"I was just asking."

"What kind of porn do *you* watch?"

"I don't watch porn! And stop trying to change the subject!"

"I don't understand what your problem is. I just asked you for a favour, okay? I'll make it up to you."

"When?"

"Whenever you want."

"Tomorrow."

"What?"

"You're off work."

"That doesn't mean that…"

"I need to go to Letterkenny."

"What the hell do you need to do in Letterkenny?"

"Shopping centre. Christmas. Daughters."

"Fuck."

"Exactly. Fuck. I need to get a move on, before I can't find the things they've asked Santa for."

"What have they asked for?"

"Something about a snowman."

"Got it."

"And I need you to look after them for a few hours. Enough time for me to go to Letterkenny, find this fucking snowman, and come back. Probably by about eight or nine. They might have to have dinner at yours."

"I can do that."

"Are you sure?"

"No. But do I have a choice?"

"You're not helping, Tyler."

"You're right, sorry."

"I still need to find a babysitter."

"Mum and Dad come back in a few weeks."

"That's not a solution."

"No, but it'll help. As will I, whenever I can."

"So, will you look after them tomorrow?"

"I'll look after them. But, I'm warning you now: I'm going to order a pizza. Or maybe a burger and fries. It's not like they eat anything else anyway."

Parker sighs. "Fine."

"Are we done now, then?"

"One more question."

I roll my eyes. "Okay."

"If you like Ms. White…?"

"I never said that," I point out. He ignores me.

"Why don't you just tell her?"

"Three months."

"Mmm?"

"She's only here for three months. And she's already been here for one and a half."

"Are you scared she's just going to leave?"

"I'm scared she'll want to stay, Parker. And I'm scared I won't be able to deal with it."

44

Tyler

When I open the door and see her standing in front of me, wearing a hoodie two sizes too big for her, her face flushed with embarrassment, her eyes wide and hopeful that she's in the right place, all I want to do is forget about all my usual bullshit, wrap her up in my arms and kiss away all her insecurities. I want to show her that this isn't just the right place for her; it's the *only* place for her. For us both.

"C-cookies." She shoves a tin under my nose. "They gave them to me at school."

I smile at her nervousness.

"You're really making an impression on those kids, Ms. White."

She smiles.

"They told me to eat them with hot chocolate."

"That's good advice."

"They're for you. To say thank you."

"Aside from the fact that you don't need to thank me for anything, are you really trying to give me a recycled present?"

She blushes violently

"No, I didn't want to… I would've made you something, but I'm no good."

I'm overwhelmed by such a sudden urge to kiss

her – to make her forget about all these ridiculous thoughts – that it's almost painful.

"You don't have to do anything for me, Ms. White."

She bites her lip nervously.

"But if you really insist on giving me these biscuits, then… I accept."

She relaxes a little.

"On one condition."

"What?"

"That you come inside and eat them with me."

"Y-you want me to come in?"

I move away from the door and pull it fully open, inviting her in. She smiles at me, torn between feeling overwhelmingly shy and happy, before stepping inside. I close the door behind us.

Do you ever get that feeling where just one movement, one step, one word, or even a second of silence, could change the course of your life? It's the way I feel right now, in the exact moment that Ms. White turns to me to show me the tin of biscuits.

I'll eat those biscuits with you, Ms. White. As long as you promise not to let me meet the same fate one day.

"Make yourself at home," I say, nodding towards the sofa. "I'll go and see if I have any hot chocolate."

"I'll help," she says, following me into the

kitchen and placing the biscuit tin down on the counter.

"It should be here somewhere. I usually buy it for the girls." I rummage around, moving a few boxes in the cupboard in search of the right one. "It should be..." I reach right into the back. "Here it is." I pull it out, showing it to her. "Could you grab me the milk from the fridge?"

"Sure."

"And the whipped cream. It should be next to the orange juice."

"Got it!" She shows it to me, putting it down on the counter next to the milk. "Anything else I can do for you, Ty?"

There's so much more you can do, Ms. White. Everything.

You can do anything you want with me. But, please, make sure to be careful; don't let me fall, shattering to pieces on the floor. Because I know that, after you, no one would ever be able to put me back together.

How do I know that? It's just a feeling, another sensation. And, this time, it's absolutely terrifying.

* * * * *

I shove another whole biscuit into my mouth as Ms. White watches me, amused.

"What?"

"You really like them, don't you?"

"I like anything to do with Christmas."

"Oh, really?"

"It's a holiday we take very seriously around here."

"So I've heard."

Her voice wavers, her eyes wandering back towards the TV, to this stupid film that neither of us want to watch, because let's be honest: there are a few things we could be doing other than watching a film on the sofa with biscuits and hot chocolate. But she's not like other women, and I'm not just that fireman with the indisputable skills.

She's *my* Ms. White, and I'm just *her* Ty.

And, trust me: that means something else entirely.

"Are you not a big fan of Christmas?"

She shrugs, sipping at her hot chocolate to avoid answering me.

"Holly…"

She turns to face me.

"It wasn't exactly one of my mother's favourite holidays."

"How come?"

She heaves a deep sigh. "We didn't celebrate Christmas, or anything else. Usually, at Christmas, we just went to a diner – you know, one of those ones which are open even during the holidays – and ate pancakes and waffles until we felt like we could explode." She smiles sadly, and I'm struck by that feeling again, of wanting to take away all her sadness.

I don't like to see Ms. White upset, and I don't like the way it makes me feel, right now, seeing her so sad.

It makes me feel powerless.

It makes me feel useless.

"We've never had a Christmas dinner. Santa Claus never came down the chimney. The Easter Bunny never left any eggs, and the Tooth Fairy never brought me a quarter."

I don't know how much longer I can resist the urge to hold her close to me.

"She didn't believe in anything. In holidays, traditions; to her, it was all just a marketing ploy, a way to con taxpayers out of their money – as if she ever paid her taxes." She looks down at the biscuit tin on her lap. She hasn't let go of them for even a second, as if it were the most precious gift she'd ever received.

And she decided to share it with me.

"I think her life was even sadder than mine," she says, tears piercing at her voice.

"I'm sorry."

"Me, too. For her. So sorry." She dries her eyes and clears her throat. "She wasn't a bad person. Just that she... That's just what she was like. So, by default, I was like that, too."

"You can always start now."

She looks at me, waiting.

"Christmas is in two weeks."

"What do you mean?"

I get to my feet, spurred on by a rush of adrenaline. Ideas begin to bounce around my mind like a pinball.

"Ty?"

I look at her, determined. "Do you trust me, Ms. White?"

She nods, anxiously.

"Then leave it all to me."

"What did you have in mind?"

I sit on the coffee table in front of her and take her hands in mine: a spontaneous but beautiful gesture.

"I'll take care of you."

"Y-you?"

I'll give you everything you've never had, Ms. White. And I'll give myself something I never thought I wanted. Something that, right now, seems like the only thing that matters.

45
Holly

When I get home from school the next day, I find a note attached to my door. I grab it with anxious fingers, my heart almost leaping from my chest.

Change of plan.

I'm going to help you spread your wings, but not in the way you wanted.

Be ready for anything, Ms. White.

I keep reading, my breath quickening.

About last night...

I really liked sharing those biscuits with you.

My hand flies up to my face, which is blushing for no apparent reason, and hurry into my apartment, before Tyler comes home and finds me outside, drooling over his note.

His car isn't parked outside, so I know he's not home. But I have no idea when he might be back, or where he's gone. Maybe he's at work, or maybe he's just popped out. Maybe he's with someone – or maybe I'm only thinking about all this because he said that there's been a change of plan.

I take off my jacket and shoes, before heading into my room to put his note in my now-empty cookie tin, where I've decided to keep all his notes. I stretch out on my bed, the tin clutched against my chest, and hope creeping slowly back into my life.

* * * * *

I spent the rest of the afternoon in my room sorting through the clothes and accessories which were still flung over the armchair. I'm not a particularly organised person: moving around so much as a kid meant I got used to living in constant chaos. I never used to waste any time unpacking when I knew we'd only be leaving again. Maybe I shouldn't waste my time unpacking now, either, seeing as my time here has an expiration date. But I know it makes no sense to keep my things bundled up on an armchair, or balled up in a corner, when I have an empty closet right here.

I've never lived anywhere particularly big, and I've never really had space just for me. My mother worked intermittently, taking whatever job she could find with no guarantors and no references. For a while, we lived in a trailer, which actually wasn't so bad. She wasn't so bad. She was my mother, so she was my whole world. It was only during the last few years, when I grew up and started to live my own life, that I realised that I wanted a stable job, that I wasn't exactly like her. It was only then that I realised our way of life was harmful to us both. It was only then that I realised how alone we both were.

I'll never know why she decided to reject my father, and I think this is something that I'll always carry with me. But I can't give up on the idea that change can make things better – just because it's the only life I've ever known. And since I've been here, I'm not only starting to see the world through new eyes: I'm starting to want a piece of that world for myself.

I finish organising my shoes on the rack at the bottom of my closet, before standing up just as someone knocks at the door. I head quickly into the living room, nervous, my heart beating a thousand miles an hour, hoping it's who I think it is. But when I pull open the door, I find the Hayes twins standing in front of me.

"Oh... Hello," I say, surprised.

"This is for you." One of the girls hands me a piece of paper. I open it, curious, and when I recognise his writing, my stomach starts to twist into knots.

Do you have any dinner plans, Ms. White?

Underneath there are two boxes:

No and *No*.

I laugh, as one of the girls hands me a pencil to fill in the box.

I mark one of the 'no's and hand the piece of paper back to the twins.

"Wait here," she says, disappearing with her sister into the apartment next door. A few minutes later, they appear at my doorstep again, and pass me another note.

Would you like to share an extra-large pizza with your local fireman?

There are two boxes here, too.

Yes, I'd love to, and *Yes, I can't wait.*

I smile, excited.

P.S. I've been thinking about you all day. I'm telling you here because if I say it in front of the girls, they'll tell my brother, and then my brother will slice my balls off with a kitchen knife.

I jot down my response.

Why would he want to cut off your balls?

The girls disappear for a few minutes, before reappearing with the response.

Because I promised him I'd never lay eyes on his daughters' teacher.

This time, my heart is beating so loudly I'm finding it hard to breathe.

But I can't seem to lay them anywhere else.

I lift my gaze the moment Ty appears behind his nieces. His eyes are piercing, fixed spellbindingly onto mine.

"Can we order the pizza now, Uncle Tyler?" one of the girls asks.

Tyler nods, his eyes never leaving mine.

"Go back inside and choose what you want from the menu. We'll be right there."

The girls head back into Tyler's apartment as he

stays standing in front of me, our eyes speaking, our hearts hammering.

"I owe you a pair of balls."

It's one of the most ridiculous things that has ever left my mouth.

Tyler smiles.

"They'll never be the same, but I can do my best."

I keep spouting embarrassing nonsense like this, but it's just my nerves talking.

"You really want to talk about my balls, Ms. White?"

"Not really. But I can't seem to talk about anything else."

"Are you telling me that you can't stop thinking about my balls?"

You. I can't stop thinking about you.

"Maybe."

"Do you want to come in? We can keep talking about my balls while we eat, if you want."

"You really think it would be appropriate to talk about your balls in front of your nieces?"

"Not at all."

"Don't you think, maybe, it would be better to talk about something else?"

"Let's improvise."

"I'm no good at improvising. I thought you already knew that."

Tyler thinks about this for a moment, then, with a voice that could melt an iceberg, says: "I don't think there's anything you're not good at, Ms. White. And I can't wait to prove it to you."

46
Tyler

"So you're the designated babysitter again?" Ms. White asks, taking the glasses from my hands.

"My brother had some urgent errands to run."

"I hope everything's okay?"

"He had to pay a visit to Santa Claus," I whisper into her ear.

"Got it."

"And seeing as he has no luck with babysitters, and his neighbour is out of the question…"

She places the glasses on the table as I bring over the pizza boxes.

"My parents will be back soon, so it won't be too much of a problem."

"Your parents?" she asks, her voice strained.

"Uh-huh." I open the girls' pizza boxes as they sit themselves at the table.

"I didn't know…"

"What?"

"You've never spoken about them. I've only ever heard you speak about your brother, so…"

"My parents are on holiday."

"Holiday?"

"For their forty-year anniversary."

"Seriously?"

I nod, and watch Ms. White do the maths in her head.

"Do I look younger?"

"I have no idea how old you are, Ty."

"Uncle Tyler is thirty-nine, and Dad is forty. I think," one of the girls says.

Ms. White looks at me.

"There are only eleven months between us. My parents are... Well, you'll find out."

Her face whitens.

"What's wrong?"

"Your parents?"

"They're not so bad when you're not related to them, don't worry."

"I don't..."

"They'll be back for New Year's Eve, so you'll be able to meet the whole family."

"I-I don't know..."

"Didn't I promise you that you'd never feel lonely?" I whisper.

She nods, frightened.

"Granddad was a fireman, Ms. White," one of my nieces – I have no idea which – takes over. "Just like Dad, and Uncle Tyler."

"Tradition," I say, sticking a slice of pizza into my mouth. "He's retired now, enjoying life. He deserves it."

Ms. White smiles.

"They've been on holiday forever!" my other niece says. "I miss them."

"Cruise around the world," I explain to Ms. White.

"Really?"

"They've never really travelled before, so they wanted to make up for it now."

"That must be amazing."

"I hope so, for their sake."

I take another bite of my pizza. Ms. White still hasn't touched her food.

"Hey," I say, nodding towards the pizza. "Aren't you hungry?"

"Yeah, sure." She smiles sadly, picking up a slice. She bites into it, unconvincingly, as I watch her, worried. Maybe the idea of meeting my family has put too much pressure on her. But what did she expect me to do, leave her alone for the Holidays? If possible, I wouldn't even leave her for another minute of her life – but I don't think it's best to bring that up now. Not after her reaction.

Maybe we should've stuck to talking about my balls.

"Hey, family!" The front door slams open and my brother Parker makes his entrance. "I finished earlier than expected, and..." He stops as soon as he notices my guest.

"Hi, Dad!" my nieces chime in chorus.

"Hi, girls. Hi, Tyler." My name doesn't exactly

come out well – it sounded more like a 'fuck you, Tyler' – but maybe that's just my imagination. "I don't think we've met…" he says, turning to Ms. White. "Although I think I've seen you a few times at the school gates."

"I'm Holly," she says, getting to her feet as Parker steps closer. "I don't think we've had the chance to talk, yet." They shake hands. "Everything's always so busy at the end of school…"

"Yeah," he comments.

"Ms. White is having dinner with us," one of my nieces explains, stating the obvious.

"I can see…" Parker glares at me.

"Why don't you have some pizza, too?"

"We actually have to go, sweetheart. You have school tomorrow."

By the way Parker practically spits the word 'school', I can tell that even Ms. White has realised that my brother has a stick up his arse.

"What's the hurry?" I ask Parker, getting up. He seems like he can't wait to leave.

"I don't want to intrude…"

I glare at him.

"Come on, Dad! Sit down!"

"Fine, but only for ten minutes."

"Was that so hard?"

"Not for you, apparently…"

I take a slice of pizza and shove it into his

mouth. "Eat, or it'll get cold. And chew carefully. We wouldn't want you to choke now, would we?"

I sit back down next to Ms. White as Parker glares at me, slowly chewing his pizza. Just as he's about to open his mouth and say something else, a knock at the door stops him in his tracks.

"Who else are you expecting?" he asks right away.

I shrug and get up to open the door.

"Surprise!"

"What the hell...?"

"I was in the neighbourhood and I thought I'd come and say hi."

"I-I don't think—"

"I brought some biscuits." She hands me a tin. "I made them myself. But, if you prefer..." She opens her coat, revealing that, underneath, she's totally naked.

"Oh, fuck!"

"Tyler!" my brother's voice distracts me from my unexpected visitor.

"Oh, my god!" She pulls the jacket tightly around her in embarrassment. "I had no idea you had company!"

"And I had no idea you'd just turn up at my door."

"Come on, girls." Parker gets up.

"Stop, don't go anywhere." I turn back to Callie. "This is a really bad time."

"I can see…" She glances inside, trying to work out who I'm having dinner with, but Ms. White is sitting with her back to the door. She hasn't even turned around once.

"Maybe I'll come back later… I'm free this evening. The kids' dad is in town, and…"

"Let's talk out here." I push her into the hallway and close the door behind me. "What the hell is wrong with you?"

"What do you mean?"

"You can't just show up at my house like this…"

"I just thought that…"

"What?"

"I thought we could have some fun together. Like last time."

"When was the last time, Callie?"

"I don't know, maybe a few months ago…?"

"Have we even spoken since then?"

"No."

"Have I ever asked you out?"

"No, but…"

"You knew all this when we slept together."

"Yeah, but…"

"My nieces are here, for Christ's sake!"

"Not just your nieces, apparently."

"What's the supposed to mean?"

"I didn't think you invited women to your

house, for dinner, with your family."

"I don't owe you an explanation."

"You definitely don't owe *me* an explanation. But I reckon you owe one to someone else…" She nods towards the door behind me and I turn suddenly.

Ms. White is standing in the doorway. She seems small again, vulnerable, and hurt. Very hurt.

And I know it's entirely my fault.

* * * * *

"Holly," I say, holding up my hands and stepping closer to her. "I can explain."

"You don't have to explain anything."

She strides past me and heads towards her front door. She pulls her keys out of the pocket of her jeans and sticks them into the lock.

"Then why are you leaving?"

"Because I have no reason to stay."

"That's not true, and you know it."

"Goodnight, Tyler."

"No, Holly, wait…" I block the door with my hand. "You know that there's a reason."

"All I know is that we're not friends. And that…" She sighs, hugging her arms around her body. "That we're nothing else, either."

"That's not true."

"She brought you cookies."

I look at her, confused.

"She knows how to make cookies."

"No, Holly, don't…"

"You should spend your evenings with someone who knows how to make cookies."

"Why the fuck would I care about baking fucking biscuits?"

"She was naked, under that jacket."

"Holly…"

"She came here for a reason."

"I didn't invite her, I swear."

"Is she familiar with your *skills*?"

I fall silent.

"Is she one of the lucky damsels in distress you've rescued?"

This can't really be happening.

"How many women have you used your skills on, Tyler?"

I can't answer her, because I have no idea.

"Do you think it's nice for me, to hear other women talking about it?"

I shake my head.

"But I told myself that there was more to you than that. There was something that…" She takes a deep breath, which seems even harder for her to bear than the guilt sinking into my stomach. "You messed me around."

"Holly, I swear that…"

"Please, let go of my door."

"Just let me explain, first."

"Don't make me call the police again. I don't think an accusation from the same person twice would be good for your career."

I take my hand away and let her barricade herself in her apartment. But it wasn't what she said that hurt me, or the idea of another trip to the police station. The thing that hurt me the most was the look on her face: so disappointed. A look that told me that she'd trusted me, and that she can never trust me again. I don't think I can bear it.

Holly closes the door, and all that's left is silence. There's no sign of life in her apartment, no sign of her. The silence is so devastating, so all-encompassing, that I'm beginning to doubt she was even here at all.

I take a few steps back and head back into my apartment. The girls are sitting in front of the TV with their pizzas, my brother standing with his arms crossed, his expression clearly stating: *you're the world's biggest dickhead.* He nods towards the kitchen and I follow him, my head bowed.

"I knew this would happen sooner or later," he says, his voice low but pissed-off, hissing through his teeth. "I knew it wouldn't be long before you hurt someone."

"Now is not the time for a life lesson, Parker."

"I didn't like what I saw."

"If it's any consolation, I didn't like it, either."

"That girl..." He says, gesturing towards the next-door apartment.

"Yeah, yeah, I know, you asked me to leave the girls' teachers alone. But, I promise, nothing happened. I never even touched her."

"Oh, I know that."

I look at Parker, confused.

"Do you know what I really didn't like, Tyler?"

"Apart from the fact I made her feel like shit?"

"I didn't like watching you throw away your only chance."

"What are you talking about?"

"I don't know whether you'll even be able to grasp this, but you should at least try."

"Try what?"

"You've never touched her, Tyler. She lives next door. She has dinner here, you spend the evenings together, and she looks at you as if you could give her all the answers in the world."

"I don't see what you're getting at."

"There's only one reason you haven't tried it on with her yet."

I shake my head, exhausted.

"And I think you need to tell her, instead of playing stupid games."

I turn quickly towards him.

"The girls told me everything as soon as you stepped outside. Notes? Seriously, Tyler?"

"What would you know about...?"

"Me? Nothing, as you can see. I've already had my chance."

"Exactly. And it was a disaster."

"I have two daughters, Tyler. Two daughters which are my whole life. How could that be a disaster?"

"I don't know, Parker," I say, rubbing my hand over my face. "Maybe it's best to just leave things like this. Maybe it's best to leave it here. Don't you think? Before I do something that could really hurt her."

"Whatever you want," he says, resting his hand on my shoulder.

"Is that all you're going to say?"

"I've done what I could."

"Wow. You're a really shit brother, you know that?"

"That's probably true, but you're pretty shitty, yourself."

I shrug indifferently.

"We're going to head home now, okay? You think about it. Maybe, I don't know... Maybe you could write another one of those embarrassing notes which she seems to like so much."

"How would you know whether she likes it?"

"The girls said she couldn't stop smiling while

she was reading them."

"They said that?"

"Yeah."

Now *I* can't help but smile.

"Maybe you can find a way of making her smile again."

"Maybe all I'll do is make her cry."

"We all know about your skills, Tyler. I think now is the time to start using them on the right person."

47

Tyler

I've tried knocking at her door. I've tried slipping an apology note underneath it, leaving a corner still visible from the hallway so I can see whether she's picked it up. But it's still there, as unwelcome as me.

There's no sound coming from the apartment, but I don't think she's gone to bed, yet. I know she's making as little noise as possible so that I don't think she's awake, thinking about everything that happened between us tonight.

I pace up and down my apartment, hoping to clear my thoughts, and stop at the window which looks out onto the balcony. I stare out of it for a few moments for no reason, when inspiration strikes. I run over to the table, where I'd left a pen and some paper, quickly scribble something down, and stick it into my pocket, heading back towards the balcony door. I throw it open and shimmy along the railing. It's a small drop – nothing that an arsehole fireman like me couldn't handle – so I scale the small wall which separates our apartments, and landing on her balcony. I wander up to the glass and take the note I've just written, before gathering my courage and knocking on the glass.

After a few seconds, Ms. White's sad face

appears from behind the curtain. I don't give her the chance to close it again and tell me to fuck off, so I show her the first piece of paper.

"What do you want, Tyler?" her muffled voice cries from behind the glass.

"Read it out loud."

She shakes her head, but stays standing in front of the door.

"Please."

"Why should I?"

I gesture for her to read the messages. She sighs, but starts to read.

I'm a dickhead.

"Go on."

And I don't deserve your beautiful, autumn-coloured eyes to ever land on me again.

I flip the piece of paper, her incredible eyes flickering back to me.

But I want them.

And I've realised recently that they're the only thing I want.

I switch to a new piece of paper.

And I promise that my skills will be exclusively at your service from now on.

I let the paper fall to the floor as Holly slides the balcony door aside.

"Tyler…"

I step closer and place my fingers gently against

her lips: the lips I've wanted to touch since the moment she first said my name.

"Before we go on, I have to tell you something. I lied, a few moments ago."

She furrows her brow.

"When I said that your eyes were the only thing I wanted, I was lying."

Those eyes are scared, now, speeding up my heart rate until it grows dangerous, out of control.

"This," I say, tracing the outline of her mouth with my finger as Ms. White parts her lips. "I want this, too. I want it so much that I think I'm going crazy."

"Ty..." Two letters which tickle my thumbs. "I'm not like other girls."

"Exactly. You're nothing like other girls."

She laughs, and I slide my tongue along her bottom lip.

"I don't know how to bake cookies," she says, almost frightened.

"Then I'll make them for you. I'll bake you all the biscuits you want."

"You know how?"

I shake my head and step even closer, as her hands land on my chest. My other hand slides to the back of her neck.

"But I can learn."

"Why would you?"

"For you."

"M-Me?"

"Remember when I said there was nothing I wouldn't do for you?"

"Y-yeah."

"It was totally fucking true."

She bites her lip and I stroke it, my eyes fixed onto her soft, warm mouth, just waiting to be mine.

"Ms. White?"

"Mmm?"

"I don't know if I'll survive."

"Survive what?"

"This," I tell her, before pressing my lips against hers. Her fingers grab onto my hoodie, my hands resting on the back of her neck. "Like fuck will I survive this," I pant, pushing my lips back onto hers, which part at my touch. "And I don't want to survive," I say, making her laugh a little, before biting gently down onto her bottom lip. Ms. White stops breathing, just as I do. I bite her again, finally tasting her, and pulling her closer against me. My tongue slides slowly into her mouth, and my beautiful Ms. White trembles in my arms. I give her time to catch her breath, my hand sliding slowly down her warm cheek, her eyes bright, seeking comfort in my own.

"Yes, Ms. White," I say, twisting a lock of her hair in my fingers and stroking her face with my thumb. "That's how you deserve to be kissed." I press my lips against her mouth. "And maybe more."

She swallows, nervous.

"My dear Ms. White, you've just become my new plan."

"Your plan?"

"My only plan."

"Should I be worried?"

"Absolutely."

She smiles nervously, and I kiss her again.

"Hey, you survived," she says, jokingly.

"For now, yeah. But I'm not sure you'll be able to survive me, Ms. White. Not once I've done everything I want to do to you."

"Are you talking about...?"

"You'll find out, Ms. White. Oh, you'll find out." I step back slowly and she watches me cautiously.

"Where are you going?"

"Into my apartment."

"What? Why?"

"We need to take things step-by-step, here."

She bats her eyelids, confused.

"You deserve every step. And I don't intend to skip a single one."

She smiles, shyly, leaning against the doorframe.

"Goodnight, Ms. White."

"Goodnight, Ty."

I clamber back onto my balcony and head back into my apartment, before my longing to pounce on her and show her all the steps of my plan in a single night becomes too much to bear.

I told her I wanted to take things slow, and that's what I'll do. Yet another 'first time' that I want only with her.

Maybe my brother isn't a total loser. Maybe he's still useful sometimes. And maybe, like he said, the time has come for me to use my skills on just one person: the only person who could truly appreciate them.

48
Holly

On the journey to school, sheltered under my umbrella, I can't help but read over the note he left me. This time, I found it stuck to the glass door of the balcony. When I opened the curtains this morning, it was there, waiting for me.

Good morning, Ms. White.

I have a double shift at the fire station today, so I won't see you for another twenty-four hours.

I don't know whether I'll survive without you, but I'll try my best to come home to you.

About last night...

Your lips are the sweetest, most delicious thing I've ever tasted.

In class, I'm euphoric; at lunch I can barely contain myself; during rehearsals, I even wear a Santa hat. When Jordan asks me what role I want to take on for the winter fair, I tell her I'll be an elf.

Wes can't believe his ears, and Jordan is shocked but pleased.

"Is there something you want to tell me?"

"I don't know," I say, nervous. "Maybe..." Maybe I need to speak to someone, to untie this knot of excitement in my stomach.

"Tonight. I'll be there at seven," she says, winking. I nod gratefully and go back to work, still happy, still euphoric, and with no intention of curbing either emotion.

* * * * *

Jordan and I sit down at a table in The Harbour, one of her favourite restaurants, apparently. The waiter fills our glasses, as Jordan suggests I order the steak, which is one of their specialities. I follow her advice – I'm so nervous I don't think I could manage even to read the menu.

"So," Jordan says, taking a sip of wine. "What's happened over the past few days?"

I bite my lip.

"He kissed me."

Jordan's jaw drops.

"On the balcony. He kissed me on the balcony and wrote me these notes, and he says that we're not friends, and that I'm his only plan."

"Hang on, let's take it step-by-step. You lost me at 'balcony'."

"Step-by-step, exactly! He wants to take things step-by-step, and he wants to make sure we take them all."

"Okay…" Jordan is visibly confused.

"Sorry. When I'm nervous I babble."

Jordan smiles. "He makes you nervous?"

"Speaking about him makes me nervous. And so does he. So does the fact that I don't know how to bake cookies, but he eats so many of them."

"Are the cookies a metaphor?"

"I haven't slept with many guys," I say suddenly, out loud.

"I'd gathered. You weren't quite so explicit last time, but I understood."

"I'm twenty-seven."

"That doesn't mean anything."

"Really?"

"I waited until I was twenty-one for my first time, and then I was with my ex-husband for years. I can count the number of people I've slept with on one hand."

"Seriously?"

"We're all different, Holly. Everyone has their own timeline and their own experiences."

"But he's been with so many women. How many do you think there have been?"

"Don't think about that."

"How can I not? How could I ever think that he would want...?" I stop myself, as the waiter brings over our food.

We thank him and wait for him to leave.

"That he'd want what?" Jordan asks kindly.

"Me."

"Why wouldn't he?"

"Because of his skills. And his gnome hunting."

"Maybe this is his chance."

"Me?"

She nods.

"I don't think so," I say, sadly. "Maybe I'm just something that has never happened to him before."

"That's a given. But I think you're looking at this in the wrong way."

I sigh, defeated. Until this morning, everything had seemed like a dream; but as the day went on, I only became more scared that I'm not cut out for these things.

Tyler is charming, funny and sexy. He could make your ovaries explode with just a smile. And everyone says that he's amazing in bed. I've never really been with a man, and I'm twenty-seven years old. I have no experience. But he's so confident, so handsome, in every way. And he'll quickly realise that he's wasting his time with me; I'm not someone a man like him would ever want. And...

"I only have one month left."

I say that last thought out loud.

"I know."

"I can't stay for any longer. I only have a three-month visa."

"I know that, too."

"It would be a mistake."

The butterflies have disappeared, my naïve hopefulness, as the sad truth takes shape before my eyes.

"I'd have to go back to Canada for at least six months. Six months, Jordan."

"Have you tried talking to him about it?"

"When I told him that my time here had an expiration date, he said that we'd sort it out. But it's right around the corner, and I still don't have a solution."

"Do you want to stay?"

"I have a job waiting for me in Canada. I have nothing here. Just a daydream."

"Sometimes that's all you need."

"And sometimes it makes you lose sight of reality."

I fall silent, and Jordan reaches her hand across the table in search of mine.

"There's always a solution, Holly. You just have to want to find it. Do you want to?"

"I don't know."

"Then why don't you work on that first?" She lets go of my hand and cuts into her steak. I mirror her, bringing a piece to my mouth.

She was right. It's really good.

"I like it here," I say, suddenly. "I like it a lot."

She smiles at me from the other end of the table.

"I feel almost... At home."

"Is he the one making you feel that way?"

I think about this for a moment. His presence, our relationship, his arms wrapped around me: they're all things that make me feel good, that make me feel at peace with the world. But it's not just that.

It's this place, the people, their way of life. The way they make me feel. All these things together make me feel as if I'm in the right place – *my* place. And I never thought that would be possible in such a short time.

I came here with no expectations, and now... Now the idea of leaving this behind is painful.

"No," I tell Jordan honestly. "It's not about him."

"In that case, I think you've already found your answer."

Maybe. But it's not enough.

"You know that if I could make you stay, I would. Wholeheartedly."

I smile at her, sad but grateful.

"And I couldn't help you, even if I found you a job at the school. It wouldn't be enough. The rules are pretty clear."

"Don't worry, Jordan. I'll work it out."

"I wish I could do more."

"You're already doing so much. You're giving me friendship and, believe me, that's one of the most amazing gifts I've ever been given. It's something I'll take with me, wherever I go."

49

Tyler

When I get home from work after being away from home – and from her – for what seems like an eternity, Ms. White has already left for school. I wanted to get back in time to wish her a nice day, but I was kept back by the same old paperwork that everyone else is too lazy to fill out.

I step into my apartment, into my once-beloved silence, my personal space, and realise, for the first time in years – or maybe for the first time ever – that I feel a huge weight pressing down on me. I slump onto the sofa, exhausted, letting my head fall back, my arms dangling by my sides, my eyes closed, tiredness seeping into every muscle. But my mind is alert, with no plans of switching off anytime soon.

I want my Ms. White. I want her now, here, in this apartment, preferably on this sofa. Or, even better, on *me*.

I haven't seen her since we kissed, for more than twenty-four hours, and I'm scared that this madness coursing through me won't stop until I see her again – hopefully in six or seven hours.

I drag myself to my feet. I could have breakfast, then have a shower. I could sleep for a few hours, make myself look presentable for when she gets home. Or I could go to sleep right away and wake up before she gets back from school, go and surprise her at the gates. Or maybe I could find a way to make today special for her.

I go into the kitchen and glance at the calendar on the fridge: there's not long left until Christmas, and there's not long until her contract runs out, either.

And then.

And then we'll sort it out later, I told her. The problem is that I'm already worried about it. I've been thinking about it before our kiss. I've been thinking about it since she told me she was on her own, since she mentioned that she doesn't really have anyone or anywhere to go back to. I've been thinking about it for as long as I've been thinking about her.

I scoff, running both hands through my hair. I can't get too caught up in thinking about this. Right now, I need to think about the present; about today; about the fact that Christmas is right around the corner. I need to concentrate on the fact that Ms. White has never really celebrated Christmas, and that I promised her I'd give her everything she's never had.

I think about this for a while, tiredness not helping my logic. But I've overcome by a longing to do something, to make her happy. Maybe I can do something special: something that no one has ever done for her. Something that will make her melt into my arms.

* * * * *

After five hours of sleep, a rejuvenating shower, and a dose of my favourite aftershave, I wait impatiently for my plan to make Ms. White happy to take shape. I had to ask someone for help – someone who's something of a celebrity around here, who's known for his great plans. Someone who can come and go whenever he pleases, because no one would ever suspect anything of him. Someone who pretends to be just a misfit, a nerd, but who is actually a genius.

"So you'll let me play?"

"Already done, mate."

"What will you say to the coach?"

"I have the coach wrapped around my little finger."

Carter raises an eyebrow, unconvinced.

"Next match. From the first minute. Skylar will be there, and you can show off as much as you want. As long as you don't let the opposition score. I can't do anything about that, unfortunately – you're the goalkeeper."

"Don't worry, Hayes. I have some tricks up my sleeve."

"I can tell..." I say, shocked at his sudden personality change.

A few months ago, Carter was just a geeky kid tutoring Niall's daughter, Skylar. He was too scared even to talk around her. Skylar can be difficult at times – she's stubborn, someone who knows what she wants, won't take any shit, and isn't afraid to throw a few punches where necessary. She's also fucking terrifying. Since they started going out, Carter seems to have absorbed some of her confidence: he walks with his head high, wears skinny jeans and unbuttoned shirts – seriously? He used to live in superhero T-shirts! He's grown out his hair, strides around with his rucksack hanging from only one shoulder, and isn't afraid to look anyone in the eye, including Niall. I'm convinced that his nerdiness was just an act, so that he could easily get past Niall. He's intelligent, no doubt – his grades speak for themselves – but I'm starting to have my suspicions about his whole naïve loser thing. Maybe I should mention my suspicions to Niall, but then I wouldn't be able to use Carter to get into the school. No one else would help me.

"What are you going to gain from playing, exactly?" I ask him, dubiously.

I don't want this to be just a game plan to get a little closer to Skylar, if you know what I mean.

"And what do *you* think you'll gain from this?" He flashes me the note I gave him.

"Mind your own business."

"Mind yours."

Mmm. I like this kid. But I can't tell Niall, or he'll start nosing around and getting jealous – of who, I'm not quite sure. Either way, he would be a pain in the arse.

"Now, off you go, before they kick you off for talking to me."

"Kick me off? You don't know who you're talking to, mate."

Wow. He's even starting to sound a little gangster.

Carter heads off towards the gates, looking around indifferently, before slipping inside, keeping one eye on the slowly-roaming security cameras, in search of anything suspicious. I wait outside, in the visitors' car park, leaning against my car, my hands in my pockets, one leg jiggling nervously. I'm not waiting for a response – I didn't really ask her a question – but I'm scared that she may have reconsidered the idea of me, of us. I'm scared that she's decided not to trust me, not to give us a chance. It's hard to keep these thoughts out of my mind, even when you're a fireman with magic skills that everyone wants to get their hands on. Because I know that, for her, this isn't the case – or, at least, it definitely wasn't the case at first. And to be honest, I'm not sure it's true even now, after the sofa, and the balcony, and my stupid notes. Because I know that she's not like other girls, and I know that this has nothing to do with her lack of experience with the opposite sex.

I realised right away, the moment she threatened me with that knife, that Ms. White was something different. I just had no idea that this 'something' could affect me so much – or that she could be affected by me. I'm not used to this: it's so beautiful, so magical. And I'm not sure whether my stupid *skills* will be enough to make me beautiful and magical in her eyes, too.

50

Holly

I head towards the gates which encircle the Abbey's secondary school campus, and he really is there, leaning against his car.

I read his note once more, and find myself blushing again.

You're mine for the rest of the day, Ms. White.

We have plans, and a schedule to adhere to.

About last night...

I couldn't think of anything but your mouth.

The note was delivered to me by a boy called Carter, who is not only one of the kids Tyler coaches, but is also Niall's daughter's boyfriend. He was the one who told me where to go.

"Good morning, Ms. White." His warm smile wraps itself around me.

"Good morning."

"I see you got my note." He gestures towards the piece of paper I'm still clutching in my hand.

I nod and lower my gaze in embarrassment. I should've shoved it into my purse.

He pushes himself away from his car and walks towards me. I lift my eyes to meet his.

"Are you ready, Ms. White?" he asks, so confident in himself, and in the effect his words will have on me.

Ready for anything, Ty. But only if you're with me.

* * * * *

I'm a little more nervous once we get into the car. I've already been in a car alone with him, but that was before he kissed me – before I became his only plan. Before his closeness made me feel so agitated, so ecstatic; before he had started to make my heart beat uncontrollably.

"How was your day?" he asks, glancing quickly over at me before casting his eyes back to the road.

"Good, I think. We had rehearsals for the Christmas show."

"Which song were you practicing?"

"*Frosty the Snowman*."

"A classic."

"Yes. That's what Wes said – it was his choice."

"Wes." His tone grows suddenly serious.

"My colleague."

"Yeah."

This time I'm the one to glance over at him.

"What kind of guy is this *Wes*?"

His question confuses me.

"I don't know... What are you expecting him to be like?"

"He sounds like someone who wants to be punched in the face."

"I don't get it."

Tyler sits in silence for a few seconds, then clears his throat. Without tearing his gaze from the road, he says: "I'd like to meet this Wes."

"Seriously? Why?"

"Because I want to meet everyone in your life, Ms. White. Just to make sure that no one comes anywhere near your apartment unless it's for pure, platonic friendship."

"Like you?"

Tyler laughs.

"I never went anywhere near your apartment looking for friendship, Ms. White."

My jaw drops open as Tyler parks the car.

"From the moment I broke into your house, and saw you in that towel, I started to imagine what it might be like to..." He glances over at me, reaching his hand out to touch my face.

"To...?" I say, inviting him to go on. I want to hear everything he has to say.

"To have you all to myself."

"T-to have me?"

"Yes, Ms. White. That's exactly what I'm thinking about."

"I don't know what to say..."

"You don't have to do or say anything. We need to take things step-by-step, remember?"

I nod nervously.

"I don't want to skip a single one. And I especially don't want to do anything you're not ready for. Okay?"

"Okay," I say, relieved.

"Now that we've got that cleared up... What do you say?" he asks, nodding ahead. "Are you ready?"

It's only when he asks me this question that I turn to follow his gaze, and realise where we are.

"What is this?" I ask, confused, blinded by the twinkling lights adorning the side of the building.

"A shop which has everything you need."

I study him, worried.

"You're about to celebrate your first Christmas, Ms. White. And we're going to make sure you do it right."

* * * * *

"Firstly, we need to choose a tree." Tyler leads me over to a room filled with trees of every shape and colour. "I know it's been fashionable lately to have a tree in some garish colour, but I think a good old classic tree – maybe an artificial pine tree – that's nice and green, with no fake snow, would be perfect. What do you think?"

"I don't know what to say."

Tyler takes my hands and turns me towards him.

"What's wrong, Ms. White?"

"I don't know."

"Does the idea of Christmas make you nervous?"

"Maybe a little."

"What about me? Do I make you nervous? Is this all making you uncomfortable?"

"I don't know," I respond, honestly. I don't want to offend him, but I don't want to lie to him, either. "There are too many lights, and it's all too bright – and there are definitely too many Christmas songs."

He smiles kindly at me. "Maybe we've skipped a few too many steps."

I shrug awkwardly.

"Okay, let's take a step back for a second. Do you want to go outside? They have some plants and a few garden ornaments. That way, we can get some air and clear your head a little."

"Okay."

"Trust me, Ms. White. We won't do anything that you don't want to do."

"I trust you."

"Let's go." He releases one of my hands, keeping the other tightly intertwined with his cold fingers. "Let me be your guide."

"What do you know about plants and flowers?"

"I have my sources. I'm a man full of surprises; if you stick around, you might be amazed," he says, laughing. But I believe every word.

I don't know whether it's the way he acts – his confidence, his charm, the way he's taking all of this into his stride – but I'm more and more convinced that Tyler Hayes is a lot. He's more than anyone expects of him – much more than I ever expected of him. I'm afraid that he wants to show me every side to him; and I'm even more afraid that I won't have enough time to discover them all.

Once we're outside, Holly relaxes, and starts to seem a little less uncomfortable. Maybe I took things too quickly by bringing her here, with no warning. For someone who's never had any experience with Christmas, it must be too much – but I wanted to do things right. I wanted to do something for her.

"What do you think about these?" she asks, gesturing towards a row of real Christmas trees, lined up and ready to be taken home.

"Old school? I like it."

"Old school?"

"Barely anyone has a real tree anymore. They make too much mess, and it's too much effort. You have to plant them, and lots of people don't even have a garden."

"I hadn't thought of that."

"But if you want a real one, then that's what you're getting."

"You don't have to, Tyler, really…"

"Stop!" I say, lifting my hand to her face. "Not another word. You've made your decision."

Luckily, she laughs.

"We always used to get a real one, too," I tell her, brushing my fingers against the branches of one of the pine trees. "When we were kids. Then my brother and I would help my dad to plant it in the garden."

"That must've been so nice."

"It was – and it still is. A lot of them are still alive, you know. They're still in my parents' garden."

"Another family tradition – like being a fireman?"

"Something like that."

I see Holly grow suddenly sad. I realise as soon as it happens, because she seems to become smaller, as if she were trying to hide herself away from the world. I wrap my arm around her shoulder and kiss the top of her head.

"You don't have to do this if you don't want to."

"It's not that."

"Then what is it?"

"I have nowhere to plant it."

"Mmm?"

"I don't want it to die."

I think I've worked out what's bothering her.

"It would be a waste."

"How about, when the time comes, I take care of it?"

Holly lifts her sad gaze to meet mine.

"I'll take care of your tree."

"Would you really do that?"

I nod, and she flashes me a weak smile.

"I'll plant it with my own two hands and take care of it for as long as I can. I promise."

Holly moves closer to me and leans her head against my chest. I pull her close to me and inhale deeply; the smell of her hair becomes entwined with the smell of the pines, of wood burning from somewhere indoors. It's a unique mix of smells which I hope I'll remember for years to come – once the memory of her begins to fade.

"This one." She points to a tree in front of us. "I like this one."

"Then that's the one you're getting."

* * * * *

We bought the tree, some lights, a few decorations, and a wreath for her front door.

"What about you? Aren't you going to buy anything?" she asks me, once we reach the till.

"I have loads of stuff."

She looks at me, confused.

"I just need to go and pick it all up from my parents' house. I keep it all in the basement there – I don't have much room in my apartment," I explain. Another, slightly crazy idea springs to mind. "Although…"

"Mmm?"

"Well, we're about to decorate your house."

"Uh-huh."

"And seeing as we'll be... Er... Spending some time together, maybe there's no point decorating *two* apartments."

"Oh."

"Only if you want to spend the holidays with the local fireman."

"Are you asking me to...?"

Spend every waking second we have left together? Yes. Because I need to. Because I want to. Because I'm already distraught at the idea of losing you.

"Spend Christmas with me? Yes."

"Wow." A voice from behind the counter makes us jump; I thought we were alone. "That seems like a pretty big step." Fiona – someone I used to go out with – appears in front of us.

"We'll just pay for everything on the till here – and we have a tree in the car, too," I say, trying desperately to end the conversation before it does any damage.

"Of course, Hayes. Whatever you say."

This cannot be happening again.

"You're always the one who makes the decisions, right? When things get started, when to see each other, when to call things off."

I glance over at Holly next to me. She looks so small, so vulnerable – and it's my fault. Again.

"We're just here to buy some…"

"*We*. I'm shocked. You actually used the plural."

I scoff, losing my patience. "Can you please…?"

"Sure, Hayes. No problem – at least, you're not my problem anymore. Apparently, you're someone else's."

* * * * *

By the time we get outside, Holly still hasn't met my gaze, or said a word to me. We walk in silence towards the car, our shoes crunching on the gravel, and our breath dissipating into the humid night air. I know I should say something – maybe I should apologise, I don't know. The truth is that I have no idea how to handle this situation.

"Holly." I move in front of her before she reaches the car door. "I'm sorry." I don't know what else to say.

"What for, Tyler?"

"For getting you involved in this mess."

"How many other messes am I going to end up involved in?"

I deserve all the accusation in her voice.

"I have no idea."

"Exactly. And you know why? Because you never have any idea of what you've done."

"I haven't hurt anyone. They were all consenting adults, and they knew exactly who I was, and what would happen. I ever lied to any of them."

"They're upset."

"I didn't expect them to be."

"No, of course not. You thought that because they agreed to... What? One night? Maybe two?"

I shrug. I can't say anything.

"...That they'd be okay with it all. That they wouldn't mind being treated like... Like... Like women who don't matter."

"I never treated anyone like that."

"Well, I don't think they agree with you."

"What do you want me to do? Do you want me to apologise to them all? Tell them that I'm sorry, that I regret it?"

Holly shakes her head.

"I don't even know why I'm reacting like this."

I know why – but I can't exactly suggest it to her.

"Listen, Holly." I take her hand, but she pulls away, and I start to lose patience. "What the hell do you want from me?" My voice lifts instinctively, and I regret it as soon as I see her flinch, taking a few steps back.

"No, no..." I step closer, but she wraps her arms around her body. "I didn't mean it. I'm sorry."

"I don't want anything. I never wanted anything. You were the one who said all those things, and did all those things, and then kissed me..." Her face flushes with anger. "I can't. Don't you get it?"

"What? What can't you do?"

"I don't want to feel like this."

"Like what? How have I made you feel?"

"Rejected. The way you rejected them. They had the right to be appreciated."

"I know," I say, ashamed.

"You had no right to use them."

She's right; and I'm only realising now how right she is.

"And I don't want to be part of this game anymore."

"Game? What game, Holly?" I step closer to her again, and grab her shoulders. Her eyes flicker up to my face. "I swear, it's not what you think. You're nothing like that to me."

She shakes her head, confused.

"You're something I never expected. You're something I never even knew existed. Do you see what I'm trying to say?"

"No."

I laugh at her honesty, at the way her gaze flashes from disappointed to hopeful.

"Those steps we've been talking about? The ones I want to take? Well... They only exist for you."

"Why?"

"Because you're my first time, Holly White."

"I don't get it."

"Trust me, I don't get it, either. But I want to try to understand, if it means understanding with you."

52

Tyler

It was a pretty quiet car journey home; I didn't even want to attempt to do anything to lighten the mood. What happened at the shop, like what happened the other night, at my front door, is the kind of thing I never thought would happen to me. I always thought I was upfront with everyone, always the gentleman. Apparently, I was wrong. Apparently for some – although hopefully not for all – I was a complete dick. And, apparently, Ms. White has finally realised this. I've finally realised it, too.

I carry the Christmas tree up the stairs, as Ms. White grabs the box of lights and decorations; I leave the tree in the hallway and head back to the car to collect the rest of the stuff we bought, as she opens the door to her apartment. She walks inside and places the box on the floor. I leave two bags next to it, before heading back outside for the tree.

"Where do you want me to put it?" I ask. I think it's the first thing I've said to her after I told her she was my 'first time'.

She shrugs indifferently.

"You'd usually put it next to the window, so that the glass reflects the lights, and you can see it from outside."

"Okay."

I heave a sigh and drag the tree over to the balcony door, before turning to face her. She's sitting on the arm of the sofa.

"Do you want me to go?"

"I don't know."

"Talk to me. Say something. Anything."

"What you said before…" Finally, she looks at me, and it feels as if I can breathe again. "It shocked me."

"What shocked you, exactly?"

"When you said that I was your first time."

I smile at her – I can't help it. Her insecurity seems to be striking all the right chords in me.

"It's true."

"I don't get it… You've been with all those women, and…"

"I was never expecting you."

"How can you say something like that?"

"Believe me, it's true. I'm not a great liar – I'm sure you've realised that by now. I mean, how long did that whole 'friendship' thing last?"

Luckily, she smiles.

"I don't want to think about it too much, or try to find an explanation. I just know that this is the way it is. I've accepted it, with everything it entails." I step towards her, taking her face between my hands. "And I want it. God, do I want it." I bend down to her lips – lips I haven't kissed for too long. For too many hours, too many breaths. "And I want this." I press my mouth lightly against hers, as adrenaline and excitement begin to course through my veins. "Jesus, I want this." Ms. White parts her lips for me, and I murmur something incomprehensible before sliding my tongue into her mouth, filling myself with the taste of her. She grabs onto my jacket, and I keep her face held firmly between my hands, as I tell her – in the most direct way possible – everything I want to say to her. I tell her that, from this moment on, her mouth belongs only to me.

Kissing Ms. White is sweet, unexpected; it's torture for my body, but soothing for my soul. Every time I feel her try to take a breath, I give her one of my own.

When I finally release her from my grasp, Ms. White runs her tongue along her lips, making all the blood – and all my thoughts – rush towards my downstairs neighbour. I think he'd been feeling left out among all the excitement.

I step back, to make sure she doesn't think I'm taking things too far, and smile at the sight of the calm contentedness in her eyes.

"What do you say, Ms. White – do you want to decorate the tree with me?"

She nods and gets to her feet, grabbing my jacket and dragging me down to her again. She reaches onto her tiptoes and I bend down to meet her.

"In a minute," she says, biting her lip – and

believe me when I tell you it's not because she's nervous. It's because of something that I've been fantasising about for a long time, now.

I plant my hands on her hips and pull her into me; my erection is still attempting to fight its way to freedom.

"What did you have in mind, instead?"

"I've thought about it too, you know."

"About what?"

"This."

She presses her mouth against mine before I can prepare myself for the fact that my world has just been flipped upside-down by something I'd never have expected to feel. Although I don't think anyone is ever ready for something like this: something so strong, so terrifying, yet so beautiful.

And we expected it less than anyone.

* * * * *

I join Ms. White in the kitchen, where she's intent on making us both a sandwich. We drank hot chocolate while we decorated the tree together; it's still not quite done yet. We just need a few finishing touches, and we still need to hang the wreath on the door, but we've made good progress.

"What are you doing?"

"What do you mean?"

"What's this?" I nod towards the sandwiches, which she's currently spreading with mayonnaise.

"I'm making turkey sandwiches, like I said."

"Yeah, but why?"

"Why what?" she asks, concerned.

"You're adding mayonnaise."

"Y-yeah?"

"And butter?"

"Butter? But I'm already using mayonnaise."

"You have to spread the butter first, then the sauce."

"I don't know what you mean."

"What the hell do you guys eat over there?"

"Sandwiches with mayonnaise?"

"I don't understand you lot. Why would you ruin a perfectly good sandwich like that?"

I open the fridge and pull out the butter. Unsalted: one of those hard, unusable blocks.

"What's this?"

"I thought it was butter, but I'm starting to doubt myself after this conversation."

"Don't move," I say, before running out of her apartment and into mine, and grabbing everything we need: butter and garlic mayonnaise. I head quickly back over to her, where I find her standing in the same position, knife still clutched between her fingers.

"It's worse than I thought."

"What?"

"We're late, Ms. White. We're behind schedule."

"Oh, really?"

"We're going to have to skip a few steps together or we'll never make it in time."

"In time?"

Before you go back to Canada, Ms. White, and leave me alone with myself again.

"Before you realise that you could do much better than a shit-talking fireman."

Ms. White takes my hands and turns me to face her.

"I don't know what else is out there, but I don't care. I've already found the best."

"You found it? You don't want to keep looking, just in case? Maybe you'll get lucky, and..." Her lips quieten my thoughts, before I can say anything else.

"I don't want to look for anything. Everything I want is already right here."

I smile at her.

"Now, please, explain to me how the hell you make sandwiches in this ridiculous country."

I laugh, grabbing the knife from her.

"Do you have a back-up liver?"

"I was born on a different continent; I never needed one."

"We could find you one – maybe second-hand."

She laughs, shaking her head.

"What's that?"

"This," I say, lifting the tub, "is butter."

"And what I had in the fridge isn't butter?"

"You could maybe use it to make a few desserts."

"Oh."

"This is salted butter, Ms. White. Spreadable. How else would you put it on the bread?"

"Okay," she says, unconvinced. "What about that? What's wrong with the mayonnaise I already have?"

I bring a hand to my chest in shock. "Please, don't joke about these things."

She laughs, rolling her eyes.

"This is garlic mayonnaise. You spread it generously over the butter."

"Are you telling me that you put butter *and* mayonnaise on the same slice of bread?"

"Now you're getting it."

I get to work, explaining to her how to make a *real* sandwich, and Ms. White never tears her eyes from me, as if I could give her all the answers in the world, just like Parker said. I like feeling her eyes on me – I like it more than I like the thought of her naked, in the shower. And it's starting to worry me.

"There you go. Now *this* is a sandwich."

Ms. White takes a bite of the sandwich I'm

holding, and chews slowly.

"Wow, you're right!" she mumbles, her mouth full.

I laugh, before biting into the same sandwich.

"I reckon this would taste better with a beer, though."

I think I love you, Ms. White.

Thankfully, that thought came from my gut and not my mouth.

"Now you're really beginning your transformation."

"My transformation?"

"You're becoming one of us."

She smiles as she opens the beer, before taking a sip and handing it over to me. I take a sip, too, hoping to drown any more '*I love you*'s which seem to be climbing up my throat, looking for a way out.

I can't say something like that. It makes no sense, you know? It makes no sense, the way I feel about her. I've only known her for two months – and, in another month, she'll be gone forever.

You get it, right? I'm fucked.

"What do you think? Am I making progress?"

You really are making progress, Ms. White. Towards one particular goal.

"You're doing really well."

She smiles and lifts onto her tiptoes, pulling herself up on my arm to reach my mouth. I let her press against me for a moment.

"Do you want to finish decorating the tree?"

"Absolutely. That's what I'm here for."

"Don't you have plans this evening?"

Plans. She's really asking me whether I have plans?

Just one, Ms. White. And I've already told you.

You are my only plan.

53

Tyler

"I need help."

Niall studies me, worried, from the door of his parents' house.

"So you've chucked the whole 'process' out the window, then?"

"The process is well and truly fucked."

"In that case…" He opens the door to let me in. "How can I help?"

"You?" I laugh, throwing my head back.

"I don't know about you, but this doesn't sound good to me." His daughter appears from behind him.

"I'm not here for you, Kerry."

"You're not?"

I shake my head. "I need your mum."

"My mum? What the hell do you need from my mum?"

The mum in question pokes her head into the hallway, as if she could sense my desperate cry for help.

"Is someone looking for me?"

I step towards her nervously and grab her hands. "I need a huge favour."

"Of course, Tyler. What can I…?"

"I need to learn how to bake biscuits."

My *ex*-best-friend – who now deserves a swift kick up the arse – bursts into sudden fits of laughter.

"Biscuits?"

I nod.

"Why do you need to learn how to make biscuits?"

"For Ms. White."

Niall laughs again, as his daughter watches, shaking her head in disapproval.

"I'm listening…" Niall's mother says.

I knew that coming here and asking for help would have everyone sticking their noses into my private life, but I can deal with it. It's a small price to pay to see Ms. White smile.

"She's never learnt to bake biscuits," I explain, her eyes immediately clouding over with maternal sympathy, "and she's never celebrated Christmas before."

"Oh, the poor girl!"

"And I want to… Well, I want to help her make up for it while she's here."

"That's very sweet of you."

"Sweet? Come on…" Niall groans like a jealous little kid.

"I'd have asked Mum but she and Dad are still on holiday, and I know that you're one of the best bakers in town."

"He's good, your friend," Skylar says, turning to her father.

"It's one of his skills," Niall comments.

"Of course I'll help you, Tyler. Actually, we'll all help."

"All?" Niall asks.

"Exactly," his mother says, firmly. "We'll all give Tyler a hand in winning over his Ms. White."

"Cool," Skylar says, sending her father into a fury.

"Cool?" Niall asks, shocked. "You find *this* cool?"

"You can tell that he cares about her, and he's trying to do something special. That *is* cool, Kerry. You could learn a few things from him."

"Traitors!" Niall moans.

"Just ignore him, Tyler. He's always found it difficult to share – especially when it comes to attention. Of course I'll help you."

"Me, too," Skylar says, determined. "Besides, I like Ms. White. She seems nice."

I smile at my friend's mother and daughter.

"Well, what are we waiting for?" Mrs. Kerry claps her hands in excitement. "Let's get to work!"

"Tell me something about this Ms. White," Niall's mother says, nudging me gently with her shoulder.

We're in the kitchen: her, Skylar, and me. Niall is perched on a stool, drinking a beer and huffing every two minutes. I don't think he's particularly happy about me bursting into his house, and I don't think he likes the fact that his mother's attention is concentrated onto me. But Skylar seems interested: in making biscuits and in nosing around in my life.

"I don't know if I should. She's a pretty private person," I say, kindly. I don't want to be rude to Mrs. Kerry, but I also don't want to betray Ms. White's trust.

"Just tell us whatever you can," Skylar suggests, "and we'll make sure we keep it to ourselves. Apart from him, maybe," she says, nodding towards her father, who's mumbling something under his breath.

"She told me her entire life story," I start, making sure not to breathe a word about her father. "She's Canadian, and she's been a teacher for three years."

"Three years..." she comments. "She's pretty young, then."

"Yeah, she is. And she's on her own."

"Her own?" Skylar asks.

Skylar recently lost her mother, and now lives with her dad, Niall. She went through a tough time – especially before moving here – but she seems to be getting better, and everyone in town is here to support her.

"She lost her mother last year. She has no other family."

"I'm sorry, Tyler."

"Me, too."

"How come she's here?" Skylar asks.

"She's part of a teacher's exchange programme – just for three months."

"Three months?" Mrs. Kerry comments.

"Exactly. I don't have much time, and I still have so many things I want to show her, and tell her, and…" I sigh inadvertently. "She's leaving in just over a month." Mrs. Kerry rests her hand on my arm. "Her visa runs out soon." I look at her, and she smiles kindly.

"I'm sure you'll find a way to make it work."

"You think?"

"Absolutely. And, if there's any way I can help…"

"You've already done so much."

"They're just a few biscuits."

"To her, it means a lot more. It means a lot to me, too."

"Why has she never celebrated Christmas before?" Skylar asks.

"Her mother didn't really believe in traditions. To her it was all a marketing ploy, and…" I take a deep breath. "You should've seen the way she stared at the tree last night."

"Tree?" Niall suddenly wakes up.

"I took her to buy a Christmas tree. She chose a real one. She's never had one before."

"That was a really nice thing to do," Mrs. Kerry says.

I shrug. "It was nothing."

"You men don't understand shit."

"Skylar," Niall scolds. "What have we said about your fucking language?"

Skylar rolls her eyes as Mrs. Kerry shakes her head in exasperation.

"It was a pretty big gesture," she continues, turning back to me. "She's never had a real tree before, and then you come along, and you take her to get one. You're learning to bake biscuits for her..."

"I just did what felt right."

"But she's leaving."

"What are you trying to say?"

"I'm not trying to say anything. But what exactly are *you* trying to do?"

"I don't... I just want to..."

"Make her stay," Niall states. "You're trying to make her stay."

"I don't know what I'm trying to do. I just know what I *am* doing."

"And what's that?" Niall asks, encouraging.

"I'm just trying to make her happy."

"And that's an amazing thing, Tyler," Mrs.

Kerry says.

I don't know whether it's amazing, but I do know that it's the only thing I want.

54

Tyler

The day after, as soon as my shift is over, I turn up at her door with a paper bag filled with ingredients.

"Hey." She smiles, happy to see me. "I didn't hear you come home. I was in my room, and…"

I bend down to kiss her. Ms. White smiles against my lips.

"Hey, Ms. White." I almost hold my breath, trying to absorb the sweetness of her lips against mine.

"What's that?" she asks, nodding towards the paper bag.

"A surprise."

"For me?"

I nod, and she opens the door to let me in. As soon as I step inside, I realise that the lights are all switched off, apart from the lights on the Christmas tree. The melody of one of the century's most famous Christmas songs is wafting through the living room. I don't say anything – I get the impression she doesn't like it when I point things out to her, especially when things are new for her. So I just head into the kitchen and put the bag down on the counter.

"What's with all the mystery?" She raises an

eyebrow, studying me, curiously.

I pull the ingredients out of the bag and place them on the counter.

"Tonight, you're going to learn to make biscuits."

Ms. White's eyes widen in shock.

"You know how to make cookies?"

"No, I'm not quite that perfect," I joke, and she shakes her head. "But I learned."

"Learned… When?"

"Yesterday, while you were busy at the PTA meeting. I went to my friend Niall's house and asked his mum to teach me how to make biscuits. I would've asked my mum, but as soon as I need her, she decides to go wandering around the world, ignoring the fact that her sons are still here."

"You really did that?"

"Uh-huh," I say, distracted. When the last ingredient is laid out on the counter, I turn to look at her.

"Why?"

"It's all part of my plan."

"Your plan involves learning how to make Christmas cookies?"

My plan involves anything that will make you happy.

"Yes."

She's not satisfied with my simple response.

Seeing as I'm already totally fucked, and she can see it, too, it makes no sense to pretend. Best to just act like the dickhead I am, right?

"The other day, you said you didn't know how to make biscuits, and that I like biscuits, so you were worried that I'd go looking for other biscuits elsewhere."

Her face grows serious.

"I don't want to eat any other biscuits." My voice drops, my breathing heavy. "I just want to eat yours."

"We're still talking about cookies, right?"

"I'm not so sure anymore," I say, "but I swear that was originally my intention."

She smiles weakly.

"You really care that much about cookies?"

About you. I care about you.

"Would you be happy if I only ate your biscuits?"

"We *are* still talking about cookies, right?"

I swallow nervously.

"Not really."

"You can eat any cookies you want, Tyler. So why do you particularly want these cookies?"

"Because I know they're the best biscuits in the world."

"You don't mean that."

"Trust me. I'm a fireman – who doesn't trust a

fireman?"

She smiles, but she still seems nervous.

"I only want these biscuits. I want to eat so many of them that I feel sick, and then..."

"And then?" she asks, anxious.

"I want to eat some more."

Ms. White's lips part and I bend down to make them mine. I slide my hands down her face, my mouth covering hers, ending the conversation.

I don't want any other biscuits, Ms. White. And it terrifies me, this thought – but it also makes me excited. I've never wanted something so much it makes me breathless at the mere thought of it.

"Can we stop talking about biscuits for a moment and say what we're really thinking? I'm getting confused," I say onto her lips, making her smile.

"I thought you came here to teach me something."

I feel a stirring below my waistband at the thought of all the things I could teach my dear Ms. White in just one night – let alone in an entire lifetime.

I slide my hands along her shoulders and down her arms, moving them onto her backside; I squeeze, and feel Ms. White shiver in my arms, resting her hand against my chest.

"Ms. White..." Her name makes me hungry, I could eat those biscuits until I explode.

"T-Tyler…"

"I'm trying not to skip about twenty steps of this plan I have in mind for you, but you're making it difficult."

"M-me?" she asks, almost shocked.

I lift her up and she wraps her arms around my neck.

"You're making everything really hard."

She trembles in my arms, and all my blood seems to rush to one particular point.

"And, yes, Ms. White. I'm talking about the thing you can feel between my legs."

Her face flushes violently, setting my body alight. I sit her down on the counter and push myself against her, proving to her just how hard we're talking. I want to show her the way she makes me feel.

Her hands roam nervously across my back, her enormous eyes staring into mine.

"Just one word, Ms. White, and I'm all yours."

She bites her lip, and I press my own against her neck.

"One word, Ms. White," I repeat, moving my hot lips across her skin. I reach her ear, whispering: "Say the word, Ms. White." My hands are splayed onto her thighs, sliding up towards her backside and pulling her into me; a nervous squeal escapes her, making me laugh. Ms. White wraps her legs around my waist and I press my poor, neglected downstairs neighbour against her.

"Ms. White." I'm almost pleading, my hands wrapping around her waist, sliding under her hoodie. Her skin is smooth, soft under my fingers, burning in anticipation, just as I'm burning up with desire at the thought of her. I reach her breasts, my fingertips lightly brushing against her hard nipples.

"Oh, fuck..." I breathe onto her mouth, before biting down impatiently. "Fuck, Ms. White..." I trace her nipples with my fingertips as she sighs into my neck. "Look at how your body reacts to mine." She gasps as I pinch them between my fingers. "Do you have any idea what you're doing to me?"

"N-no..." Her voice is strained.

"Oh, really?" I press my erection between her parted legs, and she plants her hands nervously onto my shoulders. "Do you want to touch me, Ms. White?" Her fingers tighten their grip on me. "I really want you to touch me. I want you to wrap your slim, sexy fingers around me."

She trembles against my body, and my erection seems to almost burst out of my trousers.

I press my thumbs against her nipples, my mouth roaming in search of hers. My tongue slides slowly into her, as her hands leave my shoulders and make their way down my chest and over my abs, before stopping at the waistband of my jeans.

"Do you want to touch me, Ms. White?" I ask,

breathless.

"Y-yes. I want…" Her fingers undo the first button. "…To touch you." She undoes the second button, then the third. By the time she reaches the fourth, I'm struggling to breathe.

"M-Ms. White…" I beg, shamelessly.

Her hand slips anxiously into my trousers, stroking me through the fabric of my boxers.

"Yes…" I moan, desperate. "Oh God, yes."

Her movements grow more confident, her hand trailing up to my waist and slipping against my skin. When her fingers touch me for the first time, I almost collapse into her. She slides her hand along the length of me, slowly, painfully, sensually, as I press excitedly against her nipples, longing to dive into her.

"Do you see what you're doing to me, Ms. White? If you keep going, I'll come right here."

Ms. White trembles again, as if the mere thought of turning me on like that is turning her on even more.

"Do you like it, Ms. White? Do you like touching me?"

She nods against my shoulder.

"Look at me, Ms. White." She lifts her head and looks at me. There's desire in her eyes: the same desire that's pulsing from her fingertips. "Tell me that you like what you're doing to me."

She nods, biting her lip.

"What about what I'm doing to you?" I press harder against her nipples, making her part her lips.

I smile, satisfied, and slip my hands away; before Ms. White can worry about what's happening, I grab the hem of her hoodie, stopping her hand from moving, and pull it over her head. Ms. White lifts her arms to help me, and I throw it onto the floor, her firm breasts and pert nipples calling me.

Ms. White studies me, waiting for my next move.

"What do you say we skip a few steps?"

A glimmer of desire flickers between us – but I can't go on unless I hear her say it.

"Do you want to take the next step with me, Ms. White?"

"I want to do everything with you."

55

Holly

His eyes roam sensually from my mouth to my chest.

"Ms. White, Ms. White, Ms. White..." his deep, dark voice only increases the heat pulsing from between my legs. "You should never say something like that to a man. You have no idea what it could do to him."

"I didn't say it to just *any* man."

His eyes cloud over; I can see his pupils beginning to dilate, melding with his irises.

"I said it to you."

His grip tightens around my thigh, his erection pressing against my leg.

"I only want to say it to you."

It took every ounce of courage I had, and all the breath in my lungs, to say that.

"You shouldn't say things that..." He shakes his head, apparently unsure as to whether to believe me and let himself go, or to take a step back and let *me* go.

I reach my hands out to his hoodie, grabbing the bottom, and pulling it up over his body, letting my fingers trail against his hot skin. Tyler pulls away from me, to let me remove it, before letting it drop to the floor. Trembling, I move my hands back to his skin; that one touch wasn't enough. I want to feel him under my palms. I want to touch this man, and I want him to touch me.

"Ms. White." His voice makes my hands and knees shiver.

I bite my lip nervously, as my fingertips trace the outline of his abs. Tyler follows their trail with his eyes, his lips parted and his breath growing heavy. He lifts his gaze to meet mine, his hands stroking my face, before his full, hungry mouth presses against me. He plunges his tongue into me, taking my breath away; his warm, hard body is pressing against my chest; his erection is brushing between my legs. I grab onto his wrists as Tyler drowns me in kisses, in stolen breaths; in strength, in safety, in desire.

"Tyler," I moan onto his mouth. He slides down my neck, his teeth nibbling gently at my skin. His hands are massaging my breasts, my fingers woven into his hair. "Tyler..." I'm begging him, now. His warm mouth trails along my collarbone, before he bends down, taking my breasts in his hands and pressing them against his face. I wrap my legs instinctively around his waist and push my hips towards him: I need this contact. I want to feel everything his body is promising mine. He closes his lips around one of my nipples, and I arch my back towards him, resting my hands against the counter to hold my weight. Tyler moves from one breast to the other, restlessly, madly. He torments me, tugging at my nipples with his lips, before sucking at them mercilessly. I close my eyes, trying to control the waves of pleasure.

"Don't do it, Ms. White," he says, as if he could read the thoughts radiating from my body. "Don't hold back." His mouth brushes against the sensitive skin of my nipple. "Let yourself go."

He grabs onto my backside and lifts me up. I hold onto him and let him carry me over to the couch; he lowers us onto the cushions, our bodies still intertwined, before laying me down and studying me.

"Do you want me to touch you, Ms. White?"

I feel my neck and cheeks burst into flames. He smiles when he sees my reaction.

"I want to. So much…" One of his hands trails slowly down my side. I can feel each of his fingers burning a hole through my skin, as he wanders down to the waistband of my pants. "I want to touch you," he says, his hand moving to stroke between my legs, through the fabric. I arch myself against him uncontrollably. "Oh, yes, Ms. White."

My heart is hammering so hard I can hear it thumping in my ears; it's so loud that I almost can't hear his voice.

He presses his hand harder between my legs, and I part them instinctively. I need him to do this: to touch me. I need him to want me like no one has ever wanted me before.

"Do you want to show me how wet you are,

Ms. White?" His words course across my skin. I feel as though I could catch fire.

I nod, breathless.

Tyler moves to one side, his hand slipping between my legs, beneath my underpants. His fingers move slowly against me, and I can't help but let out a moan, biting down hard on my lip.

"No, Ms. White. Don't do it. I told you: I want to know whether you like what I'm doing to you."

I nod again, and he smiles a little.

"It's all part of the plan, Ms. White."

"I-I like it."

"What?"

"Your hand."

His fingers press gently into me.

"Oh, God..." I moan.

I feel him pressing harder, this time with just one finger, until he slips slowly inside me. I grab onto his arm.

"It's okay?" he says, bending down to kiss me.

I nod again, as he pushes his mouth against mine, his tongue sliding gently between my lips, making them part. I open them for him, and Tyler slides his tongue into my mouth at the exact moment I feel him push his fingers deeper inside me. I moan onto his lips, my fingers clawing at his arm. His breath fills my throat.

He moves inside me, penetrating me slowly, as his palm starts to brush against the most sensitive part of me.

"Do you want to come like this, Ms. White?" His lips brush gently against mine.

I nod, and he smiles, satisfied.

"And do you want to touch me, while I...?" I feel another finger slide inside me, and curl my body in pleasure. "Like that... God, like that..." he breathes onto my lips. "Is this turning you on, Ms. White?"

I don't know whether I'm more excited by his fingers, the fact that his body is pressed against mine, or the things he's saying to me – and the way he's saying them. Maybe it's the fact that he's so confident in what he's doing, the devastating effect he has on me and my body, on my mind.

"Yes," I pant.

"Do you want to come in my hand, Ms. White?"

Adrenaline, excitement, desire, and the uncontrollable longing to make this man mine makes me let go of everything.

"Only if you come, too."

His eyes light up, like headlights in the fog.

"You want to..."

"Touch you," I tell him – because I want to touch him so much it could kill me. I want to feel him again; I want to stroke his soft skin. I want Tyler to feel everything I'm feeling right now.

I reach down between his legs and slip my hand

into his boxers, squeezing it tightly between my fingers. Tyler lets out an excited moan, which only sparks a flame inside me.

I move my hand up and down the length of him; Tyler watches for a few seconds, euphoric, before turning his gaze to meet mine, pressing his mouth against mine. His tongue dances around mine, his fingers sliding relentlessly in and out of my body. I keep moving my hand, waiting for him to crumble at my touch.

"You'll kill me like this, Ms. White," he breathes onto my lips.

"You'll kill me first," I tell him, before a long-awaited heat starts to seep through my body. A few seconds later, I find myself trembling beneath him, allowing my body to just let go, my mind to wander with it.

"Fuck, yes," Tyler groans, his mouth covering mine as he echoes the movements of my hand.

"Ms. White. Fuck, Ms. White…" His voice fades into a strained moan, his breathing stopping for a few seconds.

We lay there, frozen on top of each other, our hands still resting on each other.

"I'd say we've skipped about ten steps, here."

I laugh, and he looks at me, his lips brushing gently against my nose.

"You'll be my downfall, Ms. White."

No, Ty. I won't be your downfall.

I've never wanted anyone before you, and now

I'm afraid that I won't want anyone else after you.
And that's the true downfall.
And it's all mine.

56
Tyler

"We've made a mess, here," I say to my wonderful Ms. White, who's smiling a little awkwardly.

I'm still half lying on top of her. The view from here is incredible, and I wish I never had to move from this sofa.

"That was so... Impulsive," she says.

"I wouldn't quite put it like that. I knew exactly what I wanted, and..." I study her, hoping to find the answer I'm looking for in her eyes. "And I want to do so much more."

Ms. White bites her lip.

"Not right now," I say, smiling. "But I'd like to."

"I'd like to, too."

Her answer provokes and immediate reaction in my quiet downstairs neighbour. I move myself away from her and get slowly to my feet, so that she can get up; I don't want her to think that I want to skip all the other steps in one giant leap.

"Maybe it's best if I help you clean up."

She sits up. Her embarrassment is palpable, her expression and her gestures suddenly awkward. She covers her chest with her arms, as if I hadn't already imprinted the sight of her into my memory. I get up from the sofa and pad into the kitchen in search of her hoodie, scooping it up from the floor and heading back into the living room, handing it to her. I don't want her to feel like this. I wish she didn't feel so ashamed, after what we've done – but some things take time.

"Thanks." She takes it from me and quickly tugs it over her head, getting to her feet.

The proof of what we've done is all over her clothes, and mine.

"Maybe I should go and get changed."

"Maybe I should do the same."

"At least the sofa's clean."

She turns to check that I'm right, then turns her gaze back to me.

"I didn't plan for this, I swear. I really did come here to make biscuits."

"I like being spontaneous."

"Me, too – it's always more fun. But I do still want to teach you how to make biscuits."

"And I want to learn."

"We could order something to eat, before we get started. It's almost dinner time. If you want to, of course…"

"I want to. Of course I want to."

I take a deep breath and try to control myself.

"Okay, then I'll be back in a minute. Don't go anywhere."

"I'll be right here."

* * * * *

I go back to her in minutes – just enough time to quickly get changed and grab the takeaway leaflets from my apartment.

"Fish and chips?"

"Why not?"

I hand the leaflets to her and she starts to scan it as I make myself at home in her apartment. She's changed, too, and tied her hair back. The bare skin of her neck calls me, like the final drop of alcohol before you start to lose your senses. I move closer to her and rest my hands on her hips, before bending down and pressing my lips gently against her neck. Ms. White shivers, before turning her head to me.

"I can't help myself. Now that I know how you taste, now that... Now that I've felt you come..." She trembles under my touch, and my downstairs neighbour starts to knock at the door. "What the fuck do I do, now?"

"W-what do you mean?" she asks, concerned.

"How the hell can I stop myself from thinking about you every second of every fucking day?"

Ms. White lets out a nervous laugh and turns her body around to face me, my hands still planted on her hips.

"Did you really like it?" she asks, her laughter eclipsed now; her face is telling me something else, and I'm not sure I like it.

"Do you really think I wouldn't? I thought you saw what happened, there," I say, nodding towards the sofa behind us.

I came in her hand like a teenager. I came almost at the mere thought of her slim fingers wrapped around my cock – the memory of it almost makes me come again, this time without a single touch. It's familiar – like riding a bike.

"To be honest, I have no idea what happened there, on the counter," she says, her voice dropping, as if she were ashamed to even say it out loud.

"I do know what happened. It's engraved into my memory, and I'll never be able to forget it. Just thinking about it again..." I sigh, stroking her face with the back of my hand. "Thinking about sliding my fingers into you..." I feel the heat of her cheeks through my knuckles. "I can't wait to do it again."

"M-me neither."

"And I can't wait to do everything to you that my very vivid imagination has been conjuring up over the past few weeks."

The nervous laughter is back, accompanied by a glimmer in her eyes. Dear Ms. White: I've only just started with you, and I have no intention of stopping, now. To be honest, I'm scared that I'll never be able to stop – but I'll cross that bridge when I come to it. Now, my only concern is to make you trust me, to make you feel comfortable with me.

"Are you hungry?" I ask her, suddenly. I'm hoping that, with a little food in her stomach, and some alcohol in her system, she might start to feel a little more relaxed.

She nods.

"Have you chosen what you want from the menu?"

"Not yet."

"Why don't you take a look while I start to get everything ready for these biscuits? We just about have time to make the dough before dinner gets here. Then we can eat, and then we can cut the biscuits and get them in the oven."

"That sounds like a good plan."

It is, Ms. White. The best plan.

And soon, you'll realise that, too.

* * * * *

Ms. White kneads the dough with her small, sexy hands. I know I shouldn't be thinking about her hands right now – we're trying to make biscuits, for fuck's sake – but the thought of those fingers on me, the feeling of their touch against my skin, is so fresh, so exciting. I can't help but stare at them, waiting to feel them again, back where they belong, the way I like.

"Is this okay?" she asks, staring at me, tearing me from my beautiful fantasy.

"It's perfect. Make sure all the ingredients are mixed in well."

"I think there are still some lumps of butter."

"Where?" I step closer and stand behind her, my hands sliding down her arms, moving to cover her fingers. "Show me what you're doing," I say, moving my hands with hers. We're kneading the cookie dough, slowly and sensually; I'll eat every fucking crumb of these biscuits. I won't let anyone else lay their hands – or their teeth – on anything that belongs to Ms. White.

I push my body gently against hers, my erection pushing against her arse.

"Why do I get the feeling you're not concentrating on the cookies?"

"Because your arse is pressing against my dick, and I can't concentrate on anything else right now."

She turns around suddenly to face me, her jaw hanging open and her eyes wide.

"It's true."

"Maybe it's actually your dick that's pressing against my butt," she says, cheekily. You can probably guess the effect it had on me, to hear the words *dick* and *butt* in the same sentence.

"That might be true, but it's still your fault."

"My fault? I never asked you to push yourself against me."

"Push myself against you? At most I'm just leaning. It's not my fault it's huge."

"H-huge?"

"I thought you'd noticed…?"

She blushes again, and I can't stifle a laugh.

"I guess touching and *feeling* aren't really the same thing…"

"Can we go back to the cookies, now?"

"Would it make you feel better to talk about biscuits?"

She turns around, hiding from my gaze.

"I don't think anything could make me feel better."

I plant my hands gently on her shoulders and spin her around to face me again.

"I'm not good at talking about these things."

"About biscuits?"

She glares at me, and I stop being a dickhead – or, at least, I try.

"Do you know what I think, Holly? I think you're too busy thinking about the things you don't think you're good at. You're missing out on all the fun."

She tilts her head as she listens to me, just as she always does: her eyes are narrowed, her lips slightly parted, as if she could find everything she needs within my words.

"Having sex is… Fuck, having sex is the best. But talking about sex is pretty good, too."

"And you seem to like it a lot."

"What? Sex? Who doesn't?!"

"I mean *talking* about sex. You do it all the time. But I guess, if you like talking about it so much…"

"But you don't like it."

She shrugs. "I've never really spoken about it. Not so openly. As for doing it…" She bites her lip nervously. "I'm not sure whether I like it."

"How can you say that?"

"I'm not cut out for it."

"Have you seen what you do to me? How the hell can you say you're not cut out for it?"

"It's you," she says, shy.

"I'm pretty sure there were two of us."

"You bring out a side to me that… I never thought I could be like that."

"This is nothing, Ms. White. We're only just getting started."

She smiles, more relaxed now.

"You shouldn't be scared to talk to me. Even if it's to tell me that you thought I'd be bigger, I won't be upset. I swear."

She bursts out laughing, bringing a hand to her mouth.

"I'm being serious, Ms. White. I can handle anything. Except one thing."

"What?"

Watching you leave.

"I can't handle the fact that you don't think you're capable of something like this – the idea that you don't think you're someone a man would want."

"I'm not interested in other men. I'm only interested in the man in front of me. And I want... I want to be the woman he wants."

And you are, Ms. White. Fuck, you really are. You're the first woman I've ever wanted, and the first who has ever brought me to my knees – and not just in the way Niall suggested. You are that woman: the one who could melt even the iciest of hearts. You've melted mine.

"I'm happy to hear it, Ms. White. Because I don't tend to go around beating people up – I'm a fireman, you know. We have a code of conduct to follow."

"And what does this code of conduct entail, exactly?"

"A load of boring stuff."

She laughs, shaking her head.

"And you are that woman, Holly. You're the woman that this fireman wants."

"Really?"

"Without a shadow of a doubt."

"Does that mean you'll only be eating my cookies this Christmas?"

Always, Ms. White. I'll only ever eat your

biscuits.

"I swear."

57
Holly

The cookies weren't so bad, in the end. Not bad for a first attempt, anyway. The decorating was the hardest part, but Tyler had brought a few tubes of ready-made icing. He told me that Niall's mother had said it was cheating, but that it was our little secret.

I can't believe he really showed up here to teach me how to make cookies – that he learned himself only so that he could teach me. No one has ever done something so sweet for me, and no one has ever... Well, turned me on like that. What happened on my couch stayed with me all night – I couldn't even close my eyes without feeling his hands all over me, his kisses, his words. This morning, I woke up still bleary-eyed from the lack of sleep, but my body was electric, as if it were just waiting to touch him again. I gulped down a coffee and ate a few cookies for breakfast, before putting some into a Tupperware tub and packing them into my purse. I didn't know why I'd done that until, after school, I found myself standing at the door of Linda's.

Angus is inside, chatting to a few customers at their table. I take a deep breath and push the door. He notices me right away.

"Holly!" he smiles. "What brings you here?"

I head over to the counter and he steps over to me. "I was on my way back from work and I thought I'd stop in for a hot chocolate."

"Good idea. Take a seat and I'll grab it for you."

I sit at one of the stools as Angus gets to work behind the counter.

"Do you want whipped cream?"

"Yes, please."

He places a mug beneath my nose, almost fill to the brim.

"I've never been a huge fan of chocolate." I take the mug between my hands and inhale the scent. "If I keep going, I'll need to book two seats for the plane back home."

"Home?" he asks, curious.

I place the mug back on the counter. "I only have a three-month visa. I don't have much time left."

"Do you miss it? Home?"

"I miss it less and less every day."

"What do you mean?"

"I have nothing waiting for me there, Angus."

"You don't have a boyfriend over there?"

I lower my gaze, trying to hide my embarrassment.

"Looks more like you've found someone over here."

"I don't know what I've found, to be honest."

As I say it, I realise that I'm not just talking about Tyler. "I just know that I like it, and I'll miss it when I'm gone."

"So you like it here?"

"I like the city, the people, my job, my colleagues, my friends. I feel... At home," I say, holding my breath.

Angus nods, smiling.

"I wish I had more time here."

"Is there no way you could stay?"

I shake my head. "I was only allowed a three-month visa. I'm not a European citizen, so I can't just come and go as I please. The rules are clear, and I have nothing to offer them that could gain me a longer visa. My contract at the school is only three months long."

"You can always come back."

"I need to spend at least six months back home before I can set foot in Ireland again. And then, when I come back, it can only be for three months."

"I wish there was some way I could help you."

I smile at him, fighting the urge to blurt out the truth about why I chose to come here; about my life, about my fear of being rejected yet again.

"It's okay. Besides, I'm not even sure that there's anything here for me."

"Are you talking about the fireman?"

I don't look at him; I'm scared I won't be able

to lie to him now that I've laid all my cards out on the table. Now that I've realised that I want something I never even knew existed.

"He's not the best, that Hayes, but I don't think he's a bad guy."

"No, he's not."

"And, maybe, with the right person..."

I smile, embarrassed.

"He likes you."

"W-what?"

"You can tell."

That evening, those cookies, his kisses, his promises: they all make me think Angus is right. But I needed to hear someone say it. I needed Angus to reassure me about Tyler.

"Take it from someone who's seen a few things over the years, and who..." He sighs: a sigh filled with nostalgia and pain. "Who's felt those things, too."

I can't tell him what happened between us, so I just thank him with my eyes, before taking a deep breath and rummaging around in my purse, grabbing the plastic tub and anxiously placing it on the counter. Angus lifts his eyes.

"They're the first batch I've ever made," I say right away. "But they're not too bad. I've already tried them."

"Christmas cookies?"

"Uh-huh. I only learned how to bake them

recently." I clear my throat. "Tyler taught me."

"Really? Our town fireman..."

"He's helping me celebrate my first proper Christmas, and he's teaching me... Lots of other things."

"That sounds like a good thing, right?"

"It is."

"In that case..." He takes the tub and opens it, before grabbing a cookie shaped like a reindeer and biting into it. chewing enthusiastically. "Wow, not bad for your first try!"

I'm overcome by a sudden longing to burst into tears, but I manage to keep it together.

"Thank you so much for bringing me your first batch of biscuits, Holly. I'm flattered."

"It was my pleasure."

He closes the tub and hugs it to his chest, my heart skipping so many beats that I could almost collapse to the floor.

"You have no idea how much this means to me."

I don't say anything. I hide behind my mug of hot chocolate, in the hope of swallowing the bitterness which is climbing up my throat.

Someone calls Angus over from one of the tables, and he excuses himself, leaving me alone for a few minutes to pull myself together. I manage to control my excitement, but not the anger which follows just a few moments later, at the thought that someone had deprived me of this feeling for all those years, out of sheer selfishness.

* * * * *

As soon as I get to my front door, the one next to it flies open.

"Hey, I was starting to get worried."

"I stopped off for a while on the way home."

He studies me curiously, but I don't really want to talk about it right now.

"I need to…" I say, nodding towards my door.

"Sure," he says, taking a step back. "Whatever you need."

"I just need a minute."

"Has something happened?"

"Maybe I'll see you later?"

"You know where to find me."

He attempts a smile, but I can sense the disappointment in his eyes.

I can't deal with this now, too. So I slip my key into the lock and open my front door, barricading myself into my apartment with the intention of being on my own for the rest of the evening – and probably the rest of the night, too.

58
Tyler

"You're not listening to me, Niall."

"Sorry. I thought we were here for training."

"I thought changing room chat was obligatory."

"That's what you think. I have to come up with a way for us to win the next match, or they'll start looking for a new coach."

"Who?"

"Have you seen these kids' parents, Tyler?"

I shrug indifferently.

"They're..." He looks around, making sure no one can hear us. "They're fucking deranged."

I laugh, in spite of everything. Thank God Niall is here to distract me from my own emotional drama – if I can even call it that. Oh, God. Do I really have emotional drama? Is this what old age is doing to me?

"Let's get back to your problem," Niall says, nervously chewing on a piece of liquorice. "So she basically told you to piss off?"

"She didn't say anything like that. Ms. White would never say that. She was weird, okay? Something was bothering her."

"And you just left her there?"

"What was I supposed to do? She asked me for

some space."

"Ouch."

"Ouch what?"

"Mate, if she's asking you for space..."

"Since when did you become an expert in these things?"

"Since when did you start asking for my shitty advice? Isn't that supposed to be one of your special skills?"

"Do you really want to talk about that now?"

"I was just curious."

I roll my eyes, losing patience.

"Okay, okay. Let's ignore your skills for a moment."

"That would be great."

"You said she was acting weird?"

"Yeah."

"Weird how?"

"Distant. Sad."

"Mmm..."

"What?"

"She's avoiding you, mate."

"Is that all you've got to say?"

"The signs are pretty clear."

"What signs? I didn't see any signs."

"Did she close the door in your face?"

I think about this for a moment, and Niall takes

my silence as a response.

"You see?"

"No, I don't see anything. And she didn't slam the door in my face. Ms. White isn't like that."

"Then what is she like?"

"What do you mean?"

"I don't know, I've only met her a few times. I have no idea what she's like."

"And you shouldn't get any ideas."

"You're such a caveman."

"Me? A caveman?"

"I hardly recognise you anymore. What have you done with my best friend?"

He's fucked. Like you. Like everyone.

It happens to the best of us.

"I don't know what you're talking about."

"I do."

"The only thing I know is that you're not helping."

"Then why do you keep talking to me about these things?"

"Because the team is boring."

"Boring?"

"They're so predictable. And they're... Well, they're losers."

"Hey! They're your team, too, in a way."

"Speaking of losers," I say, catching the ball from him. "I think you should play Carter on

Sunday."

Niall studies me, suspiciously.

"What? He's not so bad."

"You think?"

"You're the one who put him on the team!"

"Just so that I could keep an eye on him."

"And what better way to do that than to use him out on the field?"

"I don't think it works like that."

"Try it. Just once. Sunday. What's the worst that could happen?"

"We could lose, and I could be hounded by angry parents in the car park?"

"I'll have your back."

"What's with the sudden interest in Carter?"

"You know I have a weakness for losers. I mean, I am *your* best friend, right?"

* * * * *

When I get home after training, something happens that I never expected: Ms. White is sitting on the stairs leading up to our apartments. It's as if she were waiting for someone. Waiting for me.

I climb the stairs slowly and stop at the penultimate step. I drop my bag onto the floor and sink down, right in front of her, waiting for her to tell me what's wrong.

"I have to tell you something."

I don't like her tone at all, let alone the words she's used. It's a classic sign that something terrible is about to happen.

"Get to the point, Ms. White. No mercy."

She sighs and lifts her sad eyes to meet mine.

"I gave away the cookies."

I furrow my brow in confusion.

"I don't get it."

"You said they were for you, but I gave them away."

Is she serious?

"I'm sorry."

"When I said they were for me, I didn't mean that no one else could touch them."

"Didn't you say that no one else could lay their hands or their teeth on them?"

I was talking about *you*, Ms. White. But I'll tell you that another time. First, let's clear this whole thing up.

"Is that why you're so sad?"

She shrugs.

"Who did you give them to?"

"Angus."

I smile and rest a hand on her thigh.

"That was really nice of you."

"You think?"

"I'm sure he loved them."

She doesn't look convinced, and doesn't look any less sad.

"What's really wrong, Holly?"

"We chatted a little – about me, about home. About what's going to happen when my visa runs out."

My hand tightens its grip on her thigh a little, instinctively.

"I still haven't told him who I am, yet. And I only have twenty-eight days left."

"Twenty-eight?" Tension leaps into my voice.

She nods, avoiding my gaze.

"I'm scared that even a hundred days wouldn't be enough. And I'm scared that…"

"That…?"

"That coming here was a huge mistake."

I can't help but feel hurt by her words – but I keep this to myself.

"You want to go home, don't you?"

Her huge, bright eyes land on me.

"I don't want to."

My heart starts to hammer in my chest.

"You don't want to what?"

"G-go back."

"I thought you were about to say that you wished you'd never met me, Ms. White. I almost had a heart attack – and I'm not even forty yet. Do you realise what a waste that would be, for humanity? If I died of a heart attack before my fortieth birthday?"

Luckily, she laughs.

"What do you say we head inside and order something to eat? You can tell me about your day, about Angus, about the things you're scared of, and the things you wish you weren't scared of."

"Don't you have plans this evening?"

"I have you."

And hopefully not just for this evening.

"Please, can we not order pizza or fish and chips? I can feel my arse growing bigger with every bite." We get up, and I take a quick glance at the arse in question.

"To me, it looks exactly the same as when you first arrived. If you want, I can check by hand?"

She laughs as she opens the door, and I walk up behind her, squeezing her backside.

"Perfect. Just as I remembered."

Ms. White turns, her expression calm.

"If anything's perfect here, it's you."

"You're right. But I'd be happy to share my status with your arse."

"My arse would be honoured."

"I love it when you say *arse*, Ms. White."

She leads me into her apartment, where I happily notice that the Christmas lights are already on.

"Can I ask you something, Holly?"

She turns to face me.

"Why were you waiting for me on the stairs?"

"I knocked at your door to apologise for being so rude to you, but you weren't in. I didn't want to go back to my apartment on my own, and I didn't know what else to do – so I just sat and waited."

"What if I'd come back late? Or tomorrow, even?"

"You'd have found me, sitting there, frozen to death. And you'd have felt guilty for the rest of your life."

I move closer to her and grab her waist, pulling her towards me.

"There's a spare key under the doormat."

"A key?"

"For emergencies."

"It wasn't an emergency. It was just a stupid feeling."

"You should never ignore feelings – especially not when they seem stupid. If you ever feel like that again, and I'm not here, then please use the key."

"Thanks, Ty."

"At your service."

59

Holly

The day before the end-of-term fair, which includes our Christmas show, Tyler is in my apartment. He's here pretty much every evening he isn't working, helping me make cookies for the bake sale. I felt uncomfortable not offering to bake anything – all the other teachers are taking part. Wes said that he'd make some of his special mince pies, and I didn't want to be the only one standing there, twiddling my thumbs. I'd be eating, of course – since I got here, I can't seem to do anything but eat. Yesterday I struggled a little to pull up the zip on my dress; I had to hold my breath all day.

"Done," Tyler says, closing the oven door and placing the mitt on the counter. "I'd say that's probably enough."

"You think?" I look around: the kitchen counters are covered in trays of cookies, waiting to be decorated. "I've never been to anything like this before. I have no idea how many people there'll be."

"Trust me," he says, his hands resting on my hips. "We have enough to last until next year, too."

"How do you know?"

"I've been going to fairs like this since I was

born, Holly."

"Does that mean you're coming, too?"

"Of course I'm coming. You're forgetting that my nieces are in your class."

"I hadn't forgotten, I just thought that... Well, that..."

"That I didn't care about the girls' education?"

I glare at him and he laughs.

"My brother has forced me into going."

"That I can believe."

"And, besides..." He pulls me into him. "I'm kind of having an affair with my nieces' teacher."

"An affair?"

"I like that word on your lips, Ms. White." He bends down to press his mouth against mine. "It sounds sweet but dirty at the same time."

"How can it be sweet *and* dirty?"

"You make it happen."

"I never thought I could be dirty."

He laughs, taking my face between his hands. "The things I think about you? They're dirty."

"You have dirty thoughts about me? When?"

He considers this for a moment. "Pretty much every three minutes. Day and night, there's no distinction. Lately, I seem to be wandering around with an uncomfortable stirring between my legs. And let's not even mention what happens at night."

"What h-happens?" I ask, nervous.

"Do you really want to know?"

I nod.

"I normally have to take care of it myself."

"You mean... Oh, my God!" I cover my face with my hands, my cheeks aflame.

"And I have to imagine..." He slides his lips down my neck. "I have to fantasise..." His warm, wet mouth is on my skin. "And hope..."

"H-hope?"

He trails back up my skin, stopping when he reaches my ear.

"Hope that, one day, you'll want to join me, and make my nights less lonely."

I shiver at his touch, at his words, as his hands slide down my back. He squeezes my backside in his enormous hands, before pressing me seamlessly against his body; against his erection.

"And then?" I ask, instinctively.

"Then... what?"

"Once I've joined you for a night, or two?"

He pulls away from me a little, his eyes searching within mine.

"What is going on in that beautiful mind of yours, Ms. White?"

"Forget it," I say, disentangling myself from his embrace and taking a step back. "It's stupid."

"Do you really think that after I've slept with you, I wouldn't be interested anymore?"

"It doesn't matter anyway, right? I'm leaving in... How long?" I say, vaguely, pretending to work it out – as if I weren't already counting the seconds I have left before I have to leave him behind. Leave all this behind.

"Can I ask you something?"

I look at him and nod.

"Do you want to stay?"

"It doesn't matter what I want." I tear my gaze away, but Tyler places two fingers under my chin, bringing me back to him.

"The only thing that matters to me is what you want."

"What about you?" I ask, nervous.

"Are you asking me what I want?"

"Yes," I say. I'm scared: of what *I* want, and of what his answer could do to me.

"If I told you, would you believe me?"

"You've already said you never lie."

He smiles, nodding. "It's true."

"I just want to know what we're doing, here."

"We're making biscuits for the school fair."

"Tyler..."

"We're doing what we want to do. Or, at least, I am. More or less. What I actually want is to delve between your legs – but I think you know that by now."

"Is that why you're here?"

"Do you really think I used biscuits as an excuse to get you into bed?"

His honesty floors me; I don't know how to handle it, and, to be honest, I don't know why I started this conversation. I don't want to know what he really wants from me. I just want him to stay for as long as I can stay, too.

"You tell me."

"The fact that I want to get you into bed is irrelevant, Ms. White. I think I've wanted that since I saw you in that towel, all wet and sexy, with that knife in your hand, ready to slice my balls off my body."

I can't help but smile at the memory.

"And I'd have let you, trust me."

I roll my eyes, and Tyler takes my hand, bringing my gaze back to his.

"But I want more."

"More?"

"Everything you can give me, for as long as you can give it to me."

"Why? Why me?"

"Because you're sweet, which means you're perfect for someone with a dirty mind like me."

We both laugh, but Tyler grows suddenly serious, and I find myself staring at his lips, hanging from his next word. I'm scared he's going to tell me exactly what I'm afraid of.

"Because I want you all for myself, Ms. White.

That's the truth. I want to do all the things I've never done with you, and I want you to do everything you've never done with me. I want it to be the first time for us both. And we get to decide what those first times are."

"That sounds like a perfect plan."

"Of course it is. It's mine. What were you expecting?"

"Perfection?"

He bends down to kiss me, and sighs.

"I think the two of us, together, are pretty close to perfection."

"But there's always room for improvement, right?"

"Absolutely, Ms. White. And I'm here to find perfection with you."

60
Holly

The day of the Christmas fair, someone knocks at the door while I'm in the shower. I turn off the water and quickly wrap a towel around my body, heading over to the door. I open it, sticking my nose out, before realising that no one is there. I see a note attached to the door and grab it, closing the door behind me, as I head back into the bathroom to read.

I'll give you a lift into school this morning. I want to make sure that your biscuits - and your arse - make it there safe and sound.

I laugh, stopping in front of the sink.

Speaking of your arse...

I can't stop thinking about how good my hands look, wrapped around it.

I blush violently, although no one can see me.

About last night...

I'm serious, Holly. Together, we're perfection.

I hug the note to my chest and enjoy this moment, his words seeping into the most intimate parts of my body, just as he intended. I glance at my reflection in the mirror and see, in that look, that smile, something I've never seen before; it's something I want. Something I know I don't want to give up.

*****

When I open the front door, laden with Tupperware tubs, I find Tyler there, waiting for me outside. He plants a kiss on my lips before taking the containers from my hands.

"Give them to me."

I let him take the fruits of our labour as I close the front door. Tyler stands there, behind me, his eyes all over my body. I feel as if I'm being undressed, without even being touched. I turn towards him, and he doesn't even bother to pretend that he wasn't staring at me with his X-ray vision.

"That colour looks good on you."

I look down at my red coat.

"I thought it was appropriate."

He smiles. "You're right. But I think what's underneath is even more appropriate."

He looks at me again. I'm wearing a green dress which hangs to my knees.

"I mean, under... Underneath..."

I roll my eyes and start to climb down the stairs.

"Appropriate for what, exactly?" I ask, gripping onto the railing as I take the stairs.

"Me."

"We're going to school, Tyler." I reach his car,

and Tyler opens it, placing the cookies on the back seat, as I settle into the passenger seat.

"I'll try to control myself until we get back."

"We?"

"We're arriving together and leaving together, Ms. White."

"I don't remember asking you to be my date."

"Oh, no? I thought it was obvious."

"You thought what was obvious?"

I watch him as he pulls out of the parking space and onto the street, his hand resting on my thigh as soon as we stop at the junction.

"What we are, Ms. White."

"Are we something in particular?"

"I don't know, you tell me."

"This doesn't feel like the sort of conversation we should be having before I have to face a whole day at school. We have the show, and the kids, their parents, the bake sale, the games..."

"Speaking of which, I forgot to mention that I'll be taking part in the fair."

"What?"

"I take part every year. Did no one tell you?"

"What are you doing?"

Tyler laughs. "You'll see."

* * * * *

"I don't believe it," I say to Anya, who's standing next to me. "And no one thought to warn me?"

"He does it every year."

"Was I just supposed to know that?"

"He's always Santa Claus. Or, at least, he has been for as long as I can remember."

"What's going on?" Jordan asks, wandering towards us. She must have overheard our conversation.

We're in the hall, getting ready for the performance, and Tyler has gone with Niall to put the finishing touches to the Santa's Grotto. It looks like Niall has offered to help out this year, and *someone* seems to have assigned him his role as an elf.

"Holly has just found out that Tyler is Santa Claus."

"He's always Santa Claus."

"That's what I told her."

"I'm Elf Number One, Jordan."

She shrugs innocently.

"Right. So you're telling me that you didn't do this on purpose?"

"You're the one who asked me for a role."

I glare at her.

"All you have to do is sell tickets and give presents to the kids. You don't have to sit on Santa's lap."

"Anya…" Jordan warns, shooting her a pointed glance.

"Maybe you can do that later, in private," Anya offers suggestively, as Jordan smacks her arm.

"Ouch!" she grumbles, rubbing her injury, before turning back to me. "Or maybe you've already done that."

"Anya, please…"

"Has he spanked you yet?"

"Oh, my God," I say, covering my face with my hands. "Please, stop."

"Come on, ladies. Let's be serious and professional, here. We're at school. We have a show to put on and a fair to run."

"But, later…" Anya winks at me, as Jordan takes her arm and drags her away.

I shake my head, still embarrassed by Anya's little speech, when the object of my embarrassment wanders over to me.

"I heard you're one of my elves."

I roll my eyes, pretending not to be bothered in the slightest.

"I'm looking forward to having you work underneath me, Ms. White…"

Pretending is out of the question, now.

"I can't wait," he whispers into my ear, before leaving me standing there, trembling anxiously in the middle of the hall.

"Wow!" Wes' voice shakes me from my daydream – a dream where I was sitting on his lap, and...

"What was that?"

"W-what?"

"That man is sex on legs."

"Wh-who?"

Wes stares pointedly at me. "Don't play stupid with me."

I take a deep breath and smooth down my dress, although there's no need. I chose a green dress because I knew I'd be an elf today. I still have to put on the striped tights and elf hat – complete with pointy ears – but I'll do that after the show.

"Oh, fuck. He is *just* what we needed."

"Who?" I ask, turning to see Tyler's brother arriving with the girls in tow.

"I mean – have you seen those genes?"

Yes, I have seen them. But if I tell him, then it's all over for me.

"Here we are," Parker says, greeting us, the girls clinging to his legs, "late as usual."

"You're not late! We're still setting up."

"Come on, girls," Wes says, calling them over to him. "The others are already backstage." He takes their hands and leads them away as Parker waves.

"They were practicing their songs all the way

here."

"They'll be fine."

He smiles at me, and I smile back.

"Is the clown that I call my brother being Santa Claus again?"

"It would appear so."

"He does this every year. He's always involved in everything."

I stay silent – I still haven't worked out what he's getting at.

"He's a good guy, Holly. Aside from being a bit of a dickhead, he has a good heart. And I probably shouldn't tell you this, but I've never seen him like this."

"Like what?"

"Happy. I would never have trusted him, in your position – especially given his history. But you did trust him, and this whole thing... It's shaken him up. In a good way, I mean."

"Why are you telling me this? Are you scared I'm going to do something, or...?"

He shakes his head. "I'm scared he's going to do something stupid, as always."

I nod slowly.

"Just be patient with him, okay? Just... Give him a chance."

"The fact that you came over here to tell me all this makes me think that you think it'll happen."

"Honestly, I feel like it's my fault. He's only

like this because of me."

"Hey!" Tyler's voice interrupts us. "Don't you muscle in on my Ms. White."

"*Your* Ms. White is actually also the girls' Ms. White."

"Are you saying that makes her yours, too?"

"Exactly."

"Forget it!"

Parker laughs, before wandering off.

"What did he want?"

"Your brother?"

"No, I'm not worried about him. He's hopeless. I'm talking about the guy who left with my nieces. What did he want?"

"That's Wes. We work together."

"Mmm..."

"What?"

"He was the one who dropped you off at home. You went out with him."

"Oh..."

"He's the bastard who didn't walk you to your door."

"Tyler..."

"I'll keep an eye on him."

"Please, no punching, this time."

"Can I give him a kick up the arse?"

"Tyler."

"You know that no one can go anywhere near your apartment, right, Ms. White? No one but me."

"I have to go. Please, try to keep all this testosterone under control."

"I can't make any promises."

Tyler walks off as Wes approaches.

"So it worked…"

"What are you talking about?"

"Jealousy always works."

"Oh, you mean… That?"

"I knew it would bother him."

"You know you're at risk of being punched in the face?"

"I've done my part. If you want, we can tell him I'm not interested in you."

I cross my arms and study him.

"Don't pull that face. You know as well as I do that our handsome fireman is totally smitten."

I bite my lip, trying to mask a smile.

"And I think, by this point, you're a little smitten, too."

* * * * *

The kids were amazing. Wes stood in front of the audience, prompting, as I helped them onto the stage, before waiting in the wings in case they needed anything. It wasn't the first Christmas show I've been part of, but I was nervous, and still am. It's all still new to me, and I don't want to disappoint anyone. I want to do my best, to make good memories of the time I spend with them. That's why I offered to take part in the fair, why I wanted to make those cookies. I wanted to feel like part of this reality. I wanted to feel like one of them. And, to be honest, I wanted to follow through with Tyler's plan to do everything I've never done before – and that includes with him, too.

He was watching with the parents during the show, sitting next to his brother. I caught him smiling on more than one occasion, and at the end of the song, he'd whistled and cheered as his brother gave a standing ovation.

We haven't had much time to talk about his family. I know that his parents are travelling around the world, and that his brother is raising two daughters. I know that their family has a tradition of working as firemen, but we never got further than that. It makes me wonder what Parker meant, and why he feels so guilty – why he felt the need to come and speak to me, tell me to be patient with Tyler, to give him a chance.

"Great job." Jordan's hands land on my shoulders.

I turn and smile.

"The kids were so shy and so sweet... It was adorable."

"Anya filmed the whole thing, so you'll be able to watch it back in a few days."

"Okay."

"Now, go and get ready. We're about to open the doors to the fair."

"I'm ready... I think."

Jordan glances behind me, before turning her gaze back to mine.

"It looks like someone else is ready, too," she whispers, before leaving me alone. I'm too scared to turn around. But you know how these things work; it's a little like one of those horror films, where you know you shouldn't open the door, because there's a serial killer waiting behind it. But you do it anyway, because your curiosity is stronger than the fear itself. So I turn and smile at Tyler, who winks at me from across the hall. He moves his head slightly, calling me over to him, to be his elf. He's already wearing his Santa costume and his biggest grin. I feel ready – seriously – to let myself go, to make the most of these last few weeks here. That way, I'll always have them with me, even when I'm thousands of miles away. Even when this all feels like just a distant dream.

* * * * *

"Ms. White! Ms. White!" The Hayes sisters appear at the ticket counter.

"Hi, girls! What have you got on your faces?"

"We got our faces painted!" one of them exclaims.

"I can see…"

"Obviously using the same design," their dad adds.

"That way Uncle Tyler can't tell us apart," the other says, sniggering.

"*Ho, ho, ho!*" His voice rings out from behind me. "What do we have here? Two butterflies?"

"We're dragonflies, Uncle Tyler!"

"Who's this Uncle Tyler you're talking about?"

"It's you!"

Tyler looks around him and shrugs. "I don't see anyone else around here, except that useless elf," he says, gesturing to Niall, standing behind him.

"*Hey, hey, hey!* Useless to who?"

"He's eating all the biscuits for the children!"

"You ate them, too, you liar!"

"Santa Claus is not a liar."

"Neither is Uncle Tyler."

"I don't know about that…" Parker comments, glancing quickly at Santa.

"So, what do we have here…?" Tyler sinks onto his knees to speak to his nieces. "Two identical dragonflies."

They laugh as Tyler looks up at Parker.

"Not my fault."

"You're their father. All past, present, and

future issues are your fault."

"Can we move this along?" Niall asks, calling Santa's attention. "There's a queue."

"That's because everyone wants to sit on Santa's lap."

"Oh, my God." Parker runs a hand over his face.

"Come on, dragonflies, let's go inside," Niall says, calling the girls. "Or we'll be here until New Year."

"Would you like to sit on my lap, Ms. White?" he whispers into my ear, making me blush so hard that even my plastic elf ears flush red. "If you want, I can keep the beard, and you can keep the ears – and those tights. Please, keep those tights…"

"You know I can hear you, right?" Parker interjects. "And if I can hear you, that means…" He gestures behind him where, as Niall said, a queue was beginning to form, filled with children and their parents, wanting to pay Santa a visit.

"You're coming home with me, anyway, Ms. White," he says again, ignoring his brother's protests. "There's no escape."

I don't want to escape. Not at all.

I have no intention of running away from Tyler Hayes; and, from the way he's looking at me, I think he knows that.

* * * * *

We get home at about six o'clock. After spending a whole day at school, taking part in all the different activities, I'm exhausted, but strangely happy.

Tyler offers me his hand and helps me out of the car. "Did you have fun, Ms. White?"

"It was a really nice day."

We start to climb the stairs, side-by-side. An anxiety hangs over me, making me lose my balance slightly in my heels. When we get to my front door, I dig around in my purse for the keys, and Tyler's hands land gently on my hips.

"Are you going to go out with him again?"

I turn to face him.

"Who are you talking about?"

"That guy. Wes."

"My teaching partner?"

His jaw tightens. "Please, don't use that word. Not unless you're talking about me."

"Are you jealous of Wes?"

His grasp on my skin is nervous.

"Should I be?"

"No, you shouldn't. But I don't think you have the right either way to ask me things like that."

"I don't?"

I shake my head. Even though we spend almost all our free time together, although he kisses me, tells me things – despite everything that happened on the couch – we've never spoken about what we mean to each other.

"Ms. White…" His voice drops. "Don't play around with me." He pushes me against the door, my back pressing against the wood. "Or I'll have to start reminding you of a few things."

"W-what?"

"Do you remember when I told you that you deserve to be kissed against the door, until your knees gave way?"

I swallow nervously. His eyes pierce through me.

"Do you remember, Ms. White?"

"V-vaguely…"

One of his hands leaves my hip and slides slowly up the length of my body, along my throat, and up my neck, until his thumb is pressing against my bottom lip.

"Let me show you what I mean."

He bends down to me, his tongue sliding slowly into my mouth in one slow movement, sensual and powerful; his hands are on my face, now, his hard body keeping me pressed firmly against the door. Tyler devours me, as if I were one of his cookies – something covered in icing, to be licked up, savoured. He kisses me as he's never kissed me before, holding me against the door to my apartment, frozen, enchanted by his cavernous mouth, his tongue, plunging into me, the heat of his body. He bites down gently onto my lips, his thumb tracing their outline as he studies me, satisfied.

"Are your knees trembling, Ms. White?" His voice seeps into my bones.

"If you let go, I'll end up with my butt on the floor – and you don't want to risk that, do you?"

"I'll keep you up, Ms. White. You and your perfect arse are safe in my hands."

He pulls away from me and scoops me up in his arms, sticking to his word.

"There are more cookies inside," I say, my voice shaking almost as much as my knees.

"Did you save them for me?"

I nod, happily.

"In that case, I can't say no."

61

Tyler

Once we get into Ms. White's apartment, she becomes suddenly nervous.

How can I tell?

"We could always just have dinner instead of eating cookies. I don't want them to run out, because I haven't made any more, and then you'd have to go looking for other cookies and I don't want you to eat other cookies."

Pretty clear, right?

"Ms. White."

"Although I'm sure that other people's cookies are much better. But I still don't want you to eat them…"

"Ms. White."

"I could always go out and get the ingredients, but that would take a while, and you're probably already hungry…"

"Ms. White."

"Please, don't eat any other cookies."

Would you believe me if I told you that this is the best thing anyone has ever said to me?

"You're still wearing your tights."

"Mmm?"

I nod towards her legs, which are still wrapped

up in her elf tights.

"What have my tights got to do with it?"

"I told you what would happen if you wore those tights."

My sudden change of topic throws her for a second.

"It's one of the reasons I can't eat any other biscuits, Ms. White."

"Because of my tights?"

"Because just the thought of someone else taking them off you is killing me."

"I don't want you to die just because of my tights."

"Are you saying that I should take them off you right now, so that my skills don't go to waste?"

She laughs nervously and steps closer to me, her small hand sliding uncertainly down my chest, over my jacket. The heat radiating from her sends the blood rushing through my body – especially into the most important parts.

"Let's make a pact."

"A pact?"

"Uh-huh."

"I like this already."

"But you have no idea what I'm about to suggest."

"You're right. But if you're the one suggesting it, I already know I'll say yes."

"You shouldn't trust an elf. You know we can

be mischievous."

"No problem." I pull my Santa beard out of my pocket and put it on. "I'm Santa Claus – my job is to spank the naughty elves."

Her hand flies in front of her face, masking a nervous giggle.

"Tell me about this pact."

"If I promise you that you'll be the only one who's allowed to take off my tights…"

"Anything you want," I say, agonised.

"Can you let me finish?"

"I could have already taken them off you, by now."

She laughs again, making me laugh, too.

"You can't help yourself, even for a minute."

"I'm not going to give you a minute, Ms. White, believe me."

"Ty…"

"Santa."

"Santa. Can you listen to me, please?"

"I can."

"As I was saying: if I promise that you'll be the only one to take my tights off, will you promise to only eat my cookies?"

"Are you serious?"

She nods, nervous. "I don't like the thought of you eating them anywhere else."

"Holly…" Her name sets my chest alight. "The

only biscuits I want to eat are yours."

I pull her close to me, showing her that my downstairs neighbour agrees with me perfectly, before resting my forehead against hers.

"I'd rather starve to death than eat anywhere else, believe me. I know it sounds crazy, especially as you already know my reputation around here; even though everyone has told you some pretty awful things about me. You have to believe me."

"I believe you."

I heave a sigh of relief, pressing my lips against hers.

"The fact that I only want to eat yours doesn't mean that it has to be right now, tonight."

She nods, avoiding my gaze.

"Hey." I lift her chin, and her sweet, dreamy eyes make my breath catch in my throat. "I like you, Ms. White. And not in the way that you like chocolate cake, or pizza with hot dog slices on top."

She smiles.

"I like you, the way you like evenings spent on the sofa, in front of the fireplace, with a hot chocolate in your hand and a blanket over your legs. I like you, the way I like the fresh morning air, which means another day has come, and you're still there. I like you like that Christmas present you've always wanted, just waiting under the tree."

"Those are all such beautiful things, Ty."

"Nah. You're the one who's beautiful, Holly. With or without tights."

"Well, you've already seen me with tights..." She bites her lip.

"Just say the word and I'll throw you over my shoulder and carry you into the bedroom."

"Over your shoulder?"

I bend down and grab her around the legs, at her knees, before throwing her over my shoulder, just as I promised.

"Ty! What the hell...?"

"You said the word."

I head towards her bedroom and bend down to gently drop her onto the bed. Ms. White props herself up right away, resting her elbows on the mattress. The room is plunged into darkness, but the light filtering in from the living room is twinkling in her sweet, nervous eyes. I kneel onto the floor and take off her shoes. My hands slide up her calves, her knees, and along her thighs, slipping underneath her dress. I reach the waistband of her tights and pull them down slowly, both of us holding our breath; Ms. White's eyes don't leave mine, even for a second. I leave the tights on the floor and let my fingers trace their way back up her now-bare legs. My thumbs press gently against her skin, my breath beginning to grow heavy.

"Ms. White." I lean closer to her, my lips resting against the sensitive skin of her inner thigh.

"Oh, Ms. White." My lips move with my fingers, pressing gently against her skin, willing her to open her legs to me. "Like this." I watch her as I climb back up to meet her, her lips parted, her cheeks flushed, her eyes lively, waiting. She wants to understand what's happening before it even begins.

"I want to eat you, Ms. White," I tell her – although I think I've made that pretty clear by now. "I want to take another step with you tonight – maybe even a few steps." I press my mouth against her legs again, my fingers following their trail, slowly approaching her underwear. Ms. White jumps a little, making me smile against the fabric. I tease my fingers around the hem, waiting for a sign that I can go on.

"D-do you want to eat my c-cookies?"

"If that's what we're calling it..." I slide my finger under her panties, touching the warm, wet skin beneath.

Judging by her gaze, and by the tension in her body, I don't think anyone has ever eaten Ms. White's biscuits before.

"I really want to do this, Ms. White. But only if it's what you want, too."

"I think I do." She stops, taking a deep breath. "I w-want it."

"Me, too." I slide my fingers further into her underwear. "So much. Trust me. I didn't want to say it before, because I didn't want to make you feel like I was forcing you." I pull her underwear down and watch as she grabs at fistfuls of the bedsheet. I drop them to the floor and stroke her slowly, my hands pressing against her thighs.

"Yes, Ms. White. Open up to me."

I feel her tremble beneath my fingers, watch her grip tighten on the bedsheet as my hot breath lands on her. I kiss her, and her hands fly to my shoulders. I kiss her again, and they weave their way into my hair. I kiss her again, this time more deeply, and her legs relax next to my head. I press my hands against her thighs and Ms. White completely lets herself go for me, letting me kiss and lick her, penetrate her with my insatiable tongue. I bite down onto her pulsing skin, sucking her, so that I can feel her taste on my mouth.

"Tell me that no one else has done this to you," I pant onto her.

"N-no-one... Never..." She's panting, too, her fingers trailing nervously through my hair, her body arching towards me, wanting to feel me more deeply.

"Tell me you like it, Ms. White. Tell me that you like my tongue inside you, you like my mouth between your legs..."

"Tongue... Mouth..." she echoes, breathlessly.

"What if I bite you, Ms. White?" I bite down gently and an excited cry escapes her throat. "Do you like it when I bite you?"

"Everything... I like everything..."

"That makes me very happy." I let go of one of her legs so that I can feel her with my fingers, too. Ms. White trembles when she feels me slip inside her, trembling even harder against my face when I suck at her again, as I feel the orgasm start to ripple through her. I enjoy it, too; I enjoy every second. I love it so much that I'm almost tempted to let out my downstairs neighbour and let him share this moment of glory.

Ms. White covers her face with her hands, her chest still heaving.

"Everything okay up there?"

She nods, not looking at me.

I lift myself up and lay out on the bed next to her.

"Are you ashamed?"

She nods again, and I smile at her sweetness. I move her hands from her face and she finally meets my gaze.

"I don't... I..."

"No one had ever eaten you like that before?"

"No one had ever done it, full stop. And I never imagined it could feel like that."

It shouldn't turn me on so much, knowing that I was the first to do that to her, but I can't help it. The caveman inside me appears every now and again.

"I never thought it could be like that, either."

She studies me warily, and I stroke her face.

"It doesn't matter how many times you've done something, Ms. White. What matters is the person you share that experience with. Do you get what I'm trying to say?"

"Maybe…"

"And, with you, it feels like I'm doing everything for the first time." I lean down to her mouth. "I can't wait to follow through with the rest of my plan. You're not getting away from me that easily."

"I don't want to get away from you."

"Good. Because I'd never have let you."

I really hope that's true, Ms. White – because I'll never be able to get away from you, either. Not even if you went to the other side of the world without me.

62

Holly

Two days before Christmas, I turn up at Linda's, clutching the nicest box I could find in town, containing my latest batch of cookies, made from scratch. I didn't ask Tyler for help – I wanted to do it on my own. I wanted to do something for *him*.

The days pass quickly, and my time is running out. I wish I could have spent more time here, had more conversations, more hugs; I wish I could've learnt more about his life, about myself. I want to know his version of events. I should've told him straight away who I was. I should've been honest, made every moment count – but I was terrified of rejection, of finding out that he was exactly the way my mother had described him to be.

I step into the café and look around for him. He isn't waiting tables or behind the counter, so I step towards it to ask where he is.

"Excuse me," I say, attracting the attention of a woman who has her back turned, busying herself with the coffee machine. "I'm looking for Angus. Do you know where I could find him?"

The woman turns to face me, and it only takes one glance to realise what I'm looking at: or, rather, *who* I'm looking at.

It's like looking at myself in a mirror.

"Who are you looking for?" She rests her hands on the counter and leans towards me.

"I'm... I wanted... I'm sorry," I say, turning and hurrying out of the café. I take a few steps on the sidewalk, but my knees give way, the rest of my body following suit.

I don't know why I'm reacting like this, why she had this effect on me. Maybe it's because I was never expecting to find a family; maybe I never expected to see so much of myself reflected in another person. I've always wondered who I looked like, as my mother and I were so different in every way: the way we looked, the way we were. And now that I know where I come from, who I really am, this was something I really wasn't prepared for. I don't think I ever will be.

"Where on Earth are you going?"

Her voice paralyses me.

"Why did you run off like that?"

I turn slowly, my eyes filled with tears, my heart throbbing in pain.

"Are you okay?"

I shake my head, but can't speak.

"I could try to call someone, I can..." I move quickly, as if possessed by something stronger than logic itself, and literally throw myself into her arms, without giving her time to react. She just stands there, her arms glued to her sides, as I hug her tightly, scared that someone could take her away from me again.

"Hey," she says, her hand resting gently on my head. She strokes my hair sweetly. "What's going on, my dear?"

"I'm here," I say, a sob shattering my voice. "I'm finally home."

* * * * *

Linda coaxed me back into the café. She sat me down at a table and placed a cup of tea in front of me, accompanied by a slice of cake, before sitting down next to me. There aren't many customers in the café; it's a quiet afternoon, so close to Christmas. I'd guess people are busy making preparations, spending time with their families, rushing out for last-minute gifts. They're probably swept up in excitement, joy – everything I've never had.

"My name is Holly," I tell her, my gaze fixed onto my cup of tea. "Holly White."

My name seems to have no effect on her, but that shouldn't shock me. My mother never took their surname, and I know that she loved to make up names, stories and facts, so that no one would ever know who she really was.

"Nice to meet you, Holly. I'm Linda."

I already knew that – but I keep that to myself.

"I used to run this place. Now it belongs to my son."

"Do you have any other children?"

"What's that?"

"I mean, do you have a big family?"

"That's a strange question…"

"Sorry. Maybe I should've warned you that I'm a little strange myself."

"I gathered."

"But I'm harmless, I swear."

She laughs, taking a few sips of her own tea.

"You're not from here."

I shake my head. "Canada."

"Oh, wow. That's a long way."

"I'm here for an exchange programme."

"Exchange?"

"For teachers. At school. I teach. Primary."

She studies me, confused.

"Sorry. I'm just nervous."

"I can see, dear. Am I making you nervous?"

I should tell her. I should make the most of this moment and tell her who I am, why I'm here, and why it hurts me so much to sit here next to her. But I can't; I can't do it. I've never particularly brave and, despite having flown halfway across the world to discover my roots, I can't seem to manage to do what I really came here for. I can't seem to take this step into a past that doesn't involve me, just so that I can build myself a future. I can't turn back time and right someone else's wrongs. I can't just insert myself into these people's lives and force them to accept me with open arms.

I can't have something that was never mine.

"I'm sorry. I really have to go."

I get to my feet, and she does the same.

"Why?"

"Because it's the right thing to do. Trust me."

"I don't understand…"

"Thank you for… This." I hug her again, this time holding her against me for a few seconds longer, before letting her go, slowly.

"Goodbye, Linda."

I grab my purse and head towards the door, stepping outside and pacing quickly towards the place I'll call home for just a few more weeks. Then I'll jump onto a plane and going back to my meaningless life, without ever looking back.

63

Tyler

In the evening, Niall drops into the station. We haven't seen each other much lately, apart from at the Christmas fair and our shitty jobs as Santa Claus and Elf Number Two, so we haven't really had the chance to catch up, update each other on our lives. As if there were anything important to update him with; Ms. White is still planning on leaving, and I have no idea how to talk to her about it without making things worse.

"So…" Niall shoves a whole mince pie into his mouth. "Things have moved along quite a bit."

"Moved along? I told you, she has no intention of staying here!"

"Last time we had this conversation, Tyler, you still hadn't even admitted that you liked her."

"And now I have?"

"Are you, or are you not, trying to think of ways to make her stay?"

"Yes, but…"

"Please, don't tell me you're doing this out of friendship or some bullshit."

I stick a mince pie into my mouth, too. Better to chew than speak at this point.

"I asked Jordan," Niall continues, sipping at his coffee.

"Asked her what?"

"If there were anything she could do to give her more time here – maybe extend her contract or something."

"Why would she do that?"

"Because my *supposed* best friend has fallen in love with a Canadian with no visa, and in a few weeks she'll be sent back home."

"And who's this *supposed* best friend of yours?"

Niall glares at me.

"I'm not in love with Ms. White."

"Then what are you doing all of this for?"

I can't find an explanation, so I eat another mince pie.

"We only have a few weeks left, Tyler. Don't waste your time eating."

"And what exactly are you doing?"

"I'm not about to lose the woman I love."

"That word again?"

Niall scoffs. "What else do you want to call it?"

"Can we just not call it anything?"

"Whatever. You're a pain in the arse, you know. I'll never understand how you got that woman to fall in love with you."

"Again with this bullshit?"

"Love is not bullshit. The things you do for love aren't bullshit, either."

I scoff, frustrated. It was a bad idea to get Niall involved.

"Besides, Ms. White isn't in love with me."

"You're really enjoying talking shit today, aren't you?"

"Don't you think that, if that really were true, she'd be looking for a way to stay?"

"Why should she?"

"Are you doing this on purpose?"

"What?"

"Being a dick."

"What do you want from me?"

"I want you to be helpful, for once in your life."

"Okay, let's put it like this. But I'm going to be frank."

"As long as it's useful."

"Why the hell would she tell you that she wanted to stay, or try to find a way to make it happen, when you haven't even told her that you love her?"

I think about this for a moment, but decide not to answer. It's not worth it.

"And why would she have told you that she was in love with you if you haven't told her yourself?"

"What is this, a competition?"

"I need to be honest with you, okay? What woman in her right mind would tell you that she was in love with you, given your history?"

"History?"

Niall slams his hand against his forehead.

"Your *skills*, damn it!

Aside from his constant mention of my skills, his little speech is actually starting to make sense.

"Come on, Tyler! Wake up!"

"I'm thinking."

"Well, think quicker, because you don't have much time. And, apparently, you're short of good ideas."

I consider what I'm about to say, before taking the plunge.

"Maybe there's a way."

"And you're only telling me this now?"

"I don't know if I can tell you."

"Are you kidding? I've been here trying to help you, and now you're keeping me out of the story?"

"It's not my story."

"I'm following…"

"Promise me that this will stay between us, Niall."

"Hey! Who do you think you're talking to, here?"

"My *supposed* best friend."

Niall rolls his eyes, then gestures for me to go on.

"There's someone who could make all the difference."

"Someone? Who?"

I take a deep breath and reveal Ms. White's secret to Niall, hoping that this won't come back to haunt me one day.

"Her father."

64

Tyler

After twenty-four hours without me, I thought Ms. White would have been a little happier to see me. She lets me into her apartment, which is plunged into almost total darkness. The Christmas lights are switched off, her expression just as lifeless. She's wearing jogging bottoms and an enormous hoodie, her hair piled up onto her head. Her eyes are tired – she looks as if she's been crying. I don't want to put too much pressure on her, so I tread carefully.

"Just tell me who I need to beat up."

Okay, maybe not too carefully.

She glances distractedly at me. I don't think she even heard what I said.

"What's happened, Ms. White? Two days ago you seemed so happy."

"Happy?"

I nod, worried now.

"Do you think I seem unhappy now?"

"You don't *seem* unhappy, you *are* unhappy."

Her wide, sweet eyes fill with tears – tears I want to kiss away before they can trail down her cheeks, but I get the impression that wouldn't help right now. So I force myself to bear the pain of watching her tears begin to fall.

"My time is running out," she says, her voice paper-thin. "And I don't... I still can't tell him who I am."

I try not to be selfish, to skim past the fact that she hasn't even mentioned me, and work out how I can help her.

"You still have two weeks left. There's time."

"I saw Linda today." She looks at me. "My... Grandma."

I smile at her.

"I have a grandma, Tyler. And who knows how many other people there are in my family..." She sniffs. "I almost collapsed today, when I saw her."

I shuffle closer to her on the sofa and scoop her into my arms. She doesn't need my bullshit, my insecurity. She just needs me to be here for her.

"I didn't think it could hurt so much."

I stroke her hair.

"Seeing him was hard, but her... I'm... She's..." She lifts her head and looks at me. "I look so much like her."

Her sad eyes chip away at my heart.

"I can't do it."

"Can't do what?"

"Tell them who I am."

"Holly..."

She wriggles out of my embrace and moves away.

"I don't want to tell them."

"I thought that was what you came here for? To find your family?"

"They're not my family, Tyler. I don't belong here."

This hurts more than any of the tears she's shed – any of the tears I know I'll shed, too.

"You have no idea how they'll react..."

She gets up and starts to pace around the living room.

"I don't want to know."

I get up, too, walking over to her.

"You're scared, right?"

She turns towards me.

"I never thought I'd follow through with this. I knew I'd never be able to do it."

"Then why did you come this far?"

She shrugs, then starts to sob.

"My mother died... I just wanted... I wanted to feel less alone."

I move closer to her and take her in my arms.

"You're not alone, Holly. I'm here. Okay?"

She nods against my chest, her hands grabbing onto my hoodie.

I clear my throat, trying to send down the knot of emotion lodged in my windpipe. "I'll be here for as long as you want me."

* * * * *

We're stretched out on the sofa with a half-empty bottle of whiskey in front of us. I'm stroking her hair as she regales me with one of her best lines yet.

"I never thought I'd be interested in someone so old."

I try to sidestep the 'old' thing, because I'm intrigued to know where this is going.

"And I'm even going out with him." She lifts her head and looks at me. "Because we *are* going out, right?"

"I'd say so, Ms. White."

"Sometimes I'm not sure."

"In what way?"

"I don't know. We spend most of our time here, you've eaten my biscuits."

"And I loved them."

"And I've come pretty close to your biscuits, too."

"Not close enough," I remind her.

"But I wouldn't say we're *going out* exactly."

"Then what would you call it?"

"It needs to be something more official."

"Official? Mmm…"

"I mean, you did take off my tights."

"Don't remind me, or I'll have to take off those jogging bottoms, too."

A nervous laugh escapes her lips.

"Well, I was actually planning to spend Christmas Eve here, with you."

She lifts herself up, sitting perched on the sofa.

"What?"

"Did you really think I was going to leave you alone?"

"I assumed you'd be with your family."

"I'll spend Christmas Day with them. I'm almost always working on Christmas Eve, anyway. There are shifts that need to be covered, and all the other guys have families, so..." I shrug, and she smiles at me.

"You have a good heart, Hayes. You're old, but you have a good heart."

I laugh and grab her waist, sliding her onto my lap.

"I've already asked to have Christmas Eve off this year."

"How come?"

"I wanted to spend it with you."

She smiles, happy again, now.

"We can cook dinner, eat, drink, wait for midnight, and then..."

"And then?"

"And then exchange gifts."

"What are you wishing for under the tree?"

"You're the best gift I could ever receive, Ms. White."

The lights of the Christmas tree are glinting in her eyes.

"And I wouldn't change it for anything."

She presses her lips against mine, her hands weaving into my hair. I wrap my arms tighter around her waist, moving her gently onto my erection, which has suddenly decided to show up – and I really mean *up*.

Ms. White sighs onto my mouth as she feels my dick pressing between her legs.

"Tyler..." she whispers, her fingers looping around the back of my neck as my hands slip under her hoodie.

"And now, my dear Ms. White, let me show you some of the advantages of being with an older guy like me."

65
Holly

The morning of Christmas Eve, Tyler knocks at my door with a takeaway coffee and a paper bag filled with breakfast.

"You're already up? And you've already been out? It's eight in the morning. And it's Christmas."

"And I'll catch a cold if you keep making me stand out here."

I open the door to let him in.

Tyler is ready, perfect and impeccably-dressed, as always. He's wearing dark jeans, a red sweater, a jacket that hangs down to his knees, a colourful scarf and a woolly hat.

"Wear something warm," he tells me, as I wander into my bedroom, coffee in hand, to go and get dressed. I'm still wearing my pyjamas. "It's fucking freezing outside."

I slip on a pair of jeans and a white turtle-neck sweater, pulling my hair into a low, messy bun. I moisturise my face and throw on some mascara, before walking back over to him.

"Sexy and delicious as always, Ms. White."

"Delicious?"

"You're making me really hungry."

"I thought you'd brought breakfast?"

"It's not the kind of hunger that a few

doughnuts can fix, Ms. White."

"Are you planning on being like this all day?"

"For the rest of my life, if necessary."

The way he says it moves something in me – something that shouldn't even exist. Especially not when I'm only here temporarily; when I have a plane ticket for Canada with my name on it; when I'm starting to doubt everything I've ever known.

"Ready?" He smiles at me.

To leave all this? I'm not so sure.

* * * * *

We go to the supermarket together, carrying the groceries back to my apartment and putting everything away, snacking on a bag of salt and vinegar chips as we go. We glance at each other a lot. We constantly find excuses to touch each other, like one of those couples who have known each other their whole lives; like one of those couples who are destined to be together forever. But we're not even really a couple. I don't even know what we are. We're not friends, we're not going out, but we're not really *together*. We're just trying not to get hurt, knowing already how much it'll hurt later on.

"You're thoughtful today, Ms. White."

"I was just..." I shake my head. I don't want to voice my thoughts to him. I just want to enjoy the time we have together, and I want to... I look at him, his eyes studying me anxiously.

I want to be with him.

"I can't wait for tonight."

"Oh, really?"

I nod. "It'll be my first real Christmas in twenty-seven years."

He moves over to me and takes me in his arms. "Then I have to do my best to make it unforgettable."

You already are, Ty. And I'm not just talking about Christmas. I'm talking about every word, every gesture, every smile. I'll never forget any of this. I'll never forget you.

"I have to go over to my brother's house for a few hours. I have some presents to give the girls, and I want to put them under their tree. Do you want to come with me?"

"I'd love to, but I have a few errands to run."

"I can come with you, if you like?"

"Go and spend time with your family. I can manage on my own."

"I'm sure you can. I can't, though."

He said it jokingly, but something changed behind his eyes. I know what he's thinking, and I know that it will get worse and worse every day, but I don't want to face it now. I don't want to ruin this moment, what we have.

I lift onto my tiptoes and press my lips against his. "We'll both manage."

But I'm not sure that's true, and, from the way he tightens his grip on my waist, I realise that he's not sure, either.

* * * * *

"Merry Christmas."

I place the tin of cookies on the counter and he lifts his gaze to meet mine.

"Holly! What a nice surprise. Are you here for lunch?"

I shake my head. "I just wanted to bring you a Christmas present. My cookies. This time, I made them on my own."

He places a hand on mine, and I just about manage not to crumble at his touch.

"Thank you. You shouldn't have."

"I wanted to."

He takes the tin and looks at it. I've also wrapped it in a red ribbon, and attached a card.

He reads it and smiles, first at the tin, and then at me.

Thanks for making me feel at home.

Merry Christmas.

That's all it says. Nothing that's not true.

"Come on," he says, gesturing for me to step behind the counter. "I want you to meet someone."

I wander behind the counter and follow him into the kitchen, where Linda is telling a story to two of the guys who work here.

"Mum, I want to introduce you to someone."

Linda turns, and when she realises who I am, she holds out her hand.

"Hi, I'm Linda," she says, pretending never to have met me.

"Holly."

"She's new in town."

"Just passing through," I say, sadly. "But I'll never forget this place. Or the people who live here."

Nothing I've ever said has been truer.

*****

After having a coffee with Angus, I step outside, pulling my jacket around my body and heading home. But after a few paces, a hand lands on my shoulder.

"Can I walk with you, my dear?" Linda asks.

I nod, and we start to walk together.

"I've been thinking about you a lot after our meeting, Holly."

"I'm sorry. I was such a mess."

"Don't be sorry." She wraps her arm around my shoulder and looks at me, stopping us in the middle of the sidewalk.

"There's something so familiar about you…"

I attempt to hold back the tears.

"Is there something you want to tell me, honey?"

"I don't know if I can."

"Of course you can. Tell me everything. I promise, it'll stay between us."

I can't stop myself. I've wanted to yell it to the world since the moment I set foot in this place; holding it back has been so painful, growing harder every day. It's a pain I can't bear anymore.

"I'm his daughter," I say, through tears. "Angus is my dad."

* * * * *

I've invited Linda back to my house. We wanted a quiet place to talk, and my apartment seemed like the best option. She gave me a lift in her car, and now she's sitting on my couch, a mug of hot chocolate in her hands, her eyes never leaving mine.

"I found out about a year ago, when my mother died. I found her diary, a few photos. Did you know her?"

She shakes her head, and I feel my sadness grow deeper.

"I think it was just a fling for her. But, for him…"

"He went to look for her."

"He said. He told me how much he loved her. And I'm so sorry."

"What for?"

"That she did this; she sent him away. She never told him about me."

"That's not your fault."

"When I found out about him, I tried to find a way to come over here. I wanted to get to know him. I wanted to know whether what my mother said was true: whether he really didn't want me. I wanted... I wanted to know who I was."

Linda strokes my face gently.

"And have you found out who you are yet, my dear?"

"No. I'm even more confused now than I was before."

"Don't you want to give yourself some more time to find out?"

In that moment, the door flies open, and Tyler appears in the doorway, clutching a bunch of roses.

"Oh... Sorry, I didn't know you had company. I'll come back later..."

I leap to my feet. "No, please. Don't leave."

Tyler stays standing at the door, his hand still resting on the handle, a question lingering on his face that I wish I could answer.

"Shall I stay?"

I nod, Linda's hand clutching mine tightly.

"There's someone I want you to meet."

* * * *

Tyler is amazing. The way he fills silences, strokes my hand when he sees I'm starting to get nervous; the way he looks at me. He got up to make everyone another hot chocolate, and as he wandered into the kitchen, Linda whispered into my ear.

"Maybe you should give yourself a chance, Holly." She nods towards Tyler as he moves around my apartment. "Maybe what you're looking for isn't your past, and everything you never had. Maybe it lies in what you still have to discover: in what's waiting around the corner."

I watch Tyler as he comes towards us, mugs in hand; he hands one to Linda, then another to me, before kissing the top of my head and settling himself down with us.

Maybe Linda's right. Maybe the real reason I came here wasn't to dig up something or someone I lost years ago. Maybe it was destiny. And maybe destiny is trying to tell me something, in this exact moment, through Tyler's eyes; through the way my heart beats with every gaze.

66

Tyler

"What's this?"

"Guinness soda bread. A classic, especially with salmon. My mother makes it at home, but we'll have to improvise."

"Do you miss them?"

"Who?"

"Your parents. They've been gone for a while, right?"

"I think this is the first Christmas we'll spend apart. Even though I'm normally working, I usually manage to pop in. It's harder for Parker, with the girls and... everything else."

Ms. White takes a sip of wine and listens. We made dinner together. After Linda's visit she seemed a little upset, so I tried to distract her with some of my usual jokes – but I think we've gone too far for that, now.

"But we both insisted they go on this trip. It seemed like the right thing to do."

"The right thing?"

"For them, and for us."

"What do you mean?"

"Parker still lived with them up until a few months ago. Mum helped him out with the girls. I moved out a few years ago, when I finally decided to find a place on my own, before I could afford to move in here."

"What about the girls' mother?" she asks carefully.

"She's gone."

Her eyes grow sad.

"Not in that way. She just left."

"She abandoned her family?"

"And never looked back, Holly. Parker was so in love with her." I shake my head, nervous at the mere thought of what happened. "She didn't want this," I say, opening my arms, unsure of what I'm gesturing to. "She didn't want to live here. She didn't want to be a fireman's wife. She didn't want him, and…"

Her hand rests on mine.

"She ruined his life. She scarred him."

"I'm sorry."

"And I… I saw him in his darkest moments. I heard him crying at night, in the girls' room. I watched his life slip away before my eyes. I saw how scared he was – he was terrified that he wouldn't be able to do it."

"That must have been horrible for him. For everyone."

I look at her, empathy pooling in her eyes, and feel my heart begin to expand. I want to tell her something I never thought I'd say to anyone, simply because I never thought that person existed. But now, after meeting her, I just want to let everything go. I want to run towards my destiny, my future. Towards her.

"I never wanted to end up like that."

She tilts her head and looks at me.

"I never wanted to fall in love, to believe it even existed. I didn't want to hope, only to... To fall. But I never wanted to hurt anyone. I never wanted to be that arsehole who sleeps with everything that moves."

"What did you want to be?"

"I wanted to help anyone who felt lonely, cheated, disappointed. I wanted to help them feel like themselves again; feel wanted, desired."

"So your skills...?"

"As much as I wish that were true... No, Holly. My skills have nothing to do with what happens between the sheets. Or, at least, they're much more than that."

"Then what are they?"

"I just wanted to comfort people. I wanted to be a distraction, someone who made others feel special. I never wanted anyone to suffer. I especially didn't want to suffer myself."

"But someone got hurt anyway."

"I was naïve to think it would never happen."

"I'm sure you never meant to hurt anyone, Tyler."

"Thank you."

"For what?"

"For believing in me."

"Thank *you*."

"I haven't done anything."

She reaches her arms wide and gestures around her apartment.

"It was just dinner."

"For the first time in my life, I don't feel lonely."

"Well, at least that means that my plan is working."

* * * * *

We're sitting on the balcony, drinking wine. I'm sitting on the chair, Ms. White on my lap, and we're both wrapped in a blanket. It's fucking freezing, but Ms. White wanted to get some air, so here we are.

It's all new to her, but it's new to me, too. And I'm not just talking about spending Christmas with her; I'm talking about the fact that there's nowhere else I'd rather spend it. I'm starting to think that there's no place in the world for me if she's not there.

"Are you cold?" I ask her, feeling her start to shiver.

"No. I think it's just the wine and the fresh air."

"Have you drunk too much?"

"I'm starting to get used to the idea of living without a liver."

I laugh, then gently slide her off my lap.

"What's wrong?"

"I need to give you my present."

"Now?"

I guide her over to the door and into the house, heading towards the tree, where I'd carefully hidden my present.

"Open it."

"I thought we were supposed to exchange gifts tomorrow?"

"This one's special."

She takes it, her eyes glued to me.

"I told you they existed."

She looks down at the pint glass, where *Drink 'til you're Irish* is emblazoned across the side, without a word.

"Remember? The first time…"

Her eyes snap up to me. "You remembered."

"Of course," I say, a little embarrassed. It didn't seem like a huge gesture, but judging by her reaction, I think I'd underestimated it. "It's just a little thing. I'll give you your real present tomorrow, and…" Ms. White literally throws herself into my arms.

"It's not little. Not at all."

I hold her close to me, inhaling the scent of her hair.

"It's the best present I've ever been given."

"Well, you know. My skills cover a wide range of fields."

She pulls slowly away from me and looks deep into my eyes. The words are there, resting on my tongue.

"Remember when I said there was nothing I wouldn't do for you, Holly?"

She nods nervously.

"It was fucking true. I'd do anything to make you stay, and…" Her lips close around my mouth before I can go on. "Holly, Holly, please. Let me…" She won't let me speak. She won't let me tell her how I feel, or what I'd do to keep her here with me.

"I want to skip all the last steps," she says, her breathing heavy. "Tonight. Right now."

"Holly…"

She reaches onto her tiptoes and slides her hands behind my neck.

"There's no rush. There's no…"

"I want to be yours, Ty." Her voice is trembling. "I-I want to feel part of something." My breathing starts to synch with her own. "I want to feel part of you."

* * * * *

Ms. White has no idea how much she's already part of me; how she burst into my life, seeping under my skin. She has no idea how much I need her, how much I need to feel her hands on me, her mouth on mine, giving me air. Giving me life.

"And I want to be yours, Ms. White."

She trembles in my arms as I lift the hem of her dress slowly up to her waist; I rest my palm against the small of her back and push her gently towards me. My hand slides up to her neck, my fingers weaving into her soft hair; Ms. White parts her lips and I kiss her. She tilts her head back, and I plunge my tongue into her mouth, suffocating her pain with my breath. I slide the straps of her dress slowly down her arms, tracing the shape of her body with my hands. Ms. White gasps, looking for air, but I can't let her take another breath, or pause, even for a second. I can't even let her think about speaking. The only thing she can do, now, is take this leap of faith with me.

I push her dress down over her hips, sliding it down her trembling legs and all the way to her feet. My hands are on her waist, asking her silently to take a step forward, leaving the material splayed out across the floor.

"Tyler…" she sighs, anxiously, when she finally draws breath.

"Yes, Ms. White?"

"Your hands."

I tighten my grip on her, my fingers becoming one with her flesh.

"These hands?"

"I love them."

I smile against her mouth.

"This is nothing, Ms. White. You haven't felt the rest, yet." I lift her up and carry her in my arms towards the bedroom. She lies down on the mattress as I slide off my shoes. I take off my shirt and join her, her hands sliding onto my chest.

"You're... *Wow*," she says, biting her lip – a lip which I take between my teeth, making her gasp. "Ty..." I push my knee between her legs, sliding my tongue into her mouth as my body pushes her back onto the bed. Her nails are digging into my shoulders, my dick pressing against the fabric of her underwear, threatening to set it alight.

I lie myself down on top of her, one hand behind her back, in search of her bra clasp. I pull it off within a second.

"You're so good..." she says, teasingly.

"One of my many skills."

I kiss her again, one hand squeezing her firm breasts; I slip slowly down her throat and down her body, before kneeling back to take off her underwear. When Ms. White is finally totally naked beneath me, all logic flies out the window; I forget to take things slowly. I quickly unbutton my jeans and tug them off, casting them over my shoulder. And, now that I'm completely naked, too, not even Ms. White wants to take things slow. She sits herself up in the middle of the bed, one hand squeezing my erection, her eyes glued to my hard dick in her hand. She moves it slowly, watching it grow between her fingers, her lips parted. I stare at her, desperate to feel those lips on my skin. As if Ms. White could read my thoughts, she moves closer. I can feel her hot breath, her hand tightening its grip.

"Holly…" I beg. "If you're going to kill me, do it now."

I watch the corner of her mouth lift, before those perfect lips press gently against my dick. She kisses the tip, her lips parted, before her tongue starts to move shyly, circling slowly. That mouth – the possible murder weapon – begins to slide seductively down the length of me. I push my hips towards her, unable to control myself.

"Holly…" I stroke her hair, her head moving towards me. "We're skipping so many steps." I grab a fistful of her hair. "H-Holly…" My breathing catches in my throat as her tongue – which we'll now refer to as Exhibit A – runs along me. "Holly." My voice bounces from the walls, grabbing her attention. "Your mouth… No."

She looks at me, confused.

"I don't think I can survive for much longer with your mouth on me like that – and I want to feel you come at least twice before you kill me." I push her back onto the bed and lie on top of her. "Then, if you want, you can keep going…" I slide my lips down her body, stopping at her breasts, tracing my tongue around her nipples, as my hand heads between her legs. "You said you like my hands…"

She nods breathlessly.

"Okay…" I delve two fingers into her heat, making her arch her back towards me. "Let's see whether you prefer my fingers…" I say, pushing into her, as she writhes around, wanting to feel me more deeply, "…or something else." I bite down on one of her nipples as she grabs onto my shoulders. My fingers move ceaselessly inside her, her breathing morphing into one long, sensual moan. "Holly…" I kiss her breasts, my hand tireless, her fingers digging into my skin. "Let's see if I can…" My thumb starts to massage her clitoris.

"Oh, God…" She moves around underneath me. "Oh, my God…" she repeats, her hands leaving my shoulders to grab fistfuls of the bedsheet.

"God won't make you come – but I will. Maybe it's best if you change name."

"Ty…"

"Oh… That's better…"

I play with her clitoris as I bend down between her legs. "Keep going. It's killing me, hearing you say my name like that. But I guess we all die someday."

"Ty… Ty… Ty…"

I suck at her, my fingers sliding in and out of her. I want to feel her trembling at my touch. I want her to say my name over and over, to come over and over.

"Ty... Oh, Ty..."

The vibrations of her voice, and the trembling of her body, seep into my bones. I keep sucking, until I feel her stop shaking. I kiss her again for a few minutes, giving her time to catch her breath, before working my way back up to her mouth.

"Ms. White?"

She opens her eyes.

"Mmm?"

I press the tip of my dick against the wetness between her legs.

"Maybe it would be better if I wear something..."

"There is no need."

"Are you sure?"

"I'm on the the pill for years and..." His eyes become huge and bright. "I trust you."

"Do you trust me?"

She bites her lip anxiously as I try to control the emotion that her words have provoked to me."

"I'm not going to give you any peace tonight."

Her eyes widen as she feels me begin to push between her legs.

"I won't be satisfied until you feel like you belong, Ms. White." I push a little deeper, her breath catching. "Not just to me, but to yourself, too." I'm fully inside her, now, her legs wrapping tightly around my waist. "You have to belong to yourself, Ms. White; it's the only way you'll find what you're looking for."

Her hands are in my hair, pulling me into her, her mouth pressing against mine. Her legs relax a little, and I push inside her, until I feel part of her, too. "Holly... Fuck..." I move my hips, longing to be at one with her; longing for something I never thought I wanted. Not until I realised what my life would be like without it. "Holly. Oh, God, Holly..." I echo. My thrusts grow deeper, relentless, as she wraps her arms around my neck, keeping me close to her. "I want you, Holly. I want you for me, and for you. I want you so much that it feels like I could die." I slide out of her, before pushing back inside her, so deeply that she cries out. "Let me die inside you. That's all I ask." I move, breathless, Holly barely able to take my thrusts. "You're so tight, so sexy, so..."

"Yours," she whispers, making me freeze. "I'm yours, Tyler."

"Mine... Oh, God, yes..." I move again, slower now. I want her to feel me. I want us to take this leap together. "Not just for tonight. Not just for a few weeks," I say, my heart hammering in my throat.

"N-no," she says, almost shy.

"You're mine, Holly. Stay here." I push deeper, reaching my limit, physically and mentally. "Let me stay here, inside you."

I watch as she lets herself go, throwing her head back and allowing her body to ripple with orgasm. I keep her close to me, not even giving her space to breathe; I'm scared that she'll take it all back, that she won't let me stay with her.

I'm fucking terrified at the thought of being in love with her, and at the idea that she might not be in love with me.

67
Holly

Tyler lets his face drop onto my chest, his hand gently stroking between my legs, my fingers playing lazily with his hair; our breathing has finally slowed, breaking the silence. Everything is calm, now. We stay here, naked, in bed, enjoying the intimacy we've created, each becoming part of the other. I always knew it would be like this with Tyler. Something inside me knew I wanted it, but was too scared to come after it.

"I can confirm with absolute certainty that you have absolutely nothing wrong with you, Ms. White." He lifts his head, his hair dishevelled by my hands, his eyes tired, small, but still glinting.

"What are you talking about?"

He slides a finger between my legs and I inhale sharply.

"You're absolutely perfect, just as I suspected. And I'm not just talking about your arse. I'm talking about the whole package."

I laugh, his hand following the outline of my curves and sliding up to my face, stroking me gently. His thumb traces my lips.

"I thought I was going to die there, at least three times."

"Don't get carried away…"

"I don't know where the hell you got this idea of being terrible in bed from, Ms. White, but I told you. Don't you remember? I couldn't believe you could ever be terrible at anything. I could tell right away."

"Oh, really?"

He nods.

"Does that mean you agreed to be my friend and help me spread my wings just to get me into bed?"

"Into *my* bed, yes."

I lift myself up suddenly, making him fall back onto the mattress.

"That came out wrong."

"So it was all just bullshit? You helping me, this whole 'plan'...?"

"No, I swear – it was all true. My main plan was to stop you from sleeping with the wrong guy."

I cross my arms and study him suspiciously.

"I couldn't stand the thought of seeing you in the arms of some dickhead. And I'm including myself in that category."

"Now I'm confused."

"I wanted you to have everything you've never had before – including a guy who could make you forget about all the others. Someone to make you feel special, and..."

"And...?"

"And who would love you the way you deserve to be loved."

"Oh... Oh... Oh..." I'm suddenly nervous. "Are you saying...? You're not trying to...?"

"Please, don't be scared."

I get up from the bed, dragging the cover around myself.

"Holly," Tyler says. "Holly, please..." He gets to his feet and walks over to me.

"I can't talk to you right now."

"What? Why?"

"Because you're naked, and you're beautiful, and you're... God, you're really good."

"Well, when you have the right tools," he says, glancing down at himself, "and the right inspiration..." His eyes slide over me, making me wrap the cover tighter around my chest. "There's no point in you covering yourself up. Seriously. I think I know your body off by heart."

"You're right. There's no point in me covering myself up." I take off the sheet and throw it to him. "It's best if you cover yourself instead."

"What the hell...?"

"I can't think straight when you're... You..." I gesture towards his erection, which is still standing perfectly alert. "So when you gave me that whole speech about size not mattering, you weren't speaking from experience."

"No."

"Cover yourself up, please!"

"I don't think so."

"I can't concentrate."

"You don't have to." He casts the cover to the floor and closes the distance between us. I can't help but look at him – I can't focus my attention on anything else. The only thing I can seem to concentrate on is…

"Are you staring at my dick, Ms. White?"

"Yes," I admit, embarrassed.

Tyler bursts out laughing, the sound so full, so genuine. It's full of colour and life – just like him.

I love his laugh. I love his smile and his mouth. I love those deep, piercing eyes, and I love his hands – God, his hands! And let's not even talk about his…

"Are you staring at it again?"

"Oh, fuck!" I cover my face with my hands.

"If you like."

"Can you stop? Can we be serious for two seconds?"

"No, not right now. Not when you look so beautiful, so embarrassed and shocked about what's just happened."

"Sex doesn't shock me."

"I'm not talking about the sex. I'm talking about what happens afterwards."

"I don't… I…"

"You what? You didn't think someone like me

could have anything more to him than a few orgasms?"

"Well, you did promise..."

"See?" He grabs my waist and pulls me close to him. "You see what you're doing to me?"

"We're naked, and you're pushing against me. It's a normal reaction..."

"I'm not talking about my dick, Holly. I'm talking about me. About what you do to me."

"Oh."

"And what I'm doing to you."

"How would you know what you're doing to me?"

He smiles, knowing already that he's right.

"I just wish everything were easier."

"Let me make it easy for you."

"What do you mean?"

"I have a solution."

"What are you talking about?"

"A way for you to stay. Here, in Ireland."

"I don't get it..."

"There's a way for you to get your citizenship, Holly. With no more bureaucracy, no more visas, and no fear of being sent back home one day."

I pull away from him, taking a few steps back.

"A parent," he says carefully – but I already know what he's getting at. "If you have a parent who was born here..."

"No." I grab the cover from the floor and wrap it around my body.

"He was born here. It would only take a signature, and—"

"I said no."

"You're his daughter. You have a right to Irish citizenship."

"Why are you doing this?"

"This? This... what? Helping you stay here?"

"I never asked you for help."

"What the fuck is that supposed to mean?"

"I never told you I'd stay, Tyler. I never said I'd find a way to stay."

Tyler studies me, confused.

"Then what was all this?" he asks, pointing to the bed.

"I don't know."

"You don't know?"

"Why do you want me to stay? Why are you forcing this so much?"

"Because I hate the thought of losing you. Don't you get it?"

"So this is just a selfish move, then."

"Selfish? You think I'm selfish for wanting you to stay with me?"

I nod, determinedly.

"I can't..." He runs both hands through his hair. "I can't believe I fell for it."

"What...?"

"I really believed it for a moment, you know. I believed you, your words, your kindness. I believed your kisses..." His face is hard, his eyes dark. "You really fucked me, Ms. White."

He takes two steps back and gathers his pants from the floor, tugging them on quickly before bending down to scoop up his shirt.

"This whole thing about needing help... I wasn't the one wanting to get *you* into bed."

His words floor me.

"You were the one who needed someone, who needed company. Did you feel lonely, was that it? You wanted to experience these *skills* you've heard so much about?"

"What are you saying?"

"I'm just telling it like it is."

He pulls on his T-shirt and sighs.

"I thought you were different. I thought that if I showed you..." He touches his chest, and my own hand flies to mine. He shakes his head, distraught. "I'd have done it, you know. I'd have given you everything you've never had. I wanted to be the one to do that for you."

A tear starts to slide down my face.

"You're the one who doesn't want it, Holly. You're the one who doesn't want to look for the things you've been missing. You don't want to take that risk."

"I can't," I tell him, stifling a sob.

"We could've been perfect, Holly. You already *are* perfect, and I'd have tried my best. For you."

He turns, leaving me in my room. I follow him out, before he can slip through the door and disappear forever.

"You already are," I say to his back. He stops, but doesn't turn to look at me. "You're perfect, Tyler. I just can't do this. I can't stay. Not like that."

He looks at me, his sad eyes shattering my heart.

"It's the only way."

"I'm sorry."

He nods, defeated. "Me, too."

68
Tyler

Two days after that *I'm sorry*, Niall appears at my door.

"Wow. They told me you looked like shit, but I didn't realise just how bad it was."

"Who sent you? And who told you I look like shit?"

"Your brother, and... Well, just your brother."

He steps into my apartment, heading for the kitchen. He lays a few Tupperware containers out on the counter. "Comfort food, from my family. They're mainly leftovers from our Christmas dinner, so..."

"The whole family?"

He shrugs.

"Are you telling me that everyone knows?"

"Knows what, exactly?"

"I can't be bothered to play your games today."

"Aren't you going into work?"

"I worked last night. I have a day off."

"A day off to do...?"

I glare at him.

"Do you want to tell me what happened?"

"I fell in love and it fucked me over. End of story."

"Oh, Jesus Christ!"

"Fuck off, Niall."

"Acceptance is one of the last steps of the process."

"I thought it was one of the first steps?"

"Not when it comes to love."

I let myself fall defeatedly back onto the sofa.

"No sign of life from next door?"

Nothing at all. I tried knocking, jumping onto her balcony, yelling at her through the window. I've been sliding those stupid notes under her door. It's as if she's vanished into thin air – as if she never existed. But I can still feel the pain in my chest: it's becoming sharper with every minute I spend without her.

"No. Nothing."

"Have you fucked everything up, Tyler?"

"I was only trying to…"

"What?"

"Keep her."

"Mmm… And you think that she doesn't want to be kept?"

"I just think she's scared."

"That's fair, right?"

"Considering her history, yes. But I thought that… I hoped that… I was convinced I'd showed her who I was…" I look at my friend, hoping that he'll say something intelligent or, at least, comforting. Although I should never expect much from Niall.

That's how desperate I am.

"Do you want to analyse the situation?"

"Do I have a choice?"

"No."

"Go on, then."

Niall paces slowly around the living room, one hand stroking his chin, as if he were analysing a crime scene from one of those trashy TV shows.

"She came here looking for her roots, for a family she never thought she had. She came here looking for herself. Right?"

"I think so, yeah."

"She found a father, a grandmother, some friends, a place to build up her life – or, should I say, *start* her life…"

I nod.

"And she found something unexpected. She found you."

I swallow, nervous at the idea that Niall's thoughts are more logical than mine.

"And, come on: you're you. A pillar of our community, with a unique set of skills…"

I roll my eyes.

"Something which terrifies people."

"I don't know whether to let you keep talking or punch you in the face."

"You're a fireman: don't forget about your

reputation."

"What are you getting at, Niall?"

"Come on, mate. You never believed this would happen to you. I'd never have believed it."

"Wow, thanks. Great friend!"

"No woman would've believed you, Tyler, given your history. Given *her* history. She's scared: scared of confronting what's standing right in front of her. She's scared of finding a family that doesn't want her. She's scared that she's fallen in love with an utter dickhead."

I can't admit that he's probably right, so I keep quiet.

"She's young, alone. You should've helped her, understood her, guided her, supported her. Instead you heaped all of your anxiety at losing her onto her shoulders."

I cross my arms and scoff. He surely can't be right about *everything*.

"You need to show her that you're serious."

"I've been honest with her. I told her I wanted her to stay. What else am I supposed to do?"

"You told her to tell her dad who she was, so that she can get citizenship, just so you can keep sleeping with her?"

"What? No!" I leap nervously to my feet.

Niall raises an eyebrow and studies me suspiciously.

"Okay, maybe I did *think* it, but those words

never left my mouth!"

"Maybe not those words exactly, Tyler, but I'm sure the words that came out of your mouth weren't the right ones."

"You've lost me." I sit back down. "I still can't believe this has all happened."

"By 'this' do you mean falling in love?"

"No, I already know that happened. I felt it, so clearly. It was devastating." I drop my head into my hands. "I don't know how I managed to ruin everything like this. One minute, we were in bed, and the next minute…"

"Oh, mate. Post-sex misunderstandings are the worst."

"I've ruined everything."

"That was predictable. We men seem to do nothing but make a mess – and it tends to cost us. Luckily, women are pretty good at putting things back together."

"You're not even ashamed to say it."

"Why should I be? It's true!"

I scoff and slump back into the sofa cushions.

"What am I supposed to do, Niall?"

I really must be in trouble if I'm asking him for help. But I've already lost her. What else do I have to lose?

"There is another way, you know… To make her stay."

"Mmm?"

"It's a bit dramatic, but, hey. We're desperate, right?"

"Very fucking desperate."

"That's what I wanted to hear." Niall sits down next to me. "You know another way someone can get citizenship, Tyler?"

It's only when Niall sits down that the lights flicker on in the Christmas tree in my mind.

"You think... You're saying that..."

"I don't *think* anything – I'm taking no responsibility for this. I'm just here to push you in a direction, whether or not it's the right one. But sometimes, you need to take a risk; to take a leap of faith."

"It could be a long fall, Niall."

"I'm only here for moral support. I can't tell you what to do."

"You're keeping yourself out of it, so that you don't get dragged down with me. Right?"

"Exactly."

"You're such a good friend."

"The best."

"I'm not so sure about that. I'll let you know once she gives me an answer."

69

Tyler

Waiting in the dark at her front door, after unscrewing the hallway lamp, is crazy. I realise that. But put yourself in my shoes for a moment: think about how quickly I've had to move to follow through with Niall's fucking process. I'm about to do the only thing I never thought I'd do.

"Oh, my God!" Ms. White's hand flies to her chest in shock. "What the hell are you doing standing there in the dark?"

"I need to talk to you."

"Does this really seem like the right way to approach someone, Tyler?"

"You'd never have answered if you knew it was me."

"That's for sure!"

She sticks her key into the lock and steps into her apartment. I keep my hand on the door, so that she can't slam it in my face.

"I could've broken in anytime, you know. Through the door, the balcony... You'd have found me there, in your house, and then you'd have had to speak to me."

"Or I could've called the police."

"Please, Holly. I'm desperate, here. Just let me explain. I won't ask anything else of you."

She sighs in defeat, before letting go off the door and letting me follow her inside.

"You have two minutes."

She takes off her scarf and coat and leaves them on the sofa, before turning to face me. In that moment, I realise what I've done; what I'm about to lose. Her eyes have lost that sparkle, that deepness that sets them apart. They're dark, empty, sad. Her lips have morphed into a thin, hard line; there's a line on her forehead that wasn't there a few days ago, highlighting the tension in her face. I can see that tension in her posture, can feel it in the air of her apartment. A few days ago, this house seemed to spill over with life.

"I'm sorry. I panicked, okay? We'd just slept together, and you... You let yourself go. You said all those things..."

Her expression grows more pained. I can see that she's biting the inside of her cheek, trying to hold herself back.

"And I believed you, you know? I believed you wanted to be with me."

"I never lied to you, Tyler. I meant everything I said."

"I know, Holly. I know." I step closer to her and take her hands in mine; the fact that she doesn't back away makes me hopeful. "You'd never have lied. You're not like that."

A weak smile plays at her lips.

"I'm sorry I made you so upset. I didn't want to make the decision for you, control your life."

"Okay."

"I just want you to stay."

She sighs heavily, flashing me a sad smile.

"Speaking of which... I thought that we could..."

"Tyler, no. Don't say it, don't—"

"We could get married. You'd get your citizenship, and you could stay."

"You can't be serious."

"That way, you'll have all the time in the world to get to know your family, to tell them about you, and..."

She drops my hands and steps back.

"Are you really suggesting I marry you just for Irish citizenship? You know that's a crime, right?"

"A crime? Come on..."

"You're a member of the law enforcement, Tyler!"

"Technically I'm just a fireman. I'm only trained for emergencies, and..."

"Get out of my house!"

"Holly..."

"How can you think that I'd want to marry you just to stay in this country?"

"Oh. Wow."

"I didn't mean that. I didn't want to..."

"Trust me, I got it. We speak the same language, even if you come from another country, and have a ridiculously sexy accent. Don't worry. I understood you perfectly."

This time, I'm the one to back away.

"I didn't mean it. It's not what you think—"

"Actually, I think we've got to the root of the problem, Holly."

"Which is?"

"That you don't love me."

She seems surprised by my bluntness, which only confirms my fear.

"So this was all just... For fun? Or was it a way for you to learn how to spread your wings? Fly away from here?"

I shake my head, holding my hands up to stop her from coming close.

"I'm such an idiot."

"You're reading too much into this."

"Do you love me, Holly?" I ask her, directly.

"T-Tyler..."

"Do you love me or not?"

"That's not the point."

"It's exactly the point."

Holly stands there silently, in the middle of her living room. She seems so far away from me now, as if she'd already climbed onto that plane. As if she'd already left. As if she were never even here.

"Have you ever even considered the idea of staying, Holly?"

"I don't want to tell Angus that he—"

"For me, Holly." My chest thumps. "Have you ever thought about staying for me?"

She opens her mouth, but no sound comes out.

"Okay." I run a hand over my face. "Okay." I step towards the front door, resting my hand on the door handle, then decide to speak. There's no use keeping it to myself anymore.

"I knew you'd hurt me, but I never thought it would feel like this. I never thought it would be so unbearable."

"Tyler…"

I look back at her. I can't help it.

"I knew all along. I knew it would end like this. But I threw myself into it anyway. For you."

She shakes her head, her eyes brimming with sadness; my heart is crying out in pain, in devastation.

"I'd have done anything for you."

I allow myself one last glance. One last moment.

"Take care of yourself, Holly."

I leave her apartment and head back into mine: my safe place. The place I was ready to abandon, without looking back, just to create a safe place for her.

70

Holly

Jordan and Anya have convinced me to come out. They wanted to distract me, but I didn't feel like seeing anyone, so we've opted for an evening in, at Jordan's, in our pyjamas. They said that I needed to just let go – I'm not even sure what they mean, but I trust them. They've reassured me that we'd be letting go together. I came over in my sweatpants – Anya picked me up, also wearing sweatpants, as is Jordan. They said that the first step to completely letting go is not caring about the way you look. Easy for them to say: they haven't just given up the man they love, told him that they didn't love him. Well, technically, neither have I, but I didn't reassure him otherwise, and for him, that meant the same thing.

"Should I pour?" Jordan asks, a bottle of wine in hand.

"Pour," Anya encourages. "I can tell we already need it."

"I thought I'd at least wait until dinner."

"I'm not really hungry," I say, quietly.

Jordan fills my glass, before then filling hers and Anya's.

"So, our dear fireman..." Anya begins carefully. She attempted to ask me about it in the car, too, when she told me she'd seen him watching from behind his curtains as I went downstairs and climbed into her car. But I couldn't even lift my head to look at her.

I decide to tell them the truth.

"He asked me to marry him."

Anya sprays a mouthful of wine all over Jordan. "What?!"

"What the hell, Anya?!"

"It's not what you think. It wasn't romantic or spontaneous."

Jordan wipes her face with a napkin. "What do you mean?"

"I don't know if I should say. I don't want to get anyone in trouble."

"You don't know if you can tell us?" Anya becomes agitated. "Now we want to know every little detail!"

"It was for my citizenship. If I marry him, I don't have to leave."

"Really?" Jordan pretends to be shocked, but Anya glares at her.

"You knew."

"Me?"

"Your *so-called* boyfriend. His best friend."

"I don't know anything." Jordan sips at her wine to avoid talking, but neither of us believe her.

"Traitor," Anya hisses through her teeth, before turning back to me. "Tell us, for fuck's sake!"

"What else is there to say?"

"What did you say?"

"What do you think?"

Jordan smiles sadly at me, as Anya heaves a sigh.

"I can't believe it. I'd never have expected that of Hayes."

"I did," Jordan says, taking another sip. "I always knew that he just needed the right push. Apparently, that was you."

"You really think that...?" I shake my head determinedly. "No, he can't."

"Can't what? Be in love with you?"

"He asked me whether I loved him."

"That's a huge step for him..." Anya comments.

"I hurt him."

"He'll deal with it. He's a big boy."

"What did you say?" Jordan asks again, ignoring Anya's comments and trying to get to the root of the problem.

"I didn't say anything."

"Why not?"

"I don't know."

"Aren't you in love with him?"

"I don't know."

"You don't know?" Anya raises an eyebrow.

"Either way, it's not enough."

"Not enough to what? Accept his proposal?"

"I can't marry him just because he's scared to lose me."

"What about you? Aren't you scared to lose him?"

"It doesn't matter. It doesn't seem like a particularly good reason to marry someone."

"Wait a minute." Anya leaps to her feet, the glass teetering dangerously in her hand. "You're doing it for him!"

My face blushes uncontrollably.

"Fuck! I knew it!"

"Want to fill me in?" Jordan moans.

"You've been in love with him since... Since you asked him for help. Maybe even before!"

I jump to my feet, too. "No!"

"You were in love with him that night, too – the night with Trevor."

"Who the hell is Trevor?" Jordan protests.

"You lied to me! You looked me in the eye and lied to me!"

"That's not true, I…"

"I already told you, you don't lie to your friends!"

"I didn't know, okay? I didn't know at the time."

Anya studies me suspiciously as Jordan sits, waiting to understand what's going on.

"I hadn't realised. It just happened. And when he asked me if I loved him, when I saw him there, ready to commit, to do this for me, I felt suffocated. I've never known what it's like to have someone who would do something like that for you."

Anya's expression softens.

"I don't want Tyler to marry me just so that I can stay, and then one day wake up and realise he's made the biggest mistake of his life. I couldn't bear it."

Jordan gets up and wraps her arms around me.

"Lucky bastard," Anya mumbles, making me smile through my tears.

"I wish I could do something, Holly. I wish I could help somehow."

"I know. Thank you." I pull away from her and take a deep breath. "But it's for the best. This isn't my place."

He's not my place – even though I've never wanted anything more.

"I'll miss you," Jordan says, sadly.

"Me, too," Anya adds, stepping towards us.

I let them both hug me, aware that I'm about to leave behind something more than I could ever have believed in.

71

Tyler

During dinner at my brother's house, I almost crumble in sadness, like a man who's heart has been shattered into pieces.

I stick a spoonful of ice cream into my mouth, followed immediately by a squirt of whipped cream, swallowing down the calories which will ruin all my hard work. But, hey – who the fuck cares? I'm no longer on the market – not after offering myself up to the only person who could ever claim rights over me.

Did you really think I'd just go back to my old habits, after she showed me everything I could have?

I can't even set foot in my apartment without suffering, like the dickhead I am. If it weren't for Parker's pity, letting me crash on his sofa for a night, I think I'd have slept under a bridge. And it's really fucking cold around here.

"Have you seen my brother around anywhere?" Parker asks.

"Who's that?"

"Tyler..."

"What am I supposed to do? I asked her to marry me, and now I don't know what to do with myself."

"Would it make you feel better if you went gnome hunting, Uncle Tyler?" one of my adorably innocent nieces asks.

"That's out of the question, honey."

"It's exactly what got you into this mess," Parker comments, also helping himself to a spoonful of ice cream and a squirt of whipped cream. He's already been through this, but ten times worse.

"Can I have some ice cream?" the other twin asks.

"No. It's getting late, and you have to brush your teeth."

"But you're eating it!" she protests.

"There's nothing left for us to do, honey. Let us get old and fat in peace," I explain, earning myself a glare from Parker.

"Come on. If you get ready now, Uncle Tyler will read you a story."

"Do I have to?"

"You need to earn your spot on the sofa somehow."

I scoff and turn back to the girls. "Off you go. I'll be there in five minutes. Choose something fun for us to read – please, no princes kissing princesses, or any of that shit."

"Do you really think that's appropriate, Tyler?" Parker groans. I shrug.

The girls disappear into the bathroom and I let

my head fall back against the sofa cushions.

"Can I offer you some brotherly advice?"

"You?"

"Do you have any other brothers?"

"Not that I know of."

"Depressed sarcasm will get you nowhere."

"You may be right, seeing as I've found myself sleeping on your sofa."

"I really don't know what that woman saw in you."

"Nothing, apparently. Otherwise she wouldn't have said no. Don't you think?"

"That depends..."

I lift my head, suddenly interested.

"On what?"

"On the reason you proposed in the first place."

"Do we really need to go through this again?"

"You did it for the wrong reasons, Tyler."

"What are you talking about?"

"The proposal. Wanting to get married."

"Mmm."

"She didn't take you seriously. She didn't believe you."

"Huh."

"Can you tell me something?"

"Absolutely."

"Why did you do it? And I mean *really*, Tyler. Why did you ask her to marry you?"

I think about this for a moment. What comes to mind first is the way she smiles shyly at me when I say something inappropriate, or the way her lips fall apart when she listens to me, as if my bullshit were actually useful or interesting. I think about the way her hands slide, trembling, down my chest, or weave their way into my hair. I think about the way she babbles when she's nervous about something, or the way her mouth curves into a smile before I kiss her. I think about the way my body reacts to the mere thought of her.

"I think you might be getting there..." Parker comments, before squirting more whipped cream into his mouth.

"Can I ask *you* a question?"

"If you think it'll help."

"Why did you do it?"

"Get married, you mean?"

I nod.

"She thought we'd done it for the wrong reasons, too. We hadn't known each other for long..."

"And then you got her pregnant. And you asked her to marry you. Then she left you."

"And there are an infinite number of memories between those three moments – things I wouldn't change for anything in the world. I wanted to marry her. I wanted children, and... I wanted her.

I didn't ask her because she was pregnant, but that's what she thought. That was the problem."

"The wrong reason..." I consider out loud. "I can't see what's wrong with us, though."

Parker smiles.

"All I can see is how perfect we'd be together; how great it would be to have her sitting around the table at Christmas, with Mum and Dad; how nice it would be to drop her off at work, or to come home in the evening and find my place next to her in bed."

"Well, they all sound like good reasons."

"Yeah..."

"Maybe you should say all this when you ask her again."

"Mmm?"

"You'll ask her again, right? You're not going to let her get away, are you, Tyler?"

"I've made such a mess."

"I'm sure that, with your skills, you'll find a way to make it right."

72

Holly

Angus places a bowl of soup and a sandwich in front of me.

"I haven't ordered yet."

"You've been staring at that envelope for an hour. You're not smiling, you're not talking. You're not *you*."

I fiddle nervously with the envelope in question, before deciding to tear it open, looking again at the plane ticket which I'd picked up this morning from the travel agent. All that was missing is the date of travel.

"It's almost time for me to go home," I say, sadly.

"Why aren't you happy about it?"

Because I don't know where home is anymore. Because I don't have a home. Because I have to leave you, and Linda, and Jordan, and Anya... And him.

I have to leave him.

Because I have to leave the best part of my life behind.

"I don't like goodbyes," is all I say, stealing one of my mother's favourite sayings. She used to use it a lot when we would move from one place to another in the middle of the night, without saying goodbye to anyone, without leaving a trace. That was how she loved to go; to just disappear. That way, she avoided any problems, never had to make tough decisions.

Which is exactly what I'm doing, too.

I guess she'd be really proud of me – maybe for the first time ever.

She never understood why I wanted a stable life, a regular job. She never understood my dream to become a teacher. She never approved of my decision to stay in Montreal, my hometown; rent an apartment, have a bank account, and pay bills with a credit card.

Maybe it was all just an illusion, trying to be myself, without her mistakes for protection. Maybe I really am just like her.

Angus furrows his brow for a few seconds. "Goodbye? So you'll never come back to visit?"

I don't look at him. I know I wouldn't be able to avoid crying. I've been so good not to burst into tears around him; I don't want to ruin it all now.

"Not for a while. I have to stay home for at least six months. That's how it works."

Angus nods slowly. He seems thoughtful, almost distracted.

"What about your fireman?"

I lift my gaze to meet his, and his eyes speak for themselves.

"What did he do?"

"He asked me to marry him."

I don't know why I tell him. I didn't mean to blurt everything out like that, make his gesture the next piece of town gossip. But it's eating me alive, driving me slowly crazy.

"Ah."

"Ah?"

"I don't know what else to say."

"I said no."

"Okay."

"Okay?"

"What do you want me to say?"

"I don't know. That I made the right decision?"

"That depends."

"On what?"

"On the reason you said no."

"It's obvious!"

"No, it isn't. Not to me."

"What was I supposed to do? It was just a way for him to make me stay. He doesn't really want to marry me."

"Did you ask him?"

"What?"

"Did you ask him why he wants to marry you?"

"I don't..." I shake my head, confused. "I didn't have to. It was clear that..." I don't know what I'm saying anymore. I feel as if I'm repeating the same excuse to myself, to everyone.

"I did the same thing," Angus says suddenly, interrupting my thoughts. "I threw myself in at the deep end. I followed a woman to the end of the Earth. I asked her to marry me, to come back to Ireland. I wanted her to live with me, to help me run this place together one day."

My emotions begin to swirl; pain, anger, helplessness, love, nostalgia, sadness... I feel them all, together. I feel as if I'm about to collapse, to tell Angus the truth.

"She told me I was doing it for the wrong reason. That we didn't really love each other, that I was just afraid to lose what we had together. She said we wouldn't have been happy, that I'd have been unhappy with her. I even bought her a ring."

I can't hold back the tears, now. They're burning, screaming, overwhelming; just like Angus' words.

"I still have it." He shakes his head. "It's so stupid, I know. Maybe a part of me hopes that, one day, she might come back."

I should tell him, now. He has a right to know that my mother isn't here anymore, that she'll never come back to him. But I'm here. I'm ready to love him. I want to love him.

"Sorry. I shouldn't have said anything." Angus puts an end to my stupid idea of telling him the truth about everything, hurting him once again, making him suffer for no reason. "I'm probably not the right person to be saying this, and I have no right to do so, but think about it, Holly. Don't make a decision just because it seems like the right one. Follow your heart. Listen to what it's telling you."

I could've listened to those words over and over again; the fact they've come from him makes it hurt more than never having heard them.

"Love is never a mistake."

"My mother always said the opposite. She told me that love was never the right decision, that I shouldn't listen to my heart. She said I should never believe men, or let any man stop me from living my life."

Angus' eyes grow sad, overwhelmed by emotion.

"I'm sorry to hear that, Holly. But your mother was wrong."

He takes my hands.

"And I'm not talking about letting someone stop you from living, but about letting yourself go. You need to give yourself the chance to really feel your emotions, to hope, to dream... To love. Never hide yourself away from love, Holly, or you'll become sad and lonely. I never want you to be like that."

He lets go of my hands and strokes my face; it's a spontaneous, sweet gesture which opens a dam inside me, leaves me in tears. Angus dries my eyes, just as a father should, and smiles at me as he reassures me. Just as *my* father should.

"You're such a beautiful girl, so full of light. Don't let yourself fade to grey, don't let them put out that fire behind your eyes, my dear. Go after your dreams. Take risks. Don't shy away from anyone – especially not from yourself."

"I'm scared, Angus. I'm so scared."

"I know, but fear is part of the process. It's not a bad thing – not always. Sometimes it's just another hurdle to jump over. Don't stop, Holly, because you have no idea what's waiting for you on the other side of that fear."

73

Tyler

Once I've made sure that Ms. White isn't home, and that she won't be home for a while, yet, I let myself into her apartment via the balcony. That way, I know no one will see me from the road.

Oh, you're wondering how I know what time she'll be back? Simple. I have a mole. Or, rather, a lookout. My good friend Carter. We've become pretty close lately – and not just because we keep doing each other favours. Carter happens to be quite the romantic – who'd have known? And he enjoys love stories with a happy ending – but he's made me promise never to tell his *non*-girlfriend, Skylar. He wants to play the tough guy around her. And I get it – I've done that, too, years ago. It's hard, being a teenager – especially when you've fallen for a girl who could take you out with a single punch, and whose dad is a dickhead like my best friend Niall.

I wander around the house, the Christmas tree we decorated together discarded lifelessly in a corner, as if to warn me that I could meet the same fate. But I don't let it scare me. I'm here with a plan, and I'm going to follow it through to the bitter end. Fireman's honour.

You trust me, right?

Probably not.

I wouldn't trust me, if I were you, but hey, who am I to give advice? I'm just a desperate man who doesn't want to lose the woman he loves. Just a man who has broken into that woman's house, because... Well, just because. Why the fuck would I know? You should have realised from the very first page, dear reader, that there's nothing trustworthy about me – despite what my friend Niall says.

I slip into her room and look around. There's the usual pile of clothes on the armchair, and a half-packed suitcase on the floor which tells me that she only has a few days left. If I don't do this today, it'll never happen.

What am I doing in her house? I'm looking for something. An idea, a clue; a little detail to help me plan the best way to do this, so that she believes me. So that she believes in us. I sink onto the bed and pull open the drawer of her bedside table. Nothing. A Kindle, a lipstick, a nail file. I close it over and rest my elbows on my knees, dropping my head into my hands and sitting there, until my eye lands on something familiar.

I grab the biscuit tin the kids gave her at school and shake it, realising that it contains something other than cookies. I mean, it would make no sense to keep biscuits under the bed, would it? I rest the tin on my lap. I don't know why I feel so nervous; why my fingers are shaking as I open the lid. But I know exactly why I'm crying as soon as I realise what this box contains.

I pick them up, reading through them: my notes. My stupid notes. All of them. They're all here. I don't even need to check. I can feel how much I want to make her laugh, how much I want to see her; how much I want to peer under her skirt, discover what pair of underwear she's wearing. How much I want to kiss her, to touch her, to please her.

I can feel how much I want to love her.

Not just for a few nights. Not for a few weeks. Not for three months.

I replace the notes in the tin and push it back under the bed. I dry my eyes on my arm and get to work. I know what to do. I know exactly which of my *skills* to make use of: my stupid face.

* * * * *

When I hear her key turning in the lock, I hold my breath nervously, waiting for her to come across my first note. I'm not exactly hiding: I'm just waiting behind the door of her bedroom. I don't want to miss her reaction.

I see her looking around, maybe in fear or confusion. I hope she's not angry – I don't fancy another trip down to the police station. She looks around at the notes plastered all over the house, her hand shaking as she brings it to her lips.

"What...?" She mumbles. "What the...?"

She picks one up, her fingers still trembling.

Because I want to kiss you until your knees give way.

She reads it out loud. I knew my Ms. White wouldn't let me down. There's a reason I fell in love with her, you know.

She takes another.

Because I want to be the only man to take off your tights.

She laughs.

Thank God.

Come on, Tyler! You can do this!

Because my downstairs neighbour only shows up for you.

I can't work out whether she's laughing or crying, but hey. I'll take it.

Unless she tells me to fuck off.

Because if you get onto that plane, we'll both die a little every day.

Now I know she's not laughing. I'm not laughing, either.

Because there's nothing I wouldn't do for you - even letting you go.

When she picks up the note from the wall opposite me, she notices my presence – although I'm sure she already knew.

Because you're my first time, Ms. White.

She takes another, reading it to herself, before glancing up at me.

"Because I love you."

I don't know whether she's just repeating what she's read, or whether she's telling me herself, but you know what? I'm happy with what her eyes are telling me. Those eyes are worth more than any stupid note I could ever write.

"You wanted a reason, Ms. White. Well, there are hundreds." I stretch my arms out, gesturing towards the walls, covered in unread notes.

I get down on one knee – because, apparently, that's what you're supposed to do – and hand her a small box.

"Ty..."

"Just open it."

She takes the box, her hands shaking. Inside is my last night, the one I wrote with all my heart.

About last night...

She reads, a tear trailing down to the corner of her mouth.

It's the last one I'll ever spend without you.

74
Holly

I look at Tyler, kneeling in front of me, my eyes filled with tears. His own eyes are glinting with emotion.

"Sorry. I used the box for one of my stupid notes."

He pulls a ring out of his pocket and holds it out to me.

"I've written down hundreds of reasons why I want to marry you, Holly. And if that's not enough, I can think of a hundred more. The truth is that there are no reasons why I shouldn't marry you."

I dry my eyes on my sleeve, his notes clutched to my chest with my other hand.

"But I just need one reason for you to say yes."

"One reason?"

"I can give you a clue if you like."

I laugh. I can't help it.

"I'm open to suggestions."

"Marry me because you love me, Holly."

"And would that be enough?"

"How could you think it wouldn't be?"

"I'd say it's perfect."

"Does that mean you love me?"

I nod, jumping when Tyler leaps to his feet and gathers me up into his arms.

"You don't even have to say it. I can feel it. And I can say it. That's all I need."

"Really?"

"Just say yes."

"Y-yes."

"Yes, you love me? Or yes, you'll marry me?"

"Yes to both."

"Oh, fuck..." He pulls me close to him and kisses me, taking my breath away. "Yes, yes yes..." he repeats into my mouth.

"You'll have to wait six months," I say, as he looks at me, pained. "We'll never be able to get it done in time. I have to go back to Canada, and then I have to stay there. If you can wait for six months, if you think you can..."

"Wait? Like fuck are we waiting."

I look at him, shocked.

"I'm coming with you."

"What?"

"Didn't you read my last note?"

"Yes, but..."

"I thought it was pretty clear."

"I don't get it..."

"I'm coming with you."

"With me?"

He nods, serious. "I'm getting on that flight."

"You'd come to Canada with me?"

"Anywhere, Holly. I'd go wherever you go."

"But what will you do in Canada? What about work? What about your family?"

"I promised you. You'd never be alone again. Remember?"

I nod, starting to cry again.

"Here. You have to stay here." He hugs me tighter, my head against his chest.

"My safe place," I sob into his T-shirt.

"So you've finally got it."

I lift my head and look at him, the words spilling from my heart.

"I'm in love with you, Tyler Hayes."

"You are?"

I nod, and he sighs.

"Since that night you punched that guy in the hallway."

"Really?"

"I didn't want you... I didn't want you to feel like you had to be with me. Like you were making the biggest mistake of your life."

"The only mistake I could make now would be to let you go. And it won't happen."

He loosens his grip on me, planting a kiss onto my lips.

"Now. Tell me, Mrs. Hayes."

"I'm not Mrs. Hayes yet."

"True. But, for now, if you wear this..." He shows me the ring.

I hold out my hand and he slides the ring onto my finger.

"I don't want to get carried away, but that looks pretty perfect to me."

I laugh and reach onto my tiptoes to kiss him, just as someone knocks at the door.

"Who the hell is that?"

"I have no idea."

Tyler scoffs, but lets me go so that I can go to the door.

"What shit timing. If it's Niall, slam the door in his face."

I laugh, before opening the door.

"Hi, Holly."

I stand there in silence, as I feel Tyler's hands land on my shoulders.

"My mother gave me your address. Can I come in?"

I nod, petrified. Luckily, Tyler holds me close, giving me courage, as Angus makes his way into my apartment.

"I've been thinking about what you said. Those words... Those exact words..."

My eyes start to brim with tears again.

"And I've thought back over a lot of the things you've told me over the past few months. About you, about your mother."

Tyler holds me tighter.

"And I thought that, maybe... Maybe... That... I don't know. It sounds insane, but there's something inside you. Something that tells me we have a bond – a unique bond. Is that true, Holly?"

Tyler kisses my head. "I'll leave you two alone."

"No!" I grab his hand before he can leave. "Don't go. Please stay."

Tyler looks at Angus, who smiles at him.

"Okay."

He takes a few steps back, but I can still feel his reassuring presence behind me.

"So..." Angus begins, uncertainly.

"Your daughter. I'm your daughter, and you're my father. I'm so sorry I lied to you, but I didn't know how to tell you. I was scared that you wouldn't want me, that you wouldn't..." Angus' strong arms wrap themselves around me, making me burst into tears.

"Oh, my God." He strokes my hair as I let my head fall onto his chest. "You're... Oh, my God. I have a daughter. I have a daughter."

"I'm so sorry. I only found out about you when my mother..."

"It's okay. It's okay."

"I wanted to..."

"Don't cry, my love, don't cry. We have all the time in the world. You're here. We're together.

Nothing will take you away from me. I promise."
I pull away from him, his hands still on my face.
"I'm so... God, I'm so happy."

"You are?"

"How can you even ask me that? I have a daughter, *you* are my daughter."

"I have to go back to Canada. I already have my plane ticket, and my visa, and the bureaucracy... But I'll come back, I promise. I want to get to know you, and get to know Linda, and I want you both to get to know me, and... Oh, God, I don't actually think there's anything left for me to tell you about myself. I talk so much, and can't stop babbling... Like right now..."

Angus and Tyler laugh.

"You don't need to go anywhere, Holly."

"I d-don't?"

"I'm your dad."

I nod, sobbing.

"You're half Irish. You have the right to stay here. You have the right to choose."

"Can I really stay?"

"You can choose to do exactly what you want."

I look at my father, then look at Ty, my eyes filled with tears, brimming with hope. I look back at my dad.

"I want to stay here... D-Dad." Another sob, followed by a sob coming from behind me, too.

"With you." I turn to Tyler. "And you." I hold out my hand. Tyler takes it, and joins us.

They both hug me. They love me. They both want me to be happy, want me to feel at home.

And, finally, I am.

75

Tyler

"Are you nervous? Your hands are sweating, but it's fucking freezing."

"What do you think?"

"I'd say you're nervous, but you also have absolutely no reason to be."

"I'm about to meet your family, Ty."

"It would've happened sooner or later, right? Aren't we engaged?"

"We've been engaged for less than twenty-four hours."

"Did you want to keep the good news all to yourself?"

She glares at me, but doesn't have time to say anything; the door to my parents' house flies open in front of us.

"Tyler!" My mother launches herself at me, wrapping her arms around my neck, forcing me to let go of a very anxious Ms. White's hand. "We were expecting you yesterday!"

"I know, I'm sorry. I got held up."

Mum lets me go slowly, realising only in that moment that I'm not alone.

They got back last night and, yes, they were anxiously waiting for me to visit, so that they could hug me after more than three months apart.

But, as you know, I was busy trying to avoid another disaster.

What disaster am I talking about, you ask? Well, last night I asked my sweet, slightly crazy Ms. White to be my wife, and against all odds and all good reason, she said yes.

I won't tell you what happened afterwards, after Angus' appearance, after all the tears and the embraces, once we were left alone again. I won't tell you because, although rumour may suggest otherwise, I'm actually a gentleman.

"Held up..." Mum echoes, her eyes flickering from me to Ms. White and back. "I can see."

"I've brought someone I'd like you to meet."

"I can see that, too."

"If you ever actually let us in, I might even be able to introduce you."

Mum steps aside and we make ourselves at home.

"Is Parker already here?"

"He's in the living room with the girls."

"Let's all go through, then."

"I thought you wanted to introduce us, first."

"I do. But I thought it might be better to do it once we're home."

"We're already home."

I scoff, before turning to my future wife.

"You'll get used to this, I promise."

She watches me through narrowed eyes, as I

turn to my mother and announce, straight to the point: "This is Holly. Holly White. My fiancée."

"Your *what?!*" My mother's voice becomes a squeal.

"You heard. Don't make a scene."

"What happened?"

"What do you mean?"

"Did you blackmail her?"

"Mum..."

"Did you force her? Threaten her?"

"Mum..."

"Did you get her pregnant?"

I scoff loudly.

"Are you telling me that this beautiful girl next to you has agreed to marry you of her own free will?"

I lean in towards Ms. White. "She likes you already."

"This isn't a joke, is it? You're not winding me up?"

"Why don't you ask her?"

My mother's eyes land on Holly, standing, terrified, beside me.

"You... Him... Seriously?"

She nods, concerned.

"Consider it a late Christmas present."

"You're kidding... This is... Oh, my God, this is..." My mother throws herself at Holly, who still doesn't let go of my hand. "My dear, dear girl..." She hugs her tightly, before planting her hands on her shoulders and staring into her eyes. "Thank you."

Holly shakes her head, confused.

"Thank you, thank you, thank you."

"I don't get it..." Holly looks at me for help.

"I never thought this would happen," my mother explains.

"Let's not get carried away, now..."

"You're brave, I must say."

"Mum!"

"Are you sure about what you're doing?"

"You're not exactly making her feel welcome, Mum."

"You're right, honey, I'm sorry. You just took me by surprise, and... I need a drink. I suppose you could do with one, too," she says, turning to Holly, who finally manages to get a word in edgeways.

"A drink. Yes, please. I'd love one. I'm getting used to the idea of destroying my liver, so..."

Or, at least, she attempts to get a word in edgeways. But you know my Ms. White – you know what she's like when she's nervous.

My mother takes Holly by the hand, dragging her along behind her.

"Your father's going to have a heart attack. Thank God you and your brother are both here.

You can give him CPR."

Once we're all in the living room, the girls leap to their feet at the sight of Ms. White.

"Holly! Holly! You're here, too!" They run at her, launching themselves onto her and wrapping themselves around her waist, under my mother's curious gaze.

"She's their teacher," Parker explains, getting up from the sofa. "Or, at least, she was."

"What do you mean *was*?" Mum asks.

"I'm only here for a few months," Holly explains, shyly, to which my mother's nervous gaze lands on me.

"It's a long story," I begin, before my father appears between us, carrying a bottle of wine and a few glasses.

He looks at us all, his gaze stopping at Holly, who's still clutching my mother's hand.

"Have I missed something?"

"Your son is getting married," my mother announces. "Please, don't have a heart attack, now. We might never get this lucky again."

* * * * *

After the initial chaos, the formal introductions, and my mother's ceaseless questions, echoed enthusiastically by my nieces, everyone finally starts to calm down as we all sit around the table for dinner.

"You only got back yesterday and you've already prepared this whole dinner?" Holly asks, looking around the table, laden with food, freshly cooked by my mother.

"She went to the supermarket at eight o'clock this morning," my father says. "And she hasn't left the kitchen since ten a.m."

"I wanted to make a special family dinner – we haven't seen each other for three months. It was wonderful to travel around the world together, but it feels even more wonderful to come home – especially with a surprise like this waiting for us…"

Mum can't seem to contain herself – joy is seeping from every pore, sparking her every word.

"Tell me about yourself, Holly. Parker mentioned you're the girls' teacher?"

"I was, but my contract has run out now."

"What do you mean?"

"I was here on a teacher's exchange programme. I'm Canadian, and my visa is about to run out…"

Mum looks suddenly over at me.

"That's not why I'm marrying her," I say, calming her down. "There's actually no need, in that sense."

"What do you mean?"

"Her dad is Irish."

Mum's eyes fall back onto Holly.

"I came here from Canada to meet him."

"Does he live here?"

Holly nods.

"I actually only found out recently. My mother passed away about a year ago."

"Oh, my dear, I'm so sorry..." My mother's hand flutters to her chest.

"I only found out who my father was after she'd died. I wanted to meet him, to find out more about his roots, about... Me." She looks over at me, her huge doe eyes so round and so deep. Everyone around the table falls silent – even my nieces. "And while I was looking for myself, I found something I was never expecting."

My mother sighs. She loves things like this. You should take a look through her bookshelf.

"So you're marrying him because you want to?"

Holly smiles, then nods.

"Are you really sure? Just because we can't handle another divorce in this family..."

"Thanks, Mum," Parker hisses, but my mother ignores him.

Her attention is trained onto the newest member of the family: a member who I know will quickly become her favourite.

"I am," Holly says, her voice shaking a little.

She's emotional: I don't think she expected all this. This warmth, this joy. She never expected to find anything more than herself. She never really believed in a happy ending where she was the main character.

She looks at my mother, her eyes bright and her smile beaming. She's just realised that she's not so crazy, after all – how could she be, when she's surrounded by people so much crazier than her?

"One hundred per cent sure."

Epilogue

So, here we are, dear readers. Thank you for coming on this journey with me, and my dear Ms. White.

After the New Year celebrations, family introductions, and various goodbyes, me and my future wife climbed onto the first of the three planes that would take us to Canada. She wouldn't have been able to get a passport so quickly, out of nowhere, even though her father is an Irish citizen. There are laws to respect and bureaucracy to follow, but I would never have let Holly go back to Canada on her own; so I took all the holiday I had left at work so that I could be with her. I want to help her sort everything out in Canada, and help her move back to Ireland permanently.

I also want to make sure that she doesn't suddenly decide to run away in the process.

Luckily, in the end, she doesn't have to stay here for six months – but it'll be a few weeks yet before she can go back. And I'll be with her every step of the way, so that she never feels alone.

I can't wait for everything to be official – for her to finally have a home, and for me to finally start the next stage of my plan: making her happy for the rest of her life.

Easy, right?

"Are you hungry?" I ask her. Her eyes have been fixed out of the window for a while.

She was sad at the idea of leaving, and a little worried. She didn't really want to talk about it. She said it was silly and it wasn't worth talking about, but I know that's not true, and our friends and families knew it too: which is exactly why I'm here right now, with a bag full of stuff.

Holly is scared of losing everything she's just found. She's scared that she'll lose herself again during the journey back home, and I'm here to make sure that doesn't happen.

"We have some comfort food."

Holly turns to me. "Comfort?"

"Well, we have a two-day journey. It's not exactly quick."

"I guess not... What do we have?"

I grab the bag from underneath the seat and open it, rummaging around for the three packages that our families made us, to try and cheer us up during the trip. "Let's see... Your dad made us some special sandwiches: two chicken wraps and two slices of raspberry pie."

"That sounds amazing."

"There's more." I look in the containers that my mother snuck into the bag. "Mum made us beef and coleslaw sandwiches, and two portions of mac and cheese."

"Wow. Do they know it's only a two-day journey?"

"There's more."

"More?"

"Niall's mother has given us two slices of her special apple pie, and turkey sandwiches with potato salad."

Holly slumps back into her seat. "My butt has no hope, does it?"

"Neither do my abs, honey. But, hey – at least we'll be growing old together, right? Fat and happy."

Holly smiles at me.

"Oh, hang on... There's more." I pull out two boxes of chocolates: one whiskey flavour and one gin flavour. "These are from Jordan and Anya. They said they wanted to sneak some bottles of alcohol in the bag, but they'd have stopped us at security, so..."

Holly laughs. "Always so thoughtful."

"I think that's everything. Let me know what you want to eat first, and I'll get the flight attendant to bring us each a glass of wine. What do you think?"

"I'd say white would be perfect."

"Then white is what you're getting. Nothing but perfection for the future Mrs. Hayes."

Her hand slips into mine, holding me close. I press my lips against hers.

"I already have perfection."

I smile onto her lips. "You do?"

She nods, determined, and I pull back from her, satisfied.

And, no, it's not because she said I was perfect that I'm happy; I don't think either of us believe that. In spite of my infamous skills, I'm anything but perfect – but she makes me want to try to be the best version of myself. Not just for her, but for the other people in my life. For my family, for my friends, and for me.

"Why don't we eat a few chocolates while we're waiting for the wine?"

I laugh as I pass her the box.

"I think we might need that back-up liver, honey."

Holly shoves two chocolates into her mouth. Needless to say, it really turns me on – everything this woman does turns me on.

"Do you know where I can get one?" she asks, her mouth full.

"No, I'm still working on it. But if we can't find one, I'll happily give you part of mine."

"You'd really do that for me?"

"There's nothing I wouldn't do for you, Mrs. Hayes."

"I'm not Mrs. Hayes yet."

I stroke the ring on her finger, before lifting her hand to my lips.

"I'm sure that can be arranged."

She raises an eyebrow.

"We could always move things along a little."

"What are you talking about?"

"What paperwork would we need to get married in Canada?"

"You can't be serious?"

"My dear, naïve, and *once*-innocent Ms. White: you have no idea what your fireman is capable of."

"I think you need to explain yourself."

I bend down to her face, one hand sliding behind her neck. I bring her close to me and bring my mouth to hers. "Maybe I need to clear a few things up for you, just to be sure."

Holly laughs, and I kiss her.

Maybe this is what love is, after all.

Finding someone who laughs at your jokes, and someone who makes you laugh at theirs. Someone who can laugh at themselves, and who wants to laugh with you. Finding someone you can be yourself with; someone you love more each day, for all that they are.

I think that's what love really is – and yes, that's coming from me. Trust me. After all, I am a fireman.

And, as my friend Niall always says: who doesn't trust a fireman?

Also By A. S. Kelly

FOUR DAYS SERIES

Rainy Days
Sweet Days
Bad Days
Lost Days

O'CONNOR BROTHERS SERIES

Ian
Ryan
Nick

STANDALONES

Last Call
The Best Man

Printed in Poland
by Amazon Fulfillment
Poland Sp. z o.o., Wrocław

63189527R00333